EVERYTHING'S CHANGING . . .

I drive the entire five miles into town with the windows down, blasting music. I'm awestruck once again by how green everything is, how lush and alive. I pass acres and acres of farmland, fresh manure wafting through the window. Then more forest, thick and dark. Finally I reach the edge of town: a sprawling school campus with a deserted old playground, a closed-down Dollar General. And then it's like I blink and I'm in the absolute center, which is marked by what might be the town's only stoplight.

I'm pretty sure I've crossed into another dimension, found the exact, diametric opposite of LA and its endless maze of streets, its superfluous freeways, stoplights, entrances and exits, signs of all kinds. The shabbiness of the buildings here—the yellowed awning of the drugstore and the dilapidated sign in front of the gas station—the aggressive plainness of the entire town seems to mock California and its obsession with newness, its ever-changing coffee shops and restaurants, billboards and beauty trends.

I hear myself whisper, "This is it?"

Also by Kate Sweeney

This One's for You

Catch the Light

KATE SWEENEY

VIKING

VIKING

An imprint of Penguin Random House LLC, New York

First published in the United States of America by Viking,
an imprint of Penguin Random House LLC, 2021
First paperback edition published 2022

Viking & colophon are registered trademarks of Penguin Random House LLC.

Penguin Books & colophon are registered trademarks of Penguin Books Limited.

Visit us online at penguinrandomhouse.com.

Library of Congress Cataloging-in-Publication Data is available.

Paperback ISBN 9780593350256

Printed in the United States of America

1st Printing

LSCH

Edited by Kelsey Murphy
Design by Monique Sterling
Text set in Janson Text

For Dad:
I write
Because we lost your lungs
But I have found your breath.

Catch the Light

1

WE DRIVE INTO CUMBERLAND, NEW YORK, LATE ON a Wednesday afternoon and—

Oh my god.

It's beautiful.

It's the time of day when the light is just starting to turn gold and we're driving through thick forest and the sun is dappling down through the leaves everywhere. There are layers and layers of shifting light. Hundreds of shades of green. Magic.

It's almost enough to make me forget why we're here. It's almost enough to make me forget my grandparents in the front seat and the tedious, awkward, ten-day road trip and the hours of NPR and the slow driving and the musty motel rooms and the subtle humiliation of my grandmother herding us together at every single state park and viewing station, wielding her ancient iPad like a Leica M10 and chirping, "Smile like you mean it."

It's almost enough to make me forget. Almost.

My sister Bea is sitting on the other side of the back seat with her earbuds in, staring out the window. She looks lost in thought and the leafy sunlight is moving across her pale, freckled face in little flickers and flashes. She's fourteen, old enough to be pissed about the whole thing, but young enough that it's not ruining her entire life.

To be clear: this whole thing is ruining my life. Not that it really matters. The grand scheme of things is much bigger than that. I get it.

But in California, I had friends. I had a boyfriend, sort of. I had a job at the photography store downtown. I had parties, hanging under the giant palm tree on the lawn after school, laying out in the hot sand at the beach on the weekends. A whole senior year shimmering off in the distance. Some days it was still hard to do anything—grief pressing down like a weighted blanket—but things were getting better.

And then, six weeks ago, a month before my older sister Hannah left for her freshman year of college in Connecticut, I overheard Mom on the phone.

I'm drowning, El. I don't think I can do this.

• • •

MY DAD DIED NINE MONTHS AGO. IF I TRY, I CAN SAY IT NOW without really feeling anything. But my mom still disappears every time it comes up. She'll be standing right there in front of you, but the self inside of her is gone.

When I heard her say this, *I'm drowning*, in a voice that crackled with sadness, I was surprised. The first few weeks after Dad died, she was blown wide open, leveled by a hurricane, splinters of her former self littering the front lawn. But then about three weeks in, she just got dressed and went to work. And that was the end of it.

I take out my camera, adjusting the shutter speed and focusing in on the tiny pieces of dust glowing gold on my window. I twist the lens and the dust blurs; leaves and sunlight emerge and sharpen.

Then the world in my viewfinder lurches and we pull into a long, bumpy driveway that winds through a tunnel of overgrown shrubs and briars. It's darker in here, too dark for photographs, the heavy greenery making it feel as though the sun's already gone down.

The car lumbers along, branches scratching across the windshield.

"Jesus," my grandpa whispers.

"Don't curse, Jack," Grandma whispers back.

"Are we really leaving them here?"

He must think that my music is on because I'm wearing my earbuds, but I turned it off a while ago. Sometimes I like to listen without anyone knowing.

If it was up to my grandfather, we would all be moving to Ohio. He's my dad's dad, not my mom's, so all of this is really hard for him. He's also been ingrained with generations of Irish Catholic stoicism, which makes emoting difficult. He likes college football and church and reading the newspaper quietly in his chair. He doesn't like New York or California, preferring the flat expanse of the Midwest, where he's lived his entire life. The thought of us moving here, with our mother and recently divorced aunt, seems like it might be more than he can handle.

He shakes his head and adjusts his glasses, swiping at his

sweaty forehead and smoothing the thin piece of white hair that stretches across his bald spot.

"This place is like a tropical rainforest," he says. As if he or any of us have ever seen one.

Eight months ago, when Grandpa was in LA for the funeral, he spent half an hour wandering around Whole Foods looking for Keebler sandwich crackers. He circled the store twice, his black dress shoes squeaking as he wove through the aisles squinting at the artfully packaged items and fuming silently. I finally convinced him to ask for help, and a bewildered teen employee led us to the organic snack aisle he'd already searched four times.

Grandpa stood there, shaking his head and holding a box of Late July mini peanut butter sandwich crackers in his hands, muttering, *$6.59 a box*, again and again like he was trying to make himself believe that any of it—the organic snack aisle; the ridiculous, fancy grocery store with the landscaped parking lot; the fact that his oldest son was dead and gone—was real. I thought he might be broken, for good, but then he just sighed and put the box back onto the shelf.

"C'mon, Mary," he'd said. "We're going to 7-Eleven."

• • •

Now in the stuffy front seat of our old Toyota, Grandma lays her small, knobby hand on Grandpa's arm. "It's going to be fine, Jack," she says. I can tell it's hard for her too, but she does a better job of hiding it. She's raised ten kids and grandmothered twenty-nine grandchildren. She's basically an emotional fortress.

Finally, the driveway ends in a clearing so big I'm shocked that there could be so much open space in the middle of this forest. The house itself is medium sized and covered in gray-brown shingles. It has two and a half stories, the kind where the bottom floor is dug into a slope in the ground. On one side an outrageous garden bursts with a jumble of vegetables and late-summer flowers. On the other side a sea of green grass stretches all the way to the distant tree line, fresh cut close to the house and long and wild farther off.

A heavy wooden front door stands in the middle of the house, facing the afternoon sun. It's framed on either side by rows of deep red dahlias, all bowing under the weight of their heavy heads.

"I guess this is it," Grandma says, adjusting her butterscotch-colored polyester skirt. It sounds like she's trying to force extra cheer into her voice to compensate for everyone else in the car.

Bea just sighs heavily and shoves her phone into her backpack.

As soon as we park in the gravel out front, the door opens and three dogs burst out: one giant and shaggy, one stocky and short haired, and one tiny and fierce and loud. All three are mutts; El found them in parking lots and walking down the road, and now, despite never having set out to be a pet owner, she dotes on them like they are her children.

Behind the dogs are Aunt El and Mom. El looks cool as ever, in ripped jeans and Birkenstocks, her face glowing in a wide-lipped smile. Mom is wearing casual clothes, no computer in sight. Her hair is curling in the humidity and her skin is pink from the sun. She almost looks like she used to before the great comet of Pancreatic Cancer ripped the roof off our life.

I open the car door, feeling like I'm inside a mirage. I'm trying to get myself to believe that this is the place I'm going to be living now and this very alive person waiting for me on the porch is my mother.

After Dad died, when Mom went back to work, it was like she stepped off a pier and ended up in another person's life. Her hours doubled, tripled, stretched out into nights and rolled over weekends. She encased herself in clients and paperwork, building a thick, opaque shell between herself and the rest of us. She said she was fine but not even her eyes peeked through.

Now she's here. Right in front of me. She pulls me into her and I can feel her heart beating where my cheek is pressed into her neck. Bea slinks up to us and El reaches for her and we're all in one giant hug: Mom, El, Bea, and me.

It's a while before we let go and look over to where my grandparents are standing stiff next to the car, the dogs sniffing all around them. They look small and out of place in this great big clearing.

El holds her arms out, as if to hug them from all the way across the yard. "Jack! Nancy! You must be exhausted. Come on in and get settled."

My mom adds, "The girls can get the bags."

Normally, as in one year ago, I would have rolled my eyes and protested. Because I've been in the car for a thousand hours. All I want to do is go inside and shut myself in a room and not talk to anyone. But things are different now, so I jump off the porch and head over to the car.

"Come on, Bea."

Of course my little sister balks.

"This is stupid," she says under her breath.

But she drags herself down the steps and follows me over.

I open the trunk and start pulling bags out and piling them onto the grass. Bea grabs her backpack and pillow out of the back seat and starts walking off toward the house.

"Seriously?" I say.

She shrugs.

"If she wants the bags inside she can do it herself," Bea says.

I turn back to the trunk, sweating as I empty the whole thing by myself and haul the bags inside. I tell myself it's good exercise. I tell myself that I'm not exhausted, that I'm not freaking out, that I'm not getting a sunburn and bug bites and possible heat-stroke. I tell myself that I'm not really moving into this house in the middle of the woods of upstate New York. Everything, even this, is temporary. I'm fine.

. . .

An hour later, I'm sitting on a bench seat at a giant slab table, watching El bring out big wooden bowls of salad and ceramic plates of grilled steaks and tomatoes from the garden. I feel a little dizzy. This past year we've been living on takeout, buttered noodles, and grilled cheese sandwiches. After the sympathy casseroles ran out, we all forgot how to cook.

El nestles the dishes amid a sprawling arrangement of candle-sticks and flower jars like each one is something precious. Until about two years ago, El lived in a cramped bungalow in Atlanta, Georgia, with my uncle Mac. They only had one dog then, Bernie, and big pots of kitchen herbs that surrounded a cement slab backyard. Everything of El's felt contained, tiny pieces of ephemera sprinkled in among Mac's towering bookshelves, offer-ings hidden among the classics.

Then they split up and El took a summer residency in upstate New York. She got a position at a community college after that, adopted Katharine Hepburn and RBG, and bought this place. In this great big house, El is everywhere, from the giant man-eating flowers to the wild paintings that jam the walls.

We hold hands as Grandpa says grace, Bea loudly sighing through the whole thing like she's the actual devil and the prayer is causing her physical pain. My mom shoots her a look across the table as Grandpa tacks on a toast with his water glass to thank El for opening up her home.

"And that garden!" Grandma adds. "How do you do it, Elizabeth?"

"It's the soil here," El says. "You can literally grow anything."

"Well," says Grandpa, "it's certainly very nice."

The whole time I'm thinking to myself, *Can we just hurry this along?* Because I want to eat everything, all at once.

Finally he's done, returning the glass to the table with a shaky, liver-spotted hand. I take a bite of salad and it's like the crunchy butter lettuce is breathing little puffs of life back into my spirit. The permanent impression of the back seat upholstery slowly starts to lift from my soul.

I look over at my mom and see it again, that color in her cheeks. I can't remember the last time I saw her sitting at a table, eating food, but here she is, chewing, swallowing, smiling, talking.

I can tell Grandpa's tired and out of sorts, but he makes a real effort, complimenting El on the food and giving a full rundown of the trip while we eat. Still, the way he talks about it, it sounds just like a list: Grand Canyon, Petrified Forest, etc., etc.

I sneak a glance at Bea and she's slumped in her chair, spearing pieces of lettuce like she's hunting them. It looks like she hasn't eaten a thing.

You okay? I mouth.

She just sighs like I'll never understand and pushes back from the table.

"I'm full," she says as she stalks off toward the stairs.

My mom watches her, visibly deflating. For a second her eyes are completely blank. Then she straightens up, turns to me, and says, "Mary, what did you think of the trip?"

"It was good," I lie, recognizing the fragility of this moment. "The Grand Canyon was really cool."

I don't tell her about the crowded, old bathrooms or the creepy motel or how numb I felt as I stood at the edge of the vast expanse of empty air.

It wasn't that the Grand Canyon wasn't beautiful or that it wasn't amazing to get to see the country. It was more that it felt like the four of us were just drifting from California to New York on an iceberg: quiet, cold, alone. Just radio show after radio show of calm, soothing, boring voices or long stretches of silence, Grandma snoring softly in the front seat. Bea on her side, me on mine.

"What did you think of the Badlands?" Grandma asks. "All those sunflowers!"

"Oh," I say. "That was cool too. I really liked all of it."

"Cool," Grandma repeats, shaking her head. "The internet is ruining the vocabulary of an entire generation."

Her fake pearls glow a little in the candlelight, the same white as her short, straight hair.

"If you want to get into Columbia you can't spend all of your time surfing the internet," Grandpa says. His eyes are small and tired behind his glasses.

"Jane, you should be helping the girls to cut back," Grandma says, turning to my mom. "Did you get that article I sent you?"

My mom's smile tightens. "I did," she says. "Thank you, Nancy. And I don't know if Columbia is on Mary's list, but I'm sure she'll get in wherever she wants to go."

It makes me a little lightheaded, everyone talking about my life like I'm not even here.

Grandma sets down her fork. "I hope she's at least looking at some of the Ivies. We want Mary to aim high, even if James isn't here to push her."

My dad's name, spoken aloud, is like an airhorn. There's a long pause as we absorb it. Mom aggressively saws the stripe of fat from her steak. Grandma takes a long sip of water. My stomach turns.

El looks at me from across the table and shrugs.

"Nancy," she says. "Jane tells me that you've been growing roses this year. It's the one thing I haven't had much luck with."

"Sheer willpower," Grandma replies, and El laughs, big and loose.

With that, the forks go back to clinking against plates, the conversation moves on to other things. I look down at my own food, trying to regain my enthusiasm, but the moment is gone.

• • •

AFTER THE DISHES ARE DONE I EXCUSE MYSELF, ANXIOUS TO BE alone for the first time in days. Aunt El walks me up the stairs to my room and gives me a big, hard squeeze, whispering, "I'm so glad you're here."

Then she releases me and says, "You don't have to take that kind of shit from your grandparents."

"I know," I say, my cheeks burning.

We both look over at Bea's closed door.

"It's complicated," I say.

"It is," she agrees.

Then she kisses my cheek and disappears back down the stairs.

● ● ●

My new room is on the third floor, at the back of the house—a tiny space with huge windows that overlook the field and the forest beyond El's yard. I feel like I could spend days just sitting by the open window watching these woods. I do for a minute and see the dusky pink sky deepen, then I flop onto the twin bed with its colorful quilt and stare up at the ceiling.

I breathe. The air feels good. Thick and clean and humid— completely different from Los Angeles. It's noisy, but instead of cars and people I can hear hundreds of crickets and frogs, all out there trying to find each other. I focus on that for a while—the sound of the night and the feeling of the air in my lungs. I try not to think about anything else.

But of course the thoughts come, one after another. I think about Bea closed up in her room. I think about Hannah, some- where in the middle of Connecticut, laughing her weird, cackling laugh. I think about our old house with the beige carpet and the stucco walls. I wonder who's going to be living there now, living our old life.

There's a knock on my door. It's my mom. She leans up against the frame, arms crossed, face wide open, eyes so deep I could fall right in. It's jarring.

"Hey, babe," she says. "Just want to check in and see how you're doing."

"I'm good," I say, not having words to describe what I really am.

"Good," she says. "I missed you."

The words feel bigger than the space they take up in the hallway. I want to say, *When? For how long?* But the questions get stuck in my mouth like saltine crackers.

I'm not used to seeing her like this, so still, just standing right in front of me wanting to know how I am. I've gotten used to catching glimpses of my mother, distractedly reaching into the fridge for a handful of grapes and then floating back up to her desk like a ghost.

"Do you need anything?" she asks.

I want to need something. Because it looks like that's what she wants.

I wish I could take a photograph of this Mom—the light of the bare bulb on the hallway ceiling illuminating the single, affectionate dimple in her cheek—to create some evidence that she was here before she disappears again. But that would be weird, so instead I just say, "I'm good," again, and watch as she nods and walks back down the stairs.

I close my door, trying to shake off the weirdness of the moment, of every moment since we've arrived, and open my laptop. I haven't spoken to Nora in days and I promised I would FaceTime as soon as I secured reliable Wi-Fi and my own room.

In the train wreck that was our last day in Los Angeles, when Hannah was already off getting wasted at freshman orientation; when my grandparents arrived in perfectly creased khakis and Notre Dame paraphernalia, dropping a steady string of subtle judgments about Los Angeles, our house, our packing progress, and our manners; when the movers arrived late and broke my favorite mug with the middle finger on it; when it took us three hours to finish packing the car to Grandpa's standards after dinner and everyone screamed at each other in the driveway and I snuck off in Nora's car—at the peak of the whole fiasco I dropped my phone into the sea. Nora had taken me to the beach for one last talk in the sand. It was well after dark by then, and as I pretended to run into the ocean in a silly, melodramatic gesture, my phone, along with all of my contacts and photos and notes and memories, somehow slipped from my pocket.

It felt like a sign. The worst kind. And the next morning I drove away with my mom's old iPhone 5c, which was not compatible with most apps and stopped getting any kind of cell service halfway between Albuquerque and Denver. After that, I bribed, begged, and wrestled with Bea for turns on her phone and took a deep dive into the Alanis Morissette and Liz Phair albums in my mom's iTunes library. Missing Nora has become a headache that's always at the back of my mind.

I hover the cursor over the little circle of face next to her name, and for a second the missing grows. But then she answers on the second ring and everything's a little loud and blurry. Her face materializes and I see that she's at the beach, but it's still sunny. And then I remember the time difference.

"Mary!" she yells. Her voice sounds like she's using a hundred exclamation points.

"Nora!" I whisper-yell back. Suddenly I'm flooded with a mixture of feelings—affection and loneliness and jealousy and longing.

"Where the hell are you?" She's almost yelling over the roar of the waves.

Nora's mom is Korean American and her dad is white. She has a heart-shaped freckle on her cheek and long black hair that is caught in the neck of her wet suit. She's been my best friend since the first day of kindergarten, when she walked up to me on the playground and, without saying a word, took hold of my hand.

"My aunt's," I say. "We just got here a couple of hours ago. I can't believe this is real."

She shakes her head.

"Me either. How is it?"

I sigh. "Weird? Different. I'm basically in the middle of a gigantic forest. No ocean in sight."

"Here," she says, turning the camera around so I can see the waves.

"I can't tell if that makes it better or worse," I say.

She flips the camera back around.

"Come back," she says.

"I wish."

Then she smiles. "I bet I know something that can cheer you up."

"Oh yeah?"

She disappears from the screen for a second and I can see

the slanted horizon and a strip of ocean that glints sharply and obscures the rest of the view.

"Guess who's here?" She sings out the question, stretching out the last word. And then I experience some momentary sea-sickness as she passes the phone.

"Mary?" I hear a deep voice as the screen rights itself and then I see him. He's just a silhouette because the sun on the ocean is so bright behind him.

I duck to the side for a second, smoothing out my hair, testing my breath. As if that matters.

"Where'd you go?" he asks, confused.

I pop back up, flustered, and I can tell I'm blushing through my freckles. He's turned himself around so that the sun is on his face and I'm hit full force with his blond-haired, blue-eyed, California golden boy good looks.

The first time I ever saw Bennett was in fourth grade. We were on the same YMCA basketball team, and at the very first sight of his long, downy limbs and swishy hair, he poured straight into my heart like concrete. *Oh*, I thought. *This is what love is.*

"Hey!" I say, a little too brightly.

"Hey," he says, a lazy smile on one side of his mouth.

There's a long silence. I swallow. I'm not sure what to say, where to begin, and suddenly it feels like the distance between us is really, really far. And then, "I miss you," he says, and I barely hear it above the waves.

It makes my stomach hurt.

"I miss you too," I whisper.

And then Nora grabs the phone back from him, yelling, "My turn!"

I'm vibrating with what Bennett just said. I'm completely melted and completely crushed and I don't think I can take another second of sitting here on this bed in the absolute middle of nowhere while my friends are all together on my favorite beach, all the way across the country.

I look down, picking at a loose thread on the quilt. The square is embroidered with the words *Chin up, buttercup!* in loopy yellow cursive.

"Nora, I gotta run. I haven't even started unpacking yet and I want to check on Bea."

She tucks an errant strand of hair behind her ear. "Okay, yeah, sure. Call me tomorrow?"

"Definitely."

"I'll be waiting, like one of those sad boyfriends who holds his girlfriend's purse while she's trying on clothes."

The wind whips up again, swooshing Nora's hair across her face. Quick as lightning, I press the computer keys to catch a picture of the screen.

"Love you, Nora," I say, and suddenly tears are pushing at the backs of my eyes.

"Love you too, Mary." She yells it over the roar of wind and then the screen goes black.

2

I WAKE UP EARLY IN THE MORNING, THE EDGES OF THE sunrise slanting in through the open window across from my bed. The air cooled during the night, leaving little droplets of condensation on the windowsill. I stand there, smearing my finger through the moisture and dust, thinking, *Okay. This is my new life. It's starting now.*

I guess maybe it started when we finished packing up the car, or when we pulled away from the curb, or when we crossed the California state line. Or when my dad was diagnosed with cancer. It could have been any one of those moments. But something about today feels big.

I throw on some clothes, a wrinkly vintage floral skirt and T-shirt that says NO. Then I tiptoe down the stairs, trying not to wake anyone. But when I get down there I see that everyone but Bea is up already, drinking coffee and eating cold cereal at various spots around the kitchen and dining room table.

My mom comes over and gives me a hug.

"Morning, Mary," she says, beaming at me in her pajamas. It's almost getting creepy, the hugging and the smiling.

I think of a morning before any of this, when Dad was still alive. My mom would be in constant motion, ping-ponging from the coffee machine to the refrigerator, stuffing a seltzer into her purse while she watered the plants, her eyes somehow never leaving her phone. She'd spill coffee on her blouse and swipe furiously at it with a Tide pen, eventually giving up and peeling her shirt off right there in the kitchen.

"Ew, gross, Mom," Bea would say. "I can see your stretch marks."

"That's rude," Mom would say. "And anyway, Dad thinks they're sexy."

Bea would pretend to barf, then storm outside to wait in the car. Mom would roll her eyes and then rush out of the kitchen, calling, "Hurry up with breakfast, girls!" to Hannah and me.

Dad would sit in his threadbare blue robe at the kitchen table, eyes glued to the morning paper, like he didn't even know we were there.

I sit down and Grandpa grunts over in my direction. Grandma, already dressed in a pink skirt and striped, matching blouse, gets up and starts fussing over my breakfast. She asks me which kind of cereal I want and I consider my choices: two different versions of hippie cardboard flakes.

"I'm good, Grandma," I say, grabbing a plum out of the fruit bowl.

"C'mon, Mare," El says. "A piece of fruit is not breakfast. Let me make you a fried egg."

I look at her, trying to decide if I should say yes or no. I don't

18

want her to have to go through the trouble; at the same time, she seems invested in feeding me. So I shrug. "Sure."

She gets out a pan, eggs, and some butter and starts cooking with her back to me. Katharine, the big, shaggy dog, sniffs her way over to investigate.

"How'd you sleep, Mary?"

I consider this and I remember the cool air, the quilt, the crickets. "Actually, I slept all right."

My grandma wrinkles her nose. "Gosh, I don't think I've gotten a full night's sleep since we left Cleveland. I'll be glad to fly home to my own bed tomorrow."

The adults start up a boring conversation about the merits of sleeping in your own bed. I zone out and watch El at the stove, in paint-covered overalls the color of the sky. I bite into my plum and it's perfectly ripe and sweet and firm. It's like eating sparkles or edible sun.

Soon my egg is done, crispy and delicious. Everyone is discussing what to do for the day when Bea trudges down the stairs.

"Hey," she says in her raspy voice. She sits down next to me at the counter and collapses her head onto her arms.

"How'd you sleep?" I ask her.

"Awful," she grumbles.

Her hair is black right now—she's in a sort of nineties-Goth phase—and it piles around her like squid-ink spaghetti. I pick up a strand that's dangerously close to my plate.

"I was thinking of going into town to explore in a bit," I say. "Want to come?"

She doesn't lift her head.

"You know what," she says. "I love you a lot but after two

weeks in the car together, I think I need a little me time."

"So true," I say. "Hey, Mom. Can I take the car for a while?"

Grandpa's shoulders tense and he makes a little humming sound.

My mom looks at him and grimaces, then takes a breath, straightens up. "Jack, she'll be fine. She's a senior in high school."

He frowns and shoves his nose deeper into his newspaper.

I put my hand on his shoulder. "How will I get to Harvard if I don't know how to drive a car?"

He chuckles. "If you go to Columbia, you won't need a car."

"I'm not going anywhere this morning," El says. "You can take my car if you want. The keys are hanging by the door. Do you know where you're going?"

I shrug. I don't really but I also don't care.

"I'll give you my phone so you can use the navigation," El says. "Just get directions to the co-op."

I run upstairs and grab my sunglasses, wallet, and camera, the feeling of impending freedom buzzing through my bones. I need to get out of here, away from my family, to see what's beyond all these trees. My aunt presses a grocery list and her co-op member number into my hand as I whisk past everyone and out the door.

. . .

I DRIVE THE ENTIRE FIVE MILES INTO TOWN WITH THE WINDOWS down, blasting music. I'm awestruck once again by how green everything is, how lush and alive. I pass acres and acres of farmland, fresh manure wafting through the window. Then more forest, thick and dark. Finally I reach the edge of town: a sprawling school campus with a deserted old playground, a closed-down

Dollar General. And then it's like I blink and I'm in the absolute center, which is marked by what might be the town's only stoplight.

I'm pretty sure I've crossed into another dimension, found the exact, diametric opposite of LA and its endless maze of streets, its superfluous freeways, stoplights, entrances and exits, signs of all kinds. The shabbiness of the buildings here—the yellowed awning of the drugstore and the dilapidated sign in front of the gas station—the aggressive plainness of the entire town seems to mock California and its obsession with newness, its ever-changing coffee shops and restaurants, billboards and beauty trends.

I hear myself whisper, "This is it?"

And for the weirdest half second as I wait for the light to turn green, absently watching two old guys chatting outside the door of Stewart's, it feels like my dad is sitting on the seat next to me, shaking his head and saying, *Holy shit, Marigold.* But then I look and all I see is the coffee-stained upholstery of the passenger seat.

I turn left, passing a few shops and a tiny diner, and pull up in front of a huge wooden clapboard building with a crooked spire coming out the top of it. My navigation tells me that this is the co-op.

I park out front, but instead of going in I head down the street, away from the stoplight, my camera—a beat-up 35 mm I found at the Salvation Army in Santa Monica—slung over my shoulder.

As I wander down the narrow road, I start to see Cumberland's charm. It's almost cute. Most of the houses have two stories, big porches, and wooden siding. Most are painted white with black shutters. The stores are small and the displays look dusty. But the lawns are trimmed and the trees are majestic, stretching out their branches in places to almost meet one another above the streets.

It's quiet in town—not too many cars or people. It's completely different from the bright, vibrant Los Angeles sprawl I'm used to. I spot a few faded Trump signs clinging to front windows and a confederate flag bumper sticker that sends a shiver down my spine.

Wandering down the sidewalk, I start to feel strange. Disconnected. Far from home.

So I take the lens cap off my camera. I focus on the way the light is once again dancing through the leaves or the way a shadow folds in and out of the siding on someone's garage. For a while I'm not me; I'm a young Uta Barth, marveling at subtle color changes and noticing the spaces between things.

I wander a little more and then I make my way to the co-op, walking up the creaky wooden steps and pushing through an ancient screen door. Inside, it's kind of old-timey, but I get the feeling that the vibe is not intentional. All of the shelving is dark, heavy wood, and the floors are old and loud.

I peruse the shelves at the front of the store, which are full of balms and oils and natural beauty products. There are three different kinds of crystal deodorant and about a hundred different bottles of oil perfume, all of which smell like patchouli.

I'm trying on a sample of tinted beeswax lip balm when I feel eyes on me. I look up and see that they're big and round and deep brown and they belong to a boy standing behind the counter. *Boy* is probably the wrong word. I think he's my age and he's tall and lanky, with the kind of body you'd have to fold up to fit in the passenger seat. He's white, like everyone else I've seen so far today. His arms look strong and suntanned and he's wearing a threadbare Velvet Underground shirt—the one with the banana on it—and his hair is dark, a little bit long and unruly, falling over one eye.

And then I register that he's watching me check him out and at that exact moment I drop the lip balm on the floor and it rolls away loudly.

I scamper over to grab it, then duck back behind the shelf, trying to gather myself. *I'm me*, I think. *Mary Sullivan*. I'm at the store, picking up things for my aunt. I'm a normal person doing normal-person things.

I smooth my hair, fix my skirt, and emerge somewhat gracefully. Then I wander around the store, through the bulk bins and along the refrigerators at the back, adding items to my basket. I avoid eye contact to counteract all of the staring I was doing before. I almost start to forget what happened. Until I get to the counter.

He's smiling at me, grinning, when it's my turn. And just my luck, there's no one behind me in line to rush this along.

"Hi," he says through his stupid grin.

"Hi," I say.

"I don't think I've seen you before," he says, and I notice that his teeth are a little crooked on the bottom. "Are you visiting?"

"Actually, I just moved here."

He looks surprised. "You moved here?"

I nod and notice the way his hands are dancing around aimlessly, touching things on the counter, straightening the pens. His fingers are long and graceful and an old watch with a brown leather band wraps around his wrist.

"Oh." He's still smiling, but it's different now, like when the sun rolls out from behind a cloud. "Cool."

"Yeah . . ." I say, dropping my eyes and dragging my finger across the wooden edge of the counter. I can't look at that smile anymore or my eyeballs might burn right out of my head.

"What's your name?" he asks, and he finally starts moving my groceries over the scanner. I brought some bags from El's house, so I start packing everything up.

"Mary," I say, still avoiding eye contact as I place a cold bottle of milk into a cloth bag that says GLOBAL WARMING: SO UNCOOL!

"Mary?" he says, and I look up to see his eyes wandering slowly over my face.

"It's short for Marigold," I say, and as soon as I say it I wish I hadn't.

"Marigold?" he says, his brows drawing together in confusion.

My cheeks flame. "Seriously?"

"Sorry." He shakes his head. "It's nice. I like it."

"Oh thank god," I say. "I've actually been walking around my whole life, waiting for male affirmation."

Shit. I can't believe I just said that. He blinks and his mouth falls halfway open.

"Sorry," I say, nervously tucking a strand of hair behind my ear. "That was so rude. I'm having a weird day."

The smile comes creeping back. "It's okay. You're right, anyway."

"Well, for what it's worth, Marigold is totally bizarre," I say, shoving a box of mushrooms onto the top of my bag and handing him El's member number. "My mom was going through a phase."

He laughs at this. Then he nods at my camera. "You take photographs?"

"Yeah," I say, and now I'm smiling. "It's the best."

"It is," he says. "Black and white or color?"

I open my mouth to answer, but a customer who I didn't realize was behind me clears her throat loudly. I lug my bag of groceries off the counter.

"I should go."

"Okay." He shoves his hands in his pockets. "See you around, Marigold."

I hesitate, wondering if I should correct him—everyone calls me Mary—but the lady sighs again, louder this time. So I give a limp wave instead.

"Yeah," I say. "Later."

I'm trying for casual but of course I trip on the threshold on my way out of the store, knocking my bags against the giant door and barely catching myself before I fall down the steps.

. . .

WHEN I GET HOME, THE HOUSE IS QUIET AND THERE'S A NOTE ON the counter:

> Went into the new office to take care of some paperwork.
> Grandpa and Grandma are napping. Be ready to help with dinner at
> 5:30. Love you—M

Back in my room I open my computer, then close it, then open it again. I don't really feel like talking to anyone, but at the same time I miss *everyone*.

I open my email, which feels so strange. Normally, Nora and I would be messaging all day long, an endless stream of jokes, memes, surreptitiously snapped pictures of ugly dogs and hot guys. But now I'm here on a faraway planet that time forgot, with no phone, so I'm using email like a thirty-year-old office worker.

I have to scroll through rows and rows of junk before I see one from Nora from a few days ago. I open it.

Mary!!!

I miss you so much. You've only been gone for five days but it feels like a year, at least. I feel like I should tell you that you're not missing anything, but you're missing EVERYTHING. JK. But not. But yes. I'm kidding. Here's what's new with me: I found a new surfing spot up past Malibu. And my dad is dating another twenty-five-year-old. That's all I've got.

I have a million questions for you and I hope you call me soon. Do you know how much it's killing me that you lost your phone? The universe hates us. Anyway, here are my questions:

How's Bea? Hannah? How's your mom? Are you still alive? Is it true that everyone wears polo shirts on the East Coast? Have you seen any cows yet?

Bennett asked why you'd disappeared so I told him about your phone. He said he'd send an email. You'd better forward all correspondence for analysis. Also, you'd better call me soon.

Love u.
Nora

I want to write her back, but I'm not sure where to begin or what to say. *The road trip was depressing. I feel like my life is over. The air here feels wet to the touch. I can't think about Bennett without wanting to crawl under the couch.* The idea of trying to string all of those thoughts together seems exhausting.

So I open a new window and paste Bennett's email into the address box. I try several different subject lines: *Hi*, and then *Hey*, and then *Hi* again, before giving up and just leaving it blank. I click down into the box for the main part of the email, and then I type:

Did you mean it when you said you missed me?

And then I click the X in the corner and delete the whole thing.

The first time Bennett kissed me, after seven years of excruciating friendship, was the day my mother told us we were moving to New York. We were sitting on my bed, watching *Point Break* for the thirteenth time, when the news just sort of slipped out.

"What?" Bennett said.

"I'm moving to New York."

On the screen, Patrick Swayze was robbing another bank.

"You're kidding," Bennett said, shaking his head a little.

"It's true." I wondered how many times I'd have to say it before it felt real. "We're leaving at the end of July."

Bennett sat there for a minute, blinking his eyes, a whole world of incomprehensible thoughts passing behind them. Then he tackled me against the pillow and said, "No you're not."

His breath was hot in my face and his eyes blurred into one big circle in the middle of everything.

And then he was kissing me and holding my cheeks. His

tongue tasted like Starbursts. His mouth was soft and his hands were warm and it was almost like an out-of-body experience, getting the thing I had always wanted.

I tug my backpack out from under the bed and pull out a stack of prints: a long strand of Hannah's hair, floating across the sky; the cushion of Bennett's palm, peppered with tiny pieces of gravel; a triangle of light on the peeling paint of Nora's windowsill.

On my phone, under the ocean, there are other pictures—slanting afternoon sun on the beach pictures; sweaty, dancing, smiling pictures; me and Nora laughing; me and Bennett almost kissing; Bea flipping off the camera; Hannah laughing until she peed her pants.

I try to swallow the fact that those are gone. Instead of crying, I tack my photographs to the wall until I'm surrounded by lopped-off parts of what used to be.

Bea's got her door open across the hall, so after a while I get up and head in there. She's lying on her bed with her earbuds in and her eyes closed. I lie down next to her. She doesn't seem startled by me, even though the music is blaring so loud I can hear it: Talking Heads. Dad's favorite. She pulls one earbud out and hands it to me, and I stick it in my ear and we lie like that for a long time.

Here's a secret about my dad: I'm starting to forget. I don't remember his smell or the feeling of his skin, and my memories curve around the empty spaces where he would have stood or spoken. Sometimes, right before I fall asleep, I try to bring him into my mind. I think of a time when I know he was there, I draw his outline from photographs. Behind my eyes, I try to color it in.

But the more I try to remember him, the more he's gone.

Lying here, on Bea's bed, I know he's in us, somewhere. In the space where the music seeps out into our ears, in the iconic drums at the beginning of "And She Was," in the place where our hair is mixing together on the bed, in our cells, our genes. But I can't get to him.

I grab Bea's hand and I pull it into mine. Her palm is soft and warm. I squeeze as hard as I can and she squeezes back, like she knows all of my thoughts, like she's thinking them too.

• • •

Dinner is delicious, real food again, and Grandma and Grandpa are leaving tomorrow so for the most part the tension has subsided. Mom and El tell us all the old stories and we laugh until tears roll down our cheeks.

But after last night, we leave Dad out of it. Even though he was there at Bea's third birthday when she poured ketchup all over her birthday cake. He was there when I shoplifted a fistful of fruit leathers from Trader Joe's in second grade. He was there when Mom caught Hannah sneaking out the window her freshman year of high school with an entire jumbo pack of toilet paper in her backpack. No one knows how to mention his name anymore.

When I think nobody is looking, I lift my camera to catch the candlelight glinting off Grandpa's wedding ring and the soft sag of skin under Grandma's chin.

Bea gives me a look and mouths, *You're being creepy.*

I wiggle my eyebrows and mouth back, *You have no idea.*

Grandpa and Grandma have an early flight, so after dessert and dishes are done we say goodbye. I get a stiff hug from

Grandpa and a squishy one from Grandma. Both of them smell a little like mothballs. We've never been close, but I'm weirdly sad that they're leaving. Like another little piece of Dad is breaking off and floating away.

. . .

THE NEXT DAY, EL MAKES US A BIG BREAKFAST OF FRENCH TOAST and bacon and convinces us all to come to the river. I put on a dark green one-piece, and Bea wears a black-and-white polka dot bikini that's cut like it's from the fifties. El loads us up with hats, sunscreen, giant towels that are covered in flowers, and canvas bags of picnic lunch food.

It's a ten-minute drive through town and out the other side. Then we park by the road, tromp across a field, and scramble down a brush-covered embankment. Aunt El leads the way, carrying twice as much as anyone else.

Mom is right behind her, and I watch as she laughs the whole way down. I study her like a scientist, trying to figure out what's different. She's lighter somehow. Like, full of light.

"Creepy, isn't it?" Bea says as if reading my mind. "It's like she got a brain transplant."

I ignore her, picking my way through blackberry brambles and trying not to fall to my death.

"Or maybe she got bodysnatched." Bea's eyes are hidden behind giant sunglasses, but I can hear the hint of bitterness in her voice.

A pricker scratches across my kneecap. A bead of blood seeps out, sticking to my skin. I wipe it off with my thumb and push ahead.

"I'm glad she's back," I say.

"I hope it lasts," says Bea.

The trail ends and we see the river. It looks deep and cool, with big, round stones all along the bank and giant rocks cropping out above the water for jumping. We have the place to ourselves. The thick layer of trees around us makes it feel like an oasis.

We lay our towels out over on the pebbled beach, and then Aunt El scrambles up on the tallest rock and leaps into the water. She's under the surface for a few long seconds, lost to us, then she emerges, her long gray-and-brown hair slicked back perfectly and shining in the sun.

"Get in here, girls!" she calls. "The water is fucking exquisite."

"Language, El!" my mom shouts, but she's laughing, and for a moment the two of them look so much alike they could almost be twins.

Mom heads up to the rocky ledge and I follow her. Bea declines, deciding instead to sunbathe. She looks like someone famous in her big, cat-eye sunglasses with her black hair fanning out around the daisies on her towel.

Mom and I scramble upward, slippery little avalanches of rocks collapsing under our feet. When we're standing at the ledge, ten feet above the water, I feel like I'm swaying at the edge of a skyscraper. The fear of letting go, of dropping into and under the rushing water, wraps around my ankle like a snake.

But I look over at Mom and she suddenly looks so young. Her smile is stretching across her face like it actually belongs there. So I grab her hand, bend my knees, and leap.

My stomach drops when I hit the water. I'm shocked by the cold that covers every inch of me. But when I emerge, breathless, the world looks different through my wet eyelashes. Everything sparkles.

Mom swims gracefully over to the edge, and I watch her pick her way back over to the towels, squeezing the water from her hair. Then I float on my back and squint up at the clouds. I can feel the water moving around me, washing one second of time and space into the next.

• • •

WHEN WE GET HOME THAT AFTERNOON I SEE AN EMAIL FROM Bennett:

> Hey Mary,
>
> How's New York? It's Thursday night and I'm bored as hell. I wish you were here. In case you're wondering, I really do. Miss you. When are you coming back home?
>
> Bennett

I read it at least ten times before sinking back onto the pillows and closing my eyes.

I think about that last month together, the in-between. Nora was on her yearly summer trip to Seoul so it was just Bennett and me for three whole weeks. We were more than friends but not really enough of anything else. Existing in a finite sliver of time. Trying to make it last. Spending hours in my room while my mom was at work, lying on our sides and kissing. Letting his hand creep up my shirt while I touched every freckle on his cheeks.

I look around at this unfamiliar room, my half-empty suit-cases spilling out clothes. How did this happen? Why does it seem so impossible to ever get back to that feeling?

I open the computer again to work on my reply. The words feel clumsy, ugly, somehow both too emotive and without any meaning.

Once we started kissing, Bennett and I didn't talk very much. My head was too crammed full of questions like *What does this mean?* and *How do you feel?* and *What do you want to do in August?* I knew that saying any of them out loud would puncture the perfect bubble we'd created in my bedroom, would move the ending of everything a little bit closer.

The first and only time we ever had sex was two days before I left. Right before it happened, he looked down into my eyes and said, *You know I love you, right?*

And I nodded and tried not to cry.

Hi Bennett,

New York is weird. Lots of trees and Trump signs. I'm taking tons of pictures, even though I'm not yet sure if this is an experience I want to remember. I really do. Miss you too.

M

I read it back a few times. It doesn't feel like enough. I used to tell Bennett everything but now it's hard to tell him anything at all.

A new email pops up from Nora:

Marigold. Whyyyy are you avoiding me?

She only ever calls me by my full name when she's pissed, so I get to work on writing her back. I tell her about my aunt's house, about the way my mom is coming back to life, about the town of Cumberland and swimming in the river. When I come to the part of the letter that would be about the guy with the long limbs and dark hair, I skip right over it. I don't even know his name.

3

MY PARENTS NAMED ME MARIGOLD ON SOME KIND of anomalous hippie kick. My older sister, Hannah, and my younger sister, Beatrice, both lucked out and were born during normal name phases, even though I'm the most normal out of the three of us.

Hannah is the kind of dramatic you might find in a Victorian novel. She's always sulking or pining, shutting herself in her room for a week because of some heartache or another. When Kristen Jameson broke up with her in the seventh grade, she forced Bea and me to participate in a full-moon ceremony she'd read about online, claiming that it was the only way she'd ever be able to "move on with her life."

She bought actual crystals, and we tried to burn all of the notes they'd passed. Hannah made me hold a letter while she did the lighter—because I was too young to handle such a dangerous tool—and it ended up burning up much quicker than any of us expected. I lost half of my bangs and ruined my favorite sweater smothering out the flames—because Hannah had just screamed, "Oh my god, fire!" and run out of the room. And still, for weeks, all she could talk about was how our failure was a sign from the universe that they needed to get back together.

Bea is the kind of person who tries to be weird at all costs. At home her room was like a costume shop—wigs and jewelry everywhere, closet bursting with old prom dresses and polyester smoking jackets.

She used to keep a collection of dead things—flowers, beetles, curled-up daddy longlegs, and a rodent skull she'd actually dug up in the backyard—which she arranged museum style on her dresser. In the corner, Frida, a full-size replica of a human skeleton that she'd discovered at the Rose Bowl Flea Market when she was eight years old, hung crookedly, grinning creepily and staring into space.

When Dad died, she put all of it, even Frida, into plastic bags and left it in the garage. My mom asked her why, but she just shrugged and said, "I've moved on."

• • •

On Friday afternoon my mom takes us to register at Cumberland Central, the local public school, which is K–12. At home there were nine elementary schools, three middle schools, and two high schools just in our district, but here there is only one school in the entire area. We park in a gigantic lot at the back with only one other car in it, a bright yellow Ford Mustang. Then we trudge our way around the giant building to the front.

The first thing I notice about the school is that it's all in one sad, sprawling, plain brick building. There's a sign out front that looks new, but everything else has to have been built at least fifty years ago. My old school was on a large campus that was a mix of new and old buildings, long breezeways, and courtyards full of planters and benches. The classrooms opened into outdoor hallways, motel style, and the lockers and lunch tables were all outside.

The second thing I notice, looking at the sign in the middle of the front lawn, is that the school mascot is the *Indians*.

"Jesus Christ," Bea whispers.

"No way," I whisper back.

We push through heavy double doors into the long front hallway and are immediately assaulted by air conditioning. Tan linoleum floors shine under hard fluorescent lights. To the left, a tiny sign that reads OFFICE hangs over a doorway that's flanked on either side by trophy cases. One whole side is dedicated to football, a giant plaque that says CUMBERLAND INDIANS STATE CHAMPS 2015 mounted at the top.

I'm startled by a booming voice as a round, balding man in his fifties appears in the doorway.

"I coached that team myself," he says. "Before I became the principal. You must be Jane, Beatrice, and Marigold."

He extends a leathery hand toward my mom. His fingers look like hot dogs.

"I'm Mr. Pearson, but everyone calls me Coach P."

Bea catches my eyes and mouths, *Is this for real?*

Hope not, I mouth back.

"C'mon in," he says, leading us through the reception area and into his office.

The room is small and square, and it looks a little bit like the trophy case outside. The walls are covered in framed newspaper articles about the football team. I see a photograph of Mr. Pearson on the sidelines, a whistle hanging around his neck, his face frozen mid-yell.

"Welcome to Cumberland!" he says as he lowers himself into a leather desk chair. We sit down in a line of scratchy seats facing his desk, Mom in the middle. She's wearing one of her courtroom suits, her hair pulled back into a bun, and she looks completely out of place in this sports shrine of an office.

"Thanks," she says. "We brought a bunch of paperwork."

She puts a thick folder on the desk, and Mr. Pearson thumbs through it absently.

"I'll have Danielle go over all of this on Monday and get your schedules settled. Everything should be all squared away by Tuesday morning. We start at seven forty-five."

Mr. Pearson rambles on for a while, producing endless, meaningless historical information about the school, mostly about the mid-eighties when he was the quarterback and led the football team to three consecutive state championships. I feel like I'm in a bad dream.

The whole time, his eyes are moving back and forth between Mom's breasts and her face. She's wearing the necklace Dad got her for her twenty-first birthday: a lucky golden horseshoe pendant on a delicate chain.

Finally, Bea snorts. "Her eyes are up here," she says, gesturing to Mom's head.

Mr. Pearson's already ruddy cheeks turn magenta. My mom gives Bea a death glare. I wish I could disappear.

Mr. Pearson clears his throat. "How about I take you girls on a tour?"

We exit the office and head down one of the three long hallways that splinter off from the main entrance.

"This is the high school wing," Mr. Pearson says, gesturing at the row of aggressively orange lockers stretching the length of the hall. "The middle school wing is upstairs, and the elementary wing is back that way."

"How does everyone fit?" Bea asks.

"There are only ninety or so kids in each grade," Mr. Pearson says. "It's a little tight but not too bad."

"Wow," says Mom, raising her eyebrows at me.

Behind Mr. Pearson, Bea mime barfs into an imaginary garbage can. I try to fight the sinking feeling that this is going to be so much worse than I'd imagined.

Mr. Pearson shows us a few classrooms that are small and jammed with old desks. A dingy whiteboard stretches across the front of each room, a synthetic American flag hanging limply at the corner. It looks like half of the windows are painted shut.

As I wander along behind Mr. Pearson, through the air-conditioned bunker that is my new school, I remember walking to class in California, cutting through courtyards and across lawns, feeling the breeze under the neck of my sweatshirt. The air here must be a hundred times cleaner than in LA, but this building is impenetrable.

He shows us the gymnasium, the cafeteria, and the sprawling sports fields out behind the school. Bea drifts farther and farther behind us. When we get to the parking lot I look back to see that her earbuds are already back in.

"We have a few really great electives to choose from," Mr. Pearson says. "Marching band, chorus, a yearly musical, and art."

Art. The word falls flat, right off the end of the sentence. Just art. Not ceramics, painting, or drawing; not newspaper or school magazine; and definitely not photography. Clearly there is no darkroom here.

In my old life, the one that made a little sense, I spent hours and hours in the darkroom, feeling the time pass in thirty-second increments and brief chemical reactions. Even on my worst days, even when my dad was sick or my mom was walking around like a zombie, leaving the burners on and overflowing sinks, even then, stepping into the dim red light had the effect of quieting my mind. It's the only thing that really works.

"I'm sure you'll love our art teacher, Mary." Mr. Pearson's voice comes bounding back into my thoughts like a giant golden retriever, full of enthusiasm. "Your mom tells me you're quite creative."

I smile and nod absently, trying to fake enough interest to read as polite.

"That sounds great," I say.

• • •

BACK IN THE CAR, MY MOM GIVES BEA A LOOK IN THE REARVIEW mirror and says, "Would you take out your earbuds?" exaggerating the words with her lips to make sure there's no confusion.

Bea does, and it's quiet as Mom pulls out of her parking spot. She backs up slowly, carefully, as though she's not surrounded on all sides by empty spaces. Then she puts the car in drive and makes her way back onto the main road.

Finally, she sighs and says, "Bea, you certainly were rude to Mr. Pearson."

Bea frowns. "Rude? Mom, he was staring at your boobs for three whole minutes. I counted in my head."

I shrink into my seat, bracing for a fight and wishing Mom would just let it go. I'm already starting to sweat, my body offended by all this unfamiliar heat and humidity, and it's taking all my energy to swallow the despair I feel at the prospect of a senior year at Cumberland Central.

"Bea," Mom says, "he's going to be your principal for the next four years. It's not worth it."

Bea scowls and turns to look out the open window. "Can't you just be on my side for once?"

I focus my attention on the hundred thousand trees flying by, willing myself invisible. But out of the corner of my eye, I see the way Mom's face softens, the wrinkle between her brows straightening out.

"I *am* on your side, Bea. I'm always on your side."

The dark green of the forest gives way to a lighter green of pastures—we're halfway home—and I burrow farther down into my seat.

Bea stares at my mom hard, violently, her eyes the color of wet concrete.

She tucks her earbuds back in. "You are so full of shit."

* * *

WHEN WE GET HOME, MY NEW PHONE IS WAITING FOR ME IN A package on El's counter. I nearly faint with relief. But as soon as I'm back in my room, sitting cross-legged on El's quilt, as soon as I'm through the welcome screen and the settings and I'm all signed back in, the numbers of messages and notifications start climbing up, up, up. Thirty, forty, fifty, sixty-seven messages from my old life. Forty-five Instagram notifications. I turn my phone over and slide it under the pillow. I can't even look.

4

SATURDAY MORNING, I WANDER OUT TO EL'S STUDIO, an old garden shed out toward the tree line. She's there making a giant painting, a thousand dots and lines coming together to form a shape that's just barely familiar.

I lie down on the navy blue loveseat at the back, dangling my feet over the end.

If she notices me come in she doesn't give it away. Instead she dips her brush into a smear of deep green, then stands for a while, arm suspended, perhaps considering her next move.

"Mary." She says it without turning around, and for some reason her voice startles me. "How are you, my dear?" She makes a long green line, right across the middle of the canvas.

"I'm good," I lie, out of habit, my lips replying to her question without involving my brain.

She dips her brush again.

"No," she says, still not looking at me. "How are you really?"

I think.

How am I?

I don't really know. I feel like I'm just drifting. I feel like I'm watching a movie without the sound. Like my life is the movie. I'm sitting here, watching, and I don't know how to get back in it.

"I'm good," I say again. "Just tired."

"Just tired," she repeats, making the line longer and longer, stretching it around the side of the frame.

"Yeah," I say, closing my eyes, feeling myself sink down into the cushions. "Don't worry about me. I'm fine."

I lie there for a long time, looking at the clapboard ceiling, listening to the scratch of the paintbrush, wishing for better words.

5

SATURDAY AFTERNOON, BEA AND I DRAPE OURSELVES across El's plush taupe wraparound sofa and read for hours. Bea's head is on the center cushion, her feet thrown over the armrest, nose buried in last month's *Vogue Japan*. Bernie, the smallest of El's dogs, is curled up in a nest of her hair.

I'm working my way through a towering stack of art books on El's walnut coffee table: Ralph Eugene Meatyard, Francesca Woodman, Kara Walker. I'm trying to get interested in El's things so I can forget that my things are packed away in storage until we find a house of our own.

The French doors are open to let in the sad breeze that periodically tries to move the air, which is like a solid object inside a world-shaped Jell-O mold. El doesn't believe in air conditioning. Neither does Mom, but it worked a lot better when we lived ten blocks from the beach.

Mom walks in, a yellow legal pad tucked under her arm, pen behind her ear. She's wearing old cutoff shorts and a soft blue T-shirt.

"Got room for one more?" she says.

Bea puts her earbuds in, turns the page of her magazine, doesn't budge an inch. She's still mad about our school visit, one in a long string of betrayals that started the day Mom told us we were leaving California.

I pull myself upright and scoot to the end, leaving Mom a spot between me and Bernie, who is making little snuffling sounds in his sleep.

Mom sits down, propping her feet on the ottoman. She takes her pen from behind her ear and starts writing on the legal pad, pausing every now and then to stop and think. I watch her out of the corner of my eye, her delicate wrists and sturdy hands. Halfway through the essay at the front of *The Unphotographable*, my eyes get stuck on the words "a stubborn conviction that what can be seen is not all there is."

My mother used to be so straightforward. Her love was right at the surface, warm hands and smothering kisses and declarations of *You girls are seriously the coolest.* She was busy, but she had a way of making time expand, so that the five-minute drive to the grocery store was almost always enough time to hit on something profound. We would be blasting Joni Mitchell, singing as loud as we could, and Mom would turn to us and say, *Did you know that enteric fermentation by beef cattle accounts for nearly two percent of US emissions? Farts and burps. We really need to stop eating beef.*

But then Dad died. And Bea's right, it's like she got body-snatched. On the outside she was the same, but we couldn't get to her anymore. Now she's back but she feels like someone else entirely. I wonder if I took enough photographs I could start to figure her out.

After a while, Mom leans her head back onto the edge of the couch and says, "It's too hot to work today."

I nod and put the book down, wiping at a trail of sweat on the back of my knee.

She leans over and tugs an earbud out of Bea's ear. "You girls want to drive to the mall this afternoon? Soak up a little AC? Maybe we could get something for the first day of school."

"At the mall?" Bea says, incredulous.

I can't remember the last time my mom, a militant environmentalist, set foot inside of one. All of her clothes are ordered from online secondhand sites or boutique stores with 100 percent recycled/deadstock/organic/free-trade/ethical-labor-made garments.

"New tradition?" Mom says.

"I'm good," says Bea, her voice indifferent. She turns the page of her magazine, her mouth in a perfectly straight line.

I can see Mom trying not to be hurt, bending her lips up into an awkward smile. Suddenly, after months in hiding, all of her emotions are right there on her face. It makes me uneasy.

"Mary?" says Mom.

Bea looks at me. I look at Mom. There's this triangular thread of tension between the three of us and I can't tell where it started.

El walks in, the screen door of the kitchen slapping shut behind her.

"Who wants to go for a swim?" she calls out.

Bea sits up and *Vogue Japan* crashes to the floor. "I'll get my suit," she says.

Mom closes her eyes and takes a long, slow breath like she's in a meditation video. Then she looks up at El, face placid as a lake. "Great idea."

She gets up and wanders off to her bedroom, leaving the legal pad behind.

I search the chicken scratch for something that means anything:

Peterson's 4pm
Check easement on Windman land
26.5 acres
Don't forget

. . .

IN CALIFORNIA, NORA AND I SPENT MOST SUNDAYS AT LIFEGUARD station 26, our spot on Santa Monica Beach. We had been going there with Bennett ever since we were kids.

Nora and Bennett had the kind of dads who pulled them out into the ocean on surfboards as soon as they learned to walk. I had the kind of dad who spent ten hours a day writing novels in the garage, so I stayed on the beach blanket for a thousand afternoons, watching the water through the lens of my camera but never going in past my knees.

By the time we were juniors, Bennett was often surfing other spots with the real surf heads or out with the kind of girls who are so beautiful they look airbrushed, even in person. Our tight triangle had loosened into more of a line, with me in the middle. But every weekend, Nora would put on her wet suit and disappear into the water, and I'd cover myself in sunscreen, a kind that smelled like coconuts, and just lie there, half asleep, half alive, half somewhere else, until she came back, dripping cold water all over me.

I'm at least a hundred miles from the ocean now, but on

Sunday afternoon I spread an old quilt on the grass between the gardens and lie on my back for hours. Instead of the waves I hear the buzzing of a hundred thousand insects in the grass around me. Instead of the ocean to keep me cool I have a sweaty glass of ice water from El's kitchen.

I finally got the guts to turn on my phone again late last night. I sat for several long minutes with my thumb hovering over the various icons, the blue light piercing the darkness of my bedroom. In the end I deleted all of the messages without reading them.

I texted Nora:

Me: Sorry. I deleted everything.

Me: I got flustered.

Me: We have to start over.

Damn it, she replied. That was some of my best work.

The only texts I actually read were from Bennett. There were four:

Bennett: Bored again. What u up to?

Bennett: The waves are crazy today. I surfed so long I almost missed work.

Bennett: The sunset tonight is unreal.

Bennett: When are you coming home?

I waited an hour, for good measure, then texted back:

Me: Sunset here happened hours ago. I wish I was home already.

• • •

THE FIRST TIME BENNETT EVER HELD MY HAND WAS AT MY DAD'S funeral, seven months before he kissed me. Dad's was the first death that any of us—Nora, Bennett, or I—had ever experienced, and Bennett seemed so shaken by it. The sunlight that always seemed to emanate from his skin was dimmed for weeks.

We were in the reception room of the Unitarian church, on one of those hard wooden benches with spindles in the back. People milled around the room, carrying casseroles and wearing solemn looks on their faces. I kept trying to get in touch with some kind of feeling, but all I got was this faint buzzing in my head.

We sat there for an hour, Nora on one side and Bennett on the other. Every time someone tried to come over—my aunt Darla with her thick lipstick and perfumed handkerchief or our precalculus teacher, Mr. Pinkerton, with potato salad in his beard—Nora would scowl at them and they'd turn right around.

And then, suddenly, a gust of damp, cold California November air pushed the side door open.

"It's James!" Aunt Darla yelled out as we all watched the door swing in the wind.

A few people gasped.

"Jesus Christ," my grandpa muttered. "Somebody get her out of here."

I watched the scene unfold as if on a screen, like I wasn't really even there.

Nora shifted next to me. "You okay?"

"Yeah," I said. "That's typical Aunt Darla behavior."

Nora laughed. "I'm getting a drink," she said. "Want one?"

I nodded and then turned my head to look out the window, at the wet cars in the muddy parking lot.

That's when Bennett slid his hand over mine. I could feel my pulse thrumming in my neck, and as he laced his fingers through my fingers the buzzing in my head went quiet. I couldn't look at him, or anyone. I just held on as tightly as I could.

• • •

I'M ABOUT TO GET UP AND HEAD BACK INTO THE HOUSE WHEN A shadow falls over my face, blacking out the sun. Before I can focus my eyes to see who it is, Bea flops onto the blanket beside me.

"Hey," I say, and she nods in greeting as she settles down onto her back. She's wearing pajama shorts and a Radiohead *OK Computer* T-shirt. She looks so *Bea* and so *not*. I turn toward her and quietly lift my camera, trying to capture the halo of light in her heap of tangles.

But the *click* of the shutter is interrupted by her hand squashing over my lens like an octopus.

"Jesus, Bea! You'll break my camera."

She lowers her hand, squinting at me.

"Why do you keep doing that?" she says.

"Doing what?"

"You know," she says.

I do. But I don't say that. Because I don't want to talk about why I suddenly need to take pictures of everything I can.

Bea turns her face back up to the sun, putting on a pair of round-face sunglasses. We lie for a while, absolutely still, listening to the garden.

"I feel like a corpse," Bea says.

"You look like a corpse," I joke.

She's quiet for a minute.

And then she says, "What do you think it's like to be dead?"

I flick at a tiny ant that's crawling up my arm.

"I think it's like nothing," I say.

"Nothing," she repeats.

"Yeah," I say, spotting a cloud that looks like a cartoon ghost.

I think the word again and again: *Nothing. Nothing. Nothing. Nothing.* I think about how Dad is nothing, and I feel a stabbing sensation behind my eyes.

"Nothing," Bea says again. "I think that sounds nice."

I can't decide if she's serious or if she's just getting into her new Goth persona. Either way, something about it unsettles me.

"Yeah," she says. "That sounds really nice."

Then she pulls at a snarl in her long black hair and smiles up at the baby blue sky.

• • •

I NEVER USED TO PHOTOGRAPH PEOPLE, PREFERRING INSTEAD TO capture the light, the patterns, the empty spaces between things. And then one day, a few months after Dad was gone, I saw Hannah through the crack in her door, lying flat on the bed with her earbuds in, her graceful legs and knobby feet dangling over the edge. And something in my head whispered, *This.*

This moment, this light, these feet and legs, this Hannah *is never going to happen again.*

And now sometimes photography feels like breathing, and other times it feels like frantically trying to gather up all the parts of my life before they disappear.

Monday is Mom's official first day of her new job at the Albany Environmental Land Trust. When I wake up she's gone, and something about it gives me this foreboding feeling. Like I'm just waiting for her to slip back into the wilderness of grief and never reappear again.

El lets us borrow her car after breakfast, and I drive Bea over to the school to pick up our schedules from an elderly office manager who is wearing a Colonel Sanders–looking ribbon tie around her neck.

We pull our schedules out of their envelopes, shivering under the blast of AC coming out of the ceiling vents.

"Everything look all right?" Mrs. Harrison asks. Her lipstick is seeping into the wrinkles around her mouth, and her long fingernails clack across the keyboard in little bursts.

I look down at my schedule: AP English, AP Calculus, AP Physics, AP World History—the typical Sullivan-family achievement track—Advanced Spanish, French 1, PE, and art. I don't even have room for a study hall.

Bea clears her throat. "Why am I in music class?"

"It's what your mom requested," Mrs. Harrison answers in a dull monotone.

"She's not even here," Bea says, looking around and crossing her arms.

"We spoke on the phone last week."

Bea frowns. "Well, what do I do if I don't want to take music?"

"You'll have to get your mom to sign this form," Mrs. Harrison says, her fingers coming to a brief stop as she reaches over to grab a paper and hold it out to us from across the desk.

"Although it's a little late because school starts tomorrow and a lot of the other electives are full."

I watch Bea's face changing colors, realizing that I need to get her out of here before she explodes. But then she just sighs and takes the form.

"Do we need to do anything else?" I say.

"Nope, you're all set." Mrs. Harrison's fingernails resume their clicking. "Have a wonderful first day, girls."

* * *

BACK IN THE CAR, I SHIMMY MY SHOULDERS UP AND DOWN, TRYING to get warm after the school AC nearly froze the skin from my body. Bea sinks down in the passenger seat, looking defeated.

"I thought you loved music," I say, treading carefully so I don't get stung by Bea's temper, which appears to still be seething right under the surface.

"Right, but music *class* is for losers," she says, twisting her tiny skull earrings. "I just wanted a fucking study hall."

I roll my eyes. "You have a study hall."

"I wanted another one!" she whines.

"Why?"

She tugs at her hair and looks at me as if I'm stupid for not getting this. "Because."

Channeling Hannah, gold-star big sister, I try to give her a look that communicates empathy. But it's really hard because honestly, I don't actually care. I'm itching to yell at her to just get over it, to suck it up like the rest of us. But instead I take a long, deep breath.

"Look," I say. "This is not ideal. I get it. But it is what it is. We're here now. There's nothing we can do."

Bea just shakes her head like I've failed some test and slowly, dramatically pushes her earbuds in, despite the fact that there's already music playing in the car. I grip the steering wheel tighter, roll down the windows, and turn the music louder. I feel like I'll never get it right with Bea, no matter how hard I try.

* * *

When we get home, I close my door and text Hannah:

Me: Bea is being difficult again.

Hannah: Just talk to her. There's usually a reason.

Me: What do I say?

Hannah: You're the big sister now, you got this.

And then: Gotta go. A very cute girl just sat across from me in the dining hall. I'm going to work my magic.

I get up, walk across the hall to Bea's room, and hover there for a while, just standing outside the closed door, listening to the grumpy silence, thinking about what I could possibly say to make anything better. Then I give up and walk back to my room.

I've been here less than a week, but already my clothes have gone from suitcase to closet to cyclone. There's a layer on the floor that could be clean or dirty. Everything is wrinkled and a little bit stale.

I try to find something to wear tomorrow, to make me feel a little less hopeless, but my wardrobe seems to be rebelling against all of the improper treatment. I dig out a sundress with a mysterious grease stain, a gold necklace in an impossible tangle. My Carole King T-shirt is missing, along with one of my four-leaf-clover earrings. Everything is ruined or lost or stuck in storage. Every outfit is missing a part, just like me.

Eventually I give up and watch Netflix on my phone until dinnertime. I shove my schedule, with its tiny Cumberland Indians logo, into the back of a notebook. For a little while I let myself forget about tomorrow.

• • •

Despite my fears, Mom is home at six o'clock, kicking off her shoes and dropping her messenger bag on the floor of the mudroom. I look at Bea and raise my eyebrows. She looks at me and shrugs.

The four of us eat dinner at the counter, stuffing our faces with big bowls of spaghetti and homemade tomato sauce with torn-up basil leaves on top. The dogs are clustered at the doorway, trapped behind a baby gate, tails thumping the ground, looking from El to the spaghetti with undying, over-the-top love and devotion.

There is so much commotion here, even when it's quiet: constant clicking of claws on the floor, a tail disturbing a water glass on the coffee table, the water spilling over a pile of sunflowers that have rolled onto the floor. The blue jays are always harassing the robins, bees fly right into the house, crows pass overhead in a loud, inky blob.

At home, Bea and I would be eating scrambled eggs and watching old episodes of the Kardashians on the couch. I'd be texting with Nora and pretending like I wasn't waiting for Mom to come home. Other than the television, the house would be eerily quiet. It would always feel like Dad was gone.

"So, how are you girls feeling about tomorrow?" Mom says, twirling her fork in a pile of noodles.

"Fine," Bea and I say in unison.

I'm still kind of trying to pretend tomorrow isn't happening.

"How very teenager of you," El says, rolling her eyes. "Did you decide what you're going to wear?"

I don't tell anyone about my disaster of an afternoon. Instead I just shrug and say, "I'll figure something out."

And Bea shrugs and says, "I have something in mind."

Then she says, "Star Trek tonight?" And I almost drop my fork.

Star Trek used to be ours, before. Mom was a Trekkie in college, and she introduced us as soon as we were old enough to understand what space was. We've watched the whole thing through at least four times (*The Original Series* and *The Next Generation*, but never *Deep Space Nine*). The last episode we saw—the season five finale—was the night before we found out about Dad. In our timeline, Data is still waiting to be rescued from the nineteenth century.

Mom smiles into her spaghetti like Bea has just asked her to the junior prom. "I have a little work to do, but I think I can squeeze it in."

After dinner, before Star Trek, El puts on Nina Simone and the four of us clean the kitchen, and for twenty minutes we move together like seaweed, swaying on the ocean floor.

* * *

BEFORE BED, WHEN BEA AND I ARE BACK UPSTAIRS, KNOCKING elbows as we brush our teeth in the tiny bathroom, I say, "I'm sorry about today."

"Me too," she says, spitting out a glob of toothpaste foam. "I mean, I fucking hate that I'm stuck in music class, but I guess I'll live."

I laugh. "I guess so."

I wipe my face on an indigo-dyed hand towel and lean against the doorframe. Bea looks young with her face just washed and hair pulled back, but tomorrow is her first day of high school. I remember what a big deal that was for me, how Hannah let me borrow one of her dresses and did my eyeliner in the downstairs bathroom. Does Bea want that kind of thing from me? She's so contained. It feels impossible to tell.

"It's hard doing this without Hannah," I say. "I feel like she always knew what to do."

Bea pulls at a blue thread at the side of her shirt. "I know. I really miss her. I miss everything."

I miss Dad, I think. But instead I say, "Me too."

It's quiet for a minute and I wait there, wanting to say more. But then the silence fills up with everything else that's missing. I clear my throat. "I should get to bed."

Bea nods, looking a little relieved. "Me too."

"Night, Bea."

"Night."

When I get back to my room, I have fifteen texts from Nora—all pictures of different outfit possibilities for her first day, which is also tomorrow. Each outfit is basically the same thing—tight jeans in different washes, cropped at the ankle, and T-shirts in various colors and necklines. Nora has a very Steve Jobs approach to fashion.

I respond: White crew neck and dark wash. It's classic.

Nora texts back immediately: I was thinking the same thing. Soulmates!

Then: Your turn.

I wearily eye my tornado of a bedroom.

Me: Nah, I'm just going to wing it.

Nora: BADASS.

Nora: How are you feeling?

Me: Nervous.

Nora: You've got this.

I fish through a pile of dresses, looking for my pajamas.

Me: DO I?

Nora: Shut up. You're gonna kill it.

Me: If it doesn't kill me first.

Nora: You just need to get through 340 more days. This time next year we'll be downing Jell-O shots and decorating our dorm room.

Nora and I are both applying early decision to UC Santa Barbara. We decided last spring, after laying out all of the college pamphlets we'd received in the mail in a giant mandala on Nora's bedroom floor. Dad had been gone for a few months by then, and it seemed like a good choice for me—staying close to Mom and Bea, Nora, home. Nora wants to study marine biology and fell in love with the program there. A few times, Bennett even said he was applying too. But that's one of the million things we haven't talked about since we started kissing.

I write: 340 days!! Then, remembering her email: What's your dad's new girlfriend like?

I watch as three little dots flash on the screen, like she's writing and rewriting.

Nora's dad is a recording engineer. Her parents divorced when we were thirteen and her mom found a pair of ladies' underwear stuffed under the front seat of his Audi. The divorce was long and brutal, and Nora slept over so much that year that we just kept the blow-up mattress inflated under my bed.

Nora: The usual, I guess. I'll tell you next time we talk on the phone.

Me: You want to talk now?

Nora: Can't. My mom is making me watch The Bachelorette.

Me: Yikes.

Nora: I know. I think she just likes to psychoanalyze all of the characters.

Nora's mom is a therapist, which, according to Nora, is extremely annoying.

Nora: But seriously. You're going to be great tomorrow.

I sink down under my covers, turning out the light.

Me: Not sure if I believe that.

Nora: But you have to believe everything I say.

In the darkness, I laugh out loud.

Me: I love you.

Nora: Ditto times forever.

Just as I'm closing my eyes, my phone lights up with a text from Bennett:

School tomorrow is going to be weird without you.

I write back: So unbelievably weird. All of it.

In the darkness, I wait for him to reply, but he doesn't. I read our texts again and again. I wish I knew how to say something that means something. I wonder if it's really possible that in just 340 days I'll be back in California. If he'll be there too. I can almost see it—the three of us sitting on the beach in Santa Barbara like none of this ever happened. But every time the edges start to come into focus, a piece of the middle disappears.

6

THIS IS THE WORST PART ABOUT OUR NEW SCHOOL:
we have to take the bus. A yellow fucking school bus with
CUMBERLAND INDIANS stamped on the side.

In California, I sometimes took the city bus, but usually
Hannah drove us to school in her 2006 Honda Accord. She'd
bought it with three years of wages from working at the public
library and had declared it, like so many other things, the love
of her life. It died the week after graduation, as if it felt the same
way and couldn't stand being left behind.

I spent my paychecks from the camera store on film and paper
and lenses and chili fries at Benders, never really thinking ahead
to the day when Hannah wouldn't be there anymore. But here I
am. Bea and I are waiting by the mailbox, having bushwhacked
our way down the driveway, when we hear the bus rumbling in
the distance.

I'm wearing a thrifted baby-doll dress that isn't too wrinkled
after a night on my floor and my old white high-top Chucks. Bea

looks just like the Goth girl in every nineties movie in her head-to-toe black—long velvet dress, lacy socks, combat boots. I look at her heavy eye makeup and her stick-straight blue-black hair, and my heart wilts a little.

Back in California, everyone *got* Bea. She always had tons of friends, despite the daily spectacle of vintage prints and strange hats. I think about how this, today, is her first impression in this new place, this place full of people whom we know absolutely nothing about. I'm worried about her.

We get on the bus, and like I predicted, it's full of mostly little kids. So we make our way to the very back and slide into a seat. We both slump down with our knees up on the seat back in front of us. We put our earbuds in, and I watch the tall corn roll by the window.

The whole time I'm just thinking: this is so weird. I'm in New York. On the first day of my senior year of high school. Riding a yellow school bus like they do in the movies. In a couple of hours my friends will all be walking into school and I won't be there. Because I'm here with a bunch of seven-year-olds.

It takes a long time to get to the school because the bus takes a circuitous route, stopping a few more times to pick up small packs of elementary and middle school kids. But finally we pull up and my heart starts beating double as I watch all the high schoolers in the parking lot heading inside.

Bea takes one earbud out to say goodbye when we get to the entrance, then pops it back in and is swallowed up by the sea of students heading down the hallway toward the lowerclassmen lockers. We don't even have the same lunch, so I know I won't see her until the end of the day. The thought makes my throat fill up with rocks.

But the crowd moves me along too, and soon I'm at my locker, organizing all of my fresh notebooks and pens and going over my schedule one more time. I look around, wondering, kind of hoping to see co-op boy in the crowd. Just one familiar face. No such luck.

I find my homeroom without much trouble, since there are only so many classrooms in this part of the building. Then I slip into a desk in the back and watch as the seats fill up.

Even though I'm pretending to write in my notebook, I see the way that each person's eyes stop on my face as they enter the classroom. There's this brief, nearly imperceptible halt to forward motion every single time someone spots me. I sink lower and lower in my seat. It's only 8:07 and already I'm exhausted.

A few rows ahead of me, a shaggy-haired guy in a ripped hoodie teases a girl with a perfect honey-blonde blowout and pokes her knee with his pencil, and she laughs. This kind of contact between groups, a stoner flirting with one of the beautiful people, wouldn't happen in California, and I find it fascinating. Then the teacher, a pasty twentysomething dude with giant forearms and a weird pompadour, walks in, and I realize that I'm staring.

"Morning, guys," he says in this voice that is trying to be deeper than it really is. "Welcome to your senior year at CCS!"

Everyone cheers. I cringe.

"This is the last one you're gonna get, so make it count. Have fun but don't be idiots about it."

He does a little cheers with his NY Jets coffee mug, then starts taking roll. As he makes his way through the list, my skin starts to itch. It's times like these when I hate my name.

But by some miracle, no one laughs when he calls it.

"Marigold Sullivan?"

ThankyouJesus.

"It's Mary," I say. And then I watch as everyone tries to look at me without really turning around.

The same thing happens in the next class, and the next. I feel like a chameleon or a praying mantis in the middle of the supermarket. Balanced atop a pyramid of oranges, just trying to *blend*.

In my old life, the one that made sense, I was always the one who was watching.

The kids here don't seem all that different from the ones in my old school. Except almost everyone is white, no one is wearing designer clothes, and all of the cars in the parking lot are shitty and old. I guess, in those ways, Bea and I will fit right in.

No one's really talked to me yet. And I haven't talked to anyone. I'm too distracted by the feeling of homesickness seeping in through the floorboards, surrounding my ankles like water.

And then I see him. I walk into my fifth-period AP English class and there he is, sitting at the back, talking to a group of seniors. He doesn't see me come in, which gives me a chance to look him over, to make a plan. He's just like I remembered, hands in constant motion, limbs taking up too much space. His brown hair is still flopping over the same eye. I sit in the back too, in the other corner of the classroom, making my hair into a curtain, trying to hide.

The bell rings and the teacher starts taking attendance. When she calls out my name, *Marigold Sullivan*, there's kind of a question mark at the end of it. I raise my hand as subtly as I can—is it possible to be invisible with your hand in the air?—saying, once again, "Mary's fine."

Then I can't resist anymore, so I look over at him, the guy whose name I now know is Jesse Keller. He's looking back at me. He's smiling with one side of his mouth, the same way Bennett does. I'm in trouble.

The teacher, Ms. Bell, is handing out the syllabus. She's probably in her early fifties, dressed in a caftan and a big, funky scarf with a thick gray stripe in her hair. She doesn't quite fit with any of the other adults here, and when she passes my desk she says, "Nice to meet you, Ms. Sullivan," and gives me a warm smile.

We talk over our syllabus, and she assigns the first thirty pages of *One Hundred Years of Solitude*. I am handed a beat-up paperback with a leafy green cover, the number twenty-six Sharpied onto the front of it. And I spend most of the forty-five minutes of class flipping back and forth through the yellowed pages and trying not to look at Jesse sitting in the other corner of the room. Then the bell rings, and suddenly, I am hit with the overwhelming, inexplicable urge to flee the scene. I rush out the door, heading for my locker.

But, of course, Jesse's behind me.

"Marigold!" he calls, and I turn around.

Again, for some reason, I don't correct him.

"Hey, Jesse," I say, resigning myself to this conversation.

"You headed to lunch?" he asks, falling into step beside me. He's so much taller than I am that I have to look up to see him form the words.

"Yep," I say, noticing the way he dodges the other bodies in the hallway. He's strangely graceful for being so angular. "Just gotta drop these books off at my locker."

"Cool."

He follows me through the throng of hungry juniors and seniors and waits, leaning like Jughead Jones against the wall, while I get my lunch out.

"Okay," he says finally. "Black and white or color?"

I slam my locker shut.

"Both, of course."

"Really?" he says. "I'm a purist myself."

I roll my eyes. "You and the patriarchy."

He laughs. A laugh so big it fills the whole hallway. "Wow."

"Yeah," I say, and I'm laughing too.

"How's your first day?" he asks, pushing off from the locker and reentering the stream of students. It feels like he's moving so much more slowly than me, but somehow I'm still struggling to keep up. It's like he's slightly out of time with the rest of the world.

"Strange," I say. "How's yours?"

He shrugs. "Turns out my little sister drew in all of my notebooks, which sucks, but I saw a Karner blue on the way to school this morning. So it sort of balanced out."

I must look confused because he adds, "It's an endangered species of butterfly."

"Oh," I say, and now I'm imagining Jesse pulling over to the side of the road to look at a butterfly and something about that is just too much to process.

We get to the doors of the lunchroom and there's this pause—this one giant second of hesitation. Jesse opens his mouth, as if he's about to speak, and my eyes catch on a freckle underneath his bottom lip.

And then I say, "Well, gotta get going!" and bolt away.

What's ridiculous is that it's lunchtime, for both of us, and technically we've both "gotta get going" to the same place. The same tiny cafeteria. Where I have no idea where to sit or what to do. Nevertheless, I power walk away like a complete idiot and park myself in the corner, at the end of a long string of interconnected faux picnic tables.

I close my eyes and take a deep breath, relieved that he hasn't followed me. It occurs to me that I have zero friends and can't really afford to be running from potential candidates right now, but I'm also just kind of worn out and want to be alone.

I slump over and press my forehead to the lunch table for one minute, feeling the coolness of it, the smoothness, the hardness. I slip my camera out of my backpack, point it at the floor, and twist the lens back and forth, watching my feet blur into the linoleum. Then I pick my head up and take out my lunch, before anyone starts thinking I'm weird.

I have lunch in a brown bag for the first time in years—courtesy of Aunt El—and it feels like the best surprise to reach inside and find each of the little, carefully packaged items: a turkey sandwich on sourdough with lettuce and radishes from the garden, a fuzzy peach and a ripe plum, a small bag of salt-and-vinegar potato chips, and an article about color that looks like it was cut from one of her scholarly journals.

I eat slowly, dragging out each part, reading the article twice, so I don't have to just sit here like a loser with nothing to do. Still, as I'm finishing my chips with ten minutes left on the clock, the anxiety starts to rise again. And this deep missing. At home, I would be eating pizza around a picnic table with my friends.

The sun would be warm on the back of my neck. Maybe Bennett would be sitting with us today. Under the table, he might be holding my hand.

I'm relieved when lunch is over and I can slip back into the flow of bodies and make my way to art class. It takes me a while to find the room because it's actually in a little annex at the back of the building. The space is big and there are tons of windows, one on top of the other, making a wall of glass at the back.

I walk in after the bell has already rung and slip into the only open seat I see. We are all sitting at long tables and I'm at the end, next to a girl I've seen in one of my classes already. She's a little bit hunched over, doodling triangles with her pencil on the edge of her notebook. She's wearing a plain, threadbare black T-shirt and vintage Levi's, and her light brown hair is cut into a blunt bob an inch below her ears. Her wrist is covered in delicate gold bangles, and she has tons of rings and three little gold necklaces at her throat.

She turns to me and smiles, passes me a syllabus. Her fingernails are blue black with little red strawberries painted on the top.

"Thanks," I say, wondering why it's so hard to think of anything else to say.

The teacher, a young woman with blonde hair and a long dress covered in flowers, starts talking about grading, deadlines, and our first unit, which is collage. Out of the corner of my eye I watch the girl's triangles spread onto the top of our table, spilling over the paper. Something about the dreamy look on her face and the clinking of her bracelets feels familiar.

The teacher finishes up her lecture, and the classroom starts to buzz with talking. I grab a magazine from the stack on our table and start flipping through the pages.

In my head, I argue with myself.

I should talk to her, to somebody.

What would I even say?

I guess I would like friends.

You already have friends.

"I was going to offer this to you, but then I figured it was way too literal," a voice cuts in.

I look up to see the girl holding up an issue of *Martha Stewart Living* with a big bouquet of marigolds on the cover. It feels like a beginning.

"Nah," I say, "I'll take it. I have no idea where to start with this project."

"Cool," she says, passing it over. She turns to the next magazine in the stack and tears off the cover. "Where are you from?"

"California," I say, and the word brings up a dust cloud of sharp memories that I try desperately to push back down. I guess this is why talking to strangers is so hard: my life is basically a minefield.

"California," she repeats carefully, like she can see my inner struggle. "Wow. I'm Sam, by the way."

"I'm Mary." I try to smile. "But I guess you already knew that.

"Cumberland is the smallest town on Earth. I bet half of the people knew your name before you even got here."

"That's kind of creepy," I say.

She laughs and it changes her whole face, the composure broken by a crooked, toothy grin. "You have no idea."

Sam works for a while, flipping through her magazines, sorting them into piles. I stop at a blurry black-and-white photograph of the ocean and tear it out. It makes a loud rip that is deeply satisfying.

Then she sighs and says, "I'm sorry."

"I'm sorry?" I ask, confused.

"Yeah," she says, her face soft and a little dreamy. "All I've ever wanted was to get out of Cumberland. It's a shame you got trapped here so close to the end."

I want to agree but I don't want to be rude so instead I say, "It's all right here, I guess."

She gives me a look that says, *You are such a liar.*

When the bell rings, she waits for me to pack up my stuff. Then she says, "Come on," and we walk out of class together.

• • •

I'M HUMILIATED TO BOARD THE BUS AT THE END OF THE DAY, BUT I'm also anxious to see Bea and make sure she's okay. She's already there, in the very last row, and when I slide in she rips out her earbuds and says, "Hey."

Her voice is tired and defeated and her eye makeup is smudged. I want to gather her up in my arms, but it's not our style. Instead I slump down and lay my head on her shoulder. She smells like home.

"Hey," I say.

She rests her head on top of mine and lets out a long, loud sigh.

"This fucking sucks, Mary."

I nod. "I know."

"These people are all so weird."

It's ironic to hear it coming from her, but I sort of get what she means.

"I heard a kid call a guy gay, as an insult," she says.

I cringe. "Yikes."

"I wanted to punch him."

I watch as she winds the cord of her earbuds around and around her finger, turning the tip bright red.

"I wish you had but I'm glad you didn't."

"I want to go home," she says, in a lonely, tumbleweed voice.

I feel my spirit drooping, the adrenaline that kept me on my feet today seeping out of my skin. "Me too."

"It's never going to happen, is it?"

Out the window, a green field full of black-and-white cows slowly passes.

"Nope."

I grab her hand and lace up our fingers. Her black nail polish is chipped around the edges, and her fingernails are bitten into stubs. Then her music is back, The Doors, and I listen to it blasting through her earbuds all the way home.

Mom is gone for dinner tonight. She texted while I was doing my boring, first-day-of-school homework: Buried in paperwork. Be home late. I tried not to read anything into it, but all afternoon, I imagined her trapped in a paper sarcophagus.

She comes in at ten, when Bea and I are on our way up to bed. She grabs us for a kiss, but Bea slithers out of her arms.

"You're still wearing lipstick," Bea says.

I squish Mom up in a hug so I don't have to see the wounded look on her face.

N<small>ORA TEXTS ME RIGHT AS</small> I <small>WALK INTO MY ROOM, STILL FEELING A</small> little uneasy.

Nora: How was your first day?

Me: Really bizarre. How was yours?

Nora: Mundane. I can't believe you ditched me senior year. I had to be lab partners with JENNY WENDLETON. She brushed her hair in class. Twice. Some of it got on me.

Me: Gross. She has nice hair tho. Maybe you can sell it.

Nora: I just threw up in my mouth. Tell me about your new school.

Me: The entire inside is Gatorade orange. Like every single locker.

Nora: *shudders*

Me: I saw at least eight people wearing camo. Including my principal.

Nora: Is it wrong that this misery fest is so intriguing? TELL ME MORE.

Me: I rode the school bus today with kindergarteners.

Nora: WHAT?

Me: YES.

Nora: Seriously?

Me: YES.

Nora: Sorry, I have to go. I'm laughing too hard to type RN.

I send her the middle finger emoji.

Me: I'm going to need a lot of therapy when I get to UCSB.

Every time I mention college it's like scratching an itch, pressing on a bruise, peeking at the future to make sure it's still there. I need to know that this part of my life is temporary, that something else is coming.

Nora: It's cool. I'll probably minor in psych.

Me: Look at you abbreviating. You sound like a real college student.

Nora: IF ONLY.

Me: Seriously.

Nora: 339 more days.

In between texts from Nora, I keep checking my thread with Bennett, waiting for something new to appear. But it's just those words from yesterday, *going to be weird without you*, which I have already analyzed too much.

Was it really weird without me? I wonder. I try to imagine Bennett—who is never not surrounded by people—feeling lonely, and I can't.

That last day together, after it happened, when we were lying there looking at the ceiling, the blanket pulled across all the parts of us that suddenly felt too naked, I couldn't think of anything to say. Bennett reached over, pried my fingers loose from the covers, and held my hand.

I listened to his breathing, slow and sleepy. I thought of all the hours I'd spent sitting alone on the beach, watching the miracle of his tiny figure emerging from the curl of a wave. He'd sail closer and then swim back out over and over again and I'd wait, a fixed point in the sand.

Lying there with Bennett, in the ocean of my bed, I felt sad and empty and full of love. All at the same time.

I wanted to say the big things that had been twisting in the washing machine of my mind for the past six weeks. I wanted to speak into existence some kind of future where I could know that this would happen again. But instead I just said, "We should get dressed."

I made the bed while Bennett found his socks. I kissed him at the back door just as my mom's car pulled in the driveway.

He said, "Call me, okay?" As if tomorrow would be another day of kissing to old movies on my laptop and not the end of everything.

I said, "I will." And then he disappeared in the gap between houses.

7

THE SECOND DAY OF SCHOOL IS PRETTY MUCH THE same as the first: a surreal bus ride, overt staring, floating up and down the long hallways like a leaf in a river.

When I get to English, Jesse's saved me a seat.

"Hey, Marigold," he says, and yeah, I guess he's just calling me that now.

"Hey, Jesse," I say, like it's nothing.

I arrange my book and notebook in a neat pile, corners aligned, to give my hands something to do. I swear I know how to talk to boys, to humans, but for some reason all of that is escaping me right now.

I look over and he's drumming his fingers on the sides of his desk, *tap tap ta-tap tap.*

Maybe he's forgotten too.

Luckily Ms. Bell walks in, her arms full of books and messy papers. She takes attendance and then we're off on an hour-long discussion of the first few chapters.

I notice that Jesse likes to talk in class, and his comments are really good and strange, like he's part philosopher, part alien.

He says: *The sentence structure is so long and suffocating—it feels like everyone is trapped by time.*

And: *He makes you think the magic is real, and maybe it is?*

When Ms. Bell isn't looking, he passes me a note that says: *Do you think it's possible to photograph ghosts?*

And I write back: *Definitely not.*

And he writes back: *Agree. But José Arcadio would probably try to do it anyway.*

He walks me to lunch again, stopping at my locker to wait as I put my books away.

"You know," he says, "I have a darkroom at my house. For black and white. Do you develop your own prints?"

And I stop mid-motion, almost dropping *One Hundred Years of Solitude* on the floor. Because, holy shit. There is a darkroom in this town.

"Marigold?" he says. He tilts his head, looking down at me. His neck is long and brown from the sun.

"Sorry," I say, pushing away from my locker and heading toward the cafeteria, still trying to get myself to believe it. "Yeah. I do."

"The enlarger can be a little finicky," he says. "I found it in my uncle's garage and it was in pretty bad shape."

I have the strangest feeling of being about to dissolve into a fit of laughter. For the first time since I got here, I actually feel hope.

"I used to work at a photography store," I say. "So finicky equipment is kind of my thing."

We are almost at the cafeteria when a herd of ninth graders heading to their afternoon classes forces us over to the side. I spot Bea, walking alone, wearing her black hair like a cloak. I try to catch her attention, but her earbuds are in and her eyes don't leave the linoleum.

When we get to the big double doorway, Jesse and I replay the exact same scene as yesterday: awkward pause, embarrassing flight across the cafeteria. When I get to my seat, I watch him lope across the room and sit down at a table with some other seniors. He sits next to a beautiful girl from my physics class, and she reaches over and tousles his hair playfully. For exactly one second, I burn with jealousy.

And then I mentally slap myself across the face. Because Bennett. California. My life.

"Anyone sitting here?"

I look up to see Sam, in a faded Backstreet Boys T-shirt, with an orange plastic tray of sad cafeteria food and chocolate milk. It surprises me enough to prevent me from overthinking my brief emotional episode.

"Nope," I say. "Just me."

She clunks down next to me and starts yammering away about our Spanish homework, like it's normal, like eating together is something we do every day.

And so I act like that too.

"Did you know that Ms. Smith is dating Mr. G?" she asks.

"What?"

"Yep." And then she adds, "Do you think his pompadour stays that perfectly intact while they're doing it?"

I smack a hand across my eyes, as though I can shield myself from the mental image. "I don't know if I can eat my lunch now."

Sam carefully unwraps a hamburger from inside of a steaming plastic package. The bun looks like a wet sponge.

"Want some of my sandwich?" I say.

"Actually, yes," she says, pushing her tray to the side. I tear my wax paper in half and slide it over to her with half of the sandwich on top.

"I do have friends," she says. "Just so you know."

"Oh," I say. "Of course. Me too. They're just not here."

"Same," she says, bringing the sandwich to her mouth. "Most of mine graduated in June. Everyone is sort of friends with everyone here, but Nicole and Fiona were my people."

"Cool," I say. "Nora and Bennett were mine. They're back in California, doing senior year without me." Just saying their names makes me instantly gloomy.

"It blows being left behind," Sam says. She rips off a tiny piece of wax paper and rolls it up on the tabletop.

"Yeah," I say, even though I'm the one who left.

Sam looks out the window and suddenly seems far away. I offer her my bag of chips, but she doesn't seem to even hear me. Then she snaps back into the present and says, "Hey, there's a bonfire Friday night. You want to go?"

"Definitely," I say, wondering where she just went and feeling slightly amazed at the fact that I actually have plans.

In art class I finish my first collage. It's pretty minimal: the fuzzy ocean, marigolds bursting out of the water, and a silent, screaming figure floating above.

Sam's collage is only half done. It's elaborate, with pieces of about a hundred different magazines all making a chaotic, stormy, violent scene. I watch her working and it's like she's back in the trance again, somewhere else completely. So I pick up another magazine and start turning the pages, looking for something that reminds me of home.

. . .

Mom skips out on dinner again, but just before bed I catch her sitting at the counter, going over some files. The kitchen lights are mostly off, except for the cans that are over the counter, which cast a soft glow onto the tiny strands of hair that have fallen out of her bun.

"Mary." She smiles, wide, but there's something in her eyes that I can't place.

I lean on the counter across from her, trying to read her face. "Everything okay?" I say.

She sighs. "Yeah, I'm sorry. I've just been so busy at work. I'm trying to make a good first impression. How's school going?"

I shrug my shoulders, feeling tired. "It's fine."

Mom eyes me suspiciously. "Fine, huh?"

"Yeah."

She looks me over once more, then sets her attention back down to her computer, her fingers firing over the keys. "How's it going with college stuff?" she says, somehow typing and talking at the same time. "Do you need any help?"

I stand up, yawning. "Nah, the UC applications aren't even open until November. I've got time."

Mom stops typing, nodding once, then closes her laptop.

"You know, I'll be the first one to tell you that Grandma and Grandpa take it too far sometimes. But you've been working your butt off for the past three years. Why not just apply to some other schools? Just to see what happens."

For some reason her words sizzle in my stomach. UCSB is the plan. Nora is the plan.

"I'll think about it," I say.

"Sounds good," she says.

I look at her eyes, trying to figure out if the purple ringing them is better or worse than before. "Hey, don't go to bed too late, okay?"

My mom laughs. She *laughs*.

"Okay, Marigold. Night."

* * *

BACK IN MY ROOM, I TYPE *COLUMBIA UNIVERSITY* INTO THE GOOGLE search bar on my laptop. Then *Brown. Wesleyan. Williams*. I look at picture after picture of well-groomed smart kids lounging on manicured grass, working away in state-of-the-art laboratories and art studios, and under their carefree yet serious expressions is the self-satisfied look of being *chosen*.

A part of me thinks, *I want that*. And then another part of me thinks, *Why?*

I close my computer and text Nora: 338 days.

I reach under my mattress and pull out my journal, a black-and-white composition book that's almost full. I try to write in it every day, ever since I started to forget. It's part practice, part punishment.

The forgetting happens a little at a time. That's the thing about losing someone. The rest of your life grows back. You go to parties, you remember that you're in love. You get distracted by one thing and then another thing and then everything.

Every once in a while, anxiety jolts me awake in the night. I think, *I'm forgetting.*

I used to go into his study and sit on the floor, reading his books and papers. Or I'd hide at the back of his closet and breathe in the smell of his clothes. I'd collect his things like prizes, stealing them from my parents' bedroom: his notecards and old receipts, the plastic bracelet that was on his arm when he died.

One day, I found his old digital recorder at the back of my mother's bedside drawer. I unwrapped the earbuds and tucked them into my ears—thinking of them in his ears—and waited. I listened to one strange, half-formed thought after another:

More violence, maybe.

A marching band, all lying on their sides.

But I didn't even recognize his voice.

Even with the writing, my memory hasn't gotten any better. I've been here less than two weeks and already it seems like I can barely remember anything concrete about my old life—the way it felt to be in our house, at the beach, in the passenger seat of Bennett's Jeep.

But I start to move the pen anyway. Instead of California, I write about Jesse's big hands and square fingernails and the way it sounds in the hallway when everyone's shoes are squeaking on the linoleum floors. I feel guilty but I fill a page, and then another, and then I have to stop because my eyelids are drooping.

I put the notebook away and turn off the light, lying down under my sheets.

• • •

A MEMORY—A FLASH—RISES UP OUT OF THE DARK WATER OF SLEEP. It's the day after New Year's, two thirty in the morning. I'm young enough to be afraid of the dark, and I have thrown up all over my bedroom floor.

My dad is there, cleaning up the vomit on his hands and knees. I watch him but he doesn't look at me. His face is angry or sleepy or maybe just annoyed.

In the dream, I want to reach for him but I don't. My heart aches worse than my belly.

• • •

I WAKE UP AND MY EYES ARE COVERED WITH A LAYER OF TEARS THAT makes the moonlight stretch and blur. I know that was a memory. One so real I can still feel it; the rejection is a sharp pain in my side. But it's not a memory that I can write down. It's not even a memory that I want to remember.

Worry gnaws at my insides. Is this all that's left? These weird crumbs of him? Or was it all like that? Was he always that irritated by me?

I want to call Hannah. To ask her what Dad was like. I need her to reassure me about the parts that were good. But it's late and she's probably sleeping.

So I take out my box of Dad things. The photograph of us walking down the beach with me on his shoulders. The sixteenth-birthday card where he wrote, *To my flower child.* The tattered Lakers shirt that used to smell like him but doesn't smell like anything anymore. I hold them, hoping I'll feel some magic. But I don't.

In a last-ditch, half-hearted effort, I pile everything in a pool of moonlight and take my camera off the desk, opening the aperture all the way, slowing down the shutter speed. I try to keep my hands very still as I focus in on the half shadow of the curtain cutting across a curl of paper. Dad's face, his lips turned up in a weak smile.

8

THE HISTORY OF MOM AND DAD IS MY FAVORITE bedtime story, a worry stone in my pocket, smooth and round from telling and retelling. It was 1992. They were sliding like minnows through the teeming halls of Shaker Heights High, when Mom tripped on the laces of her low-top Doc Martens and ran into Dad, who spilled an entire can of Coke in her hair. Six months later they were driving to California in a beat-up Jetta: Dad with his Buddy Holly glasses and record collection, Mom with her red lipstick and Barbara Boxer T-shirt. Midwestern life was not for them. They were a pair of sparkles looking for romance, palm trees, enough city lights to blot out the stars for miles around. So they drove west. And they lived happily ever after.

• • •

ON FRIDAY MORNING I WAKE UP TO A TEXT FROM BENNETT: Hey beautiful.

A warm feeling spreads into my bones and millions of things to say in return flutter through my mind. But all I end up writing is Hey.

Immediately after sending it I want to take it back, to write more, to say *I miss you*. But we are one for one, exactly even, so I'll have to wait for next time.

I walk into the kitchen to see Bea slouching over the counter like a sad houseplant while El flips pancakes at the stove in paint-splattered work pants.

"Where's Mom?" I say, already knowing the answer.

"A work emergency," El says, and Bea grumbles, "Whatever that means."

Mom hasn't been home for dinner all week. The Starship *Enterprise* is stuck in Farpoint, at the very start of its journey, and it feels like New Mom is already a flop.

I try not to feel disappointed. In between the late nights she still looks at me like she wants to know what's in my head.

"Try to cut your mom a little slack," El says, grabbing the plates down from the cupboard. "It's her first week at a new firm. The sharks are circling."

"The sharks are always circling," says Bea.

"Yeah," I say, sitting down on a stool next to her. "That never used to stop her before."

El turns around with two plates bearing identical stacks of steaming, fluffy brown pancakes with melted butter on top. Her wide mouth is smiling but her eyes are stern, like we've hit some kind of nerve.

"Well, none of us are who we were before," she says, setting the plates down in front of us and turning back toward the fridge.

She's uncharacteristically quiet for a moment, rifling around inside of it, but by the time she returns to the counter, syrup in hand, her face has softened back into its usual relaxed half smile. "Anyway. What are you girls up to tonight? Friday and all."

"Nothing," says Bea. "Absolutely nothing."

I poke her with the tines of my fork. "No bonfire?" I say.

"It's a bonfire–slash–pep rally," she says. "I don't trust hybrid events and I'm not peppy."

"To each her own," El says, a forkful of pancakes halfway into her mouth. "Want to watch a movie or something?"

Bea shrugs. "Maybe."

She swirls a piece of pancake in the syrup, around and around, but it never quite makes it into her mouth.

• • •

That afternoon, Sam drives me to her house. She lives out in the country, on the opposite side of town. Her house is a split-level, wrapped in vinyl siding, with a huge, neatly mowed lawn that's bordered by dense forest. There's an aboveground swimming pool in the back and a Saturn in the driveway with a faded MAKE AMERICA GREAT AGAIN sticker on the back.

"My mom's boyfriend is obsessed with Trump," Sam says. "He's such a douche."

She takes me inside, up a set of carpeted stairs, and into her kitchen. The vinyl floor is peeling up in one corner and the air smells like scented candles. An ancient basset hound lounges on a brown fleece dog bed in the corner, next to a table with diner-style chairs and a glass angel centerpiece.

"That's Ralph," she says, walking over and giving him a

scratch under the chin. "He's almost as old as I am."

Sam opens the fridge and grabs two Cokes, then turns and leads me back downstairs. Her room is on the side of the basement that's mostly underground, so there isn't a ton of natural light, just two smallish windows up toward the ceiling. When she closes the door behind us, it feels like we're in a different world. The furniture is perfectly mismatched, from different eras of the past, a Lucite desk chair and a curvy wooden lamp, pink rosebud sheets and pillowcases. The walls are covered with ripped-out pages of *Vogue* and *Paper*, and the space above the queen-size bed is painted with a mural of a million lines, all splintering out in different directions, meticulous and wild.

Sam sits on the bed and I sit at the desk, tapping nervously on the top of my Coke can. I'm not sure how this is supposed to go. I think about Nora and me, slouching at the kitchen counter, chatting while her mom made doenjang jjigae at the stove. A sliver of melancholy lodges in my chest.

"This is weird," Sam says.

"So weird," I say. "I think I forgot how to make friends."

"Me too." Sam's phone vibrates next to her on the bed. She frowns and turns it over.

"Have you heard from your old friends much?" I ask.

"Barely," she says, pulling her hair up into a tiny bun on the top of her head. "Mostly just updates on the group thread. I think they forget that I'm still stuck here."

"They'll come around," I say, even though I don't know them.

"Maybe," Sam says. For a second she looks almost as lost as me. And then she tosses her phone on the nightstand. "Anyway," she says, a mischievous look creeping over her face. "I saw you walking to lunch with Jesse Keller every day this week. What's that about?"

I choke on my soda and the bubbles explode up my nostrils.

"Oh my god," I say, completely flustered. "Nothing. He's in my English class. It's right before lunch." I pause. "And anyway, I sort of have a boyfriend."

It's the first time I've used that word out loud, and when I add up the handful of words Bennett and I have said to each other since I left California, I'm not even sure if it fits anymore.

Sam leans forward, eyes wide. "Ooh. A boyfriend in California. Tell me everything."

"Ugh." I sink down in my chair, thinking about Bennett's tan, freckled, angular cheekbones, three thousand miles away. "I wouldn't even know where to begin."

"I bet he surfs," she says. "I bet he's unbearably hot."

"Yeah." I laugh, shaking my head. It feels funny to think of Bennett in those terms, and yet they do seem to fit. "Both of those things. But it's not like I'm going back there anytime soon, so it feels a little hopeless."

"Tragic." She gives a deep, dramatic sigh and then falls back on the bed. I take another sip of my Coke and it's painfully sweet on my tongue. "What about next year?" Sam asks.

I shrug. "I have this plan to go to UC Santa Barbara with my best friend, Nora. And yeah, he used to talk about going there too. But that was back when we were just friends."

I say this casually, like I haven't imagined it all in perfect detail: greasy takeout, sand in the sheets, an entire year of sleeping side by side on one of those tiny freshman mattresses.

"Anyway, it's kind of weird to talk seriously about the future with someone you've only been seeing for a couple of months."

"But would you want him to? If it wasn't weird?"

I close my eyes and remember the feeling of Bennett's big hand wrapping around mine.

"Yeah, I guess I would."

"Well, don't rule it out then."

I smile. "Okay, I won't."

Sam sits up, leaning against her headboard and pulling her knees up to her chin. "What's it like to grow up in LA?" she asks.

I take another sip of my soda, not even knowing where to start. For one second, a wave of sadness threatens to melt me into a puddle of pathetic on Sam's pink carpet. But somehow I swallow it back down. "I guess it seems like anywhere else until you realize that it's not."

I look outside Sam's tiny window, where the sun is starting to slant into the grass. "It's pretty quiet here."

"Quiet like death," Sam says, rolling her eyes. She sets her Coke down and turns to look over at the mosaic of cutouts on her wall. "I'm counting the minutes until graduation. I'm going straight to New York City to get lost in a crowd of people and noise."

"Hm," I say. For a second, I let myself imagine that future— what it would feel like to just disappear. "That sounds kind of nice."

"There's not even a museum here," Sam says. "The closest one is in Albany, and it's full of dead white guy paintings and marble sculptures."

I wrinkle my nose.

"We had a class trip to the city last spring, and I snuck away to the Brooklyn Museum to see a Kehinde Wiley show." Sam sighs. "I almost got suspended, but it was totally worth it."

"Wow," I say. "I've never even been to New York."

"Really?" Sam says. She looks at me in utter disbelief.

I laugh. "Yeah, really. My parents weren't about to drag all five of us across the country. But I've always wanted to go."

Sam jumps up onto her knees. "Oh my god, Mary, let's plan a trip!"

The idea hangs there for a second, sparkling in the dull basement air.

We talk until it's dark, about LA and Cumberland. I tell her about Berda Paradise Thrift Store on West Sunset, and she tells me about the Tulip Festival in Albany. We talk about In-N-Out and hot surfers at Zuma Beach and camping by the Cumberland River.

When it's time to get ready for the bonfire, Sam shows me her closet. And I nearly die. It's full. *Full.* Of the most amazing vintage. Dresses, jeans, sweaters. A red leather bomber jacket, hunter green Beatle boots.

"Where did you get all this?" I ask, in awe.

"Thrifting is kind of my passion," she says, moving hangers across the bar.

I pet a pink cropped mohair sweater lovingly. "Show me the ways of your magic."

She lets me borrow the sweater, and I'm thinking that this means we're friends now. And I feel relieved. Like one small tangle in this giant snarl of loneliness is coming undone.

• • •

When we get to school the sky is just finishing its transformation to night. There's a tiny sliver of pale violet on the edge of the horizon, but up at the top the sky is inky black and covered in stars. The bonfire is already lit, and kids are gathered around the edges and clustered on blankets across the field. I take a deep breath in, smelling burning wood and dewy, fresh-cut grass.

At home the bonfire smell was always part sea salt. And we wouldn't be caught dead at a party hosted by our high school. Instead we would drive to Malibu, stopping at the 7-Eleven for firewood, and sit in the cold sand while the fire heated our cheeks.

Here in New York, Sam and I wander through the crowd and she starts introducing me to way too many people. It's the first time I realize that she's popular, even though she seems to always be alone.

And suddenly, just like that, I'm popular too. It feels strangely good. People are talking to me instead of just staring. Asking me questions, making jokes. I'm laughing and smiling and flirting and almost glowing in the heat of the bonfire.

But after a while it all starts to blur and I stop feeling like myself. Everyone is asking me about California. What do you say about a place you're dying for?

Eventually, when I feel myself starting to drift, I turn to Sam. "Hey," I say. "I'm gonna go sit down for a while."

"Yeah, of course," she says. "Do you want me to come?"

I shake my head. "I'm good."

"Okay. I'll come find you in a bit," she says, and then she's pulled back into the throng.

I walk away from the crowd and find a spot just outside the circle of firelight. I sit down on the grass, not really caring that it's wet, and lie back until I'm looking at the stars. And wow. There are *so many*.

My phone vibrates in my pocket.

Bennett: I'm at our spot

He's sent a photo of his perfect toes in the sand.

I think of the way it felt that last day, his cheekbone pressing into mine.

I want to write, *What are we to each other?*

People in stories always stay connected by looking at the stars at the same time. But Bennett is in LA, where there are no stars. Just a sheet of smog and a layer of orange, the lights of the city reflecting back down.

And anyway, it's not even dark there yet.

I hear a sound in the grass and I look up to see Jesse, half of his face illuminated by the flickering light of the bonfire. He catches my eye and his smile breaks, wide across his face like a meteor.

"Hey, Marigold."

I prop myself up onto my elbows and push the hair from my face.

"Hey."

He sits down next to me and lies all the way back, his brown curls flopping into the grass around his head like a crown. He's quiet for a while, looking at the stars, his usually wild hands contained by his pockets.

I lie back down and thread my fingers through the damp grass. My cheeks grow warm from the effort of trying to think of something—anything—to say.

"So," I stammer. "Cool bonfire."

Wow. That was really not good.

"Yeah," he says. "I mean, we have it every year. But it's nice."

"Nice," I repeat back.

Oh god.

And then his hand escapes from his pocket and he reaches out and tugs the sleeve of my sweater. It's so sudden that I don't see it coming. My pulse hammers in my wrist.

"What is this sweater?" he says. "You look like a stuffed animal."

Jeez.

I shake my head, laughing. "Nope. Not how you talk to girls, Jesse Keller."

He laughs. "I meant it in a good way. It's cute. Soft."

That word, *soft*, makes me feel strange, like I'm floating a quarter inch off the ground.

I blink over at him and he lets go of my sleeve. For a while, neither one of us moves. The light of the bonfire dances, the crowd around the edge seems to sway.

"This light is so good," he says. "I wish I'd brought my camera."

"Me too," I say.

"I guess you'd need a tripod though," he says, looking over at the flickering shadows.

"Definitely."

The pace of conversation is slow, like a waltz. Jesse pulls the sleeves of his own sweater down over his hands and turns his head to the side to look at me fully.

"Who's your favorite photographer?"

"Uta Barth. Her photographs"—I pause, thinking of the blurry squares of trees and windows, shadows, light—"look the way I feel."

"Huh," he says, and he's quiet for a while. We're both just staring, eyes moving over each other's faces. I notice a scar under his left eye, in the subtlest relief against his otherwise smooth skin.

"Who's yours?" I ask.

"Garry Winogrand."

Of course. The patron saint of the white, cis, male photographer. I shake my head.

"What?" he says.

"Nothing." I say.

"I guess it's a little obvious," he says, shaking his head. "But he's the best street photographer ever. His photographs are magic."

"You're not wrong about the magic part," I say. The people in Garry Winogrand's photographs feel like they're actually moving, like they might lurch right through the plane of the page.

"And he's not so different from Uta Barth."

I frown. There couldn't be two more different photographers in all of art history.

"What?" he says again. "Light is light."

I look back up at the stars. They're absolutely everywhere.

"Yeah," I say. "Light is light."

Then we're quiet for a while and I'm thinking about the light and Garry Winogrand, but I'm also thinking about Jesse right next to me, his long body soaking up the dew just like mine.

And I'm thinking about Sam and New York City and the wild mural on her wall. It feels like a miracle to have found these familiar people in the land of football and Fox News. Or maybe Cumberland isn't what I think.

Jesse taps his fingers silently on the blades of grass.

I want to find a way to ask him about the darkroom, but it feels so loaded.

So we just lie there and a minute passes, or maybe ten. It's hard to tell. Out of the corner of my eye I see Sam drifting away from the crowd. I think she's looking for me.

"I should go," I say, sitting up.

"Yeah," he says, looking dazed.

I stand, brushing off the back of my jeans, and he tugs my sleeve again.

"See you around, Marigold," he says.

• • •

THE REST OF THE NIGHT IS A LITTLE SURREAL. THEY CALL OUT THE name of each sports team and the kids from that team actually run around the bonfire while everyone cheers. Off to the side, Jesse stands with a group of his friends. The girl from his lunch table is there, along with some kids from the cross-country team. Jesse is right in the middle, but somehow he seems a little bit separate from everything.

Sam and I watch from the hood of her car, drinking hot chocolate from Styrofoam cups. The megaphone calls out, "Varsity girls' field hockey!" and a group of girls in orange-and-white sweatshirts charge the fire with their arms raised.

"How does nobody fall in?" I ask.

"I don't know," Sam says. "But they do it every year and it's never happened."

"Sports are weird," I say.

"Yeah, no shit," Sam says. "Totally bizarre."

. . .

When I get home all the lights are on and Mom and Bea are yelling. Their voices hit me in a wall of sound when I walk through the door. My mind is loose from daydreaming all the way home to nineties music in Sam's car, and for one second I consider sneaking up the stairs and riding this one out up in my room. But I don't. I have to somehow keep these last pieces of my family from flying apart.

When I walk into the kitchen the yelling stops. I see Bea, red faced, crying, leaning back against the counter in a pink, matching Minnie Mouse pajama set. Her hair is piled on top of her head and she looks so mixed up—part teenager, part little kid, part punk—and I can see that she's crushed, anger and deep sadness warring on her face.

She looks at me and says, "Hey, you're home."

The sentence is without inflection, flat as a pancake.

"Yeah," I say. "Everything okay?"

I look from Mom to Bea and back again. Mom looks tired, frustrated, in wrinkled work clothes, her briefcase spouting papers at her feet. She's looking at Bea like she's a twenty-thousand-piece puzzle.

"Perfect," Bea says. Then she slinks out of the kitchen and stomps up the stairs.

Mom rubs her forehead. "Bea—" she calls, like she knows

she doesn't have anything better to say. Then her head drops, like someone cut the string that's been holding her upright, and she starts to cry.

I stand frozen in the doorway. I feel like the moment has gotten away from me. I should know how to fix this. I'm the big sister now. But my feet are glued to the doorway, in between these two rooms.

"Hey, girls." El walks in the kitchen door, earbuds in, T-shirt covered in splotches of deep green paint. When she sees Mom she says, "Oh shit."

I'm still wearing Sam's hunting jacket, still holding El's front door keys on their rabbit's foot keychain.

"I've got this," El says, waving me away and reaching for the kettle. I wonder if she can see the way I'm just about to break. "Why don't you go get ready for bed?"

I look at my mother, crying into a macramé place mat, and then I turn and leave the kitchen. When I walk up the stairs, my steps are heavy and slow.

Bea's door is closed, but it's not locked. I open it and she's under the covers, eyes closed, like she's willing the world to go away. She looks small in the yellow lamplight.

I climb in next to her, like I used to when we were young. I lie facing the wall with my back pressed to hers, spine to spine.

"What happened?" I say.

Bea is quiet for a long time. I can feel her rib cage expanding against me, a little wider with every breath as she tries to calm herself down. I try to sync my breathing up to hers, as if this will help me understand.

Finally she says, "She's getting away from us again."

I think of the way we both pretended not to watch the door all week long, while doing our homework at the kitchen table or doing dishes in the giant farm sink. And suddenly I feel so angry I'm burning up.

"How did we get here?" she says.

"I don't know," I say. "I don't know."

"She said it would be different but I'm stuck here alone, just like I was in California."

These are the words that stick me right between the ribs. I can still smell the bonfire in my hair. How did I not see how much she needed me?

"I'm sorry, Bea," I say. "I'm here."

"It's okay," she says, but even as she says it she's shifting her weight toward the edge of the mattress. *I'm sorry*, I write with my finger on the wall. *I'm sorry I'm sorry I'm sorry*.

"I miss Dad," she says. It's the first time I've heard anyone say that word in months.

"Me too," I say. "So much."

"I don't know if I'll ever be happy again," Bea says, and my heart snaps in half.

I turn around and wrap my arms around her, pulling her into me.

"It's okay," I say. "I'll help you."

"That's stupid," she says, sniffling. "How can you help me?"

"I don't know," I say. "But I will."

9

HERE'S ANOTHER SECRET ABOUT MY DAD: I'M NOT sure if he ever really liked me at all.

Of course, *of course*, I know that he loved me. I can see it in some memories, the ones I have remembered until they don't even feel real anymore, like a bumping piggyback ride under an electric, iPhone-photo blue sky.

But even before the dream, the lasting, indelible impression in my memory, the final taste in my mouth, is one of indifference. The thing I remember most is watching the closed door of his backyard office where he was always writing.

Yes, there were jokes and car rides with the windows down and secret trips to Arby's when Mom had to work on the weekends. But even then—even in the fullest, freest moments—I'd catch him staring into space, I'd notice his absent responses: *sure, yeah, right, of course*. It always felt like part of his brain was plotting his escape.

• • •

THE NEXT DAY, MOM AND BEA DON'T TALK TO EACH OTHER AT ALL. Bea seethes quietly, like an underwater volcano. Mom slinks from window to window, listlessly watching the yard. They move around the house on opposite tracks, an invisible energy field keeping them separate.

I text Hannah.

Me: Bea and Mom are fighting. I need some words of wisdom.

Hannah: Make them watch Steel Magnolias. It will cure everything.

Me: You're so weird.

Hannah: It's called eccentric. I'm working on a paper but I'll call later. You got this.

She keeps saying that but I'm pretty sure I don't.

• • •

EL INVITES ME ON A WALK IN THE WOODS AFTER BREAKFAST.

"Bring your camera," she says. "I'll bring some pens."

"Bea," she calls up the stairs, pulling on her boots. "Come walking with us. There's an entire deer skeleton just waiting to be added to your treasure collection."

"I don't do that anymore," Bea calls back.

We push and cajole, but in the end it's just the two of us, walking side by side under the leaves.

"How are you feeling?" El says.

"I'm fine," I say.

"You're always saying that."

It's cloudy today and wet and there's a pinkness to the air. The light is thick. It feels like dusk, even at eleven in the morning. El doesn't say anything for a long time. It seems like we are in some kind of gentle standoff; she's not going to ask me again, but she's also not going to say anything else until I give up the goods. Finally, when the house is far out of sight, I give in.

"I'm worried about Mom and Bea," I say.

El stops, wiping her brow with a green handkerchief. "Me too." Then she turns to me and says, "This is the hard part."

"What is?"

She leads us into a clearing, settles onto a stump, reaches into her bag for her sketchbook. The whole time I'm wondering what she could possibly mean. But then she finds a blank page, tapping it once with her index finger, and says, "When it looks like it should be over but it's not."

I stand next to her, fiddling with my lens cap.

I wonder if that's what this feeling is. Showing up in a new town where no one even knows it happened. New school, new locker, new friends. Underneath my backpack and my sundresses, I'm walking around with a hole in my side. But no one here can see it.

Maybe it will be better now that every part of our life is gone. Maybe we won't know that Dad is missing because we won't know where to look.

El takes out a tin of watercolor pencils. She runs her fingers over each of them before selecting a color. She's not really looking at me at all, and it feels like some kind of therapist/lion-tamer trick to get me to keep talking. It works because eventually I do, aiming my camera at a spot in the distance, twisting the lens in and out.

"I keep thinking that if I can just get through this year then

I'll get my life back," I say. I bring the camera away from my face without taking a picture.

"I'm not sure it works like that," El says. Her expression is cloudy, thoughtful. I want to ask her, *How does it work?* But a drop of rain breaks through the treetops, falling onto the place where her hand is drawing a thick blue line, and suddenly it feels like our talk is over.

"Well," she says, folding up her glasses. "I guess we should go back."

She takes her finger and rubs the splotch of rain into the page, spreading the color around. Then she closes the notebook, wipes her finger on the front of her jeans, and leads me back through the trees.

• • •

THE AFTERNOON DRAGS. I'M BORED AND CAN'T STOP THINKING about California. I'm thinking about shopping at the flea market and picking Pixie tangerines out of the tree in the backyard. I'm thinking about sitting with Nora in the front seat of her ancient VW Beetle, eating Shrimp Crackers and listening to the Shins. I'm thinking about kissing Bennett and the way his mouth always tastes like mint and limes. I'm thinking about how it almost never rains in LA and we're always lamenting it while secretly happy with endless sunny days.

For a while I try to photograph the rain making tracks on my window. Then I write in my journal but not about Dad. Everything is present tense—Sam's fuzzy sweater, Jesse's fingers nearly touching my wrist, the new void Bea opened up in my heart last night, right next to the old one.

Finally, at one o'clock, I knock on Bea's door.

"Come in," she yells.

She's going through her bursting closet, pulling out long black dresses and piling them on the bed.

"What are you doing?" I ask.

"Working on my Halloween costume."

"Already? It's barely even September yet."

She sighs like an old lady. "At this point it's all I have to look forward to."

Stab. Another guilt skewer, right between the eyes.

"Hey." I look down, twisting up my fingers. "I'm sorry I went out last night. I would have stayed in if I'd known how you were feeling."

"Don't," she says, sounding annoyed. "I'm fine."

She picks up a lace maxi dress and tears it down the seams, an unreadable look on her face. My fingers itch for my camera. Like if I looked at Bea through the lens, maybe I would understand.

"Okay." I'm not sure of what else to say. "Let me know if you change your mind."

"Yep."

She turns back to the closet, suddenly immersed in looking for something on the top shelf. I look around the room, trying to find a reason to stay. But Bea's back in her own world, like she's already forgotten I'm there.

• • •

Nora sends me pictures all day long:

She's drinking a mocha Ice Blended outside of Coffee Bean: I got your order, is that pathetic?

She's watching K-dramas and making a sad puppy face: Wish you were here.

She's up to her ankles in the Pacific Ocean: Bennett is hanging with the cool kids so it's just me today.

I miss her so much. I think about actually calling her, about telling her what happened last night—Mom and Bea and the latest chasm that seems to have cracked open between them. She would know what to say to make me feel better. But then I would have to tell her about the bonfire and about hanging out with Sam, which feels weirdly like cheating. So I just say: I'M JEALOUS. And: Me too. And: Tell him to stop being such a sellout.

And I think she can tell I'm half-assing because she says: What's up pup? You're not yourself today.

I stare out the window, at the dramatic purpley-gray sky and the raindrops pelting violently against the glass. I wish I could just ask, *How many days to UCSB?* But something about my talk with El has shaken that idea loose.

Me: I don't know. Things are just weird here.

Nora: I'm sending you a hug. Can you feel it?

I type, *I can't feel anything today.* But then I delete it and write: I'm sending you one back.

• • •

After dinner, Hannah calls on the house phone. Everyone gets a turn and I'm last. I've been sitting on my bed staring at my phone for an hour, willing Bennett to text me. My message window is open and I keep pulling it down to refresh the messages. Refresh. Refresh. Refresh.

I'm trying to forget an image I saw this afternoon on someone's Instagram story, Bennett's arm around some girl's waist. It was a group shot but it still filled my belly up with lead. I kept clicking through the story again and again, my eyes snagging on the way his fingers curled into the bare stripe of skin just above her hipbone.

I should just quit all social media. It's a constant California parade, a flashing neon sign that says: LIFE IS GOING ON WITHOUT YOU.

Bea comes in and thrusts the phone toward me, then turns and leaves in the curt manner with which she's doing everything today.

"I'm lost," Hannah says when I answer. "Who is this?"

"Mary." I roll my eyes. "You dork."

"Hey!" she protests. "It's not my fault. I keep getting passed back and forth. I'm losing track."

"Well," I say. "Now you know."

"My second-favorite little sister." She sighs. "How are you? I miss you."

It's so good to hear her voice. It's been weeks. I've been the big sister for way too long.

"I miss you too, Han. This shit is unreal," I say, settling back onto the bed.

"I know. Bea was just filling me in on everything. You have to ride in a yellow bus?"

There's absolute horror in her voice.

"Oh yeah," I reply. "It's awful."

She sighs again, deep, dramatic, familiar. "Mom is the worst."

"Truth." I close my eyes. "Seriously though, Han, I need your help."

"Bea and Mom?"

"It's worse than before," I whisper. "I don't know how to fix it."

"It's okay, Mare-bear. It's not your job to fix it."

I frown, my fingers tracing the edges of a quilt square that's covered in strawberries. I remember Hannah's big sister magic. She definitely would have solved this already.

"Isn't it?" I say.

"No. Definitely not." I can hear Hannah rummaging around. I try to picture her, in a nondescript dorm room, her desk littered with colorful pens. "Look," she says. "Things are just hard right now. You have to try to be there for Bea but know that she probably won't let you."

"Then what?"

"Just be relentless. You'll figure it out."

But I'm not really sure if I will.

I clear my throat. "What about Mom?"

"What do you mean?" she says.

It's so weird having to explain things to Hannah. Normally she would already know everything. And anyway, I wonder if it's even possible to describe the way I felt this morning as I watched Mom at the kitchen counter, furiously typing on her laptop next to a plate of untouched, hours-old toast.

I keep trying to compare and contrast my different versions of Mom. The one who stopped existing when Dad did. The one who was so far gone we needed a search party. Then this new person who is smiling and leaping into the river but also not home and then crying last night at the kitchen table.

"I don't know. I can't stop worrying about her," I finally say.

Hannah sighs, as if she can hear all of the noisy thoughts

tumbling around my mind. "She'll be okay. She's just figuring things out. Give her some time."

I can barely think it, but the words come out anyway. "What if she's not okay?"

Hannah pauses and I hear a soft rustle like she's wrapping herself up in her immaculate white duvet, the way she used to on winter mornings. "Then we'll figure it out."

Downstairs, I hear a burst of laughter echoing around the kitchen and I remember that Mom isn't alone. At least not right now.

"Okay," I say. I lie back on my gingham pillowcases, trying to stuff the anxiety back down. "Tell me about college."

After the past few days, I feel desperate for information, details. Something that can make my plan for the future feel real again.

Hannah pauses, and in my mind I can see her twirling her long princess hair around her finger, thinking of the right superlative to use. "It's kind of the best and kind of the worst."

"Exactly the answer I would expect from you," I say.

"What does that mean?" she says.

"Nothing." I laugh.

She ignores me and launches into a long description of her freshman dorm and her hot RA, the cafeteria that has a soft-serve ice cream dispenser. I use these details to repopulate the vision of my own future. Me and Nora eating sundaes for breakfast, listening to lectures on feminist thought. Still, as soon as the picture is formed, all of the outlines start to wobble.

"Sometimes," Hannah says, "I feel like I've been here forever."

And then I remember Dad and my dream. The other secret

I've been keeping. I want to ask Hannah about him. Just to make sure. But I can't seem to get the words out.

I glance over at my phone, at the foot of the bed, and see that there's a text. From Bennett.

I unlock the screen, and it says: Facetime? And suddenly all coherent thought flees my mind.

Oh my god. Oh my god.

"Hey, Han?" I cut into her monologue. "I gotta go. I think Mom needs the phone."

"Yeah, okay," she says. "I should go too. Call me anytime though, okay? I really miss you. And take care of Bea. She's not as tough as she looks."

"I know. I will," I say. "I miss you too."

I run the phone back downstairs to the cradle faster than the speed of light and then I'm racing to the bathroom, pulling my hair down from its ponytail and pinching my cheeks. That's what people do when they need more color, right? It doesn't feel like there's time for makeup. I've been waiting so long for these particular stars to align and I don't want to miss my window.

I spend a minute propping my phone on my quilt in an effort to find the exact most flattering angle, then I take a deep breath and try to lean casually back against the headboard.

Bennett answers the call right away and he's sitting on his bed too, looking sun dazed and perfectly rumpled. I can practically smell the salt and sunscreen on his skin.

The screen freezes for a second, then starts working again as he reaches up to run a hand through his hair. "Hey, Mary."

"Hey, Bennett," I say, trying to keep my smile small and not creepy, despite the wild happiness I feel seeing his face again. It makes me think of *before*, when we'd never even kissed, when I'd ring Bennett's doorbell and his dad would say, "Bennett, your girlfriend's here!" and I'd try to hide how much I liked it.

"It's good to see you," Bennett says as one side of his mouth lifts into his signature smile.

My heart thuds to a halt. It's a few seconds before it picks up again, before I can say, "Thanks. You too."

"How's New York?" he says. "I wanna know everything."

I'm quiet for a minute, trying to figure out how to distill the one million different experiences I've had since I got here into something that could possibly make sense to another person.

"It's . . ."

depressing, exhausting, strange, beautiful, awful, boring, weird

"All right."

He laughs. "That's it?"

I shake my head.

"No," I say. "It's just really complicated, I guess. It mostly sucks. But some things are nice."

When I say it, I'm talking about swimming with my mom and walking with El and the way the air here is like something you can touch, but as soon as the words leave my mouth I think about Jesse. Shit.

"How's California?" I say, anxious to shift the conversation somewhere else.

He sighs, shaking his head of golden hair. "Eh, it's fine. School is school. We won our first water polo game . . ." Pause. "I miss you."

And there it is again.

But it's not *Let's make a plan.* It's not *Be mine.*

There was this time, in the history of Nora and Bennett and me, when Nora and I started saying, *I love you.* It was middle school and all the girls were saying it and I absolutely did love Nora. I loved Bennett too, but the feeling had a different kind of sting to it. *I love you* wasn't the kind of thing that I could ever say out loud. So we made up this game where we'd say, *I love U————nicorns. I love EU————phemisms. I love U————niversities,* stretching the *U* out until it hurt a little. It's been a while since we've played that game. But in another way it feels like we're always playing it.

Now I say, "I miss you too." And then, to push off the unbearable hugeness of the feeling of missing, I say, "And animal-style french fries."

Bennett grins and says, "I miss your feminist critiques."

And I say, "I miss stealing your water polo parka."

Bennett says, "I miss stealing the granola bars out of your backpack."

And I want to say, *I miss feeling your eyelashes on my nose.*

But instead I laugh and fall back onto my bed, and he laughs and falls back onto his, and the sound of him hitting the sheets hits my heart right over the head with a rolling pin. For the one millionth time I want to say something more meaningful than this.

When he said, *You know I love you, right?* I didn't say it back.

Now I look at the sun-colored hair curling at his neck and think: maybe because the *you know* before and the *right* after made *I love you* seem so much smaller than the thing I was feeling.

"I miss kissing you," Bennett suddenly says, rolling to his side.

And, just like that, we are back in familiar territory.

I clear my throat.

"I miss kissing you too."

I can barely get the words out. I can't believe I'm here, lying on Aunt El's guest bed, my bare toes resting on a quilt square with the word *Yes!* embroidered in red, hearing Bennett, who is thousands of miles away and yet looking close enough to touch, say those words to me.

He's quiet for a minute, just watching. I'm perfectly still.

"I miss your skin," he says, and my heart rate picks up, even faster than before, from jackrabbit to hummingbird. "It's soft and it smells so good."

I blush, deep, all the way down my throat.

"What is this sweatshirt you're wearing?" he says through his crooked, adorable smile. Something about his expression makes me think again about how we used to be, before New York, before kissing.

Once we got to high school, Bennett mostly stopped sitting with Nora and me at lunch. He sat with the water polo players or the surfers and walked through the halls, always in the middle of a big pack. But he still came to my house on Sunday nights to do homework and watch old movies. He'd still spend Saturday afternoons with Nora and me at the beach. And whenever he passed me in the hallway, he'd look at me and smile like we had a secret.

He's smiling like that now. Like even though we are on opposite sides of the universe, part of him belongs to me.

Then Bennett's face gets a little bit mischievous and he says, "I can't even see your neck."

I know what he's really saying. And I know that I have a T-shirt on underneath my sweatshirt—a threadbare Tom Petty and the Heartbreakers tour shirt from my dad—but it still feels like I'm doing something a little bit dangerous when I pull my arms through the sleeves.

I drop it awkwardly to the floor, and then I'm sitting there in my oversized T-shirt, hair sticking up everywhere, thinking: this is the world's least sexy striptease.

But Bennett is grinning.

"That's good," he says, raising an eyebrow. He pulls his shirt off too and then he's sitting there, sun-browned skin, looking up at me with his tumbled turquoise eyes. "But I think you can do better."

"Oh yeah?" I say, and I'm not sure I can. My pulse is pounding way too loud, all the way up in my ears, and for the first time in a long time, I wish we could go back to the solid ground of friendship. To take smaller steps out into whatever this is. To make sure we don't forget anything this time.

I close my eyes and remember the feeling of Bennett pulling me down the street on his skateboard, the warm sun on my face, his hot hand wrapped around my wrist, the uneven road rattling my teeth, lurching and flying forward, skinning my knees, laughing until my stomach hurt.

I wish I could say, *I packed those granola bars for you.*

But I can't, so instead I grab the hem and tug my shirt up over my head.

10

THIS IS WHAT I REMEMBER ABOUT DAD DYING: EVERY-
thing.

I remember how hot and dry it was in our living room when
Mom sat us down to tell us he had cancer. Dad was at the hospital already, trying to shake an infection. The afternoon sun was
slanting through the front window of our house and the backs
of my knees were sticking to our green leather couch and I kept
swallowing and swallowing, wishing I had a glass of water.

I remember Hannah driving us the forty-five minutes to and
from the hospital every day after school. She was on a Beatles
kick and would blast the White Album so we wouldn't have to
talk. We'd just stare out our windows as we inched forward in
the rush-hour traffic, the sun setting over the side of the freeway.

I remember how fast my dad turned from pasty Irish peach
to translucent white, like he was having some strange camouflage
reaction to the linens on his hospital bed. I would sit for hours on
the mauve vinyl ICU waiting-room chairs, pretending to do my

homework until my neck ached. It felt like the days were going too slow, then too fast, then too slow again.

I remember taking Bea to get a new dress for the memorial. She got her first period in the dressing room, and I remember fishing a tampon out of the bottom of my backpack, finding it beneath the textbooks, coated with crumbs and hidden by gum wrappers, handing it under the door, and going up to the register to buy her a new pair of jeans.

"Don't tell Mom," she'd said.

* * *

"So," Jesse says as he floats through the crowded hallway on Monday.

And I'm not kidding, the guy floats, like he's an iridescent bubble and the rest of us are just particles of air shifting around him.

"So," I say, clunking along slightly behind him.

He clears his throat. "Do you want to come use my darkroom sometime?"

"Yes."

The answer escapes my lips before I can think it through, before I've left a socially acceptable pause to indicate nonchalance. The word rushes out because of the film piling up on my dresser and the restlessness of waiting way too long to see what's inside. Not because of Jesse.

And then I think, *Is it because of Jesse?*

And then I think, *No, you idiot.*

And then I think about Bennett sitting there shirtless, smiling his smile, and my stomach plummets to the ground.

Jesse nods and looks as if he's fighting a cocky grin. Something about the way his upper lip curls makes me want to reach over and touch it.

Jesus, what is happening to me?

"Okay," he says, unaware of the inner meltdown I'm experiencing.

Inside my head all the lights are blinking, *Danger! Danger!* It's basically Chernobyl in there.

"How about tomorrow?" he says. "I'm not working and I'm done with cross-country at four thirty."

Again, the word *yes* just tumbles out.

Not *yeah, sure.* Not *lemme check.* Just *yes.* I'm such a frigging moron.

But part of me is still chanting it like a cheerleader: *Yes, yes, yes.*

• • •

WHEN SAM SITS DOWN AT OUR LUNCH TABLE SHE SAYS, "YOU LOOK funny."

"What?" I say, still feeling part giddy, part guilty.

"You're smiling too much," she says.

She almost sounds like Bea.

"I'm just . . ." I search around for a way to explain that won't trigger an endless chain of questioning. "Having a good day?"

She rolls her eyes. "Yeah, okay, Mary."

I bite into my almond-butter sandwich to avoid further discussion on the topic, and there's a lot of almond butter on it, so by the time I swallow the subject has changed and we're talking about an Amy Winehouse documentary on Netflix.

"It's weird," Sam says. "It's like she was living this incredible dream life and at the same time she was completely trapped by it."

"Yeah," I say. "I can't imagine what that must be like."

"I don't know," she says. "Sometimes I just feel restless. Do you ever feel that way?"

And I'm sure that sometimes I do, but right now the dominant feeling in my life, this deep, visceral longing for home, is the literal opposite of restlessness.

I look at Sam's face and for one second see something that looks like sadness. Then it's gone. She tucks a strand of hair behind her ear.

"Hey," she says. "Want to come over tomorrow and study for calc?"

And, somehow, we're back to me and the topic I'm once again trying to avoid, evade, squash. But, even in my own mind, it's looming over everything, big and tacky like the Hollywood sign: I'm hanging out with Jesse tomorrow.

"I can't," I say, taking another big bite as I try to whip up a lie. "I promised Bea we'd hang."

I don't know why I don't tell her the truth. It would be the logical next step in making a friend: reveal information about yourself. But I'm still trying to figure out why I just acted like such a weirdo in front of Jesse. I can't handle any questions right now.

I also haven't talked to Bennett since Saturday, when I sat there half naked in front my computer screen, breathing hard until he said, *Oh shit my mom is coming* and closed his computer halfway through goodbye.

Later on, he texted me: Do you have any idea how beautiful you are? and I wanted to write back: *Tell me what you're really thinking.*

It's awful to long for something when you don't even know if it really exists.

"No worries," Sam says, opening her sketchbook. I don't think she detects my lie, and I'm relieved. I'll tell her. I will. Just not yet.

• • •

THE NEXT DAY I WAIT FOR JESSE AFTER SCHOOL, READING *One Hundred Years of Solitude* under a maple tree near the student parking lot. I feel guilty as I watch the big, dirty yellow school bus, where I know Bea is sulking, making its way to the street. It's been four days since I promised her I'd make things better, and I've barely made it past her bedroom door.

But an hour passes and then I see Jesse, leaning against an old VW Rabbit, all angles and elbows, his long legs crossed at the ankle, hair wet from a locker-room shower, and I forget all feeling. Like, literally, the feeling leaves my limbs.

He drives us to his house, which—like most houses in Cumberland—is out in the country. As we're barreling past the muddy green fields I think, *Does anyone here actually live in town?*

We head down a long, winding dirt road that's lined with trees and meadows and gentle afternoon light. My window is down, my hand tracing shapes on the breeze. I can smell the tall grass. I can hear the tires rolling over the gravel. El said this morning that this might be the last hot day of the year, and I'm trying to savor it because I don't know what comes next.

"I should warn you," Jesse says, his hand working the ancient gearshift. "My family is a little strange."

"Don't worry," I say, thinking of Mom in her work-paper shell. "Mine is too."

"My parents moved out here in the nineties from Chicago— major hippies," he says. "My dad built our house. It took him five years and they lived in a yurt the whole time. Even in the winter."

"Wow," I say, realizing that his family is an entirely different kind of weird than mine. "What do they do now?"

"They actually founded the co-op, so now they manage it, and we also own the hardware store next door. They kind of trade off working and taking care of my brothers and sisters. It's a lot."

My brain gets stuck on *brothers and sisters*. Plural. Huh.

"There are six of us," he explains.

"Wow," I breathe.

He runs a hand through his hair and the downy part of his cheek turns pink. "I know. It's weird."

"How old are they?" I ask, picking at the disintegrating vinyl at the edge of my seat.

"Maggie is two, Finn is five, Anna is seven, Will is eleven, and Katherine is thirteen."

He rattles them off on his fingers, and I'm struck by the sheer number of syllables in the list. Even the sound of his family is big.

"Are you guys religious?" I ask, and his answering laughter makes embarrassment pink my cheeks until they're matching his.

"Not like that," he says. "I think it sort of just happened."

"Cool," I say, trying to recover.

"Yeah, it's all right," he says. "But it makes life pretty chaotic."

Finally we pull into the long driveway and his house emerges from the trees, bit by bit, as branches and leaves roll out of our way. It's tucked back into the woods like a real-life gingerbread house. There's a big porch across the front and firewood stacked up next to the door and a big rack with eight pairs of rubber boots in size order.

When we get to the front door, he stops. He looks at me. And the sun striping over his face makes a perfect triangle between his long nose and thick eyelashes.

I'm so absorbed in the light on his face that it startles me when he blinks.

"You ready?" he asks.

"Of course," I say, though really I have no idea if I am or not.

Before he can turn back around, the front door is thrust open by a chubby, blonde, naked toddler. Her round body is deeply tanned, like she spent the entire summer running around in the sun.

"Jethee!" she screams, holding up sticky hands.

"No way, Mags. If you want me to pick you up, you gotta put on pants."

He reaches down and messes up the hair on the top of her head, just the way that a big brother in the movies would do it. Their brown eyes are exactly matching.

"This is Maggie," he says. "She's a nudist."

A tall, strong-looking woman with shoulder-length brown hair and a wide smile appears in the doorway. Her eyes are blue but her lips are all Jesse. She's wearing ripped jeans and a shirt that says EAT THE RICH.

She scoops Maggie up with one arm, resting her sideways like a rolled-up yoga mat on her hip.

"Sorry, guys," she says, kissing Jesse on the cheek. "She escaped mid-change." She shrugs as if to say, *You know what I mean*, and then extends her hand to me. "Hi, Marigold, I'm Lena," she says. "You two want a snack?"

"Don't worry about it, Mom," Jesse says. "I got it."

His mom disappears down a hallway before I can really think about the fact that she knows my name already, and Jesse leads me through a great big living room that's full of couches, funky lamps, and artwork and littered with toys and books and broken crayons, colorful chunks partially ground into the rug.

I follow Jesse into the kitchen, which overlooks a big backyard that seems to melt into the forest, with a ramshackle playhouse and several bikes scattered among the trees.

"Fair warning," he says. "We are a lentils-and-carob kind of family. But do you want a something to eat?"

"Maybe just some water," I say.

He fills two glasses and then grabs a couple of apples from the counter.

"Just in case," he says, somehow carrying all of it in the crook of one arm.

He motions with his head for me to follow and I do, through the back door, across the yard, and over to another structure—an oversized shed without any windows, just vents at the top.

"This," he says, tossing an apple into the air and catching it with a lopsided grin, "is my darkroom. My dad and I built it last summer." He sets everything down on the outside rail and leads me inside.

The smell hits me first, the familiar sour, vinegar scent of the developer. I look around at the trays, neatly stacked on the counter, the bottles of chemicals and boxes of paper lining the shelves, the immaculate metal sink, and I realize that Jesse is a whole other kind of guy from what I'm used to. He's neat. Careful.

And then I notice his photographs, hanging at the back wall of the room like shirts on a laundry line. And wow. They're as close to street photography as you can get in a town like Cumberland. They're all people—at the gas station, in the supermarket, in front of the Elks Lodge. But he's right. They're also about the light.

"Wow," I say again, out loud this time. "These are so good."

"Thanks," he says, looking down at his hands. "It's pretty hard to do street photography in Cumberland."

"You pretty much nailed it, though," I say, stepping closer to the prints. "It's almost like you made a new genre."

"Well, Uta Barth," he says, elbowing my side. "I can't wait to see what you're bringing today."

I jump, surprised by his touch, almost kicking over a jug of fixer. Jesse tosses me a developing tank, and I somehow catch it as I fish the film out of my backpack. He gets the chemicals all ready on the counter while I line up my reels in a neat row. When everything is done, he looks at me. And I see round brown eyes, thick lashes, tiny scar, dark curls, big hands.

"You ready?" he asks me for the second time today.

I don't think I am.

I nod. And he flips the lights. Suddenly I can't even see my hands in front of my face.

But somehow, without my sight, I notice even more of Jesse. His deep, even breathing, the rustling of his T-shirt right next to me. I think I can even feel the warmth of him radiating out through the air.

His movements are adept beside me, and I can tell he's done this a million times. And I have too, but here, in Jesse's darkroom, I'm clumsy. I barely get the first reel loaded before I accidentally drop the second one on the floor. The wire clatters against the floorboard.

"Shit," I say.

Right as he says, "I got it!"

And we both bend down at the exact same time, our heads colliding like we're in a Three Stooges movie. He reaches out to steady me and his fingers wrap around my bare arm in the darkness.

His hand is warm and his forehead is kind of leaning against mine and I can smell his breath and I swear to god it smells like flowers. Like the kind in the Greek myths that are designed to lead you to your death.

I start feeling desperately around the floor, and when my fingers close around the reel I shoot up like a geyser. "Got it!" I half shout, which is way, way too loud for this tiny space.

"Cool," he says, and I can feel him rising off the floor, up, up, up to his regular height, towering in the blackness above me.

Somehow I get the rest of my film onto the reels and into the tank and then he flips on the safelight and we are back on solid ground.

He looks different in the red light, the angles of his face somehow sharper without the color to smooth them out. He's looking at me like I look different too, and his lips quirk up into a new kind of smile. I turn to the counter and start adding chemicals to my film.

He says, "Tell me about California."

But it feels like he's really saying, *Tell me about you.*

"Oh man," I say, still working on my tolerance for hearing that word. "I miss it."

I shake the developing tank gently, agitating the chemicals.

"It's so different, louder and brighter. More people. Less humidity. Neon sunsets. But I think what I miss the most is just having a life that makes sense. Like, a life where I go to my school with my friends. Where I can bicker with my sisters and complain about my homework and feel like everything isn't falling apart all the time."

Jesse nods, and we're both quiet for a while, turning our tanks in our hands.

"Why did you move?" he says.

I pour the developer out and add the water, unsure of what to say.

"I mean, you don't have to tell me if you don't want to," he says, behind me at the sink.

"No, I want to," I say. "It's just hard to know where to begin."

I start to turn the tank again. And then the words just come tumbling out.

"My dad died about nine months ago. He was diagnosed with late-stage pancreatic cancer in October and everything happened really fast."

I pause but he doesn't say anything. He doesn't say, *I'm sorry for your loss*, which has to be the single most awkward sentence ever invented. He just keeps working, hanging up our film and wiping the counter.

"My mom kind of threw herself into working, and we all tried to go back to normal. But I guess it eventually just got too hard. We don't really have any family in California. My aunt El lives out here, so my mom decided we should move."

"Oh," he says. "I know El. She's friends with my mom."

I smile. "I could see that."

We go outside for a while to let our film dry, and Jesse crunches into his apple. Out in the trees at the edge of the yard, a deer appears like an apparition. It steps into a spot of sunlight and bends its long, graceful neck down to the ground.

"Whoa," I say.

"What?" Jesse says.

"That deer."

Jesse laughs, setting his apple down and taking a step toward it. "We are pretty much overrun with deer around here. They're like the rats of upstate New York."

"No way," I say, watching as the deer streaks off into the woods.

"Yep." Jesse nods. "But people here love hunting, so that keeps the numbers down. Wait till the first day of the season. About two-thirds of the school will be out."

"That is bizarre." I shudder. "Do you?"

"Nah," Jesse says. "My dad took me once when I was about twelve. We sat up in this tree stand for hours, freezing our asses off. Finally a deer came along and my dad handed me the gun, and as soon as I had the shot lined up I started crying."

I lean back against the railing. "So you're a pacifist then?"

Jesse shrugs. "I guess. Luckily, he's got Will, who at the age of eleven can already skin a deer with his eyes closed."

I close my eyes, trying not to vomit at the thought. "I can't."

"Cumberland is a weird place," he says. "I love it. But I can't wait to leave."

I laugh. I like that he loves it here. "It seems like everyone I talk to is just waiting around until they're old enough to get out."

"It's like some weird purgatory," he says.

I look up at the one million green leaves dancing above our heads.

"But it sure is pretty," I say.

Back in the darkroom, we're quiet as we cut the film and get ready to make our contact sheets. It's one of my favorite parts, when you put your negatives on the light table for the first time and remember what was on the film, but backward. Mine: window screens, raindrops, long shadows on vinyl siding, El's blurred elbow against a sharp tree line. Jesse's: people and Cumberland and painterly light.

"So what's your plan?" I ask. "For getting out."

He sighs a deep sigh that tells me it's complicated. "I want to go to the city next year. NYU or maybe Pratt." He shrugs his shoulder and his whole body follows in this wave of melancholy mixed with nonchalance. "But with six kids it doesn't seem likely. I'll probably end up at Hudson Valley Community College."

He flicks at an invisible piece of dust on one of his negatives.

"I'm applying for scholarships, though."

He goes to move around me, and for a second his hands ghost over the tops of my shoulders, not quite touching them. I shiver, and then they're gone and he's setting out the trays and mixing more chemicals.

"What about you?"

"I've been planning on applying early to UC Santa Barbara. But—"

I don't know. The thought seems to appear out of nowhere.

Up until now, The Plan has been the one fixed point in my life that gives order and meaning to everything. Nora and me together at UCSB. But now that Nora isn't here and I'm not there, everything suddenly feels so unsettled.

"Honestly, I don't know," I admit. "My grandparents want me to apply to an Ivy League school, and I think my mom secretly wants me to end up at some small, elite liberal arts college."

I straighten a box of paper, amazed that I'm still talking.

"I've been taking all these AP classes and studying for all the tests. But honestly I don't know if I really care all that much."

"Must be nice," Jesse says. I feel like an asshole. I lean into the countertop, trying to explain.

"I just mean, if I got into Harvard it would be great and all, but would I have really earned it? I'm just living the life that's been predestined by my white, upper-middle-class ancestry."

Jesse laughs, but it feels forced. "So . . . the patriarchy."

"Yeah." I shrug, my cheeks burning. "Part of me feels like, why am I mindlessly walking this path just because it's what I'm supposed to do? But I get that there's privilege in that too."

Jesse hands me a squeegee. "So what would you do if you didn't go to college?"

"I don't know."

I feel embarrassed, having rambled my way out into this thicket. I've only known Jesse for two weeks, but already I can tell he's working a hundred times harder than I ever have and I just told him that I don't care.

It's not even true. I do care. I just suddenly don't know. The future feels like a big blank. Like someone has come along and blotted everything out.

We make our contact sheets without talking much. And despite our awkward conversation, despite the magnetic, meteoric presence of Jesse, I somehow manage to slip into my quiet place. Enlarger, developer, stop bath, fixer. Ten seconds, thirty seconds, a minute at a time. Repeat, repeat, repeat. Images emerge under the waves of developer, like forgetting in reverse.

In the middle of my contact sheet there's a square of solid black from the night of my dream. The frame looks empty but I print it anyway, hoping for some tiny gray blur of recognition. Even if the memories are turning sour, I still want them.

There was this period of time, before we knew about the cancer, when Dad was sort of in between. He wasn't writing anymore, but he was still in that place that nobody could get to. I'd get up in the morning to get ready for school, and he'd be half asleep in his favorite chair, watching old movies. It was confusing, knowing he was right there but not being able to reach him. And then we found out he was sick and we finally understood.

But sometimes now I feel like I'm in between, stuck somewhere between what my life used to be and whatever comes next. When I'm here, I can't get to anybody and nobody can get to me.

When the developer is done, there's nothing on the paper but a black rectangle. In my mind, the in-between starts to stretch further and further back in time, turning into something else.

Jesse and I work for hours, drifting closer and farther apart. The space is small; our elbows graze as we agitate the chemical trays, our hands brush at the sink, the light table.

I don't know how much time has passed when we start to wake up from the haze of the darkroom. Or how we know we're done. But after what feels like forever, Jesse looks at me and nods, and I nod back at him, and he says, "I think we've been here for a while."

"Yeah," I say.

I'm dazed. Happy.

Then he takes one big, deep breath, one big, slow step across the space between us. He's standing in front of me, his feet on either side of mine, his belly a half inch away from my solar plexus. He brushes a piece of hair out of my eyes and then puts his hands on the table. He tilts his head down, an inch. Less. And I'm like those Greek sailors, the scent of the flowers drawing me up onto my tiptoes, tugging my eyelids down.

Wait.

"Wait," I say.

And his head snaps up, his hand rubs the back of his neck, and a door closes on the other side of his face.

"I'm sorry, Jesse," I stammer, feeling so disoriented by the chemicals, by the red light, by Jesse's big, melancholy eyes. "I can't."

"Okay," he says.

"I have a—" I pause, searching around the corners of my mind for the right word. "I have someone. In California. It's complicated. I don't even know what it is but I don't think that we should—" I'm babbling and I must sound completely incoherent and before I can stop it I think of myself, with the worst-ever Saturday blues, sitting there almost naked on my bed.

Jesse gives a little laugh, but his face stays closed. Completely shut. The moment is done.

We clean up without talking much, and Jesse is so careful. Every drop is wiped, every bottle is set exactly in its place. It's like he's reversing everything that just happened.

I wish I had somehow brought up Bennett before. At the co-op, at the bonfire, when Jesse asked me about California. Any time other than the moment he was leaning down to kiss me.

When we finally open the door again it's night. The crickets and frogs and fresh air hit us like a wave.

"Do they do that all year long?" I ask, more to myself than anything.

"Nah," Jesse says, stepping outside. "Probably just another week or two."

"Can we do this again?" I ask, worried that everything is wrecked.

But his smile is back and it hits me right at the back of my knees. I almost fall over from the force of it.

"Yeah," he says. "I have to work tomorrow, but how about Friday?"

I blink up at him. I still see everything.

11

THE NEXT DAY JESSE FINDS ME AT MY LOCKER BEFORE
the first bell rings. The chill of fall arrived this morning,
and he's wearing a caramel-colored Carhartt hoodie jacket and a
bright red beanie. I don't exactly know what swooning is, but I'm
pretty sure I'm doing it. My knees actually feel weak again at the
sight of the dark curls spilling out around his ears.

"I'm sorry," he says.

"For what?" I say.

"For last night," he says, pulling off his hat and running a
hand down his face. "I should have known. I feel like an idiot."

"No," I say. "You're not. It's fine."

I'm trying to pretend like I wasn't thinking about it all night,
the rush of standing with his feet on either side of mine. This
morning I woke up to a text from Bennett that said:

The ocean was stormy and gray today. Reminded me of
your eyes.

I feel like a jerk.

"Look," Jesse says. "Can we be friends? I'd really like to be your friend."

"Yeah," I say. "Of course. Me too."

And I'm so relieved. Because I really, really want to.

The bell rings. He stuffs his hat into his pocket, turns on his heel, and follows the crowd of kids rushing off to homeroom. I stand there at my locker, a little breathless, my forehead resting against the cold orange metal for a while before I remember that I'm still wearing my backpack, that I still need to put my jacket away.

I'M DISTRACTED IN ENGLISH CLASS, LOOKING OUT THE WINDOW AT the flat light and the gray sky. To be honest, *One Hundred Years of Solitude* is starting to bum me out. It's all about fathers and sons, about the deep ties between the generations. It's hard to read right now, when my connection to Dad is disintegrating like old skin.

Still, there's something about José Arcadio Buendía that reminds me of him, the determination with which he locks himself inside his study, the ferocity with which he searches for something that shines, something that transcends his small life.

This is the part of Dad I'm struggling with—this growing knowledge of his discontent, the idea that maybe he wasn't just sick, maybe he was truly miserable.

By the time school is out, the sun is back and it's warmed up again. Bea has detention because she called one of her classmates a "fucking racist imbecile" in the middle of a US history debate. She is the coolest person I know, but I'm still worried that she hasn't made any friends yet.

Sam offers us a ride, and she and I hang out in the art room while we wait. I watch her disappear inside a charcoal drawing, and I look through another stack of magazines, ripping out all of the palm trees.

After a while, we go out to the parking lot and sit with the windows down, listening to a cassette tape Sam has in her car. The boys' soccer team is practicing; the guys are little dots over on the far end of the deep green field. Even from here, I can see that their shirts are off.

Sam has her sketchbook out and she's working on an intricate abstract drawing in pencil.

"I know it's pathetic," she says. "But I could sit here and watch them all day."

"I know," I say. "I feel like a creep. But, at the same time, I think I'm actually drooling."

"Seriously," she says.

She looks down at her notebook, darkening a line.

My phone buzzes with a text from Nora: Worst day ever.

I frown and write back: What's up?

The little gray dots appear and disappear a few times.

Nora: It's complicated.

I text the obligatory: Do you want to talk? But for some reason I hope she doesn't. For once I just want to be here, in Cumberland, in the car with Sam.

Again, the dots appear and disappear and I can feel her indecision. I should just call her. It's been days since we've talked. But before I can do it a text appears.

Nora: Nah. I'm good.

Me: Are you sure?

Nora: Yeah.

Me: Ok. I love you.

Nora: ILU2.

Sam sets her notebook down. "Did you know that Cindy Sherman used to collect prosthetic body parts?"

I laugh, sliding my phone into my backpack. "Actually, I did. She's the coolest."

The cross-country team runs by, also shirtless, and I spot Jesse, at the head of the pack, looking like he was made to be in motion. His torso is long and his skin is deeply tanned and he has this look on his face like he's reciting poetry in his mind, like he's about to take flight. For a second I think about Bennett in the waves.

"Let's just pretend like we're doing research," Sam says. "Like Cindy Sherman."

"Okay," I say.

But ogling Jesse after everything that's happened still feels a little bit wrong.

"Hey," she says, as if she is reading my mind. "What is going on with you and Jesse?"

"Nothing," I say, shaking my head. "Nothing, nothing, nothing."

"Whatever you say, Mary," she says.

• • •

LATER THAT NIGHT, I FACETIME NORA, BUT THE PHONE JUST RINGS and rings. I text: Everything ok?

Nora: Grandparents in town. I'll text you later.

Me: Ok. I'm here if you need me.

Nora: I know.

Me: 331 days.

It feels like a lie.

Nora: Can't wait.

12

IT'S STRANGE BEING IN A PLACE WHERE THINGS ACTU-
ally happen in the fall. For example, the bees start acting
bizzarro, clumping up on the ground and just lying there or clus-
tering around the mouth of my soda can as I sit in the cold grass
with Sam and Jesse, reading *Song of Solomon*, our second book for
English class. Milkman Dead searches for his father's treasure
and I search for any piece of my father at all, closing my eyes and
sifting through the darkness of my mind.

Another thing that happens in the fall are the leaves. First
one or two, hiding in the green, and then by the time the week
is out every single tree is sunset red or dandelion yellow. Every
single one.

Things happen in California. An entire day of fluffy dandelion seeds blowing through the air or a week of smoke from a
wildfire pouring into the city, turning the sun orange and raining
down ashes. But there's not a lot of rhythm to it. The seasons are
just suggestions.

Weeks pass, and when Jesse isn't at the co-op, the hardware store, cross-country practice, or babysitting his many siblings, we work in the darkroom. Sometimes we talk and sometimes we don't. We move around each other in the darkness like electrons, charging the space but never, ever touching. We hang our pictures side by side and watch patterns emerge: light, objects, sometimes people—mine up close and his far away.

Mom is gone a lot. Back into the comfortable routine of work and work and work. But it's different from last year; when she's home she is fully alive. She learns how to make lasagna, she smiles with her eyes. I watch her more closely than ever, not sure if I can trust it. I watch her and the worry never fully recedes. It's always there under my skin, a whirring, humming sound.

Bea is skeptical. Angry. The storm cloud phase lasts and lasts. Like with my mother, I look for signs. She makes friends with some fellow outcasts. I find cigarettes in her backpack.

El teaches me how to paint, and sometimes on Saturdays we throw easels into the back of her Subaru, setting up in the tall grass by the side of Cumberland's twisty back roads. El says it's called painting en plein air. Sam comes and sometimes Bea does too, blobbing black paint onto her canvas. I love this different way of watching the light: slower, less frantic. My skin turns brown again, like it was in California, and freckles sprinkle my nose.

Bennett texts me every day.

I saw three gray whales this morning. Wish you were here.

We lost our game. Come cheer me up with cheese fries and the Matrix?

I drove by your house today. The lemon tree is blooming.

Observations. Half-formed thoughts. Nothing more, nothing less. It makes me think of the time when he used to tell me everything, before kissing, when words were easy.

We FaceTime almost every Sunday afternoon, but I don't ask him a single question. We mostly just lie there, talking across the surface of things, recapping water polo games and trading jokes, or not talking at all, our eyes roaming over each other's skin.

Nora and I text too. All the time. But sometimes it feels like our conversations are more and more frivolous, like we have less and less to say, the growing collection of separate experiences beginning to overshadow the catalogue of shared ones. I wonder if she feels it too.

The UC admissions window gets closer and closer, but I don't fill out my application. I don't write my essay. I don't ask for recommendations. When the guidance counselor tries to flag me down in the hallway, I pretend I don't hear her and walk the other way. Every time someone asks me about my application, I say it's going fine. At night, in my bed, I try to think about the future, but it feels like looking at the sun.

• • •

Jesse, Bea, and I are watching *Poltergeist* on El's sectional the day before Halloween. It's become a Saturday tradition, the three of us watching movies after Jesse's morning shift, Bea stretching out in the middle of the couch and eating all the popcorn.

Halfway through the movie, right as the parapsychologists appear, Bea sits up and says, "Let's have a séance."

Mom is in the office today, working on a major contract. When she left the house, Bea said, "Have fun," in this way that was halfway between sarcastic and malevolent. I dropped a banana into her purse and said, "Make sure you eat lunch," as if sending a piece of fruit would somehow keep her tethered to earth.

Bea pauses the movie, bouncing up and down on the couch with a kooky grin.

The truth is, I'm almost sick of ghosts. Bea's been making me watch horror movies every night for weeks, and it feels like they're everywhere: creepy woods, burned-out houses. Meanwhile, in real life, Dad is blurring into oblivion like an arm in an Uta Barth photograph.

"No thanks," I say.

Jesse wiggles his fingers, spooky style, and says, "Come on, Marigold. Sounds like fun."

Two against one.

Jesse and I go up to my room and sit on the floor while Bea gathers supplies. I get my box of Dad stuff and hold it on my lap. Jesse leans against the bedframe with his long legs folded into triangles. I'm trying to ignore the fact that his hair, which smells like cedar and lemon, is touching my quilt. Right at the words *Love hurts*.

"Do you believe in ghosts?" Jesse says.

"No," I say. "Do you?"

He lifts one shoulder. "I think I believe anything is possible."

"You said your family isn't religious, right?"

"Actually, we're sort of Quaker. I just didn't want to freak you out with too much information all at once."

I laugh, wondering why every new detail of Jesse's life feels more surprising than the one that came before it. "That wouldn't have freaked me out."

He grins. "You never know."

"Do you like it?" I ask. My family isn't religious, and I've always been interested in what it might be like to believe in something like that.

Jesse's thoughtful, tracing his finger through a square of sun. He's wearing a red flannel shirt today that looks soft and worn, the cuffs fastened at his wrists. "Sometimes, when I'm sitting in meeting, my mind gets really quiet and all I can think about is the sound of the birds outside the window. I like that."

I close my eyes for a minute, listening to the birds in El's yard. "Sounds nice."

"What about you?" Jesse asks.

"My mom was Jewish and my dad was Catholic and both of them had enough bad experiences to scrap the whole thing when it came to us. We were just raised with the big old void of commercial holidays." I stretch my hand out on the floor, into its own square of light. "But that has very little to offer when your parent suddenly dies."

Jesse's hand hovers near mine, like he's thinking about grabbing on to it in that awkward way people do when someone mentions the death of a loved one. I think if he touched me, after all these weeks of not touching, I might fall apart.

But then Bea busts through the door, arms full of candles.

"Sorry, guys," she says. "I forgot that Domino's mom is picking me up at four."

Domino is one of Bea's new friends. She's in tenth grade and says things like, "Fuck everything," and skips a lot of class. I don't like her. But I'm trying to be glad that Bea doesn't seem lonely anymore.

Bea dumps the candles into a heap on the floor. Then she turns and walks out, and Jesse and I are all alone in this great big house.

Jesse starts picking up the half-melted candles and putting them in a circle between us. I set my Dad box down, without opening it, sort of off to the side. It takes forever to get the candles lit because I keep losing my grip on the button of the lighter and then it gets too hot and I burn the two lines of the wheel into the pad of my thumb.

I guess we could just stop, go back downstairs, and put on the movie. Go walking in the woods with our cameras.

But then Jesse clears his throat and says, "Should we hold hands?"

Our eyes meet across the candles for one, two, three blinks. Until I almost forget what he just said. I see his lips moving before I register more talking.

"I mean, it's how they do it in movies," he says, pushing his hair out of his face. His eyes are the color of El's walnut table.

"What movies?" I ask.

He laughs. "All of them."

"Okay then," I say. "I guess we probably should."

I reach my hands out toward him, careful not to set my sleeves on fire. I wonder if Jesse can see that my fingers are shaking. He meets me in the middle and presses our palms together, and our fingers interlace, one over the other.

There's something about holding hands like this, our lifelines matching up. It's not just the fact that I haven't touched a guy in months, even though every Sunday afternoon I watch Bennett in the blue light of the computer screen. Touching Jesse feels different.

"Okay," he says. "Now what?" And he's grinning.

"Be serious," I say, but a smile is threatening to hijack my lips too.

"Should we say some words?" he says.

"I guess so?" I say.

He takes a deep breath and closes his eyes. I close mine too.

"Um, universe—" he starts, and his voice wavers a little and it's just too much. I burst out laughing and then he's laughing too and our hands break apart and we are both rolling on the ground holding our stomachs, nearly setting our hair on fire.

"We are failures," he says.

And then I get an idea.

"Wait a minute, okay?" I say. "Don't go through my stuff."

"Promise," he says, crossing his heart, and suddenly the image of Jesse rifling through my underwear drawer makes me blush the length of my body.

I shake my head and run across the hallway to Bea's room. I rummage around under her bed until I find her Ouija board and then come running back.

"I thought we could use a little help," I say.

"Extra spooky." Jesse grins. "Bring it over."

I clear a space in the middle of the floor and arrange the candles around the board. Then we sit again, across from each other.

"Okay, so what should we ask it?" he says, brushing the hair from his eyes. "Should we go serious or funny?"

S-E-R-I-O-U-S. I trace the letters on the board, suddenly feeling too embarrassed to talk.

I look across the circle of candles at Jesse with his rumpled clothes and calm face, perfectly perfect. I realize he's watching me, waiting for an answer.

"Serious," I say.

He swallows.

"Okay," he says. "Ask it a question."

• • •

On our last day in the ICU, after my dad had suffered through his last breath, his last heartbeat, the last gurgle of his stomach, the doctors asked us if we wanted to see his body. Because I guess it's important for a sense of closure.

"If you don't," Mom said, "it might be harder to heal."

I sat in the stale yellow light of the waiting room, feeling numb as a rock, like my brain had been soaked in lidocaine. I couldn't make myself get out of the chair.

But now I have this intermittent feeling that he's not really dead, that he could be anywhere. Sometimes I think he's the birds, the red robins or pink flamingos or the ruby-throated hummingbirds. I think of the way he used to cruise around Los Angeles, immune to the traffic, eyes glued to all that neon, and I think that he really would like to float from flower to flower, drinking up the color.

Sometimes I think he's become a part of the ocean, just a molecule in an endless chain of millions. Maybe he's a salt or maybe he's a water. Or maybe he got up and left the hospital when nobody was looking and he's still out there, hammering away at the keyboard, listening to The Doors.

• • •

I close my eyes and take a breath, pressing my fingers lightly to the edge of the pointer. Jesse does the same. As I say the words I feel like I'm coming out of my skin.

"Is my dad out there?"

And then I add, "Anywhere?"

There's a long silence after that. I can hear us both breathing into it, our muscles straining as we try to touch the pointer so, so delicately.

Some people are the kind of people who surreptitiously move the Ouija board pointer to freak everyone out. Apparently Jesse and I are not those kind of people. It stays in the center of the board, right over the letter *T*, and I just sit there, feeling the red flush of embarrassment and disappointment slide over my face, sending blood rushing against my eardrums.

My phone starts vibrating on the dresser, which brings me back to life. I forgot that I have a date with Nora. We are supposed to text our way through *The Craft*, but I think I've lost my stomach for Halloween movies.

The phone buzzes and buzzes.

"Are you okay?" Jesse says.

I realize that I'm just sitting there, staring. I don't remember when I let go of the pointer.

I clear my throat, avoiding Jesse's searching eyes. "I'm fine," I say. "That was stupid."

Across the circle, Jesse's usually confident face falters. I can see him searching around for a way to salvage this situation. "It wasn't stupid," he says gently.

I blow out the candles and fold up the Ouija board. Jesse stands up and brushes off his pants. The ceiling of my room is slanted under the roof, and suddenly Jesse seems too big as he hovers near the doorway.

"Do you want to finish the movie?" he says awkwardly,

smoothing down the front of his shirt. I can't tell if he wants to stay or run screaming down the road, or maybe it's a little bit of both.

I force out a yawn. "I think I'm kind of tired."

"Okay," Jesse says. He puts his hand on my shoulder and squeezes once, looking into my eyes. His hand feels heavy and his stare feels even heavier. I smile, but I think he can see my sadness anyway.

• • •

MOM COMES HOME AT NINE, ROSY CHEEKED AND SMILING.

"Everything okay?" she says.

"Yep," I say, even though it's not. "How was work?"

She sets down her messenger bag. "Good. Long. We ordered from an amazing Thai place in Troy. I want to take you girls there."

"Sure," I say. Suddenly, I feel jealous in a way that I don't understand. I wonder if the banana is still in her purse.

On my way to bed, I stop in Bea's room. She's back from Domino's and she's wearing her skeleton pajamas, her bony ankles sticking out the bottom. I watch her fussing with a needle and thread, earbuds in, and try to remember what it was like to be fourteen. But then she looks up and sees me, and her face gets older somehow, and I remember that I'll never know what it's like to be Bea.

"How did it go?" she asks.

I look down at the woven rug. "I don't think séances are really my thing."

I can feel Bea looking at me, like Jesse did, like she can see all the cracks. But she doesn't say anything.

I walk over to the bed, which is covered in an elaborate spider costume, dotted with pins. The fabric is layered, lace on top of something silky, black on black. Delicate strings weave together between the arms to make the web.

"Wow," I say. "That is incredible."

"Thanks." She sighs wistfully. "It's almost done."

"Just in time."

Bea picks up the dress very carefully and carries it over to El's sewing machine, which she has sequestered in the corner of her room.

"Can I get a ride to Garrett's party tomorrow night?" she asks, without turning around. Her voice is casual, like she's not asking me to bring her to a senior-class house party on a Sunday night.

"Seriously?" I ask, incredulous. "There's no way Mom will let you go."

Bea turns around, crossing her arms. "Mom doesn't care."

"Oh." I shake my head. "I think she definitely will."

"That's not what I mean," Bea says, narrowing her gray eyes, mouth in a line. "She doesn't care about me."

The words sneak under my skin like a splinter.

It's been a long time since the night I promised Bea I would try to help her be happy again. But lately it feels like she's somehow unreachable.

Then I blink and Bea's face is back to normal. Cloudy with a 10 percent chance of rain.

"It's not like she's even going to be home when we leave," she says. She finishes a seam and pouts her bottom lip out, like a sad kitten. "Please? I gotta get out of this house."

I know she's playing me, but at the same time I think I know what she means. I owe this to her. "Yeah," I say. "Sure."

And just like that, she smiles her old Bea smile again.

Cumberland Central teachers have an annual professional development day on the day after Halloween, which means that all the kids are free to go wild on the holiday itself. Apparently it's also tradition in Garrett Murphy's family—started by his three older brothers—to throw a rager on Halloween night.

The next afternoon, Sam comes over, and she and Bea and I get ready for the party in my room. Sam and I dress like retro housewife vampires in floral housecoats we got at the Goodwill in Bennington. Bea puts on The Zombies and fusses over her spider costume while El teases our hair and paints blood down the sides of our chins.

The candles and Ouija board lie abandoned in a heap under my bed, next to my box of Dad, where nobody can see them. Not even me.

Last night I had a flash of another dream: Dad's fingers on my arm, yanking me back, out of the street, away from the rush of cars.

"Jesus, Marigold. What are you doing?" he half yelled, his voice that isn't his voice full of anger and fear.

I called Nora this morning to explain flaking on last night's long-distance movie date, but she didn't answer. It's not the first time I've ditched out on plans or just watched the phone ringing when she's called, but yesterday was different. If I'd tried to talk to her after my séance failure I might have lost the white-knuckle grip that's holding everything together and shattered into a million sad pieces.

Still, I woke up this morning, and for the first time in a long time, she was the only person I wanted to talk to. All day I've walked around under a cloud of guilt and stale sadness.

But now I feel all right. Almost festive.

Bennett texts: Send me a picture of your Halloween costume.

And I send one of my pointed teeth and red lips.

• • •

BEA, SAM, AND I ARE HALFWAY OUT THE DOOR WHEN MY MOM walks in, carrying a stack of files that nearly covers her head.

"Wow, Bea," she says, dumping the files and putting her hand over her heart. "That costume is stunning."

Bea looks at her and actually smiles. "Thanks."

Mom pulls off her boots and sets her bag down on the counter. "Where are you girls going?"

I look at Bea and Bea looks at me.

"Trick-or-treating," Bea says, just as Sam says, "To a Halloween party."

Mom pulls one more file out of her bag, sending a shower of yellow Post-its to the floor.

Sam looks at me and mouths, *Sorry*. Her face is red all the way down to her neck.

"Will there be parents there?" Mom asks.

"Yes," Bea says, just as I say, "I think so."

"Girls," Mom says. "Sit down."

We do, and Mom looks from Bea, to me, to Sam and back again. Then she sighs, deep.

"Bea, honey, you're only fourteen years old. That's a little young to be going to a party with seniors."

Bea groans. "It's not just seniors. Everybody is going to be there."

Mom bends down and starts picking up sticky notes off the floor, doing her yoga breaths.

My brain is going to fall out of my head if this meeting doesn't end soon, one of the notes says.

Tacos for lunch? says another, under a drawing of a taco with skinny little arms and legs.

It's weirdly thrilling to see these mundane details of my mom's mysterious other life spread out on the floor. I forget that she gets bored, has friends, eats lunch. But somewhere inside the thrill is a little bit of envy. Maybe even anger.

She shoves the stickies back into her briefcase and gestures to a tote bag that's filled with fun-size Snickers. "Why don't you stay home with me and El? We're gonna watch movies and eat all this candy."

Bea rolls her eyes. "Right, because you're all about quality time these days."

I can feel waves of embarrassment coming off of Sam, who is sitting beside me, right at the edge of her stool. I want to say, *Yes. A train wreck is coming. Run for your life.*

"Bea—" Mom says, already resigned to the impending explosion.

Desperation and anger battle it out on Bea's face. I can see it expanding inside of her, looking for somewhere to go. I wish I could reach over and calm it down, or open my mouth and fix this somehow. But as usual, I feel frozen to the spot.

"Come on, Mom," Bea says, deflating a little. "Please."

"I'm sorry, Bea," Mom says, firm. "The answer is no."

Bea looks down at the counter like she's either holding back tears or trying to burn holes in it with her eyes. Her neck is red under the perfect, delicate lace of her carefully sewn costume. If I squinted I could probably see smoke seeping out of her ears.

"Fuck. You," Bea breathes. Then she scoots off her stool and stomps upstairs.

Mom turns away from us, hands on her head, breathing deep. Sam looks like she is trying to disappear into the floor. "Wait for me in the car?" I say to her, sliding out of my seat. But by the time I get to Bea's bedroom door she's already locked it.

"Bea," I plead. "Let me in. I'll stay home too."

"No," she yells. She sounds like she might be crying. "Don't. I don't want to talk to anyone right now. Especially not you."

"Me?" I step back. "What did I do?"

"Forget it," she says. "Just go."

I pound on her door a few more times, but there's nothing but silence.

• • •

AT THE PARTY, I MOPE AROUND, FEELING LIKE A TRAITOR. SAM keeps trying to pull me out of my funk, but I can't stop picturing Bea in her couture spider dress, skinny arms dangling down in disappointment. I should be home with her, under the covers, plotting our way out of there.

I leave Sam dancing in a tangle of bodies in the living room and make my way out to the front porch. The air is freezing, colder than it ever gets in California. I zip up my jacket and pull my hands inside the sleeves, but when I sit down on the top step, my bare legs are like popsicles and my whole body starts to shake.

I just keep thinking, *How did I get here?* I'm at a person named Garrett's house somewhere in the middle of upstate

New York and everyone is drinking PBR and dancing to satellite radio and I'm out on the porch taking deep breaths to combat the waves of homesickness that are slamming into me, one after the next.

I feel ridiculous, crying in this costume, and I'm cold and I can't fill back up after yesterday emptied me out. I feel like I'm letting everyone down, Bea, Nora, even myself. I feel like I'm turning into someone I'm not.

Even worse, all of my memories are starting to warp. And I can't seem to shake the feeling of sitting in front of that Ouija board in the vast, humiliating silence.

A car streaks by, much too fast for this quiet road in the middle of town. For a second the world is illuminated and then it goes dark again.

Here's the worst truth: Dad isn't the birds. He isn't the ocean. He isn't a salt or a water. My dad is dead.

The screen door slams and I look up to see Jesse ambling toward me in his best zombie impression, until he finally sees my face and lurches to a stop. He stands there, mouth open, stuck at the beginning of a sentence, looking almost as perfect undead as he does when his heart is pumping.

"Are you okay?" he finally says, sitting down on the step beside me. The wooden boards groan beneath the weight of him.

I open my mouth, but any possible words are washed away because suddenly the trickle of tears has picked up momentum and now they are absolutely waterfalling down my face.

So he wraps his arms around me, scoots my whole body across the top step to fit right under his long arm. I blink my eyes again and again, trying to stop crying.

"It's almost been a year since he died," I say when I remember how to talk again. It's so weird how, more than three hundred days later, grief is still waiting with its land mines.

Jesse doesn't say anything; he just twists my hair around his palm, his chest expanding and contracting against me in long, even intervals.

Inside the house, "Monster Mash" comes on and everyone starts singing. And the ridiculousness of this moment hits me like a sledgehammer.

I crumple forward then, truly falling apart, my chest heaving against my knees. It's like I'm on a roller coaster and I just crested the tallest drop and before I can even whisper, *oh shit*, I'm plummeting down, down, down. No end in sight.

Dad is dead is dead is dead, I keep thinking to myself, thinking of all the ways that the word *dead* careens outward, crushing everything in its path.

The river of tears hops its banks; snot and mascara soak my tights.

Jesse just sits there, his hand flat against my back, rubbing these big circles.

And then I hit the bottom and the cart slows, my breath slows, everything slows. Jesse's circles slow too, and then his hand is just resting on my back, warm and heavy. I feel empty. There's a faint humming in my hollow chest, like the sound of Aunt El's refrigerator.

"I'll drive you home," Jesse says.

"Okay," I say into my knees. I'm embarrassed to look up and show him my sad, melted makeup when he's being so dashing and kind. He tosses me the keys and goes inside to let Sam know we're leaving. I find his car parked along the side of the muddy road and sink into the passenger seat.

• • •

When we get to El's house all of the lights are off except for a faint blue glow coming from Bea's window. Jesse parks the car and turns off the headlights, and then it's just us under the moon. It's a waxing gibbous, the kind that could trick you into thinking it's full.

"I wish it were easier to photograph the moon," Jesse says, his voice slow and sleepy.

It feels easier to talk now that I'm invisible in the dark of Jesse's car. "There's a lot you can't photograph," I say.

"Dreams," he agrees.

"Ghosts."

"God."

"Memory."

"Still," Jesse says. "Sometimes it feels like it's worth a try."

"When did you start taking photographs?" I ask, wanting to know how he found the thing he's perfect for.

Jesse leans his seat back and folds his hands behind his head. "When I was little," he says, "I was scared of the dark."

"Really?" I smile, leaning my seat back too, and I think of little-kid Jesse hiding under the covers.

"Yep," he says from his side of the darkness. "My grandpa was a machinist, and he was obsessed with photography. He used to build his own cameras in the garage.

"He made me one, and he told me that I could trap light inside of it during the day and then I could keep it in my bed.

And then, even in the darkest of darknesses, I'd have a little light with me."

"Wow," I say, wishing it were really that easy.

"He was an incredible photographer. His pictures felt like living things."

Even in the dark, I can sense Jesse's constant movement, the bouncing of his knee, his fingers playing the piano on the edge of the car door, right under the window.

"He took me to my first Garry Winogrand show when I was ten. I was a goner."

"Never to recover," I say.

"Yep," Jesse says. For a second the motion stops as he gets lost in the memory. "We went out for pizza afterward, and I made him take his camera out and explain how every part worked." He pauses. "Anyway. He had a heart attack and died a year after that."

"Shit," I say. I lift my hand, reaching across the console for his arm. The fabric of his jacket is thick and cold, and I'm not sure where to hold on. He turns his head to look at me, but the shadows make it hard to see the expression on his face.

"I should get home," he says. "I have to work at seven thirty."

I take my hand back and raise my seat, folding back in on myself. "Sure," I say. I feel like I'm waking up from a dream.

"Night, Marigold," Jesse says. And then I walk back to the house through the sea of moonlight.

13

THE NEXT MORNING I WAKE UP TO AN ALL-CAPS TEXT from Nora—her first contact since I bailed on Saturday night.

THE UC APPLICATION WINDOW IS OPEN!!!!!!!!!!!!!!!

At first I'm relieved because it seems like I've been forgiven. But I think about UCSB and all of the things I haven't done yet. *Shit.*

Shit. Shit. Shit.

I text back: YESSSSSSSSSSSSS!!!!!

I hope five exclamation marks is enough to sell it.

We suffer through a silent breakfast, and then Bea, El, Mom, and I go looking for houses. After working all weekend, Mom takes the day off. It's the first time I've seen her in daylight hours in so long, and I study her, looking for clues. She's humming. She looks whole. El blasts Fleetwood Mac, and Mom plays drums on the dashboard with a couple of pencils she's dug out of the center console.

In the back seat, the vibe is much gloomier. Bea sulks, still refusing to speak to anyone. Nora's text gnaws at my stomach.

I stare off into the trees, trying to imagine the future. I can't even make out the lines anymore.

We pull onto a long dirt driveway and wind around until we see a big, old farmhouse with peeling paint.

"Looks nice," Mom says.

Bea scowls.

Our real estate agent is waiting out front, looking overly eager in a bubble-gum-pink fleece jacket. She and mom have spoken a few times since we got here, but this is the first time that Mom has found room in her schedule to look at anything in person.

She leads us inside and we wander through the echoey rooms as she goes on about closet space and hardwood floors. Bea breaks off and climbs the stairs, and I follow her up and into one of the bedrooms.

"This house smells like mice," I say.

"Dead mice," she says.

"I'm sorry," I say.

"I know," she says.

She reaches over and grabs my hand and we stare out the window, into a yard full of dead grass. I focus my eyes on the window dust, then on the scene outside.

"Where do you want to live?" I ask.

"California," says Bea.

She tries to drop my hand, but I don't let her.

"The sooner we pick a place here," I say carefully, "the sooner we get our stuff back."

Bea sulks. "I don't want our stuff back."

"Yes you do," I say. "What about all your wigs?"

Bea turns around and walks over to the closet. She opens the drawers of the built-in dresser one by one. She's wearing her hair in a braided crown, and I think she's gotten taller lately. She is growing like a weed, a climbing rose. Wildly, right under our noses. She's almost a real person now. Already more complicated than I could ever hope to understand.

She turns back around and crosses her arms.

"I guess it would be nice to have my wigs," she says. Then she walks back down the stairs and out to the car.

On the way to the next house, El says, "I think that last one probably has a rodent problem. But wow, that kitchen was beautiful."

"What did you girls think?" says Mom.

I look at Bea and she looks at me. Something shifts.

"It might be nice to live closer to town," she says.

"Then we wouldn't have to ride the bus," I agree.

"Okay," says Mom, trying not to smile too hard. "I'll tell the Realtor."

My phone buzzes in my pocket. It's a FaceTime request from Bennett. I reach in, and the way it vibrates against my fingers makes me remember the feeling of Jesse's cold jacket. I wince.

"Everything okay?" says El, eyeing me through the rearview mirror.

"Fine," I say, trying to breathe the panic out of my body without anyone noticing.

My questions for Bennett are multiplying, evolving, growing ever more vague. I'm wondering, *What do I want us to be?* I want to know, *What do I want you to want?* I don't have any answers, so I bury them all. I wait for my phone to stop ringing and then I turn it off.

● ● ●

In the first days of November, every leaf falls to the ground. We look at more houses, but none of them stick. Mom works late almost every night, but when she's home she and Bea bicker, right to the edge of explosion. I watch, feeling helpless. It's like I'm in limbo, suspended out in the middle of so many things, and I can't do anything.

Jesse works at the hardware store all week long, then goes on a trip with his parents to look at schools in New York City. I walk through the woods and try to figure out the best way to photograph the naked trees.

Sam comes over on Saturday to paint in the dining room while I pretend to work on college applications. She covers her palette in blues and greens, but most of the time she just stares out the window at the dead grass and the gray sky.

"Are you all right?" I say, the third time her paintbrush clatters to the ground.

"Are *you*?" she retorts, looking pointedly at my computer screen, where the cursor has been blinking in my empty essay doc for the past half hour.

I cross my arms. "I asked you first."

"Fine," she huffs, setting her brush down.

I close my computer, relieved to focus on someone else's life for once.

"Well," she says as she pulls her hair back into a tiny, smooth bun at the nape of her neck. "I've been looking into art assistant jobs and internships for next year and I feel like I'll never get one. I don't have any experience." She stops, frowning. Then she picks up her red sweater from the back of El's dining room chair, folding it neatly and setting it on the table. She turns to the window again. "And I live in the middle of fucking nowhere."

"But you're talented. And prolific," I say, gesturing to her backpack, which is bursting with notebooks and pens and crunched-up papers. "And you're fun to be around. Someone will hire you."

"I hope so," Sam says. She slouches down in her chair. "I just really need to get out of here. Sometimes I get scared that it's never going to happen."

It feels like there's so much she isn't saying, but I also know that we both have our secrets. That's just how it is with us.

"It's going to happen," I tell her, but she just nods and picks up her brush again, plunging it into the paint.

• • •

THAT NIGHT, NORA FINALLY CALLS ME BACK AND WE WATCH THREE episodes of *Top Chef* together. It's a relief to hear her snarky comments, to laugh like there isn't a growing cavern of distance and time between us. When she brings up college, I play my part. I pretend I'm sticking to the plan. It could still be true. The future is wide open.

14

"YOU SAID IT'S ALMOST BEEN A YEAR," JESSE SAYS ON Monday, as we're walking toward the cafeteria.

His words startle me out of my thoughts, a continuous loop of the blank look on Mom's face last night as she stared into the lamplight like a luna moth.

"When did it happen?" He turns his head to look at me, and it feels like he's peering through the clouds on my face.

"November tenth."

"That's tomorrow."

"Yeah."

"What are you going to do?"

The bodies ahead of us seem to slow down, like cars on the freeway, merging in and out.

I shrug. "I don't know." Even though we all know it's coming, nobody in my family has even mentioned it.

My hands search for my pockets and, finding none, swing aimlessly around my sides looking for a place to stop.

"Well, I'm here if you don't want to be alone," he says. His eyes are dark and serious.

"Okay," I say, looking down at the tan linoleum floor.

In the center of my chest, a pinprick of light starts to make its way in.

• • •

Jesse sits with us at lunch now. We are a constellation of three, just like Nora, Bennett, and me, and it makes me feel like I've fallen through a tear in the universe, into a parallel timeline.

Only Nora and Bennett are still here, hanging by a thread of texts and FaceTime—a photo of my favorite kind of donut, the dip between Bennett's ribs.

"How was your trip?" Sam asks Jesse, biting into a rectangular slice of cafeteria pizza. She's wearing a bright green wool sweater today, with big wooden buttons down the front, and a thick gold necklace, her hair parted exactly in the center. Her eyes look tired, bluish rings underneath.

"Good," Jesse says around a mouthful of SunButter sandwich. But there's tightness behind his eyes too. It feels like we are all full of secrets. But today, for once, I have a good one.

We wait for Jesse to say more, but after a while it becomes apparent that he's not going to. He's tired, spacey, hidden behind his dark hair. So I turn to Sam, a sly smile on my face. "Guess what?"

"What?" she says. The tips of her fingers are covered in ink.

"I talked to El last night and she says you can work for her."

Sam sets down her slice of pizza. "Seriously?"

I smile. "Yep."

Her face cracks open under a giant, crooked smile. "Oh my god, Mary, that's amazing!" she says, jumping up and down a little in her seat. Then she pulls me into a suffocating hug, and for once I feel like I've done something right.

When she gets up to return her tray, I poke Jesse in the ribs. "What's up?" I say.

"I don't know," he says, running a hand through his hair.

"Was it NYU?" I ask.

"I don't know," he says again. He sighs, his shoulders sagging under the weight of something heavy. "It was beautiful. The darkroom was a work of art. But the financial aid meeting didn't go that well. I thought my dad was going to faint."

"Shit," I say. I look down at the table, brushing away the crumbs. I try to think of better words to say, but nothing feels quite right.

"What's happening with you and college?" he says. His eyes move over my face.

I shrug and say, "I'm figuring it out." It sounds so believable that I almost think it's true, until I remember sitting at my desk last night, tearing my entire folder of college printouts into shreds. I feel like the scum at the bottom of a lake.

Jesse picks up his Empire apple, spins it around on the tabletop.

"You're so lucky," he says. "You could go anywhere you want."

I can tell he's being earnest, because Jesse Keller is always earnest, but the truth in this statement makes me uneasy.

• • •

THAT NIGHT I STOP BY THE CO-OP, JUST AFTER CLOSING. JESSE, IN a navy blue sweater that droops down below his wrists, is stocking the beauty products, and I sit on the counter for a while, researching scholarships on my phone.

This afternoon, painting with Sam on Turnpike Road, I couldn't shake our lunchtime conversation and the tired look in Jesse's eyes. My own future is losing focus, but Jesse's seems so clear. He needs to go to NYU. We have to make it happen.

Now I kick my heels against the counter, bookmarking another scholarship application.

"You're going to be writing essays from now until the end of time," I say.

"I like writing essays," he says, emptying a small box of shampoo bottles and placing them gently on the shelf.

I shake my head. "You would."

He tries to peg me with a biodegradable packing peanut, but it catches an updraft and floats slowly to the ground at my feet.

"It will be worth it anyway," he says. "You should have seen that darkroom."

"I will see it," I say. "Next year when I come to visit and you're showing me around."

He looks at me for a long time, like he's trying to tell if I'm for real. I suddenly feel a little exposed.

"You don't have to do this," he says. "I can figure it out myself."

I straighten, feeling defensive. "I want to."

He tucks a piece of hair back behind his ear, working his jaw back and forth. "I want to help you too," he says.

"I know," I say. "You will."

Jesse lets the tension build for one more second, like he knows I might be lying, then a smile breaks through his cryptic expression and he tosses another peanut into the air.

"So," he says, turning back around. "Tomorrow."

He could be talking about our physics quiz or his end-of-season cross-country banquet, but I know he's really talking about my dad.

"Yeah," I say, setting my phone on the counter. "Tomorrow." I feel like I finally might be ready to face it, right on time.

I watch Jesse's hands as they straighten rows of bottles, turning the labels to the front.

"Is there somewhere you'd want to go?" he asks carefully.

"I don't know," I say, looking down at my hands.

Dad was cremated the week he died. We left the cedar box that held his ashes on the mantel above our nonfunctioning fireplace for weeks, and the whole time I secretly wondered if it would be creepy to open the lid and take a picture of what was inside.

"I wonder which is worse," Bea said one afternoon as we sat, pretending to watch a movie but really just staring at the box of Dad between the spider plant and the Russian nesting dolls. "Being incinerated in an oven or rotting in a coffin."

"I don't think anyone feels that part," I said, a shiver working its way down my spine.

A week later, Mom drove us up to Big Sur, and we pulled over at a lookout point on Highway One and dropped his ashes into the sea. As we careened back around the hairpin turns of the Pacific Coast Highway, all of us still crying, Hannah said, "Did you know that ninety Americans die of traffic-related fatalities every day?"

And Bea said, "Driving over a cliff on our way home from scattering a dead person's remains. That would be ironic."

And the whole way back, I imagined myself down at the bottom on the rocky beach, trying frantically to pick up all of the tiny pieces of Dad and closing them back up in the box.

Jesse picks up a tube of lip balm, rolls it between his palms. His sweater has a homemade elbow patch. His hair is falling into his face.

"There's not a grave or anything, but maybe we could go to a cemetery," I say. "Just to see what it would have been like."

"Yeah, sure," Jesse says, getting to his feet. "Anything."

He turns out the lights and I follow him out to the back of the creaky old building, to where his car is parked next to El's Subaru in the darkness.

The next day, the tenth of November, Mom leaves for work at the crack of dawn, just like she always does. I walk with Bea through the doors of the school and then I circle back around to the parking lot, where Jesse is leaning against his car, waiting for me. I feel guilty leaving Bea, even though when I invited her to come she just rolled her eyes and said, "That sounds stupid."

Since Halloween, she's retreated further into herself. The earbuds are always in. The door is always closed. Her eyes are storming all the time, at me, at Mom, at the universe. I know she's feeling something, just like me, but I don't have the words to name it and I don't have the guts to bring it up.

Nora texted me this morning: Thinking of you today.

I said: Thanks. I love you.

For one second, I let myself ache over the weird distance between us. And I then turned off my phone.

Jesse drives us out to a cemetery that's just past the edge of town. The shocking green of the grass rolls out like a carpet under the gray sky and the naked trees, and it's so beautiful that when I get out of the car I think, *Cumberland has gotten me.* The wind blows bitter cold against my giant thrifted down jacket, but the damp color of the landscape spreads over everything, making it hard to feel anything else.

We walk down a gentle slope and hop over a small wooden fence, Jesse leading the way in his caramel-colored jacket. There are hundreds of grave markers here, partitioning the landscape into neat rows. Some are from the 1700s, thin and dull, small and hard to read. There are newer graves too, thick stones with ornate script and marble that shines like glass. I wonder if these losses are still fresh, if they keep finding new ways to sting like mine does.

This morning I woke up to a glimpse of my father, caught through the window of his study, a line between his brows, the glare of the sun right over his eyes. As I walk through the cold grass, I try to bring back that memory, to think of what came before or after, but all I can see is the flash of his forehead, crinkled with frustration.

We wander around without talking for a while. I don't know how this is supposed to go. No one has ever shown me. I almost wish my family had planned something. I could have been with Bea and Mom, maybe even Hannah, following El through the woods. Maybe we could have talked about him. Maybe I could have admitted that I don't even know who he was.

Jesse pulls a bunch of greenish-white daisies out of his

backpack. We stopped at the gas station on the way over, and they were sitting in a sad plastic bucket near the door for $3.99. "We should bring something," Jesse had said, pulling a crumpled wad of singles out of his pocket.

He pulls the bouquet apart now and hands me some, wadding up the cellophane and shoving it into his pocket. I turn and start walking toward the tree line, dropping one on each grave I pass until I run out. Dad isn't here, but we might as well leave flowers for somebody.

After a while, Jesse stops and looks at me as if to say, *Well?*

I can see my breath puffing against the cold air like white smoke—the holy kind.

"This isn't working," I say. I can't feel my fingers.

The push and pull of remembering and forgetting is starting to exhaust me. I feel like I'm trying to gather up all the pieces of Dad that still make sense, but even then, even when I think I have them, they disappear or turn into something else.

Jesse squints against the sun, which has emerged from behind the curtain of gray. He puts his hand up to shield his eyes, like he can't quite see me.

"Working for what?" he asks.

And then for one second I can't feel anything at all. The numbness in my hands threatens to take over every part of me. I think of all the dead bodies under our feet.

"I don't know," I say, my teeth chattering. "Let's get out of here."

He nods and we weave our way back to the Rabbit, Jesse's long strides and my short ones. I drop into my seat and wait for the heater to kick in. It almost feels colder inside the car, and

I rub my hands together, trying to warm them with my breath while Jesse adjusts worn-looking knobs and sliders, blasting us with various intensities of freezing air.

He drives us back into town and pulls over in front of the diner. I'm moving slow, so he comes around and opens my door. He stands there over me, one hand in his pocket, one arm on the car door, his eyes darting between mine like he's speed reading.

Cumberland is the kind of place where they'll know we're ditching if we go into the diner at ten a.m., but Jesse doesn't seem to care. He tugs me by my sleeve, through the doorway of the restaurant. It's all counter and booths, and it's warm and smells like cinnamon and butter. We sink into the last booth, next to the kitchen, and I peel off my layers, feeling itchy from the red wool sweater I've been wearing. I watch as Jesse pulls off his sweater too. His shirt tugs up to expose a corner of skin that looks warm and smooth and reminds me of how alive he is under his many layers.

"Sorry," he says, as if all of this is somehow his fault.

"Nah," I say. "It could have worked. I think the problem was me."

Jesse picks up a packet of Sweet'N Low and starts spinning it on the Formica tabletop. "What do you mean?"

I shake my head, not sure how to describe this feeling of emptiness. "Never mind," I say, almost too quietly to hear.

The waitress comes, wearing a scallop-edged apron over her jeans, and we order coffee and muffins.

While we wait for our food, Jesse builds a house out of sugar packets. I stare out the window, following the slanting lines of the telephone wires that crisscross above the street. I'm thinking about the graveyard, embarrassed by my complete inability to feel emotion. It's like every day I find something new about myself that's broken.

"What was your dad like?" Jesse asks, relaxing against the booth.

And somehow, his question doesn't knock me to the ground. "What do you want to know?" I ask, wondering if I might still be numb from the cold.

"Anything," he says.

Right as I'm about to speak, the waitress drops off our coffees. I smile at her and Jesse nods and they chat for a minute while I pour in cream and sugar and clink my spoon around my cup. I smile and nod in all the right places, but mostly I feel too shaken up for talking to strangers.

When she's gone I take a deep breath and start telling Jesse about my dad. I start at the surface because that feels easier.

"He liked art. And music. Neil Young and the Velvet Underground. He loved being in the car, which is weird for LA. He had a beat-up Honda, but he drove it like a Ferrari. Even just to pick us up from school."

I wrap my hands around the mug, and the warmth seeps into my cold fingers. Then I look down into the cup, and for some reason, I keep talking.

"But he liked to be alone," I say. "He might have liked that more than anything. He had this whole other side of his life that we couldn't be a part of." I look at Jesse, feeling the truth bubbling up from my guts. "Sometimes I wonder if he regretted having us."

My secret lands between us and in my mind it's like a bomb

blowing down all the walls of the diner, but Jesse's face is blank, open, a smooth plane. He barely even blinks.

The waitress comes back with our muffins, and just like that my admission comes and goes. Now Jesse knows almost everything.

I spread my paper napkin across my lap, trying to pretend like my hands aren't shaking.

"Tell me about your dad," I say.

"My dad," Jesse says, tearing off a corner of his muffin, "works way too hard." He leans forward a little, rubs his forehead. "I try to help out as much as I can, but he is definitely the kind of guy who likes to do it himself. That's why I feel so bad about this college thing. I think it's hard for him that I want something he can't really give me."

He looks down at the table, wiping away a few errant crystals of sugar. "But we'll figure it out," he says, almost to himself.

"You will," I say, and he smiles a little.

"For what it's worth," he says, "I think I get your point about college. It's wrong that we give power and meaning and money to this stupid system of prestige."

His hands keep moving, spinning his plate around and around.

"But at the same time," he says, "it could make a big difference for me. I'd be the first person in my whole family to ever go to college."

There's a long beat of silence after that, during which I scramble for the right thing to say.

"Anyway," Jesse says. "None of it really matches up. I get that it's not easy."

I swallow, looking down at the table, at the plate that's still spinning and spinning between Jesse's long fingers, then up at his hair, which has fallen all the way over his eyes. We sit there for a long time, in the space of the conversation left open by my inability to speak.

Finally he looks back up at me, shakes the hair from his face, half smiling, composure regained. "What do you want to do next?"

I crumple my napkin, relief spreading warm through my limbs, and set it carefully on my plate.

"Anything," I say.

When we're back outside, the air doesn't feel as cold as it did before. The clouds are gone and Jesse drives us out of town in another direction. We cross the Vermont border, then hike along the river with our cameras. I take photographs of the light on the water, the edge of Jesse's sleeve against the deep blue sky. We find a town with a used bookstore, and we read the first sentence of as many books as we can. We walk down the crooked side streets, our breath making clouds in the air.

By the time we head back to Cumberland, the sun is already setting. It's a different kind of sunset than I've ever seen, pale and diffuse against the winter trees. Subdued, like my spirit as we wind around the endless curves between here and home.

The closer we get to Cumberland the emptier I feel. The magic of the afternoon leaks out of the improperly sealed windows. I'm exhausted and I have no idea what awaits me at El's. I can't face the thought of trying to talk about Dad with anyone. Especially Mom. And I can't face the thought of trying to think of something to say to Bea when I see her Dead Sea eyes.

Jesse sighs.

"What?" I say.

"I wish I could fix it," he says.

"You can't," I say, looking out the window at the gentle colors of the sky stacking up like china plates.

I turn to watch his dark eyes, which are glued to the road, his hand on the gearshift as he works the gears all the way down to first, to stop at a lonely intersection in the middle of two deserted country roads. He looks over at me while the car idles, nods his head. "I know."

I smile. "Thanks for today though. I can't be sure, but I think it helped."

"Yeah?" he says, and his smile is small, subtle, like the light pink streaks in the sky. Like the crepuscular moon hanging just above the trees.

• • •

THE WHOLE WAY HOME, I'VE BEEN PREPARING MYSELF FOR SOME kind of big, awkward moment with my mother, but when I get to the house the kitchen is empty. The living room is empty. No light under her bedroom door.

I can't tell if I'm relieved or angry or hurt or anxious, but as I stand in the middle of the purple-blue darkness, I can't remember the last time I felt this alone. Suddenly tears are springing up into my eyes. I mash my palms against them. I step back, lean back against the counter and breathe, waiting for the skin of ice to freeze back over everything inside, numbing it all out.

I open the fridge and see a big pot of chicken soup inside. Stuck to the side of the pot is a green sticky note with a drawing of a heart. El is in Saratoga, teaching her Wednesday-night design class, but somehow she's also here trying to hold us together with food.

"Bea!" I yell upstairs.

"What?" she yells back down.

It feels like we are miners inside of a great big cavern.

"Want some dinner?" I yell.

"No," she yells back.

I close the fridge and rest my head against the front of it. I could stay down here, wait for my mother. Turn the lights on and let the dogs into the kitchen. Drag Bea out of her room.

But not today.

When I get upstairs, Bea's door is open. She's lying on her bed in purple scrubs, reading Jane Austen.

"How was it?" she asks. Her voice is flat.

"Fine," I say. "Weird." Then, "Wanna hang?"

"Nah, that's okay," she says, her eyes on the book, moving back and forth across the page. "I kind of just want to be alone."

Something in her voice tells me I've messed this up again. And I feel so frustrated because I don't understand how I did it.

So I cross back over to my side of the hallway, flip on my lamp, and close my door. And then I'm alone in my room that's not really my room. In this house that's not really my house. Out there, Bea, Hannah, Mom, all of the people in my family are just orbiting around the same void, silently, separately, each of us on our own path.

Right before I fall asleep, my phone vibrates with a text from Bennett:

Drove to the top of Malibu Canyon last night and actually saw some stars. Made me think about your dad. Made me think about you.

Before I can think about what I'm doing, I open the video chat. He answers on the second ring and the screen is all darkness and I think, *For once, it is dark where both of us are.*

"Hey," he says. "Everything okay?"

"Yeah," I say. "I just—"

But I stop there because I have no idea what I'm doing or what we're doing or what I want us to be doing.

"I know," he says, after it becomes clear that I'm not going to be able to finish my sentence.

I look into the black screen, trying to make out the shape of his face. "Can you just stay on for a little while?"

"Yeah," he says, his voice scratchy and tired and sweet. "For as long as you want."

I set the phone on my pillow and lie there, listening to the sound of Bennett breathing until I fall asleep.

15

THERE'S A STRANGE AWARENESS TO HAVING A CRUSH, especially one you know you shouldn't have. It's the feeling—the hope—that at any moment that person could be watching you, could notice the way you scrawl your notes left-handed, the way you stretch your arms wide like the sun when you've been sitting for a while. You see yourself through their eyes and you start to look different.

And they start to look different too. Soft focus blurs out all the weird and ugly parts. All you see are perfect details, like the freckle on the back of a wrist, a soft earlobe. Sometimes, it almost looks like they're glowing. You wonder if everyone can see it. Or maybe it's just you.

Two weeks before Hannah comes home for Thanksgiving break, a few days after the graveyard, I wake up and realize that I have a crush on Jesse Keller.

I feel stupid because it seems so obvious, this suffocating crush. It's been here for weeks, months, biding its time.

And blaring right on the other side is Bennett, is the way I woke up the day after Dad's anniversary to the still-dark ceiling of his bedroom, the way I hung up the phone and lay in my bed wondering what I was doing until I was almost late for school. I feel like I'm stuck in my own spiderweb.

I try to act normal around Jesse, but every time I speak to him I feel like it's written across my forehead in black Sharpie: I HAVE A CRUSH ON YOU.

"Marigold, do you have a pen?"

"Sure. Also, I have a crush on you."

"Can you help me with my essay?"

"I've been imagining you without your shirt on."

Being in the darkroom with him is like being in a closet with the sun. I'm sweaty and I can't look at him, even when the lights are off. I'm surprised he hasn't exposed all of my film.

"Marigold," he says, pulling at my sleeve. "You're acting strange."

"I am?" I say, dropping my tongs into the stop bath.

"You are." He laughs. "I can't decide if I like it or not."

He asks me to help with his college portfolio, and I hold each of his photographs gently, looking at the world through his eyes. I'm a horrible editor because I think every single image should make it in.

He asks me if I want help with mine and I agree, even though I have no idea where I would send a portfolio if I made one. We look through the stacks of pictures I've taken since I've gotten here, and I almost don't recognize them. This feels stupid. It feels like a lie.

"What are you thinking?" he asks me.

My eyes stall on the curve of his cheekbone.

"Nothing," I say.

16

At home, I make a different portfolio, photographs of my dad:

A faded, yellowed Polaroid from college. He's wearing a button-down shirt and horn-rimmed glasses, singing in a band. The light glinting off his glasses is completely obscuring his eyes, but there's motion in his body—life—and I can almost imagine the song, loud and drunk and slightly offbeat.

A snapshot from his twenty-first birthday. My mom is holding out a cake that says HAPPY BIRTHDAY JAMES in pink frosting, and he's leaning over the top of it, about to kiss her. His eyes are closed, trusting, utterly oblivious to the fact that he's in danger of setting his shirt on fire. And she's laughing and leaning in to meet him in the middle.

An outtake from a family portrait in our backyard. I'm a chubby three-year-old with cherub curls, and Bea is a wad of blanket in my mother's arms. Hannah sits next to Mom, a stupid, happy smile on her face in a peach-and-white smock dress. I've escaped the scene, and my arms are crossed defiantly over my little barrel chest. Dad is leaning over me, laughing, his eyes full of amusement and affection. It looks like he loves me. Like he thinks I'm the funniest person in the world.

The first few times you look, the photographs fill the void, but after a while they start to feel like lies. There aren't any pictures of Dad's voice when I walked out into the street.

· · ·

I'M SITTING AT THE DINNER TABLE WITH JESSE'S FAMILY ON Saturday night, eating lasagna with soy cheese and whole-wheat noodles. His dad is home and he sits at the head of the table, a veritable giant of a man with a big beard and Jesse eyes. He is, for lack of better words, devastatingly handsome.

The table is raucous and full of life, everyone talking over each other and shoveling food into their mouths.

"Dad," says Finn, "can I get a new bike?"

"Dad," says Anna, "Finn is kicking me under the table."

"Dad," says Katherine, "can I be excused?"

Every time someone says *Dad*, I feel a little stab right behind my eyes. And every time Mr. Keller answers in his calm, deep, resonant voice, something physically aches in my chest.

But I also feel like I'm melting, lost in the sea of voices and big eyes and thick brown hair. It's like returning to a place that's forever gone, a place you wouldn't know exists until it's not there anymore, only it's the wrong house, the wrong dad, the wrong sisters, the wrong table.

Last week, we finally settled on a house, a great big empty

one in the middle of town, four blocks from school. It feels like we'll never be able to fill it up like this.

. . .

After we wash our way through a mountain of dishes, Jesse leads me up to his room. It's a tiny, triangular space that would have been the attic in a family with fewer kids. I don't know how Jesse can stand cramming his six-foot-two self up here all the time.

The ceiling and walls are covered in black-and-white photographs. Little strings of Christmas lights line the places where the eaves come together. There's a twin bed with a fluffy white down comforter and plaid flannel sheets and a desk and chair by the nearly floor-to-ceiling window at the end.

I sit down on Jesse's bed, and a cloud of his scent wafts up and surrounds me, like I'm in the forest after the rain. He leans back against his bed, his hair falling onto my fingers, and I surreptitiously rub one curl between my thumb and forefinger to feel the softness of it.

Before I can stuff it down, a memory escapes: Bennett, in my room, sand sprinkling from his hair onto my face. Last week I texted him a photo of a photo I'd taken a month before I left, a film-camera selfie of the tops of our heads against the wall of my room. He texted back a photo of the photo of the photo. I texted back a photo of the photo of the photo of the photo, and it felt like in this way we were drifting away from each other without really letting go.

I drop Jesse's hair, pull my hand back, cross my arms.

He stands up again, almost as though he can hear my

thoughts. Sometimes I wonder if he knows about the things I'm trying to hide.

He starts moving around the room, getting ready. He takes a gray sweater out of his drawer and pulls it on over his head, and I look away so I don't get caught staring. We're going to a football party tonight, which is something I never would have done in California.

Then he puts on some music and sits back down and we just listen for a while. He's tapping the beat onto his legs with his hands, and I'm looking at the patterns in the ceiling-board knots.

After a while he says, "Marigold?"

I hum a sound that's kind of like *yeah?* without really lifting my head. I'm wearing a plaid wool skirt and thick tights, and my feet are sliding against each other in that slippery-tights way.

Jesse reaches up and runs a hand along my calf, stilling my leg.

"I like the way these feel," he says.

And when I lift my head to look up at him he's turned toward me, the weight of his gaze almost pinning me back down to the pillow. I swallow hard, feeling suddenly like I'm in a tiny boat in a stormy sea, trying to keep myself from flying out into the waves.

The moment stretches out long, neither one of us willing to break it. I'm having a staring contest with Jesse Keller. I'm lying on his bed. I have no idea what I'm doing.

"Jesse!" His mom's voice on the stairs breaks the spell and I jump up from the surprise of it, bouncing Jesse's hand off of my leg. He flies all the way up to standing, banging his head on the roof.

"What's up, Mom?" he says, rubbing the back of his head.

"Ouch," he whispers to me with his perfect, pouting mouth.

"What time are you leaving?"

He looks at me, tilts his head, a little bit of wonder still in his eyes.

"Soon. We're gonna pick up Riley on the way."

"Can you come help me put some things in the garage before you go?"

He sighs. "Sure. I'll be right down." He looks at me and says, "You wanna wait here?"

And yeah, I really do.

"No snooping," he says.

He narrows his eyes like he really means it and I nod slowly, and now I know that Jesse has secrets.

I really, really want to snoop, but instead I move over to his desk chair and flip through the binder of contact sheets on his desk. It's full of potential portfolio candidates, and there are red circles (Jesse) and green circles (me) throughout the book.

When I get to the back I notice the pocket of the binder is stuffed with the torn paper we use for test strips in the dark room. I never save these, tossing them into the heap of scrap paper under the work bench, but here they are, little striped pieces of my photographs in gradations from white to black.

Under the test strips there's a small print, four by five, that I've never seen before. It's me, walking in between gravestones, dropping daisies on the top of two at the same time, my arms outstretched on either side of me, the flowers frozen in midair, dropping through time. My hair is tangling out of the collar of my coat, stuffed half in, half out, a black-and-white cloud.

"I thought we weren't snooping," Jesse whispers over my

shoulder, so close I can feel his breath, startling the bejeezus out of me. I smack my head back into his face, his teeth.

"Jesus, Marigold. First you go through my stuff, then you assault me?"

I whip around to see Jesse holding his mouth, but the edges of a smile are creeping past his hands.

"I wasn't snooping," I say, slamming the binder shut. "I've been through these millions of times."

"Sure," he says. "Ready to go?"

"Yeah," I say, feeling how truly small the room is with both of us in here heating it up.

• • •

As we're driving to the party I notice that there's something different between us. It's like we charged up all the air in Jesse's attic and now it's following us around, threatening to storm.

When we get there, I grab a beer, to take the edge off and give my hands something to do. The PBR tastes like dirty bathwater, but I sip it anyway, slowly, feeling the stale bubbles break on my tongue. Jesse, always responsible and the sober driver tonight, leans over and finds a ginger ale in the back of the fridge.

I look through the kitchen window, and there, in the driveway, Bea is circled up with a group of juniors, smoking a cigarette. Next to her is Domino, long blonde hair pulled into two buns on either side of her head, eyes glued to her phone.

I'm wondering what my move should be when Bea looks up, right into my eyes. A dare.

I want to grab her by the hair and drag her the four and a half miles back to El's house, but lately the thread between us feels delicate, so instead I lift my hand that's not holding a beer up into a wave. She nods and then turns back toward the circle.

"Mary!" Sam shouts, banging through the kitchen door and jumping into my arms, koala style.

"Sam!" I say into her hair, with at least five exclamation points. I guess this is me now. If Nora could see it she would probably die.

Jesse hovers near the doorway, watching. Sam slides down and jumps up onto the counter. She's wearing green leather pants and a vintage Garfield T-shirt under a giant red wool cardigan. She looks between Jesse and me as he awkwardly salutes and backs through the doorway, into the living room.

"What's going on there?" she asks.

I shake my head. "I have no idea."

She smirks. "Yes you do."

I smile in spite of myself, leaning back against the cupboards and taking another sip, feeling my cheeks get warm.

"What about you?" I ask. "We never talk about your love life."

She peels the label of her beer with her thumbnail. "Love is overrated."

"You think so?" I ask, thinking about the only time I've ever been in love and what a mess it's become.

"I mean, I like kissing people. But when you live through three divorces—" She shudders. "Just, no."

We laugh, even though there's something heavy about it. Then Sam looks away, over at the kitchen door.

I finish my beer and open another, and we sit on the counter-top kicking our shoes against the cabinets. We talk about Sam's future New York life, the way she's already looking up rooms on Craigslist. Then we're being snarky about all of the football players and making up ridiculous songs that don't make any sense. I feel myself relaxing into my bones.

Sam hasn't mentioned her old friends much, and I wonder where they are. She's one of the coolest people I know, but sometimes she just seems so alone, floating on the breeze.

"Hey, I've been meaning to ask you. What's happening with your friends—you know, from before?" I ask.

Sam sets her beer down on the counter and straightens her shoulders. "What do you mean?" she says.

"I guess you just haven't brought them up in a while."

I wonder if they're drifting like me and Nora, who now only talk about TV and clothes.

She looks down and chips at her nail polish. Hunter green with microscopic yellow daisies. "I haven't really heard from them all that much. I guess maybe we weren't as close as I thought."

"Oh," I say, thinking that it's weird how far you can end up from the people you love.

"I mean, it's okay," Sam says. "I do have a lot of friends. Or a lot of people I know." She sighs. "But there's knowing and then there's *knowing*. You know?"

She's getting that look again, lonely and distant.

"I think so," I say.

"But, yeah," she says, bumping her shoulder against mine. "I've been missing out."

I rest my head on hers and for a while we just sit there, leaning on each other. Then a group of people clambers into the kitchen, and music comes blaring in through the open door.

"Wanna go dance?" she asks.

"Yeah. In just a second," I say. I hop off the counter and make my way to the living room, leaving the last few sips of my second beer, which was getting warm and undrinkable.

I spot Bea sitting on the edge of the couch, earbuds in, looking at her phone.

I sneak up next to her and pull one out. "What are you doing here?" I say. I'm trying to sound like a cool and approachable older sister, but the words come out more like I'm a stressed-out mom.

"Chill," she says. "Domino's sister is coming to pick us up in a minute."

"I mean, it's fine," I say. "But why didn't you tell me you were coming?"

She shrugs, then looks back at her screen, where Mark Knopfler is playing a wild guitar solo without the sound. A text pops up.

Domino: Time 2 go.

"That's me," she says, taking back her earbud and standing up, patting me on the head. "See you tomorrow."

I watch her weave back through the crush of bodies until she's out of sight. It feels like she's slipping through my fingers like sand.

Sam comes over and pulls me up off of the couch, out of my moping, and into the very middle of the room. It really is surreal, being in a house that smells like cigarettes and looks like it's straight out of the nineties—fake flowers, velour wraparound couch—stuffed to the seams with white kids dancing to hip-hop music. At first I just stand there, watching everyone move around me. But then I feel the one and a half beers glittering through my veins, turning up the volume of everything inside. And I decide to just let go.

Then I look up and Jesse is next to me doing funny moves like the lawnmower and making the bed, and with his long, lanky self he looks ridiculous and amazing, like a giant puppet. And then we start dancing together, right up against each other, until he tugs my hand and starts spinning me, out and in and out again and my face is flush against his chest and I'm breathing hard and lit up like I'm phosphorescent and not just beer buzzed.

It feels like someone cranked up the heat, and I notice that the windows are all fogged even though it's cold enough outside for ice crystals.

Ice crystals, I think. *Is there anything more beautiful? Is there anything more beautiful than this place?*

It goes on like this for a few songs, everyone dancing in a big mass in the living room but me and Jesse dancing together. Then we take a break and I go with Sam to the kitchen to get another beer because I just want to keep this feeling going. Jesse. Friends. Belonging. Dancing. I open my throat wide and gulp it down.

"Whoa," Sam says. "You are not fucking around."

"Nope," I tell her.

Then I march back into the living room to find Jesse, who is leaning in the doorway looking like a frigging supermodel, one single curl falling between his eyes. I grab his hand and his eyebrows raise up up up and I tug and say, "Let's go outside."

He says, "It's freezing out."

And I say, "I'm burning up in here."

And I run my index finger across the inside of his wrist.

He follows me and we are still attached as we step out the back door and into a wall of cold.

"Holy fuck," I say, teeth chattering. "You were right."

"I'm always right," Jesse says.

I sway a little on my feet and say, "You and the patriarchy."

It's dark out here except for a spotlight coming off the garage. We're on a rickety porch that looks like it's going to give way any second, collapsing us into a heap of deadly splinters.

Jesse is laughing at my joke in the way that he laughs, the way that completely fills any space, even though we are outside and technically the space goes on forever. But his laugh reverberates out, looking to see how far it can go.

I step back until I'm leaning against the wall, and Jesse's body slants over me, one hand on the siding next to my face.

"Marigold," he says. "What are we doing out here?"

I stare right up into his deadly brown eyes and my breath leaves me in a little puff of steam. He blinks. Once. Twice. Then he tilts his head and looks up into the night sky.

"Look," he says. "Orion's Belt."

He takes a step back so that I can see.

"You have no idea how lucky you are to have seen these stars your whole life," I say.

He steps a little closer again, halfway back to where he was before. "Are you saying I'm *lucky* to be in Cumberland?"

I shrug. "I feel pretty lucky right now, don't you?"

I reach out and grab his jacket, pulling him all the way into me, my ear to his chest.

"You're still shivering," he says. "Want to go back inside?"

I look up at his full-moon eyes, his long, straight nose, his wide, full lips, and I shake my head.

And then I'm standing up on my toes and he's leaning his head down and the world is absolutely spinning, not just from the beer. I close my eyes just as his winter-dry lips brush mine. A brush, and then a press.

"Wait," he says, his lips a millimeter away.

My eyes are unfocused and my hands have drifted up into his dark hair.

"What?"

He pulls back another inch.

"What about that guy?"

I shake my head. "What?"

"From California."

Fuck. *Bennett.* Somehow, for the past hour, I've completely forgotten he exists.

"Oh," I say, breaking my eyes away from Jesse's, buying time, an inch of privacy to figure this out. "He's, um. We're—"

The door behind his eyes closes again.

"That's what I thought."

"No, wait," I say, feeling desperate. "It's not. We're just. It's complicated."

He lets go of me, retreats back a step, which feels like a mile. My winter-numb knees give out, and I sink to the ground in sad slow motion. My face burns with disappointment and cold.

He crouches down so we're eye to eye and peers into my soul.

"You're drunk," he says.

And I'm not just drunk; I'm humiliated. I want to crawl under the porch and curl up until I freeze to death.

He presses a warm knuckle to my cheek.

"And you're freezing, Marigold. Let's go inside."

I shake my head, totally dejected.

But he grabs my hands anyway and pulls me up, and I try not to puke on Jesse Keller as he herds me back into the house.

17

THE NEXT MORNING I WAKE UP TO A WORLD OF HURT. My head is throbbing and spinning, my mouth is dry, and my heart has completely failed. I think I need a new one.

The first thing I think when I wake up is: *Oh my god what have I done?*

Then: *I've humiliated myself.* And then, blaring beside it: *I kissed him.*

I kissed him.

I kissed him and I can still feel the indentation of his lips. The pressure. The way I wanted to push my tongue out of my mouth and lick.

And then I remember Bennett. Shame and guilt spread everywhere. I'm the worst friend. I'm the worst almost-girlfriend. I'm scum. Garbage. An entire nest of spiders.

I lie for a long time under the quilt, sliding the blocks of corduroy and silk between my fingers. I stay in bed until I think it will be noticed, until the dry desert of my mouth can't take it anymore, and then I shuffle downstairs.

I'm afraid of the initial encounter, that El or my mom will just look at me and know. They'll smell the alcohol coming out of my skin. But when I get to the kitchen no one is there. Again.

I pour myself a large glass of water and rummage around the cupboard until I find some ibuprofen and then lurk my way back upstairs, trailing my fingers across Bea's door as I go. What I really need right now is a movie marathon, the two of us bundled up next to each other on the sofa all day long. Like we used to with Hannah last year when Mom was gone.

But when I finally get the nerve to go back and beg for Bea to cuddle up with me, I realize that she's out too. So it's back to bed with my hangover and my humiliation.

From every angle this looks bad. I think about Jesse's hair flopping down onto my forehead, right before we kissed. The way he looked when he deposited me next to Sam on the couch, like he couldn't get away fast enough. The way he didn't say anything the whole ride home.

I get my phone, check my messages, my Instagram, my email. Nothing. Not even a coupon or newsletter or spam. I've officially hit rock bottom.

I start to type a text to Nora: *I really fucked up.*

But then I think about all of the things we haven't said to each other in the past few weeks, and I delete the message, letter by letter.

And then, somehow, the video chat starts ringing. Bennett is calling me.

Shit. I catapult off of the bed, as if he can see me already, and take stock of my Freddy Krueger makeup and beehive hair. There's no way that I can answer this right now. But for some reason I feel like I should.

I open up the message window and type: Call you in five?

Then I go to the bathroom and scrub my face, brush my hair and teeth, and give myself a pep talk in the mirror.

"Chin up, buttercup," I whisper.

For extra protection, I get back in my bed and crawl down under the covers.

"Mary," Bennett says when he answers, and he is smiling the sweetest, sleepiest smile.

"Hey, Bennett."

He rubs his cheek. His hair is ruffled like he just woke up.

"It's pretty early in California," I say.

"It's pretty late in New York," he replies. "You still in bed?"

"Long night," I say, and I immediately wish I hadn't.

"Oh yeah?" Bennett says, raising an eyebrow.

And all I can think of is the press of Jesse's mouth on mine. And now I'm sweating and I can't think of anything to say besides *I kissed someone else*. I look around the room, as if I'll find some inspiration in the green bureau, the vase of cedar branches, the painting of a lightning storm.

"What happened?" he asks.

"Nothing really," I lie.

There's a long pause after I say it, during which guilt, thick as tar, oozes over every inch of my insides again. His blue eyes turn a little stormy and his forehead creases. A look I used to love.

"Mary," he says. "What are we doing?"

And finally, four months later, one of us has asked the question. I shake my head. "I don't know."

"Me neither," he says. His shoulders drop. And then, "You know, I liked you for so long before things happened with us. Practically forever."

Hearing him say this is surreal. It's everything I've ever wanted to hear.

In the month when Bennett was kissing me, I was obsessed with questions of *when?* and *how?* It seemed like one day he was safely ensconced in his pack of water polo teammates, utterly unreachable during business hours, and the next he was alone in my room, melting himself into me. The whole thing felt impossible and perfect. Both at the same time.

But now something about his confession feels wrong. I can't comprehend this alternate timeline, where he could have been mine all along.

Bennett continues on, not noticing the way my face is frozen with something that feels like panic. "I was always picking you flowers on the way back from the beach," he says, pushing his hair out of his eyes. "And then I'd leave them in my car because I didn't want things between us to change. I had this feeling like if we got together it could wreck everything."

I try to clear my throat, remembering all the little bunches of dried-up daisies in the back of Bennett's Jeep, feeling like I can't breathe.

"And then, when you told me you were leaving," he says, lying back on his pillows, looking up, "I couldn't help it."

I reach down and trace his profile with my finger. Outside my window, the clouds are heavy and low.

"But sometimes I wonder if it was a mistake," he says, and a little part of me crumples up.

"What?"

Inside of my chest, my heart is still beating, but I'm not sure how.

He rubs his forehead, frowns. "I don't mean it like that. It's just—ever since we—I don't know. Sometimes it seems like you're even farther away than you are."

For a second I see myself, adrift and alone, thousands of miles away from Bennett, California, Earth. I think about all of the ways I've been disappearing, just like Dad. I think he might be right.

"I'm sorry," I say, not sure how to fix it.

"I just—" he says again. "Are you ever even coming back?"

On the screen, he looks both big and small. Despite everything else I've forgotten, I can still remember the weight of his arm on my side, the warmth of his neck against my forehead. I want to say *yes*.

But instead, for once, I tell the truth. "I don't know."

Bennett closes his eyes. "I should go," he says.

And suddenly I feel desperate, like I'd do anything to make him stay. But the screen goes black and I burrow down all the way under the covers so that no light can get in.

Just when I'm about to cry, I hear heavy Doc Martens thumping up the stairs and there's a sharp knock on my door.

"Hey, loser," Bea says when she pushes it open.

I blink back my tears, trying to pretend like my whole world hasn't just been popped into a particle accelerator. "Hey, Bea, what's up?"

"I think I'm ready for a new look," she says, her fading black hair pulled back into a messy knot on top of her head. "You wanna help?"

And honestly, nothing has ever sounded better.

· · ·

"I'M THINKING SIXTIES HOUSEWIFE," BEA SAYS AS WE FLY AROUND the curves in El's Subaru. "Polyester dresses the color of sherbet. Big hair."

I'm starting to really love this drive to civilization, thirty minutes on a good day, forty-five million farms and trees.

"What's with the change?" I ask. I'd begun to wonder if Bea's Goth phase was going to be permanent.

"I'm just sick of being sad," she says.

I nod, noticing how the hangover makes me a hundred times sicker of my own sadness today. "Me too."

Sam texts us an annotated list of all the best thrift stops in the greater Saratoga Springs area and asks about my sad departure from the party. I dictate a text to Bea, who types it into my phone as I drive: Life is exploded. I'll explain everything tomorrow. Bea raises an eyebrow but doesn't ask what it means.

We arrive at the first spot, a giant Goodwill. The parking lot is almost empty, so we pull into the closest spot, sliding on our sunglasses like VIPs. Bea breathes in deeply when we walk through the door.

"I just love the smell of old clothes."

"Me too, Bea," I say. "Me too."

And just like that, we're back on again, filling the cart with wacky florals and brightly colored cigarette pants. There's this synergy between us, a shared goal. Find the treasures, the deals, the things that nobody else sees. Other people's trash is our triumph.

We find Bea another wardrobe, a new disguise. I find red cowboy boots and a long velvet dress.

"Remember when we went to the Salvation Army in Florida?" Bea says.

"I got my leather fringe jacket there, how could I ever forget?"

"I think this is even better than that."

I grin. "You might be right."

We're at the third thrift shop, and I'm starting to lose steam when Bea sidles up beside me. "Do you ever think about Dad?" she says, without any segue at all. She's flipping through the hangers of ladies' jackets at high speed, trying to look casual, eyes never leaving the rack.

"Of course I do," I say, moving along behind her, sliding the hangers from right to left: purple parka, camel trench, green pleather moto, yellow windbreaker. "Do you?"

"All the time," she says. "I can't stop."

She turns away from me and fingers the strap of a robin's-egg-blue handbag hanging on a rotating rack.

"On the anniversary I tried to go to school, but I ended up leaving after homeroom." Her voice is quieter than usual, almost at a whisper. "I walked all the way back to El's house."

"Jesus, Bea," I say. "Why didn't you call me?"

She shrugs but doesn't turn around. "I don't know. I was just walking and walking. I didn't even know where I was going. I felt like my toes were going to fall right off. I saw three deer and about a hundred birds. But I didn't see Dad."

I want to fold her into my arms. But instead I stop her hand on the rack and turn her to me, my hands on her shoulders. Her eyes are big and sad.

"Why don't we ever talk about him?" she says. "It feels like we're just letting him disappear."

"I know," I say. "I feel like that too." And suddenly my sadness is swelling again, threatening to spill over.

I want to tell her about the one million ways I'm scared that Dad is already gone. About how all I remember is his muffled yelling, "Five more minutes," out the study door.

But instead I rest my forehead against hers. "Don't do that again," I say.

"Okay," she says. And then, "We should talk about him."

I nod. "We should."

She nods once, her forehead against mine, then squeezes my hands and drifts off down the aisle like a ghost.

• • •

WE EAT ICE CREAM FOR LUNCH AND GRAB A JAR OF LAVENDER HAIR dye on the way back home. The Goth black has faded to gray. Bea doesn't want to be sad anymore. Both of us know it's not really that easy, but we pretend anyway.

When we get home we throw the clothes into the dryer and I get ready to dye Bea's hair. El comes in from her studio and lays down a hundred old towels in the downstairs bathroom. The dogs, who think they are getting a bath, clamor around the baby gate.

"I haven't dyed my hair in twenty years," El says. "Maybe I should try it."

"Maybe I should too," says Mom, from under a stack of files in the living room. It's the first time I've seen her since yesterday morning.

"Ugh," says Bea. "No."

In another week, Hannah will be home for Thanksgiving break. I wish she were here now, to take before-and-after photos and read aloud from magazines while we wait for the dye to set. Instead I take the photos, sending her a text that says: Guess what color is next?

And she texts back: No wait for meeeee!

I say: Too late hahaha

And for a minute everything feels normal again.

Bea's leaning her neck back over the tub and I'm working the purple into her hair, my hands covered in crinkly plastic gloves, when she says, "This has been a very good day."

"Against all odds," I say. And I don't even care about any of the messes lurking under the surface.

18

MONDAY COMES WITH MY FIRST POST-PARTY SIGHTING of Jesse, where he meets my eyes for exactly one-third of a second and abruptly turns around and heads back down the hallway, confirming that my fear is true: things between us have gotten weird.

Our *Song of Solomon* paper is due in English. Jesse won't look at me all class long, even though I'm sitting right next to him. I don't look at him either, except for out of the corner of my eye, where I register his basic geometric shapes and listen to the tapping of his pencil.

He walks me to lunch without saying anything. And when the silence gets to be too much, the void where our voices would go overflowing with the jarring raucousness of all the other students in the hall, I blurt out, "Darkroom today?"

And he looks at me like I said it in French, his head tilted to one side. And then he looks away and says, "I have to babysit."

I must look crushed because he immediately adds, "How about tomorrow?"

"Sure," I say, ignoring the voice in my head that's telling me to just leave him alone.

Right before we get to the cafeteria, I hear Ms. Simpson, the guidance counselor, calling my name. Jesse seems more than happy for the interruption, and before I know it he has disappeared off down the hallway, leaving me for dead.

"Hey, Ms. Simpson," I say, walking toward her like there is actual concrete in my boots.

"Mary!" she says, a little out of breath. She is young, in her twenties, with long, stick-straight blonde hair and big white teeth. "I'm so glad I caught you. We're a little behind on college stuff and I wanted to set up a time to meet."

She leads me into her office, which is basically a small, windowless closet, plastered with motivational posters that look like they were purchased on Etsy. Ms. Simpson is very tall, maybe even six feet, and I don't know how she can stand it in here all day long. She half sits on the edge of her desk, and I hover near the doorway, ready to escape.

"I was looking at your SAT scores," she says, beaming. "Way to go! You'll have a lot of options for next year."

Her voice seems to bounce off the walls of the office as though we are in some kind of echo chamber, *next year next year next year next year* drilling into my brain. One minute in and already I feel like I'm starting to panic.

"Did you know that the SAT was created by a eugenicist?" I deflect.

She seems a little stunned.

"I—didn't know that," Ms. Simpson says. But she collects herself, smiles, unrelentingly positive. I imagine her in a cheerleader uniform, waving her pom-poms up and down. "I mean, there are a lot of meaningless hoops to jump through in this process. But we gotta do what we gotta do."

Everyone keeps saying things like that. And I get it. I do. But every time I try to begin, the whole world disintegrates and I find myself staring, slack-jawed, at my computer screen for hours on end, or folding brochures into paper cranes, feeling more lost than before.

I glance out into the hallway, which is almost empty by now. "Look," I say. "Thank you so much for your offer, but I think I have it under control."

"Um—" she says, like she senses I'm about to make a run for it. "Let's make an appointment, just to be sure we have our ducks in a row."

"Really," I say, inching back into the hallway. The edge of my vision is starting to swim. "My mom is helping me. It's all good."

"Mary—" she says, but I'm already halfway down the hallway.

· · ·

JESSE SITS AT HIS OLD TABLE TODAY, AND ALL THROUGH LUNCH I keep stealing looks over at him. He seems fine, talking and eating and looking perfect in his oatmeal-colored sweater, like nothing even happened. We've been attached at the hip all fall, and it's a little jarring to remember that he has other friends, that he tells jokes that can make an entire lunch table laugh.

I wish I could just walk over and say, *I'm sorry. Can we try again?*

But then I remember the feeling I got when Bennett hung up the phone. Like some vital part of me was being severed. I can't seem to get that word, *mistake*, out of my head. It seems like such an ugly word for one of the most meaningful moments of my life.

"What's happening?" Sam asks when I visibly wince for the fourth or fifth time.

"What?" I say.

She takes a giant bite out of her soggy, rectangular slice of pizza. She chews it slowly, eyebrows raised, waiting for me to spill. Around me, the cafeteria feels too loud. Everyone is talking, moving, laughing, smiling. Out of the corner of my eye, Jesse and Riley Erickson actually high-five.

Finally, Sam sighs and says, "You're acting weird. And you still haven't told me what happened on Saturday."

I drop my head to the table, my hair spilling everywhere. I feel like the Bea of a week ago, when she was Goth from head to toe. I don't want to talk about it, but I'm also sick of partitioning the truth out in little pieces, this person getting this part, that person getting the other.

"I tried to kiss Jesse," I mumble, almost hoping she doesn't hear.

But obviously she does because she smacks the table, which makes my teeth knock together, and yells, "I knew it!"

I cringe, peeling my forehead from the sticky tabletop. "Yep. I was drunk and a complete idiot and he shut me down and then dragged me inside and left me on the couch like a bag of old laundry."

"Oh," she says. "That's what that was about. He definitely looked pissed."

She's quiet for a while, and I replay the pathetic scene in my head, feeling the burn of embarrassment at the back of my eyes.

"But why would he—"

I look up at Sam, then back down at the table, where my lunch sits untouched inside of its bag. "I know I haven't updated you on Bennett in a while, but we've been *video chatting* for the past four months."

Sam's mouth drops open. "Wow, Marigold. Wow."

I cover my eyes with my hands, my stomach turning over. "I know. I'm a mess."

"This is why I don't do love," Sam says. "Although . . ."

"Although what?" I say.

Sam looks out the window, toward the line of trees at the edge of the football field. She's smiling in a way that I've never seen before, twisting a piece of her hair.

"Nothing," she says.

"Come on," I whine. "I told you."

Then she laughs and says, "Did you know that all of the models in El's class are naked?"

"No," I say. "That is—wow, that would be hard for me."

"I think it's a little hard for everyone." Sam snorts. "If you know what I mean."

I roll my eyes. Sam is grinning.

"But how's it going?" I ask, trying not to laugh on principle. "Apart from the nudity."

Sam sighs and now her smile is sweet again.

"Good," she says. "Really, really good."

• • •

IT FEELS LIKE FOREVER SINCE I'VE TAKEN THE BUS HOME WITH BEA, and one day into her new look, she seems like a different person.

Her hair is in a violet heap on top of her head, and she's wearing a pink wool jacket and a polyester dress with yellow daffodils all over it.

I haven't talked to her about the football party. I don't know how to do it without ruining this rare happy streak. Instead, as I walk down the aisle toward our seat in the back, I dig my camera out of my backpack and take a picture of the strip of sunlight falling across her knee.

"Ready for winter, I see," I say as I slide down into the seat next to her.

"You gotta keep a little sunshine in your heart, Mary. Otherwise you'll never make it."

"Fair enough," I say, amused and a little perplexed. "How was your day?"

"You know what?" she says. "It was all right."

We pull out of the parking lot, and everything starts whipping by in shades of brown, mud puddles and dead grass and naked trees.

"What do you think Dad would say if he saw us riding this bus?" Bea says.

"I don't know," I say, trying to remember something good. "He'd probably laugh his ass off."

Be smirks. "So true."

A flash of Dad's irreverent smile flutters through my mind like a falling leaf.

"He'd probably speed up to the door in his beater and insist that we jump out."

"No child of mine is going to ride in that piece of shit," Bea says, making her voice all deep.

Remembering this part of Dad with Bea is like looking into a fun house mirror; for a moment I can see all the different sides of him at once. It feels like, in the empty expanse of my memory, Bea and I are building something new.

"Get in, girls," I say, my voice deep too. "We're going to the goddamn movies."

Then we collapse against the seat and laughter washes away the sting.

19

THERE ARE KINDS OF RAIN THAT WASH EVERYTHING clean. In California, the rain would come in a yearly burst to clear months of exhaust from the buildings and asphalt, to turn the grass from brown to green, to make the air fresh again. It covered the sky in gray, only to make it bluer than ever before.

The rain in New York in November is not that kind of rain. It spreads the ice and mud around, makes the brown even browner, the cold even colder, drives the chill into your bones.

Bea is suddenly the kind of person who takes on the rain with a vintage floral umbrella and a smile, and I huddle beside her at the bus stop in a black puffer jacket, black corduroys, and a frown of deep dejection. How quickly things have changed.

After school, Bea gets a ride to Domino's and I wait for Jesse under the awning, full of anxiety and devoid of hope.

It's silent in the car for six whole minutes, except for the sound of Jesse's fingers fluttering on the gearshift, the windshield wipers struggling to squeak across the glass, and my breathing, which sounds loud and a little desperate. I think that the ball is in my court, but I can't make any words come out.

Finally, when we are almost at the end of the gravel road, I say, "I'm sorry."

And then, "I'm the worst."

For good measure.

Jesse laughs. He laughs. And I almost feel relieved. But the laugh is different, thin. It barely fills the tiny car.

"Marigold," he says, running a hand through his dark waves. "It's okay. You were drunk."

"I was drunk," I repeat in my best robot voice, feeling like this is going downhill fast.

"You didn't know what you were doing."

I nod slowly. Even though I *did* know what I was doing. I felt every cell of his November-cold lips on mine and have replayed it a million times since in my mind. But I can't say that, so I just nod and watch the rain streak over the dirt and gravel, down into the little gully beside the road.

"But I don't want to do that with you if you're with someone else," he continues. "It's not right."

I want to say, *I'm not with someone else.*

I wonder if that's true. But either way it doesn't feel like the right thing to say here. It doesn't feel like Jesse even wants that anymore. So again, I just nod. I keep everything I want to say inside, and I take the out he's giving me.

"I get it," I say. "I'm really sorry. That was messed up."

He nods. Sharp, like a soldier. "Thanks," he says, his voice formal and far away.

I suddenly feel like a tired swimmer, miles from shore.

"And also," he adds, pulling his sweater sleeve down over his hand in that way that he does, "I don't really like to do that kind of thing unless I mean it."

"Oh."

An icicle lodges itself in my heart.

Jesse reaches over and squeezes my arm. It's a kind gesture, completely devoid of romance.

So I say, "Can we just forget about it?"

"Sure," he says. "I already have."

• • •

LATER, I RUN INTO MOM IN THE KITCHEN. SHE'S LEANING AGAINST the counter, eating almond butter out of the jar with a spoon. Lately, her comings and goings have begun to smooth out into a steady rhythm. Monday late, Tuesday early, Wednesday late, Thursday early. She's mostly gone on the weekends, but bit by bit, it feels like she might be coming back to us.

El floats between the counter and the stove, bending over something that smells delicious, seemingly lost in thought. I pull out a stool and sit down at the counter, needing the warm noise of the kitchen after the cold quiet of Jesse's car.

But then Mom says, "College applications are due soon," raising her eyebrows like I'm supposed to be excited. And if I weren't so lonely I would turn right around and walk back up to my room.

"I know. I've been working on them," I lie. Right to her face. It feels easy, like I'm telling her the time.

At the stove, El makes a little humming noise.

"What's on your short list?" Mom asks, then shakes her head.

"God. I can't believe it's November and we've barely talked about this. Your dad would have killed me."

I try to remember the last time she mentioned him like this, when his death wasn't the subject of the sentence. I tuck the words away into my folder of evidence.

"It's okay," I lie again. "I've got it under control. UCSB, of course, and Columbia. And also Sarah Lawrence and Williams." I rattle off the names of some colleges, hoping she won't see through it.

Despite everyone's insistence, I haven't spent a lot of time thinking about the future. I've been out in the yard, taking pictures of the house through the windows like a creep. I've been in Jesse's darkroom, building a fake portfolio for a list of schools that doesn't exist. I've been avoiding Nora's texts and calls, avoiding Ms. Simpson's anxious emails, and writing nonsensical strings of letters into the text boxes of the Common Application. I feel like a malformed part on a conveyor belt; everyone around me is just gliding toward the future at a steady rate, a good clip, and it feels like when I get to the end I'm just going to tumble off, to fall down into nothing.

Mom beams. She looks so relieved. "You can use your emergency card for the application fees. Let me know if you need help."

"Sure, Mom." I feel relieved too, but part of me already wants to rewind the conversation, to do it differently and tell the truth.

She drops the spoon in the sink and screws the top back onto the almond butter. "I'm gonna go lie down before dinner. I'm exhausted."

She stretches her hands up over her head and I remember

how long she is, what it felt like to be small, reaching my arms around her middle.

"I'm so proud of you, Marigold," she says as she shuffles up the stairs.

Fuck. The lies sit in a heavy pile in my stomach. I keep stuffing them down, adding more. I wonder where it ends.

I pick up the spoon and rinse it off, dropping it into the dishwasher.

"You okay?" El says. She watches the doorway where Mom has just disappeared, fingers tapping at her lips.

"Yeah," I say. "I'm good."

"That was quite a list," she says. "Good for you."

"Yeah." I scrub my hands down my face. For some reason it's a lot harder to lie to El. "I don't know," I say. I feel suddenly fragile. One crack away from splitting wide open.

"It's okay to be lost," El says. She looks at me like she can see right through my delicate shell. "It makes sense. But I don't want you to mess everything up because of it."

"I won't," I say. And maybe it's true. Maybe I just need a little more time.

"Okay," she says, turning back to the stove. "I'm here if you want to talk it through."

• • •

That night, when I'm done with my reading and I'm sick of stalking Jesse's outdated photos on social media, I open up the UC homepage and click *Apply*. I scroll past all the preliminary information: birthdate, address, etc., etc., coming to a section of short-answer questions.

1. Describe an experience where you have taken part in a group effort, displaying leadership, solving problems, and positively influencing others.

I think about the nightmare explosion group effort that is my family and my utter failure to hold things together. And I actually laugh out loud.

My phone buzzes against my desk.

Nora: SUBMITTED!!

I pause for a moment, fingers hovering over the screen, trying to think of what to say. I miss Nora like crazy. I am so sick of lying. I hate that all we ever do is live-text through our old favorite shows.

I bring up the FaceTime app and find Nora's name. I almost press it. But then I remember all of the lies that I've already told and I feel suddenly exhausted.

I open up the text window again.

Me: AMAZING! I'm almost done. These short answer questions are killer.

Nora: Need any help?

Me: I'll figure it out.

Nora: Real talk: I miss you.

Me: I really miss you too.

I fall asleep with the computer open, the cursor still blinking in the empty answer field of question number one.

20

THE NEXT WEEKEND, IN THE ABSENCE OF JESSE'S glow, I try new things like sleeping all day. The more I slip in and out of sleep, the harder it is to get out of bed. Katharine and RBG curl up on the floor beside me, thumping their tails on the rug. A box of chemicals and paper arrives from my old photo store in LA, just in time to remind me that I'll probably never set foot in Jesse's darkroom again. I shove it into the corner of my closet and climb back into bed.

Saturday passes, then Sunday. My application to UCSB, due in eight days, stays untouched, a perfectly empty canvas. My phone periodically chirps with texts from Nora, subtle attempts to check on the progress of my application. I'm running out of vague responses, so after a while I stop texting back.

I finally get the nerve to call Bennett, but he doesn't answer and I'm relieved because I don't know what I would say if he did. I listen to his voicemail recording: *Hey, this is Bennett, leave a message*, and it's over so fast. I want to listen again, like maybe it will give me some kind of clue as to what happened last weekend. But then I realize that the beep has gone by and it's my turn to say something and I can't so I just hang up the phone.

All week long there's been nothing but silence between us. It's a little disappointing how, after one disastrous moment of honesty, we've gone back to not talking at all. Part of me just wants to let it go because even if I've blown it with Jesse forever, I know now that things are never going back to the way they were in California. But suddenly I miss it more than ever, the neon pink bougainvillea and the hot, crowded sidewalks and the easy quiet of Bennett, Nora, and me.

On Sunday afternoon, Sam texts: Want to go for a drive?

The sun is sinking low, even though it's only four o'clock, and something about it makes me feel so blue I can't even think. I imagine riding through the twilight in Sam's car, the way the world would glow in the headlights. I almost consider getting up, putting on real clothing. But then I would have to talk about this hollowed-out feeling.

I text Sam: Maybe tomorrow, but I don't really mean it.

• • •

HANNAH COMES HOME ON MONDAY NIGHT AND LUGS A SUITCASE and a giant mesh bag of laundry up to my room. She flops onto my bed like it belongs to her, picking up a dirty sock from the bedspread and wrinkling her nose.

"Ew," she says.

"I've missed you too," I say.

"What, are you moping?" she asks, looking over my pathetic ensemble of baggy black sweatpants, oversize black T-shirt, and navy cardigan with a giant hole in the elbow. She frowns in utter disapproval, as if she herself is not the queen of moping, and then continues on without waiting for me to answer. "And where is Bea? This isn't going to work. We need movies."

She gets up, tugging me with her, and pushes me out of my room. "You go make the popcorn," she says. Then she turns and pounds on Bea's door. "BEA!" she screams. "You've got ten minutes to get your pathetic little ass downstairs!"

She parks all of us—including Mom and El—on the couches and makes us watch *Heathers* and then *Home Alone*, talking ceaselessly through both movies.

"That outfit is fucking amazing."

"Bea, stop hogging the popcorn."

"Is it weird that being left at home to build elaborate booby traps to ward off robbers is kind of my dream scenario?"

I'm annoyed, but something about it is also comforting, and after a while I realize that her constant babbling is filling the awkward, empty spaces and easing the tension, word by word. Nobody is fighting. Jesse and Bennett become a little numb spot in my mind.

Everyone else falls asleep, and eventually it's just the two of us.

"I can't believe Macaulay Culkin is forty-one," she says, looking at her phone.

"Did you just google that?" I ask.

She shrugs. "What? I wanted to see if he was hot as an adult."

"Jesus," I say, shaking my head.

"You know you missed me," she says, turning off the TV and gathering the cups and bowls on the coffee table.

I stand up and stretch out my arms.

"You have no idea," I say.

· · ·

THE NEXT NIGHT IT SNOWS FOR THE VERY FIRST TIME. THE FLAKES are big and fluffy and they cover the hard ground within a matter of minutes. Ice crystals splinter up the windowpanes. Thin piles of white line the twigs and branches, glowing periwinkle in the twilight. From my room at the top of the house I watch the whole world transform.

In the morning, I'm awakened by someone poking me in the back.

"God, it's like she's dead," I hear Hannah whisper.

"It's six in the fucking morning," Bea whines. "Who the fuck cares?"

I feel Hannah lean down to my ear. "Wake up, Maryyyyyy," she whispers.

I open one eye.

"You are so creepy," I rasp. I sit up, squinting around for something that will help me understand why my sisters are doing this. "What is this? It's still dark outside."

Hannah sighs. "You guys are way too grumpy." She makes a swoony pose with her arms. "It snowed! It's beautiful. We have to go out and play in it."

I groan and lie back down, hiding my head under the blankets.

"Nope." Hannah is using her Mom voice now, and I know we are in trouble. "I don't know what has been going on around here but you two need some fresh fucking air. I can't handle another day in mope town. You have ten minutes to get up or I'm coming

215

up here and pouring a glass of water on your greasy little heads."

I don't have the right clothes for this, but I pull on leggings under some heavy jeans, two pairs of socks, a wool sweater, and a giant down parka I find in El's coat closet. Hannah meets me at the back door with a hat and a mismatched pair of fuzzy mittens.

As soon as I step out the back door, snow makes its way under my cuffs and stings my ankles. But after a while it's like we're little kids again, making love potions out of the lemons that grew in our yard, but instead we're making an anatomically correct snowman. I'm breathless with laughter and the cold.

I run inside to get my camera and try to photograph the slice of lavender hair tumbling out of Bea's polka-dot beanie, yanking my mitten off with my teeth. My finger is about to press down the shutter release when Hannah comes up behind me and shoves a handful of snow down my back. It burns hot and cold against my skin, which is sweaty from laboring in the snow.

"Asshole!" I scream.

Hannah and Bea high-five and double over in laughter, but I'm fast and I catch both of them before they can stand up again, scooping armfuls of powder into their hair.

Hannah shrieks and Bea emits a long, loud stream of *FUCK*s.

"Justice!" I shout, and run for the house.

When we're back in pajamas and our wet clothes are in the dryer, El makes us waffles and hot chocolate with mini marshmallows, and we watch the Keira Knightley version of *Pride and Prejudice*. By the time Mom comes home we are half asleep on the couch like cats.

"I brought Chinese food!" Mom announces, and suddenly, despite the snow piled up outside El's expansive living room windows, it feels like a Sunday night in California—a Sunday night before everything—Mom chiding us to get our butts off the couch, Bea complaining about setting the table, Hannah organizing the takeout containers in the exact right order. I ache for my dad. Any version of him. Even the one with faraway eyes.

We sit down at the table and everyone is talking at once, even Bea. She's smiling and stuffing her face with shrimp dumplings.

"Jeez, Bea," Mom says. "It's like you haven't been fed in weeks."

And instead of making some snarky comment, Bea just says, "You are so weird," and she's actually kind of laughing as she says it.

And then I see it: Hannah has magically restored the balance. It's like she was the Jenga piece whose absence made the whole tower tumble. And now she's fixed it again. She doesn't even have to try.

• • •

DAD WAS A THANKSGIVING PURIST. HE ALWAYS MADE A FEAST, Midwestern style, with white-bread stuffing and canned cranberry sauce. He'd spend the whole day in the kitchen, sweating and cursing, while the rest of us watched the parade. Then we'd go around and say what we were thankful for, and Mom's would be cheesy and Dad's would be funny and we'd groan and laugh and finish the whole thing off with a canned-pumpkin pie in a foil pie tin.

These memories—the facts—hold together like they're frozen in ice. I can see them from the outside but can't get anywhere near the people. What I want is to burrow right into Dad's brain, to hear what he's thinking. Or even just to sit next to him and feel the heat of his skin.

• • •

On Thursday I wake up early and join El in the kitchen. The room is half dark, the sun still hovering at the horizon, just behind the tree line. I lean against the dishwasher while El makes me a cup of tea from a jar of dried herbs on the counter. Then she hands me a peeler and a brown paper bag full of apples.

"Any progress?" she asks, dumping cream into her coffee.

"On what?" I say, still feeling only half awake.

"Anything," she says.

Sometimes conversations with El feel like some kind of word game, like I'm just blindly following along, waiting for something to be revealed.

"Well," I say, pulling an apple out of the bag. It's dusty and lopsided and still clinging to a little piece of branch. "My portfolio is getting more and more abstract."

El raises her eyebrows. "Art imitating life."

"Or life imitating art."

"Either way."

She rifles around the cabinet and pulls out the flour. "What else?"

"I've been trying to photograph the trees," I say, looking out the window. "But it's not really working. The light feels so flat. Even when it's not."

El frowns, looking me over. "Maybe it's something on the inside," she says.

There's nothing on the inside, I want to say.

I sip my tea, watching as she sprinkles flour onto the countertop and takes out a disk of pie dough from the fridge.

"What can I do to help?" she asks.

"I don't know," I say. "I'm so lost I don't even know where to begin."

El hands me wooden brush. "Here," she says. "Wash the apples."

"That's it?" I say.

El laughs. "One thing at a time."

She turns on the radio and we finish the pies and then Hannah comes downstairs and we watch the parade. In the afternoon, all five of us elbow our way around the kitchen, making all the sides—hot, fluffy mashed potatoes, buttery brussels sprouts, homemade cranberry sauce—and a golden chicken with crispy skin, in the name of new traditions. Then we sit at the table, which Bea has decorated with candles and dried lavender. The food is steaming in El's ceramic dishes and she sits at the head of the table, still wearing her red apron, with flour on her cheek.

"I'm thankful for you girls," Mom says.

"I'm thankful for my divorce," El says.

"I'm thankful for the Beatles," Bea says.

"I'm thankful for Megan Rapinoe," Hannah says.

When it's my turn I'm suddenly overcome with a wave of sentimentality. "I'm thankful for my family," I say.

"Gross," Bea says.

"You're such a suck-up," Hannah says.

"Fine," I say, rolling my eyes. "I'm thankful for the snow."

LATER, WHEN WE'RE LYING IN BED, THE BLUE LIGHT OF THE MOON on snow coming in through the curtains, Katharine Hepburn asleep between us, I turn to my sister.

"Hannah?"

"Yeah?"

"I wish you could just stay."

She sighs. "I know. I'm sorry."

"It's okay," I say. "It's just that everything is so much better when you're here."

Between us, Katharine Hepburn stirs, lifting her head and thumping her tail on the bed, as if to ask us to quiet down. Hannah reaches over to scratch behind her ears. "That's just because I'm something new. A distraction."

I shake my head. "Most of the time Mom's not here, and Bea won't come out of her room. They fight all the time. I don't know what to do."

She's quiet for a while. Katharine Hepburn jumps off the bed and lumbers out the door, leaving a big space in the middle of the mattress.

"Why do you think it's gotten so bad?"

"I don't know," I say, tugging at the corner of the blanket. "It's like there's nothing holding us together anymore. I don't know how to fix it."

Hannah pulls me over to her side, squeezing me into a tight hug. I burrow my face into her neck and she rests her chin on the top of my head.

"It's okay, Mary. None of us do," she says, combing her fingers through my hair. Then she whispers, extra quiet, "Did you know that for the first two weeks of school I didn't even go to class?" She pauses, and I wiggle out of her arms to look at her face in the moonlight. The shadow of the windowpane makes it hard to read her expression. "I almost got kicked out. But I couldn't bring myself to get out of bed or get dressed. My roommate thinks I'm a total freak."

"Wow," I whisper. I remember that first phone call, how upbeat she sounded, recounting all of the details of college when she'd barely even left her room. "Why didn't you tell us?"

She rolls away, facing the wall. "I don't know. I think I was embarrassed."

I start writing letters on her back, *A, B, C, D*. I wonder if now I'll need to worry about Hannah too.

"What changed?" I ask.

She doesn't say anything for a long time, as if she's gathering up courage for the rest of the story. *This is how you tell the truth*, I think to myself.

She finally says, "I've been seeing a therapist at school, and I'm actually taking medication now. But it still comes in waves, you know?" I watch her side moving up and down with each breath. "I think it will for a while, for all of us."

I nod, even though she can't see me, and then she says, "Don't tell Mom, okay," just like she's said about ten million less serious things.

"I won't," I say, kind of relieved that Hannah has secrets too but also feeling like this is a big one.

I think for a while about my sister, living this whole other life. Taking medicine for depression. I think about how, even with all of that help, she still feels the ebb and flow of sadness just like me. I wonder if there's any pattern to it or if it's just random. I wonder if it will ever stop.

I wonder if Hannah's forgetting, like I am. I wonder what she thinks about the in-between. She's always seemed to know everything before I did, but this feels so mysterious.

"Can I ask you something?"

"Sure."

I take a breath. Hold it. "Did Dad like us?"

She laughs. And I can't tell whether to be relieved or insulted.

"Of course he did."

"I just remember—" I whisper, rolling away to my side of the bed, staring at the half-open doorway. "It just seems like sometimes he didn't."

Out in the hallway, something creaks, loud enough to scare me if I hadn't heard it happen a thousand times before. *Just the house settling*, El always says. This house is always settling.

"I think it's just complicated," Hannah says eventually, and her voice is sleepy like she might drift off at any moment.

"Yeah," I say. "I know."

But she's already snoring softly on her side of the bed, leaving me all alone with my doubts.

21

ON SATURDAY HANNAH GOES BACK TO SCHOOL, AND on Sunday we move into our house in town. I pack up the parts of me that have spread all over El's house, the books and hairbrushes and single socks. I take down the photographs, old and new, New York and California, from the walls of my temporary room. I pack up El's patchwork quilt.

Bea and I ride with El, and we hardly talk the whole way to town. I wonder if she's going to miss us or if she's glad to be alone again.

Our new house is big, way too big for our family of four. All of our California furniture looks strange inside, as if the time in storage has warped it, made it smaller and louder. Who puts a green leather couch into a house from the 1800s? Or a lamp with giant lips painted onto the shade? All of the pieces that Mom and Dad picked out with such gusto, that seemed to fit our kooky Westside bungalow, are totally absurd here.

The floors are obnoxious hardwood; every single board

seems to creak and groan. The cupboards are old and smell faintly of mildew. The ceilings are high and the light pours in, but it's drafty and cold and Mom says the heat costs a fortune, so we have to keep the thermostat at sixty-eight, which is freezing.

Bea loves it.

"This house," she says, "is definitely haunted."

"Just like *Beetlejuice*," I say.

But I'm not scared. After the Ouija board incident, I know that ghosts don't exist.

Sunday afternoon I'm upstairs, sitting on the chilly floor of my new room, staring at the pile of boxes pushed up against my bed. They've been waiting at Public Storage in Albany all these months, and now they are here, ready to be opened.

In California my room was small and packed with ephemera, tchotchkes, photographs, poems. I hadn't even lost anything yet, but already I was trying so hard to remember. This new room is big and empty. Every sound I make echoes around it, reminding me that I'm the only one here.

Bea has been blasting music all day from Dad's record player, which she rescued from the donate pile back in LA along with five boxes of old vinyl. I listen to the Staple Singers coming through the wall, and it feels like, maybe, the months of eerie silence are coming to an end.

It's only three forty-five, but already it feels like my room is getting dark. The white walls glow a solemn thistle color, the shadows long and diffuse.

When I peel the tape off the first box and peer inside, I'm immediately transported back to July, to the late, demoralizing nights spent cramming my life into boxes, Nora and me sitting in the middle of my wrecked room, our legs sticking to the carpet as we organized and reorganized, like maybe if we focused enough on just this one task we could pretend the next part wasn't coming.

"Do you think they have Sephora in upstate New York?" Nora had asked, laying lip-gloss tubes carefully side by side in a box that used to hold my mom's old business cards.

I looked around my room then, at the thousands of little things crowding every surface—pens, photographs, costume jewelry, empty PEZ dispensers—and something inside of me broke.

Nora saw it happen, a flood of tears getting ready to burst through the dam. She sat up straight and snapped the lid back on the business card box.

"Fuck it," she said. "Let's just stuff everything in."

Now, here I am, on the other side, and somehow I haven't called or texted Nora in over a week. I think I've hit my quota on lying; every time I pick up the phone my fingers just stop working. But, god. I miss her.

I sort through the box and its jumble of things I haven't seen in months: binders of old negatives and stacks of prints, yearbooks and old English-class novels, photo booth pictures and broken shells. I pull out these items, one by one, brush my fingers across the surfaces, wipe away the crumbs and dust.

I touch each book and photograph, trying to remember why it was important. But after a while my things start to feel like they belong in someone else's life.

I unpack for a long time, until the sun has completely vanished from the sky and the smell of takeout is emanating from the kitchen. I can hear Mom and El chattering downstairs, but I can't bring myself to join them. Instead I lie on the hardwood floor, staring up at the cracked ceiling, surrounded by snow drifts of my old things.

I'm stuck in between, just like Dad. Here and there, then and now. I can't figure out what I'm doing wrong, but I know for sure that something is not right.

For the first time since leaving LA, I actually want to forget. I want to forget the wild sunsets and the flowers that bloom year round. I want to forget what's happening with Bennett. I even kind of want to forget Nora.

But my old life is where my dad resides. There isn't a trace of him here, not even in the photographs or the weird furniture that's awkwardly trying to fill out our living room. California is where he lived, where his body displaced actual air, moved through real space and time. How can I ever let go of that?

The UCSB application is due today, and I didn't even write the essay. I feel my hold on the future getting looser and looser. I'm not sure if I even mind.

As if to taunt me, my phone starts pinging with a series of texts. They're from Bennett.

Bennett: I'm sorry about last weekend.

Bennett: I freaked out.

Bennett: Can we talk?

Bennett: I don't want to lose you.

And one from Nora.

Nora: Where are you?

I turn off my phone before anything else can come in.

• • •

THE NEXT MORNING, BEA AND I WALK TO SCHOOL. WE TRAVERSE A few blocks of houses and skirt around the football field and then we're there. Even though the air is freezing enough to burn my skin, the walk is a hundred times better than the bus. We push through the front doors of the school, cheeks stinging, out of breath, and I literally feel the new leaf turning over.

In English class, Jesse looks at me and smiles.

After school, I walk around town with my camera, taking pictures of the gray sky and the dirty white houses. I blur the landscape like Uta Barth, and everything becomes a soft gradation of white and brown. By the time I reach the co-op, my fingers are burning from the cold.

I push open the heavy doors and Jesse's the only person in there, leaning against the checkstand, reading a magazine. His body is a thing of beauty draped so casually like that, his brown hair tucked back behind his ears. His lips are turned downward in concentration, like a wilted heart.

He looks up and I see the jolt of recognition ruin the perfect scene. But I'm sick of this dance we're doing, from across every room we're in. So I approach him cautiously, trying to smile.

"Hey, Jess," I say, the abbreviation tumbling out in a weird attempt at familiarity.

But it works, and the corner of his mouth slides upward, his body settles back into the lean.

"Hey, Marigold," he says.

"When's your shift over?" I ask, still having only made it halfway across the room.

He looks at the watch on the back of his wrist, and I wonder at the perfect curve of the round bone there.

"A couple hours."

"Come for dinner?" I say, and bravery tips the next words out. "I miss you."

His face stretches in the strangest way, my words working their way across it, but it doesn't leave any discernible sign of his reaction.

I want more from him. Even though I don't deserve it. I wish everything wasn't happening so out of order.

"I want you to see my new house," I say.

"Sure," he says. And it feels like he's smiling, even though he's not.

"Awesome," I say, scribbling down the address on the back of an old receipt.

* * *

As soon as I'm out the door I run all the way home. When I get there, I streak past Bea, who is lying on the couch reading *Jane Eyre*, and up the stairs, telling her, "Jesse's coming for dinner," as casually as I can. But it comes out kind of frantic, half hysterical laugh, half yell.

When I get to my room I survey the sad piles. Then I start heaving things into boxes. Forget my old life. Jesse Keller is coming for dinner.

I arrange some shells on my windowsill, tack up some photographs, make my bed with my fluffy down comforter, and lay El's quilt over the top.

Carpe diem, it says.

Yes.

Mom texted earlier: It's gonna be a late one, and for once I'm actually glad she's not here. I boil some water and dump a jar of pasta sauce into a small pot as Bea eyes me from the kitchen table.

"Jesse's coming for dinner," Bea says as she wiggles her eyebrows up and down. "Hubba-hubba."

"Shut up."

She picks up her homework, smiling creepily, like a cult leader. She's wearing pink today from head to toe, and looking at her without the heavy black eyeliner I'm reminded of how young Bea is, how all of this being alone must be so hard on her.

"I'll give you two a little privacy," she says. She starts to turn, but I stop her with my hand.

"Don't be stupid. I want you to eat with us."

She steps back and spins her pen around her finger. The pen cap is pink and fluffy, just like her sweater. "Really?"

"Yeah," I say. "Just don't embarrass me."

A sly smile creeps from one pale cheek to another. "I make no promises."

• • •

Twenty minutes later Jesse arrives, bringing a gust of cold into the kitchen. He's wearing his usual jacket and beanie, and his cheeks are red from the winter air.

"Let me take your coat," Bea says.

"Oh, uh, sure," Jesse says, and then there's this awkward little dance as he tries to twist out of it. Bea's standing slightly too close, her arm outstretched like a butler.

What are you doing? I mouth.

Being polite, she mouths back, rolling her eyes.

"Thanks," Jesse says, handing over his coat. He leans down to pull off his boots while she rummages in the closet for a hanger.

"We're just so glad you're here," Bea says, winking at me.

I open the fridge and bury my head inside of it, pretending to look for the parmesan cheese, which is already on the counter. I'm trying to tell myself to *just be cool*, but I'm so scared of blowing it again, and why has Bea suddenly turned her quirkiness all the way up to ten?

We sit down at the table, and luckily Jesse tucks right into his food, shoveling in mouthful after mouthful of steaming pasta, seemingly unaware of my nerves and Bea's over-the-top hospitality.

"Wow, Marigold," he says after a while. "This pasta is really good."

Bea raises her eyebrows and gives me a thumbs-up under the table, and I try not to cringe.

She sighs. "She was working on it all afternoon."

I grimace. "I wasn't. Jesus, Bea, you are so weird." For a second I imagine walking away from the table and locking myself inside the coat closet, right next to Jesse's jacket, but then he turns to Bea with a dazzling smile.

"Hey," he says, "I finally started listening to *My Favorite Murder*. It's kind of amazing."

"Right?" Bea says, her own smile turning kind of shy. "Did you hear the episode about the Kentucky meat shower?"

Jesse shivers. "Gruesome. What did you think, Marigold?"

"I'm taking a break from gore for a while," I say.

Bea pushes back from the table and winks at me again. "This has been fun, but I gotta go finish my homework."

"Is something wrong with your eye?" I ask.

"Nope," she says. "I was just trying to—"

"Never mind," I interrupt, pushing her toward the door with all of my mental force. "Let me know if you need any help."

"Bye, Jesse!" she says, and then, thank the lord, she turns and starts skipping down the hallway.

"See you later," Jesse calls, laughing, then he picks up his fork and takes another huge bite.

• • •

WHEN WE'RE DONE EATING, I CLEAR THE TABLE AND JESSE STARTS on the dishes. I try not to stare as he unbuttons his cuffs and rolls his shirtsleeves up to his elbows. But I do, and it must be minutes before I jolt back to life, thinking, *That's not what this is about.* Because he's here. In my kitchen. His laugh sounds real again. And I'm not going to mess this up.

We load the rickety dishwasher together, and it feels like we're back in the darkroom, like we're synchronizing our movements. It almost feels like music is playing, even though it's not.

"How's your family?" I ask, squeezing detergent into the dispenser.

"Okay," Jesse says. He stops to dry his hands on a towel. "My mom threw her back out right before Thanksgiving, so things were kind of a shit show for a few days. My break was basically spent stocking snow shovels and trying to pacify Maggie and Fin with old episodes of *Mister Rogers*."

"*Mister Rogers*?"

Jesse grins, wiping down the counter with a dishrag.

"My parents are kind of weird about television. *Mister Rogers* is pretty good though, once you get into it. Trippy." He laughs. "Riley loves it."

"Huh," I say, trying to imagine Jesse and Riley, who is the captain of the soccer team, on the Kellers' enormous couch, watching children's shows from the nineties.

"Maybe you just need to experience it for yourself," he says, sweeping some crumbs into the sink. His hair is falling into his eyes again, making him a little hard to read.

We finish cleaning up the kitchen and then linger for a while by the doorway. Neither of us has gotten Jesse's coat yet, and I'm trying to think of excuses for him to stay. His phone dings and he pulls it out of his pocket to read the notification, frowning a little.

"Ry wants my physics notes," he says, right as I finally get the guts to ask, "Do you want to hang out for a while?"

It's awkward for a second as all of our words crash together.

"Oh," I say, reaching for the door of the coat closet. "You should probably go do that then."

"Nah," he says, and he slides the phone back into his pocket. He looks at me with his old smile, the one that's like the sun. "It can wait till tomorrow."

• • •

UPSTAIRS, I SIT ON MY BED AS JESSE DRIFTS AROUND MY ROOM, eyeing my things, looking through stacks of old prints and picking up seashells. Behind my closet door, a tower of half-empty boxes waits, but out here the space feels sparse and quiet.

Jesse stands at the wall of my prints, staring at all of the disembodied arms and legs and teeth and eyebrows.

"Why do you take pictures of parts of things?" he asks.

I watch the light spreading over the back of his flannel shirt, soft on soft. His shoulders rise and fall with his breaths, graceful and even.

"Because it feels like something," I say. "Even when nothing else does." I'm surprised by how easy it is to tell the truth when he's not looking right at me.

"What about you?" I ask. "Why street photography?"

He picks up one of my seashells, gently smoothing his thumb over the back of it. "Because it makes me feel like I'm going somewhere," he says. "Even if I'm not."

He puts down the shell and pulls at his sleeve. I try to think of a way to respond, but nothing fits.

"Look," he says carefully, still turned toward the wall. "I'm over what happened if you are."

"Yeah," I say, even though I'm worried that I'll *never* get over what happened between us. "Can we be friends again?"

"Friends," he says slowly. "Yeah, I'd really like that. But—" He finally turns around to look at me. "Let's be honest with each other, okay?"

I nod and look down at my hands, tracing the love lines, trying to think of something honest to say. Bennett's texts from last night are still there on my phone, unanswered, unresolved. And I don't think I want just friends with Jesse, even though I said otherwise only a second before. My feelings about everything are so tangled up it feels like he's already caught me in a lie.

Finally I say, "I missed you. A lot."

He sits down next to me, a respectable distance away, and I want him closer.

"Yeah," he says, clearing his throat. "Me too."

In her room, Bea puts on a record and the Beatles come floating through the wall. We lie back on my bed, across it with our feet on the floor, and listen: "Hello, Goodbye," "Strawberry Fields Forever," "Penny Lane." Jesse is drumming along with his fingers on his legs, and I'm keeping my breaths slow and steady, pretending that the four inches between us isn't making my arm hair stand on end.

I want to reach over and run my finger the length of his arm. I want to trace the curve of his upper lip, the shell of his ear, the slope of his nose. But I know I can't. I probably never will.

More than ever before, I wish I could just let go of Bennett. Of everything. I wish I could just sink down into this. Jesse in my big, half-empty room.

I try it for a minute and then another. I move into another part of my mind where nothing else exists.

I'm nearly asleep when Mom knocks on my door. The record is finished and we've just been lying in the quiet.

"Oh," she says when she sees us. "Hi, Jesse."

He leans up on one elbow and half waves. "Hi, Jane."

She frowns a little, crossing her arms. Her reading glasses are pushed up on her forehead, like she just stopped working.

"You two should probably keep this door open when you're in here."

"Sure," I say, sitting up. "Whatever." I try to think of the last time she told me what to do and come up completely empty. "I didn't hear you come home."

"I've just been working downstairs," she says, gesturing behind her.

She's still in her work clothes, but they're wrinkled now; her hair is coming undone.

"Did you eat?" I ask, trying to figure out if she looks any smaller. For a while after Dad died, Mom was most definitely shrinking.

"Yep," she says, nodding absently. And honestly, if anything, she looks a little bit rounder at the edges. "That leftover pasta was great," she says. "Thanks."

"Good," I say, sizing up the circles under her eyes.

"Anyway," she says, like my inspection is making her uncomfortable. "Jesse should probably head home soon, yeah?"

When my mom pads back down the hall, Jesse rolls his head to the side and looks at me with sleepy eyes.

"Darkroom tomorrow?" he says.

And the edges of the world start to soften and everything but Jesse Keller seems to disappear.

22

I HAVEN'T DREAMED ABOUT DAD IN AGES, WHICH DULLS one ache and worsens another. But Bea keeps talking about him. Ever since the thrift store she brings him up in subtle ways, always in the conditional, as if he were almost still here:

Let's listen to something Dad would like or—

What do you think Dad would order for dinner if he were at this restaurant right now?

I play along, continuing to shape this new-old Dad, one who lets himself belong to us, in my mind:

Actually, I think Dad would roll over and die all over again if he were forced to eat in a restaurant called the Burger Den, I say.

That or he would die from the effort of trying to read through all of the items on the menu, she says. *It's a frigging novel.*

How can there be fajitas, meatloaf, and stir-fry all at the same restaurant? I say in my Dad voice.

Get in the car, girls, we're going to Wendy's, is Bea's reply.

Mom doesn't participate. She's home more and more, colorful and smiling, but sometimes it seems like she can't even hear us.

. . .

THE NEXT DAY, IN THE DARKROOM, JESSE IS DIFFERENT. He obsesses over his portfolio. He prints and reprints, adjusting the enlarger times by a second, then less. He agonizes over what to keep in and what to take out. Outside, we can hear his brothers and sisters shrieking in the snow. I watch him with a kind of envy and wait for my own apathy to lift.

"What are you thinking?" he says.

"About what?" I ask, thinking about all of the messed-up half-truths that are hiding in my messed-up brain.

He looks at me forever before he says, "College."

I shrug, feeling like my skin is too tight. Last night, in my room, everything felt perfect, but now there are sharks in the water again.

"I'm working on it," I say, even though I'm not. The lie makes me think of Nora, which makes me feel a little unsteady on my feet.

I want to just be honest with him. I promised I would. But it's hard to watch him struggle so much, to want so much—applying for every scholarship he can find—when all I feel is profound confusion.

I don't even recognize myself these days. In California my life was a continuous thread, each part connected to the next. Here I'm a pile of incongruous impressions. Failing. Forgetting. Falling apart.

An image emerges in the tray of developer: a reflection of a blur of a part of nothing.

• • •

THE DARKROOM IS HEAVY, BUT EVERYWHERE ELSE, THINGS WITH ME
and Jesse are so light.

"There's a party on Saturday," he says mid-lope in the hall a
few days later. "Think you can handle it?"

"Get over yourself," I say.

He tugs at a strand of my hair.

"Not until you get over me."

My face flushes, and I pull at the neck of my blue wool
sweater.

"You're an idiot." I gaze off down the hallway with its sea of
upperclassmen until it becomes an abstract thing, an undulating
series of waves. "Actually, I think I'm over parties for right now."

"Fair enough," he says, his smile still light and mischievous.
"What should we do?"

"We? You're so presumptuous."

"Me and the patriarchy," he says, and I can't contain the
laugh that slips through my teeth.

Somewhere, deep down in the bottom of my backpack, my
phone starts vibrating. I think about Bennett, who has been
calling every day this week, and suddenly feel like my head is in
a vise.

"How about a movie?" Jesse says.

I try my best to ignore the subtle vibration of impending
doom and say, "You've found my weakness."

Jesse looks at me for a long time. "If only that were true," he
says.

• • •

AFTER SCHOOL, I RIDE THE BUS OUT TO EL'S HOUSE, TROMP through the crust of old snow covering her yard, and flop down on the studio couch. The tiny room is peaceful and quiet, except for the whir of the space heater and the trickle of water at the sink, where El is cleaning her brushes. Inside, my emotions are loudly clashing, lightheaded excitement and steel-toed guilt.

"You're smiling," El says. Busted.

I try to sound nonchalant as I say, "I think I have a date with Jesse Keller. Or maybe it's not exactly a date." I pause, replaying the conversation in my head, the feeling of Jesse's hand, in slow motion, reaching for my hair. "But maybe it is? I can't tell."

El lets out a little yelp and pumps a fist in the air. "Yes! I was rooting for you two."

Then she turns and studies my face a little more, taking off her apron and hanging it on the wall. Today she's wearing white from head to toe. If she stepped outside she'd blend right in.

"You're also sort of grimacing," she says. "What's going on?"

I look up at the ceiling and all of its feathery cobwebs, feeling duplicitous. I wonder if I should just go live with the spiders.

"Things with me and Bennett are still a little unresolved."

"And . . ." El says, hands on her hips, waiting for more.

I pick at my black fingernail polish. "I'm not sure what to do."

"Huh," El says, arranging the brushes in her dish rack. A loud bunch of crows flies across the square of window, interrupting the quiet. "Well, what do you want?"

"I don't know," I say, burrowing my chin down into the neck of my sweater. "Sometimes it feels impossible to let Bennett go. But I like Jesse too." As I say it, a smile sneaks, uninvited, back across my face. "I really, really like Jesse."

El sighs. "Sounds like quite a tangle." She comes over to the couch and perches on the edge.

El has always been a self-proclaimed love-triangle expert. Her high school years and most of her twenties were seemingly full of escapades and entanglements. When we were younger she loved to tell us stories about frenzied marriage proposals and awful first dates while Uncle Mac would sit in the corner of the couch, still as a stone, frowning into his book.

I wonder if she'll tell me a story now, something to make this all feel silly, but she just stands back up after a moment and says, "Although I bet if you were really honest with yourself, you'd know what you want."

I close my eyes, feeling tired. Every time I open my mouth it seems like another half-truth comes out—to Jesse about Bennett, to Bennett about Jesse, to everyone, even myself, about college, as I barrel toward deadline after deadline I know I'll never make. The lies keep piling up and it's hard to imagine ever shoveling myself out from under them. "Be honest with myself. That sounds hard."

El laughs out loud. "The hard part is being honest with everyone else."

* * *

On Friday, I wake up and the world is white. School is canceled and work is canceled, and I pull my covers over my head and hide for a long time.

Bea has been sleeping extra late, barely making it to school on time, and I think she might be sneaking in and out of her window at night. She feels closer these days and also further away. She'll lie with me for an hour watching cat videos, snuggled into the crook of my arm, but she won't tell me any of her secrets.

She's still not really talking to Mom, but she's more polite about it. When Mom asks her a question she'll answer with one or two words and then wait until Mom's back is turned before scowling or rolling her eyes. Sometimes I wonder if Mom even notices the anger glowing right underneath the surface. She doesn't seem to notice anything as much as she used to.

When I get down to the kitchen, it's just Mom and me. I study her as she moves around the room, making pancakes, humming Rod Stewart. She looks so much like herself: reading glasses sliding down her nose, loose strands springing out of her top-knot, lips in a tight line of concentration. But something about her is utterly different.

"How's work?" I ask, handing her a measuring cup.

"You know?" she says, looking up. "I think I'm finally settled. Not quite one of the guys, but I'm working on it. How's school?"

I smile and try not to imagine the ten unread emails from Ms. Simpson right at the top of my inbox. "It's good. Just trying to get ready for my finals."

Mom nods, sifting the flour. "Did you get your UC application in?"

I spit out yet another lie, "Yep," and turn toward the stove, hoping to hide my grimace. It's been so long since I've talked to Nora, since I've told the truth to anyone. I feel like an ostrich with my head at the center of the earth.

But Mom is oblivious, cracking the eggs and carefully stacking the shells on the counter. "You know, I'd be happy to help you with the others if you want. I could read over your essay today if I get through these depositions."

I step into the dining room to grab the napkins, pausing to catch my breath right outside the kitchen door. "Actually," I call through the doorway, "I know you've been busy, so my English teacher's been helping me out. They're practically done. I think I'll throw up if I have to make one more change."

Lie lie lie. I'm buried so deep in them I can't see the sun anymore.

Mom chirps, "Okay, love. Let me know if you change your mind." And for a second it kind of blows my mind how easy it is to keep this going.

I step back into the kitchen, napkins in hand, and busy myself with setting the table while Mom works at the stove. I make a silent promise that tonight I'm going to sit down and think. Figure it all out, or at least some of it.

I get the orange juice and syrup out of the fridge, and Mom brings over a plate of pancakes that look a little like misshapen bricks. Their consistency is kind of like glue, but I pretend not to notice. For a while we sit at the table and trade sections of the local paper, eating and talking about what a travesty the world is becoming. It almost starts to feel like *before*.

I read aloud a letter to the editor with the title "Blue Lives Matter." It's ranting and racist and it makes me shudder. LA has its own kind of racism, but you wouldn't see a letter like that in the *LA Times*.

"How did we end up here?" Mom says.

And I almost say, *You. You blew up our life.*

But instead I say, "It sure is surreal."

After breakfast I put on my parka and boots and try to photograph the snow, but it feels too white, too reflective, too foreign today. I can't tell if I'm trying to remember or forget anymore.

All day, El's words echo through my mind: *The hard part is being honest with everyone else.*

But I'm not just thinking about Bennett and Jesse. I'm thinking about Nora.

. . .

When I've done everything I can think of, unpacked and reorganized my boxes, finished my homework, spent an hour making wacky outfits from my recent vintage finds, I finally slink to my room and unearth my forgotten phone from under a pile of prints on my desk.

There are seven texts from Nora and three from Bennett. Ouch.

Nora's last text says:

I'm worried about you.

And Bennett's is only slightly better:

Still alive?

I cringe. I've been a horrible friend. The worst coward.

I sit down on my bed, next to a quilt square that says *Today is the day!* and I pull up Bennett's number. I start with the easiest apology, hoping to work my way up:

Me: I'm sorry I haven't texted you back.

It's one o'clock in California. I wonder if Bennett is in class, if I'll have to wait for his reply. But almost immediately I can see he's writing something back, and then it pops up on the screen: No worries.

And then I write about a million different things:

You mean a lot to me but I can't do this anymore.

I want to be your friend.

I met someone else.

Call me.

Again and again I type the truth. Every time I delete it.

Finally, I give up and write: I love Eucalyptus and then hit send.

He sends me back a photograph of just his lips, smiling wide.

I sit for a long time, phone in hand, letting myself fill up with shame. And under the shame is a layer of heartache that's so strong I almost can't breathe. I miss my friends. I miss myself. I don't know if I like who I'm becoming. Then I scroll back through Nora's texts, forcing myself to read them all.

Are you okay?

Did something happen?

Where are you?

I read the ones that came before that, all of times I let her go on about UCSB without saying anything. I should have told her a long time ago. After the darkroom, when I felt the very first streak of doubt. That's what she would have done.

I find her number in my favorites and press call. It rings seven times before she answers.

"Hello?" she says. Her voice is flat. Zero exclamation points.

"Hi," I say, and now my heart is fluttering in my chest. I feel like I have a murmur or maybe I'm having a heart attack, but either way it's hard to say anything.

"What's up?" she says, and it sounds like she is doing something else, like watching TV or scrolling Instagram, only halfway here.

I want to pull her back to me, but I'm not sure how.

"Nora," I stammer.

"What?" she says, sounding a little irritated now. I wish she would just get all the way mad, yelling and screaming at me. It's what I deserve.

I try to think of what to say next, how to begin. *I've been lying to you for months* feels impossible to say.

"I'm sorry," is what I come up with instead, a generic Band-Aid that feels entirely insufficient. I lie my head back on my bed, following the hairline crack that spreads out from the corner of the ceiling with my eyes.

"For what?" Nora says, anger finally starting to creep into her voice.

"For everything," I say, feeling like a coward.

"Everything what?" She sighs. "Look, I'm a little busy right now. I just wanted to make sure you're okay because I haven't heard from you. But I should go."

"Wait," I say. It's now or never. "I have something to tell you."

Nora is quiet on the other end, but she doesn't hang up.

This is it. My ears are ringing. I follow the line on my ceiling back and forth, as though trying to hypnotize myself. And then I say it, each word dropping like a heavy stone.

"I didn't apply to UCSB."

Silence. I can't even hear her breathing. One million hours pass between my admission and Nora's response, each of them painful and hopeless. In my mind I shrink down, slip into the crack, disappear forever.

Then, finally:

"Okay."

I wait for more, but nothing else comes.

"Okay? That's it?" I can hear the desperation in my voice. It sounds pathetic.

"Yeah, that's it," she says, and I can already feel her receding. "Look, I have to go."

And then she's gone. Just like that.

• • •

THAT NIGHT, I HAVE A DREAM, STANDING IN OUR OLD KITCHEN, MY head against my father's thick, warm chest, which is full of cancer, breathing in the scent of sweat and the damp dish towel on his shoulder. I wake up, in the pitch-black middle of the night, grabbing at the cold winter air.

23

IN THE MORNING BEA IS UP EARLY, BLARING THE VIOLENT Femmes. Saturday: my date with Jesse, the first day of life without Nora. It's funny because we weren't really talking for weeks, and everything sort of seemed fine. But now I'm not fine at all. Inside, I feel lopsided, like a whole part of me just up and left when I wasn't looking.

I knock on Bea's door and it's a long time before she peeks out, pushing the tip of her nose through a sliver in the doorway.

"What?"

"Let me in, loser."

"No."

But I'm bigger than her, so I reach up and push the door open, forcing her to the side. I walk right over and flop onto the bed like she invited me.

"Where have you been?" I ask, thinking about last night and the night before that but also about the way that she hasn't been inside her eyes lately.

"Out," she says, closing the door and walking over to the bed.

Bea's room in the new house is a little smaller than mine, but it's still huge and full of light and cold air. Everything is lavender—bedspread, lampshade, rug. We even painted one of the walls.

Her records have taken over most of the room, stacked on the floor in piles that stretch the length of the longest wall. Dad's record player sits on top of two milk crates in the corner. It makes me jealous, the way Bea's room is full of Dad and mine is empty.

"You know," I say. "Eventually Mom's going to come back online and you're going to be in trouble."

"I'd like to see her try," Bea says, lying back next to me, crossing her arms. "She's basically missed a year of my life."

I turn my head to look at her profile. She's staring at the ceiling, making one of my favorite Bea faces, the one that lets a little bit of light in, nostrils flared, like she's willing herself not to cry.

"I know," I say, my hand inching over until it's a millimeter away from hers. She pulls at a thread on the comforter. Her cheeks are pink.

"You know why she's doing this, right?"

"Doing what?" I say, annoyed that Bea is deflecting, right when it felt like she might open up.

"Late nights, weekends. Tuesday nights with us and Wednesday nights at work."

I think about the blue circles under Mom's eyes, all of the little signs that she could be drowning again. "I think she's just struggling right now."

Bea's raspy voice is hard when she says, "Keep telling yourself that, Mare."

I turn my head to the ceiling and lie quietly for a while,

watching the bands of light bending up through the thick window glass. In my mind, I take a photograph.

Next to me, Bea sulks and seethes. Sometimes I envy her relationship to anger, so straightforward and clear. But other times it seems like it's eating her alive.

I pick up a strand of her wavy lilac hair, wrap it around my finger.

"What's going on with *you*?" I ask.

"Me?" she says. "I'm fine."

"You're never home anymore."

"So?"

I try to think of something convincing to say. Something sisterly that she won't hate. But I know that there's no way to ever outsmart her.

"Just be careful," I say.

She rolls her eyes. "I will."

I sit up, feeling like I'm missing a page in the manual they give big sisters on how to avoid calamity. Maybe Hannah accidentally took it with her when she left.

"You want to go downstairs and watch a movie?" I ask, a last-ditch effort.

"Nah," Bea says. "I'm good. I have some stuff to do."

"Fine," I say.

"Good talk," Bea says.

Then I slink back to my room to waste the afternoon.

For a few hours, I drown my sorrows in three episodes of *Top Chef* with no Nora on the other end of the line. It's still morning in California, and she is probably at station 26, bobbing up and down in the freezing-cold water.

The night my dad died, after we had talked to a million social workers and gathered our things from the ICU waiting room— late, when everyone else had gone to bed—Nora came to pick me up. We drove around in circles, through the long, flat streets of our neighborhood, and when I couldn't stop crying she pulled over and held me and said, "I've got you," again and again and again.

Nora and I have ridden out hundreds of heartbreaks together, both of our families falling apart, boys ripping out our hearts, all kinds of rejections and disappointments and failures. No one else but Nora will ever know what Dad looked like, shrinking in that hospital bed. I'm worried that I've ruined the most important friendship of my life.

I feel obsessed with the question of what happened, of what's going on with me. Last night, every night, I've tried to think about next year. I google lists of colleges, art schools, gap-year programs. I look at hundreds of websites, thousands of photographs of people my age who know what they are doing. But I don't feel like any of them. I don't feel like anyone.

• • •

JESSE PICKS ME UP AT SIX AND WE DRIVE AN HOUR TO THE THEATER that shows art films. All week long there's been an energy between us, the space just filling and filling, until it's overflowing like a broken sink. It's filling up the car now too, and I have to crack my window and let in the sharp December air so that some of it can escape.

I watch the landscape roll by, the lonely farmhouses and hillsides of naked purple branches. In LA the winter was rain and oranges. Here it's crisp snow and diffuse light and air so cold it creeps in through all of the seams.

"What did you do today?" I ask, watching Jesse tap his fingers against the wheel.

"I babysat and then worked on some scholarship applications," he says. "It was pretty dull. How about you?"

"Same," I say, my fingers tapping too.

He raises his eyebrows.

"You worked on some applications?"

"No," I say, laughing. "I mean my day was dull."

"How's it going though?" he asks.

"Better," I lie.

In that moment, I want to open the car door and throw myself right out.

• • •

WHEN WE GET TO THE THEATER, JESSE TRIES TO BUY MY TICKET. But then the bored-looking twentysomething at the counter says, "That will be thirty-seven fifty," and his whole face turns white.

"What," she says, snapping her gum. "It's a double feature."

"I've got it," I say, grabbing two twenties from my wallet. "Feminism and all."

Jesse's face goes from white to red and he gently pushes my hand away from the counter. "No," he says. "I'm good."

I feel trapped, like there isn't any way forward that won't ruin the evening. But then Jesse smiles his Jesse smile and says, "You can get the snacks," and we are out of the rough patch, sailing smoothly again.

I get us popcorn and candy and soda and we are practically the only two people inside the theater. We sit in the exact center and our voices seem to echo into every corner, even when we whisper. So we just sit quietly, swimming in electric tension, until the lights go down.

The first movie is *Raging Bull*, a black-and-white film about a boxer who moves as gracefully as a ballerina. Halfway through, the black and white breaks into a color section of home movies shot on Super 8. The whole world transforms; the young wife jumps into a sky-blue swimming pool.

"See?" I whisper. "How could you not love color?"

He turns to look at me, and a wash of brilliant grass green reflects off his cheek.

"You're winning me over."

"Me or the movie?"

His lips stretch into an easy smile.

"Both."

He tilts his head. Something about the way he's looking at me sends pins and needles down the length of my spine. It's one move in a series of moves in a week-long game of checkers, each hop having nudged the line between us ever so slightly toward the unknown.

For the rest of the first film, I'm overwhelmed by Jesse's physical presence beside me. He shifts and swallows, crosses his ankle over his knee, bumps my leg and tenses. The inches between us feel stiff with potential energy, a rock at the top of a cliff, the ground crumbling.

We're ten minutes into the second film, *Goodfellas*, the end of the second excruciating and sweet hour of sitting side by side in the darkness, when his arm brushes mine on the armrest and stays, pressing against me from elbow to wrist. He's wearing a flannel shirt and I'm wearing a fuzzy cardigan, but I swear I can feel his hot skin, even through all that thick fabric. On the screen, a young Henry Hill runs from a row of cars he's just set on fire. In the darkness, my cheeks burn.

The next few minutes pass by in a blur of color and breath and the press of Jesse's arm. And then he lifts his hand and curls his pinkie through mine, like he's making a promise.

Everything stops, except for the pounding of my heart in my ears, which drowns out Ray Liotta's voice blaring through the speakers.

And then his hand is moving to cover mine, and somehow, by some magic, my hand is turning itself palm upward. It happens in the slowest of motions, like a lunar landing, the way his hand touches down on mine, all of the fingers in just the right places.

And then we're holding hands, for real, in the dark.

For the next hour, I am consumed by the point of contact between us. Jesse adjusts our hands so he can stroke my wrist with one finger. I move mine so I can trace the lines on his palm. He tucks his thumb up under my sleeve and my pulse flutters against it.

When the movie is over we look at each other with starry eyes and stumble out to the parking lot, holding hands until the engine turns on and Jesse has to put the car into gear.

It's late, and the ride home is long and quiet. The moon is a tiny crescent and it follows us, trailing out my window, making a stream of light in the snow.

We're almost there when my phone rings. It's Bea. Normally

I wouldn't answer, but Bea never calls me unless she needs something. And she almost never needs anything from me these days.

"Hello?" I say, and my voice feels too loud as it breaks the sleepy silence. Jesse's eyes flicker over, from the road to me and back.

"Mary?"

Her voice on the other end is hard to hear. It sounds slow and strange, like a warped record. Like she's drunk. Her breathing is heavy because maybe she's holding the phone too close. It's loud in the background, music and the talk-yelling of drunken kids.

"Where are you?"

"I'm at Matt's house." She says it like it's a question, like she's already forgotten the place where she snuck her stupid self out to and managed to get wasted at.

I'm annoyed, but a swell of worry is rising in my throat. "Are you sure?"

"Maryyyyy," she says, like a half-asleep valley girl. "I don't feel good. I need you to come rub my back."

"Jesus." I try to keep my voice steady, but I'm starting to freak out. "I'll be there in ten minutes. Don't do anything stupid."

I hang up and look at Jesse, feeling the magic seeping out of the moment like air from an old pool float.

"We have to get Bea. I'm so sorry. Do you know where Matt's house is?"

He nods and puts a heavy, warm hand on my knee.

"Don't worry," he says. "We got this."

He drives the rest of the way as fast as one can while being careful of ice and deer. We pull up at the house and it's a rager cliché—beer cans and cigarette butts all over the front porch, some ridiculous Top 40 song blasting onto the lawn.

I open the door, and to my relief, she's right there on the couch—there will be no frantic search through a house full of my drunken classmates. Her head is lolling to the side, trying to bop in time with the music, and her eyes are halfway closed. Her three-quarter-sleeve lime-green dress looks rumpled and is riding up her thigh.

Domino sits on the arm of the couch, talking to Lenny, the third in their ridiculous crew. Both girls have their long, claw-like fingernails wrapped around cans of hard cider. It's like they barely notice Bea is there, fourteen years old, seconds away from passing out.

I stride over to the couch, anger flaring in my cheeks. For a moment, even with Jesse right behind me, I'm so mad I forget to be embarrassed. I shake my head at Domino and Lenny. "Seriously?" I say.

Then I turn to Bea and grab her hands. "Time to go, Bumblebee."

"Mary," she says, stretching the word like bubble gum. "You came."

"Yup," I say, unable to look at Jesse, who I can feel standing right behind me. I give her hands a yank. "Time to get up, buttercup."

She heaves forward, and after swaying a bit, she manages to stand with some support. Jesse creates a path through the bodies that have suddenly started swarming the living room to dance to some song everyone loves. I follow behind with Bea leaning on my shoulder.

We're out the front door and down the steps before she

suddenly crouches down in the snow and says, "Hold my hair, I'm gonna puke."

I look up at Jesse with hot cheeks and shake my head.

"It's okay," he says. "I'll be in the car."

I gather her smooth lavender hair into my fist and rub her back while she vomits clear liquid into a puddle at her feet.

"I'm sorry," she mumbles. "I'm sorry."

It's only half a mile to my house, so we manage to make it home without any more puking. But Bea is sleepy by the time we get there and more ornery than before.

"I'll just sleep here," she says, sitting on the porch steps. "It's cool."

"You'll freeze to death, doofus," I say, "and then Mom will come out here in the morning and ground your dead body."

"I don't care," she says, closing her eyes. "She's probably not even here."

"I got it," Jesse says, tugging me aside by my coat sleeve.

"Ready, Bea?" he says.

"For what?"

Then he crouches down and picks her up, like she's one of his many little sisters, gently cradling her in his arms.

Bea seems to fall asleep almost instantly, snoring quietly into his shoulder, and he somehow gets her up the stairs and into her bed without waking my mom. I get a washcloth and wipe her face while Jesse grabs a mixing bowl from downstairs to leave by her bed. When she's all tucked in we stand in the doorway and high-five.

"I'll probably end up sleeping in there," I whisper. "But I've gotta go get my pajamas."

Jesse nods and says, "Walk you to your door?"

And I thank the universe that he is still being sweet after an hour with my crabby, vomit-crusted little sister.

We tiptoe down the squeaky hallway to my bedroom. He stands on the threshold leaning with his arm above my head, looking like a cowboy/movie star in his plaid flannel shirt, and our bodies are just inches apart. We'd be breathing the exact same air if he weren't ten feet tall.

"Marigold," he says, and he draws it out, lingering on the vowels. I watch his chest move in and out, closer to mine and then farther away.

"Yeah?"

"Break up with him."

I tip my chin upward so I'm looking in his eyes.

"I already did."

The twinge of guilt from the lie is small and sharp. But it feels more like stretching the truth. Bennett and I are over. I just haven't been able to say the words yet.

And then whatever force that's been keeping Jesse and me separate snaps like a toothpick. His hands are in my hair and mine are in his and we crush our mouths together in this way that feels a little unhinged, like we might never get the chance to do this again. But—

Oh my god, his lips feel good on mine.

We're moving backward into my room and he slams the door shut with his foot in this way that is somehow totally silent. And I'm not surprised because I'm realizing that Jesse does everything exactly right: taking pictures, picking flowers, talking about T. S. Eliot, walking through the hallway, kissing. Especially kissing.

My knees hit my bed and we topple over onto it, banging heads and laughing against each other's teeth. He pulls back just enough to smile and say, "Sorry."

And then the kiss completely changes. What was once wild and desperate and a little bumbling becomes painfully slow and sweet, a hundred little kisses and then a few deep ones and then he takes my bottom lip between his teeth and it changes again, into this haze of heat and want.

His hands are both sliding up under my sweater, under my shirt, and I don't even think before I'm tugging it all up over my head, tugging his up over his curls. I can feel the button of his corduroys, sharp against my belly. I can feel his chest, hard and warm against my skin.

I want to say *Wow*.

But I can't because we are kissing again and his tongue is sliding into my mouth; his hands are everywhere and I couldn't get a single syllable out if I tried. My bra is gone and we're under the covers before I can even think. All that exists is kissing. All that exists are Jesse Keller's hands on me.

And then—

Wait.

"Wait," he says, right as I'm thinking it, and I don't know whether to be relieved or crushed, but another part of me wants to cry in frustration.

"Your mom," he says.

"Bea," he says.

And then he says, "I've never done this before."

"I don't believe you," I say, thinking of the way his fingers finessed the clasp of my bra.

"No. I mean yes. I've done this before. I just haven't done what comes next."

Oh.

"Okay," I say. He's tracing the line of my collarbone with a long pointer finger, and I'm trying to pretend I'm not still breathless.

"To be clear," he whispers in my ear, "I want to. With you." I shiver. "Maybe in this very bed."

I nod, vigorously. *Yes, Jesse Keller, I want that too.*

"Just maybe when your mom isn't home."

I nod again, speechless from the little kisses he's pressing to my eyebrow, the circle he's traced around my belly button.

"And maybe when this"—he motions between us—"has had a little more time to sink in."

"Okay," I say, unable to come up with any more words right now.

"I like you, Marigold. I really, *really* like you."

I smile. "I really, *really* like you too."

"Then it's settled."

He presses one more kiss to my lips and then pushes up from the bed. It sends a little gust of cold air over me and I burrow down under the covers.

"Night, Marigold," he says, and I'm mesmerized by the way his long fingers push the little shirt buttons back through their holes. If I were brave, I'd reach under my bed for my camera and swallow up the lamplight glinting off his square fingernails.

"Night, Jess," I say, closing my eyes as the door to my bedroom clicks shut.

As I stumble around my room, lips still stinging, looking for my pajamas, a little seed of guilt starts to take root. But I push it down, down, down, not willing to ruin the feeling of Jesse finally being mine.

Tomorrow, I promise myself. *I'll talk to Bennett tomorrow.*

24

ALL THE NEXT MORNING I FLOAT AROUND LIKE A lovesick cartoon character, my feet drifting inches above the ground, a little circle of hearts flying around my head. Bea, in contrast, is a thumping, grouchy, hundred-pound rhinoceros. She's pale yellow with gray circles under her eyes, and even the lavender of her hair seems faded.

"Are you okay?" says Mom, who somehow is completely ignorant to the many transgressions of her daughters in the past twenty-four hours.

"I think I'm getting sick," Bea moans, and she lumbers back up to bed.

I know I should lecture her, as is my big-sisterly duty, but I can't bring myself to do it and kill this high I'm riding. I made out with Jesse Keller last night. In my bed, which still smells like a forest at Christmastime.

I almost text Nora about a hundred times before I remember

that we aren't speaking. It's still strange that things like this can happen to me without her knowing.

So I settle for Hannah instead. When I text her the news, she does not disappoint, sending an entire screen full of emojis and about a hundred gifs of people freaking out.

I mean of course he wanted to kiss you, she says. You're the best person I know.

At this, the guilt threatens to bubble up again, and I scroll over to Bennett's name. But then another text comes in.

Hannah: Don't overthink it.

Hannah: I can practically hear your brain melting down

So I put it off for an hour. And then a few more.

• • •

EL'S BEAT-UP SUBARU PULLS INTO OUR DRIVEWAY AT NOON, AND she honks the horn.

"Let's go, Sullivan girls!" she yells.

She's been in and out, dropping off pots of soup and bouquets of cedar boughs, but it's been weird not having her around more. I feel like she was the anchor, keeping us all from floating out to sea.

"I hope you've got your long underwear on," she says to a sulking Bea as we all pile into the car.

El's got this plan to "really do the holidays" this year. I think it's because last year was the most depressing Christmas ever. Mom was working all the time, so Hannah and I drove Bea to get a tree. The three of us decorated the house and bought each other presents. We baked and frosted hundreds of cookies that dried up, stale and crumbling on the counter because nobody felt like eating.

El flew out the day before Christmas Eve and she tried to lift our spirits, but it was her first Christmas since the divorce, and under the thin layer of cheer, we were all just too sad. We put on the movies and listened to the music and pretended we weren't dead inside. But everything was just a replica of itself. Nothing felt like anything.

Apparently the first step in really doing Christmas is getting a tree. El drives us out to a tree farm that looks a lot like a regular forest, and we hike through a foot of snow with a bow saw and toboggan. El says that this is the authentic way to get your tree, rather than driving to some lot in downtown LA with hot tree farmers who carry your Douglas fir to the register, but I'm not sure I agree.

We hike for what feels like forever, Mom and El leading the way, arguing over the trees. Bea and I struggle along behind them, whining like puppies.

"How about this one?" Mom points to an enormous tree that's got to be at least six feet tall.

"It's too big," El says. "It'll take up half the living room."

"That's the point of living in a house with twelve-foot ceilings!" Mom argues, and in their exchange I catch a glimmer of what they must have been like growing up.

Mom turns to us and says, "What do you think, girls?"

I shrug.

"I'm freezing." Bea says. "And I don't really care."

Mom looks at us, frowning. "Come on, girls, just have an opinion."

"Fine," I whisper under my breath. Then I paste a smile across my face, even though I can't feel my toes. "I think it's perfect," I say.

"All right!" Mom says, beaming.

El insists that we all have a turn sawing at the tree trunk. When it's mine and I'm lying down there, in the cave of sharp needles, my cheek pressed to the snow, I'm surprised at how good it feels: the sound of the saw against the trunk, the feeling of sweating in the freezing cold under a tree that smells like Jesse.

We finally get the tree back to the checkout area, and the man at the counter eyes our crooked cut and gives us a condescending smile. He's young, maybe twenty. He's wearing a bright orange hunting jacket and he's got a cigarette dangling between his lips.

"Let me straighten that out for you, ladies."

El bristles.

Mom rolls her eyes and says, "No thanks, we're happy with it."

And then she walks right on over to the car without looking back.

• • •

THAT'S HOW WE END UP, AN HOUR LATER, WRESTLING IN THE LIVING room with a tree that badly wants to topple over and kill us all. It takes all four of us to hold it up, even once we've gotten it into the stand. El rummages around the garage for some gardening wire, which we wind around the top of the tree and then around the curtain rods for stability. But it's still crooked, and now a couple of the upper boughs have broken off, leaving a hole.

Mom brings out the Christmas box, and Bea and I work at

the obnoxious amount of tape at the edges to pry it open. It's stuffed with ornaments and tangled lights and littered with tinsel, and there's something about the feel of the cardboard, the smell of the dust, the messy way the word *Christmas* is scrawled on the side in Dad's handwriting.

For one shimmering second, the ineffable feeling of home hangs in the air: lounging on the green couch, surrounded by crumpled wrapping paper, eating peanut butter cups and watching Dad curse over assembly instructions. And then the heat clicks on and it's gone.

I close my eyes, trying to stretch it out for one more second. I want to say, *Bea, did you feel that?* But the memory is already back in the void, if it was even a memory at all.

We decorate the tree and drink hot chocolate and play the original *Very Special Christmas*, the red one with the Keith Haring drawing on the front and the Bruce Springsteen song, Dad's favorite.

Bea invents another game: What do you think Dad would say about this fucked-up Christmas tree?

Maybe it's just hungover.

We should have left it out on the lawn.

I always wanted to be that guy who died in a freak Christmas-tree accident.

• • •

LATER, I TEXT NORA: CAN WE TALK AGAIN?

I don't even know what I would say, but I miss her. I hate myself for doing what I did. And the worst part is that I don't even know why I lied. I think of all of the applications that I haven't started, am never going to start. I imagine Nora at UCSB orientation, without me. It makes my stomach hurt.

• • •

THAT NIGHT, I CAN'T FIND MY BRASS CHARM BRACELET, THE ONE that Bea is always stealing. When I poke my head into her room, I catch her sneaking back in from the roof, one pajama-pant-covered leg slung over the windowsill. She smells like cigarettes and the cold.

"What are you doing?" I ask, my arms folded across my chest, shivering a little.

"None of your business," she says, jumping to the ground.

"Seriously?" I ask. "It's been less than twenty-four hours since I rescued your wasted ass, and you're, what? Sneaking out again? Smoking on the roof? How stupid can you get?"

Anger swirls through my bloodstream, into my cheeks.

"What are you, Mom?" She slams the window shut behind her but a chill lingers, fighting the warmth of the lamplight. She laughs. "She's probably not even home right now. It's Sunday night, right? She's probably *working*."

"What does that even mean?" I ask, feeling like I'm missing the thread somehow.

"Nothing," Bea says, throwing the cigarettes into the back of her desk drawer.

"I just don't get why you're always pushing it, Bea," I say, shaking my head.

"Yeah, I know." She sits down on her bed, pulls off her jacket. Her voice sounds tired. Old. "You don't get me. You probably never will."

I walk to the door, feeling like I might explode if I stay in here a second longer. "Whatever it is that you're trying to fix, you're just making it worse."

She shrugs. "Yeah, maybe that's the point."

●　●　●

LATER, IN MY ROOM, I'M TRYING TO TACKLE THE FIRST THIRTY pages of *Swann's Way* for English, but really I'm thinking about Jesse. The paragraphs are thick and the sentences are long and circular, and my thoughts keep pulling back to the feeling of his hands on my skin.

And then, as soon as I sink down into that feeling, the thought of Bea climbing through the window breaks in, like a bucket of ice water over my head. It feels like she's one spin away from something big, and Mom thinks that coming home for dinner three times a week and getting a giant Christmas tree is somehow going to fix it. I want to grab her shoulders and shake as hard as I can. I want to say, *Snap out of it.*

I pick up the book again, I plod on, past swirling thoughts of Jesse and Bennett and Nora and Bea and Mom, as Proust perseverates on his childhood bedtime for almost all of the section. And it's exhausting, but after a while I think somehow I actually get what he means. I think I understand the way he's clutching at his past. It reminds me of how my fingers get sometimes, tight and shaking on the lens of my camera.

When I was younger, ten or so, I used to have these dreams about my father. He'd be in his study, working like he did, only one day he'd stop coming out completely. I would climb into the orange tree in our backyard to try to peek into the window, past the hanging fuchsia plants and the hovering hummingbirds, past the old, wavy glass in its teeny panes. I could see that he was building some hulking thing out of metal and wires.

I'd carefully climb down the trunk and tiptoe through the dry grass, over to the door, knocking quietly.

He'd crack the door and peer out, with glazed eyes and a dreamy smile.

"What are you building, Dad?" I'd ask.

"A rocket ship," he'd say.

"Why?"

"I think I'm just ready to fly away."

The rest of the dream would change every time. He'd stay in his study and I'd sit among the roses in the garden, devising a plan to ruin the ship, or I'd sneak in through the window and steal all of his wrenches, or I'd run into the house and search every room for my mother. And then he'd lock the doors, cover the windows, buy new wrenches. Every dream was a race, him versus me. I'd always wake up before I knew who'd won.

25

I'M PRETTY SURE MOM AND DAD WERE IN LOVE, BUT lately I've been rethinking the bedtime story.

There was this one time, on a road trip to Montana when I was ten, when they were fighting so badly that she told him to leave her by the side of the road in the middle of Reno, Nevada, and he actually did it. Really, there were a lot of times like that.

There were good times too. Matching Halloween costumes and kissing in the kitchen while Bea shouted, "Disgusting!" Even if I can't remember them, I think there were times when Dad was really there.

But happily-ever-after just seems so definite. In real life, maybe they would have made it and maybe they wouldn't. The thing about the ending that we got is that we'll never really know. On some level, they're just suspended in time forever, stuck in 1995, lunging toward each other over a birthday cake that says *Happy Birthday James* but never really getting to the kiss.

• • •

MONDAY AT SCHOOL, I STILL HAVE HEARTS IN MY EYES BUT I'M TRY-ing to be cool. I wear my wool skirt and black tights like I did that night in Jesse's room, and I count the minutes until English class.

When I get there, Jesse is as perfectly long limbed and non-chalant as ever, and halfway through the discussion he passes me a note that says, *You're beautiful.*

On the way to lunch he holds my hand, and just before we get to the doors he pushes me into a tiny alcove and kisses me full on the mouth. His tongue tastes like honey. I forget where I am.

Until I get to the table and my phone vibrates with a text from Bennett: Have I told you how much I love Unicycles? I jam it down to the bottom of my bag. Jesse looks at me and frowns.

All through lunch, Sam seems just as lost as we are. It's like we're three little clouds floating around the table.

"There's something different about you," I say.

"There's something different about *you*," she replies.

Under the table, Jesse squeezes my hand.

• • •

BEA AND I WALK HOME AFTER SCHOOL AND MOM IS THERE, ALREADY making a big dinner. She's got a chicken tied up, ready to go into the oven, and she's peeling potatoes, humming along to the radio. Even though it's weird, the feeling of her in the kitchen, with the heat on and Christmas music playing, hits some deep and long-forgotten part of me.

I think, *This is why we moved here.*

Beside me Bea rolls her eyes as if she can read my mind. Devil child.

"Need any help?" I ask.

"Nah," Mom says, opening the oven. "Why don't you girls go get your homework done so that we can just relax at dinnertime?"

"Sure thing, Mommy dearest," Bea says, in a voice that's full of stinging nettles.

• • •

BACK UPSTAIRS I'M STRUGGLING TO FOCUS ON PROUST AGAIN, AND my brain is once more wandering into memories of Jesse's eyelashes and teeth and earth-brown eyes, how he kissed me at his car this afternoon, my back against the cold metal door. But I feel like there's some vital truth about my life to be uncovered in this book.

I think about the way my old life is disappearing. There's this big, dark void at the edge of my mind where California used to be. The more I try to remember, the bigger the void becomes. I know that the empty space is where my father would go, where cracked sidewalks and skinned knees and lemonade stands would go. I've been trying to hold on to that space for the memories, willing them to come back.

But my new life keeps filling it in. Every day it fills up with fresh snow, hot baths, kissing, creaky hardwood floors, giant windows edged in ice crystals. Every day there's less and less room for him.

I'm almost at the end of the chapter when I find the passage:

And so it is with our own past. It is a labour in vain to attempt to recapture it: all the efforts of our intellect must prove futile. The past is hidden somewhere outside the realm, beyond the reach of intellect, in some

material object (in the sensation which that material
object will give us) of which we have no inkling. And
it depends on chance whether or not we come upon
this object before we ourselves must die.

I read the paragraph again and again. And something about
it crushes me. I think it's the thought that all of my efforts have
been for nothing, that my dad will continue to disappear whether
I try to remember him or not. That it's out of my control. That
maybe, by sheer luck, I will someday find some forgotten object,
some forgotten taste or smell that will conjure him back, multi-
dimensional, fully intact. And maybe I won't.

I sit back in my chair and try to rub the stars out of my eyes.
I'm so sick of crying. Then I shut the book and shove it into my
desk drawer.

● ● ●

Mom calls us down at exactly six. Bea and I thump down the
stairs, our footsteps in time, and I wonder if she's feeling as heavy
as I am.

Mom's set the table with yellow placemats and lemon-printed
napkins, and she's filled our plates with chicken, mashed potatoes, and roasted green beans. Outside the snow is brown and
half melted, but inside the kitchen glows.

I sit down and try to ignore the Proust-shaped hole in my
heart. I pick up my fork and knife. I cut little bites, chew, swallow.
I try.

The eating part of dinner is mostly quiet. Mom tries to ask us
a few mom questions like:

How was your day?

How is school going anyway?

What are you up to this weekend?

And we give teenage answers like *fine* and *okay* and *nothing.*

But the conversation keeps stalling. There's this tension in the air and I can't place it.

Finally, my mom puts down her fork, and just as it clatters against her plate she says, "I need to talk to you girls about something."

Everything stops. My heart, lungs, brain, fingers holding on to my knife. The last time she said these words was the beginning of the end of everything.

I look at Bea, who is stirring her fork around her mashed potatoes, looking down at her plate and shaking her head, not at all surprised.

"It's not bad," Mom says, playing with her napkin. I notice that her hair is down today and it's almost grown past her shoulders. "It's—"

There's a long pause. A forever-long pause. A Grand Canyon–sized pause that fills me up with dread.

"I met someone," she finally says, so quietly it's like she's whispering.

Immediately, the mashed potatoes turn to concrete in my stomach. A block of ground-up, hardened sand.

"What?" I say.

"I met someone," she says, as if I really didn't hear her. "I met a—guy." She sounds like she's literally choking the last word out.

In her seat, Bea smiles a weird smile. "I *knew* it," she says. She sounds vindicated and sarcastic, but underneath it I can tell she's disappointed.

Then my mom just starts rambling through the entire thing in these short little sentences.

"He works at my firm. His name is Jake. He's really amazing. He has a daughter who goes to Sarah Lawrence, Mary."

This last little piece, directed at me, as if to win me over, jolts me awake.

"He works at your firm?" I ask, and there's something unrecognizable in my voice, like it's coming from another person.

Suddenly, all of the obsessing, the mapping of schedules and meals, the counting of hours, the searching of my mother's face, snaps into focus. And I feel so ridiculous. I thought she was floating away from us. And she was. But she wasn't alone. She wasn't lonely.

She's been lying to us this entire time.

"Must be serious if you're finally coming clean," Bea says. Her face is flat, unaffected, perfectly bored as she sculpts little hills and valleys into her food.

Mom opens and closes her mouth for a few false starts before she says, "It is."

I feel dizzy, like the earth is turning much faster than usual. "I need to—" I can't finish the sentence. I set my fork down quietly, push back my chair, and walk out of the room, up the stairs.

• • •

THE NIGHT OF DAD'S FUNERAL WAS THE LONELIEST I'VE EVER FELT.

Hannah, Bea, and I were piled on the couch watching *Real Housewives*, but I was somewhere else. This layer of gauze had been hanging around me like a mosquito net, making the world fuzzy and distant. The characters on the TV buzzed like flies, and I couldn't understand what they were talking about.

Mom walked in, looking exhausted, and grabbed the keys out of the little ceramic bowl by the door.

"I'm going for a drive," she said. "I'll be back in a while."

Something about the way she said it made my heart sink. Bea shifted against me, pinching my leg with her spidery fingers.

"Promise?" she said.

Mom's eyes misted over. "Of course," she said. "I'd never leave you."

• • •

BEA KNOCKS ON MY DOOR A WHILE LATER, BUT I DON'T ANSWER.

I can't get over the fact that she knew and didn't tell me. Is that how far apart we've drifted?

I feel more alone than ever, all the way out to sea. But somehow, instead of feeling sad, I feel a strange sense of calm.

All fall I've been trying to hold on tight. My sisters, my mom, my memory. And now, with this last lie, it feels like there's really nothing left to do.

I listen to Mom doing the dishes in the kitchen, creaking her way up the stairs, washing her face. I listen to Bea thumping around her room, The Zombies coming through the wall. My phone buzzes next to me on the bed, with message after message from Hannah.

Mom just told me

Are you okay?

Call me if you want to

I lie awake all night long, feeling the strange nothingness in my guts.

• • •

I watch the next day come, washing shades of gray into the night-black sky. There's no pink or purple at all, just slate and ash, a blanket of clouds from horizon to horizon. I let it dampen everything: Mom's footsteps on the stairs, the sounds of coffee making, Bea's alarm.

Then I roll out of bed, pull on jeans and a black hoodie, shuffle down the hall, and wash my face and brush my teeth. Underneath everything, all the way at the bottom, I can feel a layer of anger start to form.

I don't want to talk to anyone today, not even Jesse. But he's there in English, smiling like a goddamn jack-o'-lantern. The sun is practically shining out through his teeth. When he sees my pale, emotionless face, my tired, puffy eyes, and my sad outfit, the light dims. He scratches at the back of his neck.

"Still coming over today?" he says.

I imagine a post-Saturday darkroom where last night has not yet happened, one where we are distracted into leaving our prints in the developer too long. It feels somehow impossible.

"I don't think I can," I say, drawing big circles on the front of my notebook with my pen.

I avoid Jesse's puzzled face and turn to the front as Ms. Bell walks in, hidden as always behind papers and books. Inside my head, I'm screaming at myself to turn around and talk to him. *Jesse is good*, I think. *Really, really good.* But I'm just so tired and the truth is that *I'm* not good. I've already screwed things up way too much. And now that everything else is exposed, I can finally see it. We are doomed.

And then class begins and then I remember Proust, the last bit of nothingness, still buried at the bottom of my desk drawer. All year I've been searching like an idiot for the truth about my dad. But there isn't one. Now I know that. Because of that stupid fucking book.

I can't sit here and listen to everyone pretending like they know anything about what it's like to really remember or what it's like to really forget. So I try to shut everything out. Ms. Bell asks a question about the book and I stare out the window and count the cars driving by on the road in front of the school. I watch as the anger starts to creep toward the surface. It almost feels like it's happening to someone else. I watch and I try to coax it back down, to stuff it back into its box.

But then I hear Jesse say, "The past is dead. Maybe forever."

And I turn to see him, lounging back in his chair like it's nothing.

"What?" I say.

I almost never speak in English class, even though it's one of my favorites. Now, suddenly, all eyes are on me. Everyone can see my unwashed hair and the rings under my eyes.

Jesse shrugs, a little awkwardly, trying to silently ask me something. I look at him without emotion, waiting for him to continue, needing to hear it.

So he keeps talking, looking down at his desk. "I mean, he's obsessed with the past and he writes so many words, but in the end it's all nothing. None of his memories are authentic. It almost feels pathetic."

That word, *pathetic*, has been simmering under the surface of my brain all night. It's the only word for it, really. I forgot California. I forgot my dad. Nora. The ocean and the orange trees and pollution-bright sunsets. It feels unforgivable.

My ears are ringing. I feel like I'm going to throw up.

Stop, I say, in my head. Or maybe I say it out loud. It's impossible to know.

But everyone is truly staring at me now.

"What?" Jesse stammers, his cheeks turning red.

Suddenly everything feels like too much. The lying. The forgetting. The way everything keeps twisting around and around.

"Can you just stop?" I say. "Just stop talking."

I think he says something back to me, but I'm already up out of my seat and through the door. I want to make a quiet getaway, but the sound of me feels like it's echoing everywhere, like there are a hundred girls running down the hallway, blinded by tears.

Of course there is no way to outrun Jesse, who is part forest creature, and before I can get to my locker he's in front of me, blocking my path, out of breath with his hands on his knees.

"What is going on?" he says. He sounds concerned. Confused.

The tears in my eyes start pouring down my face, and I can't even figure out why I'm crying. I feel like a roll of film that's been left in the sun, all the way exposed, completely opaque.

Jesse puts his warm hands on my cheeks, and I could almost melt right into him. I could fall asleep, right here, on my feet. Wake up when things are a little less confusing. But then a wave of sickening anger crashes over the top of the exhaustion.

Somewhere in my mind I know that I'm not angry at Jesse. I'm angry at Mom. I'm angry at myself. But that little voice in my head that's always saying, *Keep it together*, is suddenly whispering, *Burn it down*.

"This is a mistake," I say, stepping backward, out of reach.

"What's a mistake?" Jesse says. He's looking at me like I'm a perfect scene that's one twist out of focus. Like he can't get me to match up with myself.

"Everything," I say. "I wish I'd never come here."

He winces a little, like he's been kicked in the side, but I can tell that he is still trying to be sweet. I can see the emotions wrestling all over his face. So I try to make it easy.

"I've been lying to you," I say. "I'm not applying to college."

"Okay . . ." he says. His brow is crinkled and his eyes are unreadable. I remember the way he made me promise to be honest, and I wonder if I've finally pushed us over the line.

But then, just in case, I say, "I didn't break up with Bennett either. I mean, we were never really together but we also never really . . ."

Jesse's face falls, all the way down.

"I have to go," I say.

And still, even after all of that, he reaches out and grabs my hand.

How does this already feel so familiar? I think when his long fingers thread through mine. And then, *What did I just do?*

"Marigold," he says. And his mouth opens and closes like he's trying to think of something to say. His eyes are impossibly big and lost. He's a million miles behind. I can see him struggling to catch up.

"I'm really sorry," I say, already regretting what I've just done. Part of me wonders if it would be possible to just sit Jesse down, right here in the hallway, to explain everything and ask for forgiveness.

But there's this itch under my skin that's growing more unbearable by the second. It's telling me to *move*.

So I untangle our fingers and walk away, leaving Jesse stunned in the middle of the hallway. Then I go to my locker, get my backpack, and make my way out the back door of the school.

I stop in the parking lot, head pounding, suddenly out of breath. I forgot my coat, and I'm shaking in my hoodie and jeans. The cold forms a film over the outside of me. I have no idea where I'm going.

And then it comes to me: I need to go to California.

That's when I see Sam's car pulling into the parking lot. She swings around the rows of cars, stopping next to where I'm standing by the double doors outside the gym. She rolls down the passenger window and says, "Get in."

"What are you doing out here?" I say when I'm inside and defrosted enough that I can move my mouth. We're driving around the lot in circles, from the gym to the soccer field and back again.

"I had a dentist appointment," Sam says. "Are you okay?"

"I don't know," I say. "I think I need to get out of here. I think I need to get out of Cumberland."

"Okay," Sam says carefully.

On the next circle, she moves her car to the exit, then turns left, out onto the street.

"Do you want to talk about it?" she says.

I shake my head.

•••

We stop by my house, where I haphazardly pack a bag of clothes, already having forgotten what December in California is like. I shove my camera into my backpack along with my beat-up copy of Proust. On the way to the Albany airport, Sam watches me nervously, out of the corner of her eye.

"Were you really at the dentist?" I ask, trying to shift her attention.

She laughs. "No. Are you going to tell me what happened?"

Despite everything, I laugh too. "No."

So we drive the rest of the way without really talking, just watching the trees fly by to the sound of the radio. When we get to the airport she leans over and hugs me across the gearshift.

"Thank you," I say into her hair.

I've waited to buy the ticket with my emergency-only credit card until I'm at the airport, to buy myself time, and I text Mom right before takeoff. I'm in the air, already a thousand miles from New York, before I think of Bea.

● ● ●

My phone is full of messages when I land at LAX.

There are ten from my mother, and I delete the entire conversation without reading any of them.

There's one from Nora, who is coming to get me even though I don't deserve it: meet u at baggage claim.

One from Hannah: call me okay?

And one from Bea: Fuck u

26

NORA IS THERE AT THE BAGGAGE CLAIM LIKE SHE promised, looking like she always does, wavy black hair spilling down her back, a neat white crewneck sweatshirt tucked into dark, slim jeans cut just above the ankle, flip-flops, big sunglasses. I never realized it before, but the look—the flip-flops in the rain—is so California.

She surveys me in my dirty sneakers and old black sweater, snarled hair and puffy eyes, and pulls me in for a hug.

"You all right?"

I nod, trying not to cry in the middle of LAX. "It's good to be back."

She lets me go, grabs the handle of my roller suitcase, and steers me toward the parking garages. I follow, a few steps behind.

Nora is quiet as we thread our way through the crowded airport. She walks fast; all of her attention seems to be focused somewhere ahead of us. We're pushing through the heavy glass doors of the exit before she finally turns to me and says, "Okay. What happened?"

And then we walk into the parking garage and the air hits me with the damp chill of a rainy day. California December. The smell of wet asphalt. The sound of traffic and seagulls and squabbling crows. I'm home.

"Let's get coffee first," I say. "Then I'll tell you everything."

Nora digs her keys out of her bag and leads me to where her rusty orange Beetle, Mary Jane, is parked between two BMWs.

I slide my hand along Mary Jane's fading paint as Nora opens the trunk, and then we have a little tussle over who will lift my suitcase inside. Nora wins and she slings my bag into the trunk, and somehow this one act, her carrying my suitcase, feels like it's going to sink the entire ship of guilt.

The traffic is the same, Lincoln Boulevard jammed like a clogged artery all the way to Venice Beach. The rain clouds are a uniform gray skin on the sky. It's quiet in the car, the weeks of silence weighing heavy between us.

I watch the world creeping by the window, the fruit sellers braving the December rain, the jumble of car wash and smog check signs, the wet and drooping palm trees. It's all just like it was last winter and the winter before that. I take a picture of the raindrop-covered window with a blurry LA in the background, and my heart feels heavy like a sopping-wet sponge.

We go through the drive-through at the Coffee Bean, and Nora orders the usual, a mocha Ice Blended for me, a latte with two sugars for herself. The entire time she seems so quiet and contained, somehow farther away even though I'm finally sitting beside her.

When we're back on Lincoln, in the slow parade of traffic, I turn to her and say, "I'm so, so sorry."

She adjusts the wiper speed, faster and then slower, as though we actually need a clear windshield to inch along at twelve miles per hour.

"I don't want to do that yet," she says. "Just tell me what happened."

I hate her slightly robotic tone of voice, reminding me that I've ruined everything. But she obviously doesn't want to talk about us right now, and I owe her an explanation for why I just showed up here. So I put my hand over my eyes and say it for the first time. "My mom is seeing someone."

"Shit," Nora says, swerving a little. She always drives with her hands at ten and two, but she takes one hand off the wheel and grabs mine.

"Yeah," I say, turning her hand over and touching her short, neat fingernails. "It's just. It's not even that, really. It's that she didn't tell us. She's been sneaking around this whole time. Working these long hours. And meanwhile everything is falling apart."

Recounting what happened, I feel the rush of stupidity all over again. Thinking my mom was struggling like the rest of us when really she was just falling in love.

I let go of Nora and touch the cold window. Ever since this morning, I have been literally and figuratively hurtling through space and time, just trying to get away, and now I can feel myself bracing for impact, about to hit the wall.

"I don't know what I'm doing with my life. I don't know who I am. Everything is so fucked up."

And then I say, "I forgot my dad." And finally, tears come.

I lean my head forward onto the dashboard, embarrassed to be crying like this in front of Nora, whom I have neglected for months on end.

She eases the car over to the turning lane and turns into the Ralphs parking lot. Then she parks in a spot in the back near the dumpsters, takes off her seatbelt, and puts her arms around me. We sit like that for a long time, heat blasting out of Mary Jane's vents, right at my forehead, Nora's head resting on my back.

I forgot how good this feels, crying out half of the Pacific Ocean in the front seat of Nora's car. I feel loose, boneless, strung out and sleepy.

"I missed you," I say, and immediately Nora stiffens.

"Yeah," she says. "Me too."

But she's let go, is already turning back toward the steering wheel, out of my grasp. I realize then that she's been crying too. She looks out the window for a minute, at the overflowing dumpster, wiping her face with the back of her hand. Then she sits up straight and starts the engine again. She backs out of the space, looking over her shoulder, and then pulls out onto the street.

The silence is even heavier than before, and the heater starts to feel oppressive. I roll down the window, letting the rain inside.

We pass the turnoff to Nora's old neighborhood, and I watch the street sign shrink in the mirror.

"Mom finally sold the house," Nora says. "She's actually in Seoul for a month visiting my grandparents, so we have to stay with my dad. But that's better anyway because he's way too oblivious these days to manage returning you to your mom."

"Your mom sold the house?" I ask, momentarily stunned. She's been planning to sell it for years now, ever since the divorce, but it was one of those things that seemed like it would never actually happen.

"Yeah," Nora says, changing lanes, the fact clattering between us as if to emphasize how far apart we've grown. I imagine Nora moving like I did, boxing up her things. I want to know how it was for her, how it felt, but I've missed my chance.

Nora's phone buzzes on the dash.

"It's probably my mom," she says. A look of frustration flits across her face. Nora and her mom are usually enviably close, and I wonder what's happening between them now. Again, I am overwhelmed by how many things I wonder about Nora, how much I don't know anymore.

As we drive, the distance between us yawns, stretches, grows by miles. I want to say, *I'm sorry*. Again and again in a loop until the end of time. But it doesn't seem like I've earned it.

My own phone starts buzzing in my backpack, cutting through the silence. Nora looks over as if to ask if I'm going to answer, but I shake my head. The way she grips the steering wheel as the phone vibrates again and again into the quiet car makes me realize how many times I've done the same thing to her.

• • •

Nora's dad's place is a bungalow near the canals in Venice Beach. This neighborhood is nothing like where Nora grew up in Marina del Rey, with its wide, flat streets and big stucco houses. The streets here are tiny and the houses are all wild colors, Yves Klein blue or lemon yellow, or minimalist white with postmodern furniture and ornate cactus gardens.

We pull into the garage of the tall, black, boxy house, and

park next to Craig's black Porsche Cayenne.

"Dad takes his motorcycle to work now." Nora rolls her eyes as she pulls my bag out of the trunk. "What a fucking cliché."

We dart through the rain to the side door and into the kitchen, which is on one side of a giant open area. Most of the house is part of this one room, under this huge, vaulted ceiling. There's a loft above us and a tiny hallway off to the left that leads to the bedrooms.

I've only been to Nora's dad's house a few times. He's always had Nora every other weekend, and she'd disappear into his world, hanging out at the recording studio or going on surfing trips up the coast. I was always a little jealous when Nora recounted their adventures, even though there was something a bit lonely about them.

Nora drops my bag on the floor by the door.

"You must be tired," she says. "Or hungry?"

She opens a drawer and throws a stack of takeout menus onto the counter. My stomach growls, and I realize that dinnertime on the East Coast has come and gone. But I hate the way that Nora is buzzing around the kitchen, barely meeting my eyes, so I just say, "I'm good."

She gives me a look and takes out her phone. "Let's get a pizza."

Nora orders, and then we stand in the kitchen and wait for the food to come, eating grapes off the island and watching as the sky gradually darkens through the enormous back windows.

It's weird hanging out in Craig's house, this sleek, masculine space with exposed beams and chrome appliances and guitars hanging everywhere. Nora's mom's house was colorful and cozy, with fresh flowers on the kitchen table. We would lie out in the backyard on hot afternoons or watch movies on a giant sectional sofa in the basement, feeling like time was infinite, like our lives would go on like that forever.

"I can't believe that both of our houses are gone," I say.

"Yeah," Nora says, opening a drawer of utensils. Again, her voice is devoid of any real emotion. She starts taking things out and putting them back again, right side up, each thing in its place. She throws out a packet of spicy mustard, a plastic container of red chili flakes. She gathers the menus into a neat pile. Nora is usually messy, relaxed, leaving stacks of books everywhere and throwing her sweatshirts onto the back of the couch. Watching her organize the entire kitchen without looking at me once feels jarring.

"You should text your mom," she says. "So she knows you're safe."

I want to shake her, to dump the utensil drawer onto the floor, to do something that will bring her anger back to the surface. I want her to yell right in my face. But instead I nod and I dig my phone out of my backpack.

There are three more missed calls from Mom, two from El. I text them both in a group thread: Made it safely. With Nora now. Call you tomorrow. As soon as the message sends my phone starts vibrating in my hand. I'm tempted to stuff it back into my bag but Nora is watching, so I answer and slowly bring it to my ear.

"Marigold?" El says. "Jesus. What the hell were you thinking?"

At first I'm surprised by her anger. El is the ultimate advocate for doing something big. And these past few months it felt like she was squarely on my side. But as the seconds tick by, I realize that I've played this all wrong.

"I don't know," I say, feeling lost again.

El doesn't say anything back. I imagine her sitting at the kitchen counter, a mug of tea in her hands, watching the crows.

I want to say, *I was forgetting*, but instead I ask, "Did you know?"

"I did," she says.

"Why didn't you tell us?" I ask, feeling betrayed.

"It wasn't mine to tell."

I'm stunned by the frankness in her voice, by how sure she seems to be that she's done the right thing.

"You should call your mom," she says, softening a little. "She's really worried about you."

"I know," I say, and my stomach is in knots just thinking about it. "I just can't. Not yet. Can you let her know I'm okay?"

"When are you coming home?" she says. Something rustles in the background. I can picture Bernie, jumping onto her lap.

"I don't know," I say honestly. "I won't stay long."

From across the kitchen, Nora wipes the countertops, which are already sparkling clean.

• • •

When we wake up, Nora's dad is already gone. Even though it's a school day, we loaf around for a while, making cinnamon toast and watching TV.

"Dad will cover for me," Nora says. "He's way too caught up in this new project to care."

She's still barely talking to me and I'm still too chicken to try to force anything out of her, so the morning is quiet and awkward.

After a while, we walk to the beach. Nora brings her surf-board, and I sit in the sand and watch as she paddles out into the waves.

I've missed everything about this beach: the grit of sand in my teeth, the steady crash and suck of the waves, the overflowing garbage cans and colorful litter. But even as I pull my hood up to cover my wind-aching ears, it's hard to feel like I'm really here.

In my backpack, my phone vibrates again.

El: Call your mom

Me: Soon

Then I open a fresh text to Jesse. Type: *I'm sorry.* Delete it.

I lie back in the sand and look up at the low clouds moving against the higher ones, gray over gray. I feel ridiculous for thinking that coming here would actually fix anything. I'm just as numb as I was before, just as lost and confused and angry. Only now I'm also in trouble and have ruined any chance I ever had with Jesse.

Nora comes back, dripping and shivering. She strips out of her wet suit and into a thick towel and fuzzy swim parka. We sit side by side for what feels like forever, quietly watching the waves.

"You lied to me," she finally says, after a hundred years have passed.

"I know," I say, burying my toes in the sand. "I wish I could take it back."

Next to me, Nora is perfectly still.

"I just don't get why you couldn't talk to me about it, if UCSB isn't what you wanted. It would have been okay."

"I know," I say. I think about the fall, about every time I could have brought it up and didn't. It all feels like a blur of forgetting and lying and trying so hard to hold things together. "It wasn't about you, it was about me. All year I felt like I was keeping this secret from myself. From you and everyone else too. But from myself first."

Nora sighs. "I knew something was wrong," she says. The hard line of her composure seems to break, finally, and her shoulders slouch away from her ears. "But I didn't know how to get to you. And then things started getting hard for me too. And—" She turns her head to face me, and in the cloudy gray of the morning, the sadness in her eyes is bottomless. "I get that you don't need me anymore, but I still need you."

"I'm sorry." I pick at my fingernails, chipping at the remnants of polish. I hate that I've broken us apart like this. I can't believe I've been so wrapped up in my own disaster, in my own life—Bea and Mom and Jesse and photography and Sam and drawing outside and the weather and the leaves—that I forgot to make sure that Nora was okay.

"I'm so sorry," I say. "I do need you." I feel more tears threatening, but I blink them back. "It's just, if I let myself think of California when I have to be stuck in New York I die of loneliness."

Nora turns and looks back out at the ocean. "I know," she says quietly. "But this year has been hard for me too. You left and Bennett kept doing his own thing and I felt like I didn't have anyone. My mom got really wrapped up in selling the house, and Dad was being Dad. Most weekends I just hung out by myself, in my room, doing homework and watching TV." She pulls her wet hair away from her face, tying it back with the rubber band that's always around her wrist. "And then you called and told me that the one thing I'd been looking forward to, the one thing that made everything feel like it was going to be okay, wasn't going to happen anymore."

"I'm so sorry," I say again, wishing I could travel back in time. "I wish I had known how you were feeling."

I feel like a jerk saying it. There were so many times that Nora told me she was doing fine but I knew better. I just couldn't be bothered to dig any deeper.

"I know," Nora says, wiping her face with the back of her hand. "I get it. I do. I just want you to know. It hurt."

I nod, wanting to scoot closer but not quite sure if I should.

"But anyway," she says, sitting up straighter. "I'm doing better now. It just took a while to adjust."

"Good," I say, pulling a string at the edge of the towel. "But it was still shitty of me to ditch you."

"Very shitty," she agrees, and we both laugh a little.

It feels like we've gotten somewhere, but the silences between talking still feel so big, like my mistakes are still taking up all of the space.

"I want to make this better," I say. "I just don't know how."

"Me either." She sighs.

Then she reaches over and grabs my hand.

"So what are you going to do next year? If you're not going to UCSB."

I swallow, twining my fingers through hers. "I don't know. I keep trying to think about it but I can't. I don't know what's wrong with me. I've missed half of the deadlines and I don't even know where to start."

"It's been a really hard year," Nora whispers. "Maybe you just need some time."

I pick up a broken shell and drag it in a straight line between our feet.

"It's been a hard year for you too," I say.

She takes the shell from my hand, turning my line into a half circle. "The worst."

I turn the half circle into a sunset. She turns the sunset into a stormy sea.

"What was it like to sell your house?" I ask.

"Awful," she says, and then we talk about that until it starts to rain.

After the beach we get coffee, and then we drive around the neighborhood for a while, go to the mall, eat lunch at In-N-Out. The rain clears up, the sun comes and goes. Everything is just how it used to be. People mill around, shopping, waiting, looking at their cell phones. Cars drive by, shiny and new, old and dented. Somewhere, west of all the buildings, the tide goes out.

We park in front of my old house, and it looks the same: scrubby little lemon tree, broken roof tiles, patchy grass, sloped lawn. I remember all the times sitting on the porch steps with Bea and Hannah, watching cars drive by. But that kind of memory is not Proust's rush of the past. It's a million comings and goings, each one hopelessly the same.

"You look sad," Nora says.

"I'm not sad," I say. "I just feel numb." And then, "How could I have forgotten him?" Through my window, I watch the house. Someone else's furniture is inside; the curtains are a different color. "I was reading this book for English class, and it talks about how we destroy our memories by remembering."

Nora sighs, turning to look at me. Her hair is piled in a messy bun on top of her head, loose strands falling down everywhere. "Do you really think it's something you can control like that?"

I take out my camera, photograph the window with my blurry house in the background. "I don't know."

A car pulls into the driveway. A clean-looking silver minivan.

"Let's go," I say, suddenly feeling a desperate need to not see who is living in my house.

Nora, sensing my feeling, guns it, and we speed off down the street.

Once the house is out of sight, Nora says, "Where to now?"

"School?" I say. "Is it too risky?"

"Nah," she says. "They'll be getting out soon anyway. You can see everyone."

That word, *everyone*, makes my stomach flop over, makes me think about Bennett.

"Yeah, okay," I say, knowing it has to be done.

• • •

We pull up just as students start swarming the lawn. There, under the giant palm tree, are all of my old friends, the ones who drifted around the outside of the knot that was Nora, sometimes Bennett, and me. Jess, Una, Celly, Martin. They all look exactly the same, as though the world has been paused this whole time.

"Look who I found!" says Nora.

And then suddenly, everyone is saying my name. It feels a lot like when I first got to New York; everyone is asking me about Cumberland, and it feels too close to describe.

So I just say, "It's small. And weird. And snowy."

Which feels so far from the truth of it. I think of Jesse, crushed in the hallway of Cumberland Central, and my heart feels like it's turned inside out.

After a while the conversation drifts. We're lying in the grass, and the sun has just come out from behind a big cloud and it's warming me. It's melting me. Like it's summer again and the past three months were all a dream.

"Let's go get chili fries," Nora says.

"That sounds good," I say.

And that's when I turn my head to the side and I see him, coming toward us, sideways and partially obscured by blurry green, the blades of grass up next to my face. It takes a minute to register his wavy golden hair and permanent crooked smile.

Because I spotted him first, I can tell the exact moment when he notices me. His slouch stiffens and his green eyes go wide.

"Mary," he says. Not like it's a question or a beginning of a conversation. Like it's just a word dropping out of his mouth.

I close my eyes for exactly one second and pull myself back to earth.

"Hey, Bennett," I say.

"You're back," he says, like he's trying to put it all together. And then, finally, his brain seems to catch up to reality and he bounds over, crushing me into the ground with the full weight of his body-slam hug. Even fresh out of school, he smells like sea salt and Banana Boat sunscreen.

It's weird to be hugging like this, in the middle of the lawn, everyone around us. Time moves backward and forward, trying to make this moment fit.

He pulls back to look at me, and his corn-silk, sunflower hair makes a tent around my face. And then there's this moment, like we're about to kiss, except our mouths are backward magnets. And I find my hands pushing against his chest.

"Can we talk?" I say.

He nods, pulling back and brushing the grass off his clothes.

I look over at Nora, who has been watching us from her spot next to me.

"I'm gonna go catch up with Celly," she says. "Be back in ten."

Somehow, in the midst of our awkward reunion, everyone has started to disperse, drifting off toward the beach or the 7-Eleven down the street. Now it's just me and Bennett, sitting in grass that's the color of his eyes.

"How have you been?" I ask, feeling nervous.

"Good," he says, smiling, not seeming to notice how weird it is to be together again. "We ended up winning sectionals, and I think I'm getting recruited by UC San Diego."

"Wow," I say, remembering the drama of the water polo postseason that scripted the background of so many FaceTime calls. "That's amazing."

"What about you?" he asks, reaching over to tuck a strand of hair behind my ear. His fingers used to leave a trail of sparks when he did that, but now I don't really feel anything at all.

"I'm not sure," I say. And then, not really wanting to get derailed by a conversation about my disastrous mess of a future, I turn toward him and say again, "Can we talk? Like, really talk?"

Bennett nods again, his face serious this time.

"We probably should have done this a long time ago," I say, surprised at how easy it is to start.

"Bingo," Bennett says, running a hand through his hair. It's longer than it was, almost down to his shoulders. Then he smiles, sheepishly. "Sorry. I'm a wimp."

I pull out a few strands of grass and twist them together, one blade on top of the next.

"We're both wimps," I say, remembering all of the calls I've ignored, all of the times I've snaked my way around the truth. I wonder about the things we might have said before, if we weren't so afraid. "But I'm trying not to be a wimp anymore. So there's something I need to tell you. A couple of things."

"Okay," he says, leaning back onto his hands. His pants are cuffed at the ankle and he's wearing his Birkenstocks with the backstrap today. Part of the sole is worn down from skateboarding down the street. He looks easy, open, and it makes me remember that before any of this we were best friends.

Still, I'm nervous, my heart pounding in my throat.

"The first thing," I say, "is that I loved you. All the way. Head over heels."

As soon as I say the words, I feel lighter. It is so good to tell the truth. Out of the corner of my eye, I see Bennett shift in the grass.

"Really?" he says. I can tell he's watching my face, but I look straight ahead, determined not to lose momentum.

"Yeah," I say. "I used to think it would swallow me whole."

He laughs and I finally look over and it feels like whatever's been broken between us is coming back together. "I think I felt that way about you too," he says.

Neither of us says anything about the way we are using the past tense. I thread my fingers through the grass, like it might help me keep myself from floating away.

The second truth feels harder to tell. But he deserves it. Jesse does too. So I look out toward the blur of cars in the street and say, "I met someone else."

Bennett doesn't talk for a long time and I turn his way again, watching emotions rush across his face. It's like one of those time-lapse videos of clouds passing over the sun, one after another after another.

Eventually he says, "I never asked you not to." It hurts a little bit, all over again, remembering this. He looks down. "There have been some other people for me too," he says. Then he looks at me and adds, "But not love."

Then there's this space in the conversation, like I'm supposed to say that too. But I'm not sure if I can. For once I'm trying to be honest.

Bennett is an athlete; his hand is steady and he sinks the free throw every single time. But for a second, he gets this look on his face, like he's lost his footing.

But then he slings his arm over my shoulder and the hurt on his face gives way to something else, and I can feel his unwaveringly sunny spirit come back, warming everything up. I feel like we're kids again, racing down the street, Bennett going slow enough to make me think I could win.

"Let's be better at being friends," he says.

"Definitely," I say.

He reaches over to mess up my hair. "We really fucked it up the first time, huh?" he laughs.

"We sure did," I say.

We watch the sun sink a little bit lower, the light melting like butter over the top of everything. Eventually Nora comes and slides in on the other side of me, and we sit for a while in the grass, Nora, Bennett, and me.

27

THE NEXT MORNING, NORA WAKES ME UP AT SUNRISE and says, "I think I know what we need to do."

She packs lunches and we load our stuff into Mary Jane, and then we drive. When we hit Ventura, my phone buzzes a text from Hannah: Callllllllll me.

One from Mom: If you're not home in twenty-four hours I'm coming to get you.

The road to Big Sur is beautiful. Route 1. Hearst Castle and dramatic cliffs and always the ocean to our left. Nora and I play each other songs and catch up on the last four months. I tell her all about Jesse, and I try not to die over the mess I've made.

I keep replaying the scene in my mind—Jesse's confused and perfect face, the burning-hot anger that made me feel possessed. Last night I called him—just once—and the stab of regret I felt at the sound of his voicemail was so sharp that I couldn't sleep for hours. But there's nothing I can do, because everything I said was the truth and it was way too late for that.

Nora tells me about life in California, and it doesn't make my heart fall out of my chest. All this time I've been waiting to get back here, to come home, and now that I'm here, now that I've felt it, I realize that home is somewhere else.

California doesn't fit like it used to. I'm a different shape now, a different texture. The part of me that was oceans and palm trees is filling up with rivers and pines. Behind my eyes, the jumble of cars and electric sunsets are turning into deep forests and wide-open space.

"Sometimes I'm not sure who I am anymore," I say to Nora, looking out the window at the blue sky and scrubby sea grass.

"You're different," Nora says, reaching over and tugging on a strand of my hair. "But you're still you."

And then we're there. Big Sur. Dramatic cliffs on one side of the road and haunted redwood forests on the other. There's a photograph of Dad down on this beach, twenty years old, looking like a Kurt Cobain wannabe with long hair and an army jacket. One of him and Mom with hearts in their eyes.

It takes us a while to find the pullout, and when we do, it's even smaller than I remembered. Just a parking spot and a bench that looks out over the edge of the world.

"I'll wait in the car," Nora says.

I walk to the bench and sit down in the damp, cold air. Beyond the edge of the cliff, the ocean is blurring into the fog, which is blurring into the sky.

"I forgot you," I say. And then, "Did you even want me to remember?"

The waves answer back in their rushing sound, rhythmic and unchanging.

I peer down at the narrow, empty strip of beach, a hundred feet below. I think about how, even now, Dad is somewhere we can't get to.

I take out my camera and photograph the gravel at my feet, the gradient of sea and air, the dizzying drop to the beach below. I make the field blurry and then sharp; I zoom in all the way down to the waves. Maybe I'll develop these later and feel nothing. Or maybe I'll discover the ghost of my dad, sitting at the bottom of the cliff reading Shakespeare, too caught up in the book to even notice I was here.

• • •

NORA AND I DRIVE TO THE BEACH AND EAT LUNCH ON A GIANT blanket. The sun comes out for real and the air warms up, and Nora intrepidly puts on her wet suit and gets into the icy water. And when I'm all alone on the beach my heart fills up with longing. I long for my mother. For Bea. For El. For Hannah. For Jesse. For Cumberland.

On the way home, Nora lets me drive Mary Jane. We make our way back down Route 1 listening to the radio and singing at the top of our lungs. When we get close to Hearst Castle, I get an idea.

"What are you doing?" Nora asks, as I put on my blinker and turn off the highway. But then she sees the sign for San Simeon, and she starts jumping up and down in her seat. "Oh my god. Seriously?"

"I knew you'd be into it." I grin.

"You have no idea!" she says, flapping her hands. "And it's December, which means the adult males are starting to return to the beach to prepare for mating season."

I pull into a parking lot and Nora springs from the car, power walking toward the boardwalk. And there in the sand, hundreds of elephant seals are basking in the last of the afternoon sun.

"Holy shit," Nora says, spreading her arms wide. "Aren't they beautiful?"

I survey the giant creatures, the males with their strange, floppy proboscises, and say, "Kind of?"

Nora shakes her head and says, "Honestly, Marigold." And finally, finally I feel like we're back.

• • •

By the time we eat dinner and are back on the road, it's almost nine. The world outside the car is quiet, sleepy. We're discussing whether or not to stop for the night when my phone starts vibrating like crazy on the seat next to me.

"Oh shit," I say. "I think I've been out of service this whole time."

My phone keeps buzzing, the number of messages going higher and higher. I feel more strange with each notification.

Nora is driving, so I open my screen to see the last one from my mom: Marigold, please call me.

And the way she's written out my name in full jolts me with panic. So I do.

She picks up on the first ring.

"Marigold. Thank god."

"What is it?"

"It's Bea."

Again the world stops. The words crush everything down to a tiny pinpoint. It's like I can't even see the trees out the window.

I hear myself say, "What happened?" But I don't remember telling myself to say it.

"She's in the hospital," Mom says. "But she's okay . . . She was out with some friends and she drank too much. She passed out and one of the kids called an ambulance. Thank god."

I'm silent. I can't think of a single thing to say. All I can think is that if I'd been there—if I'd stayed—this never would have happened.

I should have been there. I should have answered my door when she knocked. I should have asked her to hang out and when she said no I should have asked again.

I think back to my first high school party, the way Hannah showed me how to pump the keg, the way she looked in my eyes and said, "Never let your cup out of your sight. Guys are fucking creeps."

Hannah would have done this right.

"El is in with her now," Mom says. "She still won't talk to me."

I can hear the exhaustion and despair in her voice.

"I'm so sorry, Mom," I say. "This is all my fault."

"No," she says firmly. "It's not. But I need you to come home now."

• • •

SHE BOOKS ME A SEAT ON THE FIRST FLIGHT OUT OF LAX, AT SIX a.m. It's a quiet drive back to LA, but my mind is blaring with all of my mistakes. We get back to the city at two in the morning and go straight to the airport. We try to sleep for a while in a seating area by the baggage claim, but the seats are hard and the arms won't go up.

Nora is draped awkwardly across the seat next to mine, her head on my shoulder. I pick up a few strands of her hair and start to braid them together.

"I am such a fuckup," I say.

Nora turns to look at me, pulling against the braid.

"What do you mean?"

I frown because it seems obvious.

"Bea. I should have been there for her. How could I have just left?"

"Mary," she says, taking my hands gently down from her hair. She's so good at this. Being here. Knowing what to say. "It's not your fault. Everything that's happening to Bea is happening to you too. You're allowed to have feelings about it. You're allowed to mess up and get pissed off and run away."

I breathe in and out, trying to catch my looping thoughts. I know she's right, but I still can't let myself off the hook. I just need to be there. I need to see her for myself. I pull my hands back, pressing them against my eyes. "If I had stayed this wouldn't have happened. I should have tried harder."

Nora shifts upright, tilts her head. "When have you ever been able to get Bea to do anything?"

I breathe out, trying to let some of the tension out of my body. "You're right," I say, even though I'm still not sure.

Nora smiles and says, "I'm always right." And then she settles against me, leaning her head against mine. My limbs start to loosen and I feel a little sleepy.

"Nora?"

"Yeah?"

"Thank you."

"For what?"

"You picked me up at the airport with six hours' notice after I was a shit friend to you all year. You took me to see my dad. You didn't have to do any of this. I didn't deserve it."

She squeezes my hand. "Remember the time you cut school and stole your mom's car because I found out my dad was banging that nineteen-year-old who works at Peet's Coffee in Ventura?"

"Oh my god." I laugh. "I didn't even have my license yet."

"You're a good friend. It's just been a horrible year."

I lean my head all the way back, staring up at the tiny black holes in the ceiling tiles. They're like stars in reverse, sucking in the dull neon light.

"God, it's been a horrible year."

"We can only hope that the next one will be better," she says.

• • •

When it's four thirty we head to security, and Nora wraps me up in a hug. I sink into her puffy North Face jacket, breathing her in.

"Ignore me again and I'll make you regret it," she says.

"I'm legitimately scared of you sometimes, you know that?" I say, trying really hard not to cry. "But of course, never again."

"I love you so much," she whispers in my ear.

"So, so, so much," I whisper back.

28

AND JUST LIKE THAT, I LEAVE CALIFORNIA AGAIN. I fall asleep twenty minutes into the flight and wake up to the stale snow of the Albany airport.

My mom is waiting under the arrivals sign, looking like a zombie again. And my heart compresses when I see her, my lungs stuck on the inhale.

"Marigold," she says when I get to her.

She reaches for me and I let her pull me in. I'm overcome by her scent, Tide detergent and Dove bar soap. It makes me remember:

Sick days coloring on the floor of her office.

Sitting still in the lamplight, her brush tugging against my unruly hair.

A night in El's kitchen, the sound of laughing so hard it hurt.

I remember that I'm home.

• • •

We drive to the hospital, where El and Bea are waiting to get picked up. They walk through the double sliding doors together, Bea as limp and pale as a snowdrop, El hearty and full of color, a whole bush of pink beach roses.

"You look like shit," Bea says when we slide into the back seat.

"You're one to talk," I reply, poking at her sallow skin.

I scoot into the middle seat, drawn to her side like a magnet. The feeling of relief, being near her, is overwhelming. She smells like hospital, but I get even closer, so that all of my arm is pressing against all of hers.

"I'm still mad at you," she says.

"I'm mad at you too," I say, even though I'm really just mad at myself.

"Fine," she says.

"Good," I say. "Don't forget to buckle your seat belt."

We drive home, past miles of cornfields, the stubble where the stalks were chopped poking up out of the crusty snow in long, straight rows. We pass a few little towns like Cumberland, with one stoplight and a Stewart's, towns that I used to never even know existed.

It's getting dark by the time we get home, and I realize that it's almost the shortest day of the year. Six months ago, I was still in California, celebrating the solstice under the stars on the beach.

Mom disappears into the kitchen while El tucks Bea into bed with a steaming mug of ginger tea. I climb under her covers and curl up next to the wall.

"I feel like garbage," Bea says when we're alone.

"I bet," I say, shuddering at the thought of Bea passed out at some strange kid's house.

I want to ask her why she did it, but I'm not sure if I'm ready for that. Instead I roll onto my back and watch the moon slowly rising over the roof of our neighbor's house.

"How could you just leave?" Bea says after a while.

"I'm sorry," I say. "I was angry."

There's a long pause, and then Bea turns over and lets out a dramatic sigh. "Finally."

"What does that mean?" I ask, shifting a little bit closer.

Bea's profile is sharp in the dusky room, all of her features small and precise. "You always make it seem like everything is fine," she says. "Even when it isn't."

I'm startled by how clearly she can see me. She's right. That's what I've been doing all year, pretending like everything isn't falling apart. But I'm not sure if Bea's way is any better, letting the anger consume everything, taking it all the way to the edge.

"True," I say. "But isn't it better than self-destructing?"

I turn to face the wall again, and Bea curls up behind me.

"I don't think that either way is really that good," she says.

She starts scratching her fingers up and down my back like she used to when we were kids. I'm close to drifting off to sleep, but then a flash of Bea, drunk and limp and out of control, comes crashing into my mind.

"What's the deal with Domino?" I say. "She doesn't seem like a very good friend."

Bea growls a little. "She's been there for me," she says, twisting the knife, and I'm hit with a wave of regret. "Anyway, all of the partying has been my idea. If anything, Domino tries to rein me in."

I'm not sure how much I believe her, but I get that this isn't really the moment to push. And Domino isn't the point of this conversation. Bea and I are.

"I'm sorry," I say again. "I haven't been a very good big sister."

Bea wraps her arms around my neck, pulling me into a strangley sort of hug.

"I can forgive you," she whispers. "If you give me ten years off the end of your life."

I squeeze her as tightly as I can. "You are so creepy."

A car pulls out of a driveway across the street, striping the wall with pink-and-red light.

Bea leans in and says, "What was it like being back?"

I twist out of her arms and turn to look at the ceiling. "Honestly," I say. "It was a little weird."

"Really?"

I close my eyes, trying to remember what it felt like to be there, surrounded by our old life but feeling somehow separate.

"Yeah. Everything was exactly the same as before. But it was like someone let the color out. Even the ocean was strange."

Bea tugs at a string on my sweatshirt.

"Did it feel like Dad was there?" she asks, her voice scratchy and tired.

I turn on my side so we are nose to nose, eye to eye. "Can I tell you something?"

Bea nods.

"I'm forgetting."

Bea takes a deep, solemn, shaky breath.

"Me too," she says.

I let my eyelids flutter closed, feeling the blankness behind them. And then I say, "The parts I remember aren't really that good."

Bea rests her forehead against mine. She grabs both of my wrists with her long, cold fingers.

"I keep having these flashes," I say, opening my eyes again. "He always looks angry or frustrated. He always feels far away."

Bea's black eyes look straight into mine, like she can see everything that isn't there. It feels so good to tell her, to be close to her again.

She's quiet for a long time, and then she says, "He'll come back to us."

And because it's Bea it somehow feels true.

We stop talking then and just lie there for a while. The tension of the past few days, months, drains out of my limbs, into the mattress, and I feel soft, like I've taken off my shell. The moon moves on, out of view. Bea starts snoring softly. I hear my mom and El downstairs at the kitchen table, and then I hear El leaving, warming up her car in the driveway and driving away.

I hear every creak of Mom's feet on the stairs, and then the door cracks open and a slice of the hallway light comes in.

"You girls up?" Mom asks.

Bea groans, "We are now."

Mom shuffles over and, without asking, climbs right into bed on Bea's side. It makes me think of being kids, all of us girls in Mom and Dad's bed.

Mom settles in next to Bea, sighing deeply. "You are both in so much trouble," she says.

A car drives by and its lights slide across the dark room, over the dresser, onto the ceiling, across the posters on the wall. The three of us lie together, breathing in the dark.

I'm almost asleep when Mom says, "This has been an awful year." And then, "I'm so sorry."

I can feel how heavy she feels in the way she says it.

"I missed your dad so much," she continues, her voice a fragile thread. "I didn't know how to function. It felt like someone turned off the world. And the only thing I could do was go to work."

Between us, Bea is so still. But I feel restless, like the blankets are suddenly too hot, too heavy. I feel angry all over again. I know she was lost. I don't need to hear it. It's all I've been able to think about for months and months.

Mom keeps going, like if she stops she'll lose her nerve. "But I should have been there for you girls," she says. "And I should have told you about what was happening with me."

"You should have," Bea says, her voice quiet.

"I know," Mom says, and suddenly this whole conversation, Mom's contrition, Bea's restraint, becomes unbearable.

"I was worried about you," I say, my fists balling up at my sides. "You were never home. And even when you were, you were so distracted. You missed months of our lives."

There's a sting in the silence that follows.

"I'm sorry," Mom says, again, sounding so sad. "You shouldn't have to worry about me."

No one talks for a long time. Around us, the house creaks and groans. I feel myself deflating, feel Mom counting her breaths, thinking of something to say.

And then Bea asks, "If you loved Dad so much, how can you be with someone else?"

And my stomach knots up all over again.

Mom turns her face away and says, "I don't know."

She's quiet for a long time. I wonder if she is going to cry. But then she says, "Can I be honest?"

And Bea says, "Can you?"

And Mom laughs a little, in spite of everything. "I have no idea what I'm doing," she says. And it feels like the first honest thing she's said in a very long time.

Then she arranges us into three spoons, her arms wrapped all the way around. She squeezes my shoulder and says, "We are all starting therapy next Monday."

Bea groans.

"And," Mom says, as we're all finally drifting off to sleep. "You're both grounded until New Year's."

29

IN THE MORNING, I WAKE UP TO BEA SNORING LOUDLY beside me. I tiptoe out of her room and into mine, where I find my phone lying facedown on the bed. I crawl under my covers and open my texts to Jesse's last message from Monday night. He said: Darkroom tomorrow? And I said: Yes!

The exclamation point seems to echo through the empty thread, tacky and loud and out of place. I type, *I'm sorry I'm sorry I'm sorry I'm sorry*, until it fills up the text box. But I know I've used up all my chances.

• • •

I WANDER DOWNSTAIRS, AIMLESSLY LOOKING FOR A DISTRACTION. I find Mom in the living room, arranging an elaborate nativity scene on our front windowsill. She's dressed casually today, in jeans, a violet long-sleeve shirt, and thick wool socks. Her hair is down and a little bit messy, and something loosens in my chest as I realize she isn't leaving today.

"Where did you get that?" I ask, gesturing to the little group of clay figurines and tiny fake trees.

"It was Grandma Rose's."

"Wasn't she Jewish?"

"Yeah, it's complicated."

She shrugs and steps back to assess her work while I sink down on the big green couch. The leather is cold on the backs of my legs, and I pull my knees up to my chest.

"Marigold," Mom says. "We need to talk."

Part of me wants to slither away, back up to my room, and lock the door behind me. But there are still a lot of lies left to clear up.

"Okay," I say, and Mom takes a deep breath.

"Your guidance counselor called," she says. "I know about your college applications."

Even though it feels like the train is finally hitting the wall and flying off the tracks, part of me is relieved. Maybe this first thread will unravel every knot, and then, finally, I'll be free of this mess.

She's still facing the window, not looking at me, when she asks, "What happened?"

In the silence that follows, the furnace chugs to life, noisily blowing hot air out of the grate in the living room floor. Upstairs, Bea thumps out of bed.

"I don't know," I finally say. "I had this plan, and then one day it just started falling apart. Everything was so overwhelming that I couldn't think about the future. At first I thought I would just set it aside for a day or two, but then every time I went back to try to figure things out, they felt bigger and more confusing."

"Why didn't you tell anyone?" Mom asks, turning to look at me. Her eyes are tired and sad.

I shrug, feeling suddenly like my mouth is full of chalk. "I was embarrassed. I felt so lost and I didn't want you guys to know."

"But this is a big deal," Mom says, her eyebrows pulling together in the middle. "You should have told someone."

I lean my head on the back of the couch, feeling tired, irritated, like it's impossible to explain any of this. "Everyone's been really busy," I say. "*You've* been really busy. Gone. I wasn't sure what was happening to you. Sometimes I couldn't think about anything else."

Mom's shoulders sag. I can see regret in her eyes and the turn of her lips; it's like she's looking back over the past few months in her mind and seeing every failure.

"I'm so sorry," she says quietly.

"I know," I say. "We don't need to talk about it anymore."

Mom turns back to the crèche, arranging the three wise men again and again, like it really matters if they're on the left side of the manger or the right.

"You know," she says. "You have a couple of weeks before some of those deadlines. There's still time to figure this out."

I sigh, feeling a dull throb start at the back of my skull. "I know. I just don't know if I can."

Mom sets the last wise man down, stepping back to assess her work, then she starts fussing again, with Mary and the baby Jesus. "I can help you if you're overwhelmed. I'm a lawyer. Writing is sort of my thing."

"That's not what I mean." I run my hands down the front of my face, the frustration growing, bubbling under my skin.

Mom drops the baby Jesus and it rolls across the floor, under the couch.

"I don't understand," she says. She looks lost, like she should be able to fix this, fix me, like she doesn't see why she can't. "You've been working so hard for this, your whole life."

"It's not the applications," I say, dropping my head into my hands. "It's me. I'm not okay."

I can hear the air leaving Mom's lungs in a big gust and then she's deflated, slouching down next to me on the couch. She puts her arms around me and I curl into her side and we just sit there for a long time, listening to the heater and the faraway ticking of the kitchen clock. Mom smooths the hair away from my forehead like she used to when I was little.

Then she leans forward and picks up the baby Jesus, cradling it gently in her hands.

"You used to love this thing," she says.

"I did?"

"Yeah, when you were two or three. You called it the baby Bejesus. We had to put the crèche away though because Bea was always trying to pull the heads off. I was afraid she'd choke."

I laugh. And then there's another big silence, everything stretching out thick and heavy between us. I shift away, crossing my legs on the cushion.

"It's not that I don't want to go to college," I say. "But I also don't know if I do. I don't know what I think about it." I take the baby Bejesus out of Mom's hands and roll it back and forth between my palms. "I feel like I'm underwater."

"Oh, babe," Mom says, pulling me back into her side. "I think I know how that feels."

I close my eyes, letting my mind soften, trying to let the words find me.

"I think I need some more time," I say. "I just want to feel like myself again. College is a big decision. I feel like I owe it to myself, to everyone, to be sure."

Mom nods, even though her face looks uncertain.

"I was thinking," I say, testing out my new plan, the one that's been unfolding quietly in my mind these past few days. "I could stay with you for a little while longer. Get a job, take some art classes with El. And then next fall I'll apply if it feels right."

Mom is frowning, and I can tell it's taking everything she's got not to immediately shoot me down. But she doesn't. Instead she takes a deep breath and says, "Okay. I'll think about it. But no more lying. From either of us."

I nod. For once, I feel like I might be able to keep the promise.

Mom clears her throat and says, "Speaking of that—" There's an awkward pause. "Do you want to talk about Jake?"

Just hearing the name makes every one of my muscles tighten, and I pull back to my own cushion again. "Not really," I say. "Not yet."

"Fair enough," she says. She straightens up and pulls her hair back, and for a second I can see a bit of her old self poking through. "I'm ready when you are."

Bea comes thudding down the stairs then, hair sticking up in every direction. "I'm starving," she says. "Can we make pancakes?"

"Yeah," says Mom, standing up from the couch. "We can."

• • •

Monday morning comes like the worst hangover—final exams I haven't studied for, classes I've missed, a paper on Proust I can't bring myself to write.

I walk into English and Jesse is already there, apparently lost in his physics textbook, the page about the conservation of energy.

To be honest, it's my favorite part of the chapter. There's something comforting about the way that kinetic and potential energy can change places again and again, reinvent themselves a million different times, never really disappearing. It's better than the religion of commercial holidays. It's an explanation you could believe in, could grow to love.

I take it as a sign.

"Hi." I send the word out into the empty space between us. It feels small.

He looks up at me and smiles. Which would be confusing if it reached above his soft cheekbones and into his eyes. But it doesn't.

The potential energy of the rock decreases as it plummets toward the earth.

"Hey, Marigold," he says. And then he looks back down at his book and the conversation is over.

I was ready for angry, but he doesn't seem angry at all, just distant. He doesn't ask me to go to the darkroom, which is fine because Bea and I are grounded anyway and I have almost a week's worth of classwork to make up. But when the lunch bell rings and he hurries out of the classroom, is swallowed up into the crowd of students rushing toward their lockers, I know where I stand.

After class Ms. Bell pulls me aside. She gives me an extension on my Proust paper, but when I sit down to write it after school I can't focus. Honestly, I don't know what to say. Proust made me blow up my life and fly across the country. I wish I'd never even heard of him.

Later, when I'm curled up with Bea in her bed, watching movies on my laptop, I pick up the phone to text Nora.

Me: Jesse is a no go.

Nora: Shit. What happened?

Me: Nothing. Nothing happened.

Nora: Just talk to him.

Me: :/

Nora: Come on.

Me: I know I owe him an explanation.

Me: And I miss him.

Me: But I don't think he wants to talk to me.

Me: I'm going to hide in my room for the rest of my life.

Me: Probably better for the general public.

Nora: You're rambling.

Me: I know. Tell me something to distract me.

Nora: My mom gets back tomorrow and for some reason my dad is freaking out. He got a new sweater and cut his hair.

Nora's parents are trying for a "family Christmas" this year, since it's the last one before Nora leaves for college. She is skeptical.

Me: Oh my god. You need to live text the entire week. Is it possible to set up a video feed?

Nora: Do you really want to witness this disaster?

Me: Wouldn't want to miss a second.

Me: OK. Gotta go. Bea and I are watching Ghostbusters and she's giving me daggers RN.

Nora: LOVE YOU!

Me: Always.

• • •

THE WEEK WEARS ON. I STARE AT THE EMPTY SCREEN OF MY COM-puter, I weather Jesse's disinterest. It's the last week before winter break, the great gray void hovering on the horizon. Soon I won't be able to see him at all.

On Wednesday I roll my pencil off my desk to see if Jesse will notice, and it skids to a stop right under his chair. He places it, exactly straight, on the top of my desk without even looking at me.

Now that everything is out in the open, I think about how it felt to lie all the time. In a way it was easy, leaving out the truth, dipping my eyes from his line of sight. But at the same time, it drained something out of me, something vital. And everything I wanted to preserve ended up rotten.

That night, every night, I type out the same text:

Can we talk?

But I just delete the words without ever sending them.

Every day I eat lunch with Sam, and she tries hard to get me out of my funk. She starts the planning for our New York City trip.

"We have to go to L Train Vintage. It's my favorite thrift store on earth," she says.

And, "My cousin Lauren says we can stay with her in the Bronx. She has five cats but we can make it work."

"Yeah, okay," I say, again and again and again.

Finally, on Thursday, when I am staring into outer space, she looks at me and says, "Don't you want to know where I was when I wasn't at the dentist?"

I am snapped back to earth. Reminded, again, that it's not just me living here.

"Yeah," I say. "Sorry. Of course I do."

"Well." She smiles. "I met a girl. In El's painting class."

I look at her: her hair is in a messy bun, her shirt is covered in paint, and she has doodled hearts all over the back of her hand.

"Oh yeah?" I say, grinning. "I want to know all about her."

· · ·

EVERY DAY AFTER SCHOOL, I HANG OUT WITH BEA. WE WATCH movies, I do her hair, we scheme about getting Jesse back. We don't talk about Dad again, but we wear his shirts and listen to his records.

"What do you think therapy is like?" Bea says.

I pull the strand of her French braid tight. "There's only one way to find out."

· · ·

MOM IS HOME FOR DINNER EVERY NIGHT. SHE MAKES FROZEN PIZZA and scrambled eggs, or heats up a pot of El's leftover chili, but we eat it together. Afterward, she works at the kitchen table, and Bea and I do homework on the couch. But really I just stare into space and think about Jesse.

She doesn't bring up Jake again, except when she tells us she'll be going out on Saturday night. I grit my teeth and Bea hisses like a cat, but underneath I think we are just relieved to know.

• • •

EVERY NIGHT I TRY TO WRITE MY PROUST PAPER, AND EVERY NIGHT I can't. I feel better after telling Bea about Dad, but it doesn't change the fact of forgetting. His smell is gone, his voice is gone. All of the memories have cooled, congealed into something generic. The Dad in my mind just doesn't ring true anymore.

Thursday night I pull out my box of photographs. I take scissors, and carefully, I cut my dad out of every single one.

I write a note: *Ms. Bell, I'm sorry. I can't write this paper.*

Then I put it all in an envelope and seal it shut.

• • •

ON FRIDAY AFTERNOON, SAM, BEA, AND DOMINO STORM INTO MY room. I am wallowing in what's left of Jesse's smell on my sheets.

"Okay," Bea says. "Enough is enough."

"Sam?" I say, confused to see her in my room.

Sam shrugs. "Bea called me."

Domino lurks in the doorway, actually looking a little shy in jet-blue coveralls with ALEX embroidered on the chest. "Hey," she says, raising one hand in a half-hearted wave. I give her the stink eye and turn back to Bea.

"Aren't we grounded?"

"You know I love a loose interpretation of the rules," she says, shrugging. "And I'm serious. This is getting pathetic."

"What is?" I ask, as if I don't know.

The light is already starting to bend, making everyone glow a little. I reach under my bed for my camera, but Bea gives me a look.

"Don't worry," she says. "We have a plan."

"Okay . . ." I say.

"Actually," Sam says, glancing around the room at the piles of papers and laundry and towers of ice-cream bowls. "Let's clean up a little while we talk."

She pulls me to my feet and Bea starts throwing clothes into my hamper. Domino shuffles all the way into my room and sits down on the floor.

"Okay," I say. "What's your big plan?"

Bea smooths out a stack of crumpled papers. "We watch for Mom's light to go out. Wait thirty minutes. Then you sneak her car out of the driveway. Just roll it backward in neutral and keep the lights off until you're down the street."

"I'm not going to ask you how you know that, Bea. You're not even fifteen yet," I say, adding a mug to a stack of small plates on my desk.

Bea lobs a crumpled paper toward the garbage can.

"You're the one who can't figure out how to work the cable. And anyway, it was Sam's idea. Now, do you want to get the guy or not?" She puts air quotes around the words "get the guy" and feigns barfing.

"Couldn't I just ask Mom to borrow the car?"

"You could," Bea says. "But you did use her credit card to fly across the country without asking first. And you blew your college applications."

"True," Domino says. And when I give her a look, she says, "What? I think that's so cool."

I shake my head, feeling my resolve crumble. "Okay, fine," I say. "But what do I do when I get there?"

"Sam?" Bea says. "This is not in my wheelhouse."

"You could bring a giant boom box," Sam says from inside the closet, where she is organizing my shoes. "Like in that John Cusack movie."

I frown. "I don't know if Jesse's mom would like that."

"Or throw gravel at his window?"

I pause in the middle of straightening my books. "Hm, maybe. Then what?"

"Just tell him the truth," Sam says. "Everything."

"Ugh," I say, sitting back on my heels.

"Come on," Bea says. "Don't be a loser."

• • •

Once everyone is gone, I sit at my desk and contemplate the plan. I think about all of the times I've messed things up with Jesse, and I'm worried that this gesture, my fumbling words, won't be enough.

I open my desk drawer and take out a small sleeve of photographs. I've been shooting so much black and white lately because of the darkroom, but yesterday these color prints came back, a few rolls of film from the fall.

There's something I love about looking at photographs that

nobody's ever seen before, not even Jesse. He's here though: the back of his head, the edge of his shirtsleeve, his little sister's sticky smile. And there are other photographs too, tree branches, windowsills, things that should be unphotographable like time and loneliness.

Without thinking, I turn a picture over and scribble on the back: *I couldn't photograph the trees.*

And then another: *I thought I might be disappearing.*

I turn over photograph after photograph, writing my thoughts.

I'm afraid.

Sometimes lying is easier than telling the truth.

I wish I'd done everything differently.

I love the curls at the back of your neck.

• • •

It's almost midnight when Bea pops her head in my doorway and whispers, "Five minutes."

I've been pacing around my room like an anxious dog in Sam's mohair sweater, repeating random phrases again and again in my head. *I'm sorry. I messed up. Please just listen.*

I wait five minutes and then descend the stairs like I'm in Cirque du Soleil, having spent a better part of the afternoon testing which boards were the quietest. I get the strangest thrill as I lift Mom's keys off the hook next to the back door.

Somehow the trick with Mom's car actually works, or I think it works because she doesn't appear on the porch shouting by the time I get to the end of the block. And then I'm free.

The seven miles to Jesse's house feel like forever tonight

because in the excitement of sneaking out, I've forgotten my coat. The cold is so cold the insides of my nostrils freeze on the in breath, and I'm shuddering by the time the heat kicks in.

Outside, the world is peaceful. The sky is perfectly clear. The stars and the moon feel far away. A crust of old salt lines the sides of the road in uniform white ruffles.

I turn out my headlights when I get to Jesse's house and park behind a cluster of giant pine trees. It's completely dark, except for one light, all the way up at the top.

I could just text him, but I'm afraid of rejection, so I grab a handful of tiny rocks and launch them into the air. They shoot up like sad little fireworks, and I watch them burst against his window and sprinkle back down to earth. In the quiet that follows I realize that I'm shivering again, partly from the wind and partly from my jagged nerves.

I don't have to wait long before his window slides open and a head of beautiful, dark, unruly hair emerges. I meet Jesse's quizzical look with a small, quiet wave. The rest of my body is frozen in space and time and temperature, the sleeve of photographs clutched at my side. The window closes again and I pray that he's coming down because I've already made up my mind to wait all night, even if I freeze.

And then the front door opens and Jesse is loping toward me with a bright orange puffy jacket in his arms.

"Are you trying to kill yourself?" he says, half whisper, half shout.

And, yep, he's still mad at me.

"I just need a minute," I say.

He pushes the jacket toward me and I slide my arms through

the warm sleeves, but I can't stop shaking. He looks down at me, deciding. I feel every lie on my skin.

"Fine," he says finally, pulling me around toward the back of the house.

It's quiet out here in the wintertime. Dark. Nothing stirring. The only sound is the crunch of our shoes in the snow.

When we get to the darkroom, Jesse flips on the light and turns on the space heater, pulls the door closed. And then it's just us in the warm light, him leaning on one counter and me on the other. I must look ridiculous in this gigantic jacket, in my canvas sneakers and fluffy sweater and meticulously applied makeup. Suddenly this move feels so obvious and over the top.

"So," Jesse says, cutting through my panic, and I can tell that he's irritated at having to be the one who starts this whole thing off, seeing as how I was the one to show up begging on his lawn.

"Look," I say. "I'm sorry."

This feels like the wrong thing to say.

"You already said that," Jesse says. His eyes look tired. "A lot of times."

"But I am," I say, my voice sounding too loud for the room. "I didn't mean to hurt you," and then, "Actually, I think maybe I did."

The admission falls like a piano in a silent movie, shattering everywhere, surprising us both.

He shakes his head, looking at me in disbelief. "Why?"

"I'm a disaster," I say, digging my hands deep into my pockets. "I try to pretend that I'm not. But I am." I look around the dark-room with its neat shelves and rows of photographs. "And you are just so good."

He makes a frustrated sound, uncrossing and recrossing his arms, his ankles. "That's not fair," he says.

"You're right," I say.

"Stop agreeing with me," he says, in a voice that must be the Jesse Keller version of yelling, louder and less musical. Anger makes the features of his face feel sharper, somehow even more handsome.

"Okay," I say, looking down at my hands. I'm messing this up. I can feel it. But I don't know how to change direction. He's looking at me like he wishes we'd never even met.

"I'm going to go," he says, turning toward the door.

"No, wait," I say, reaching for his sleeve. I need to do something, anything, to get him to stay. So I say, "I saw Bennett in California."

Jesse stops and his shoulders deflate. He pulls his arm away and leans his head against the door.

"Not like that," I say. "I told him about you. I ended it."

I wait for him to respond, but he doesn't. He just stands there, looking down at his feet.

"I'm sorry I lied," I say. "But nothing happened between us. Not for a really long time."

"I know that," he says, turning back around, tugging on his hair. "Obviously. But you lied. Again and again. Were you even making a portfolio?"

"No," I say, tears threatening the backs of my eyes. I try to think of a way to explain, but all of my practiced arguments don't seem to fit. "Everything was falling apart and I didn't know what to do. My mom was gone and my dad was disappearing and my future felt impossible and I just wanted you. You were the only thing that felt good. You're my favorite person I've ever met." I grip the edges of the counter, feeling the metal bite into my skin, willing myself not to cry.

Jesse looks up at my eyes and then back down at the floor. He looks wounded, vulnerable. His hands are shaking. "You're mine," he says quietly.

Then he seems to gather himself again, looking toward the door and shoving his hands deep into his pockets. "But Jesus, Marigold. What you said in English class, in the hallway. I had no idea about any of it. I felt so foolish." He shakes his head. "It was like we were in two different relationships."

"I know it felt like that," I say. "But it wasn't. I was there. Everything that I felt was real."

"But so much of what you said was a lie. I just don't know how I can trust you again." His eyes are heavy and tired.

I look into them, willing his mind to change. "You can trust me."

But he's already somewhere else. "And then you just disappeared," he says. "For days."

"I just—" I say. "I needed to go home."

"Home," he says. "Yeah. I get it."

"Please." I choke on the word, and the tears are coming now, hot and pathetic. "Don't give up on me. I hate needing people but I need you. Even if we can't be together."

He stands there for a moment without saying anything, eyes fixed on some point above my head. Then I take a step toward him and his body jerks back, like he's been sleeping, like he's just waking up. He shakes his head.

"I don't know," he says, opening the door.

And then he's gone. It happens so fast that I almost don't believe it. I stand there for a minute, trying to calm the gallop of my heartbeat, the shaking of my knees. *I have to get back in the car*, I think. *I have to drive home*.

I wait for a long time, until I'm sure he's not coming back. Then I turn off the heater and the light and I leave my photos in the middle of the counter. And then I close the door behind me. Through the trees, a million stars shine down.

• • •

THE NEXT MORNING I WAKE UP TO AN EARTHQUAKE. FOR A SECOND I think I must be back in California. But it's not an earthquake, it's just Hannah jumping up and down on my bed.

"Surprise, LOSER!"

I bring my arm up to shield my eyes from the sunlight streaming in through the window. I feel like I never want to see the sun again. "Jesus," I say, my voice scratchy. "You almost gave me a heart attack. How did you get here already?"

"I got a ride back with my friend Zoe. And also, it's noon." Hannah reaches down with her fingers, trying to pry my eyes open.

I groan, swatting her hand away. "I was up late."

"So I heard."

"Whoops," comes Bea's voice from somewhere that I can't see because my eyes have still not focused yet. I want them both out of my room so I can go back to sleep and stop feeling this ache in my chest that is getting worse by the second.

"Tell me everything," Hannah says, pulling me upright. I shake my head, catching sight of Jesse's jacket crumpled up in my chair, suddenly feeling like I'm about to cry. Last night comes somersaulting back in a flood of despair. Hannah squints her eyes and bites her lip, obviously confused. The sunlight glints off of a tiny hoop in her nose.

"Tell me everything what?" And now Mom's here too, poking her head in the doorway.

"Nothing!" the three of us say in unison. Perfect conspirators.

Mom rolls her eyes as I quickly try to blink back my tears. "Whatever," she says. "Anyway, I'm making grilled cheese if anyone wants one."

Bea crosses her arms and sniffs the air. "Are you sure you're not burning them?"

"Oh shit." Mom turns and runs out of the room.

"Language!" Bea yells.

"Oh lord," Hannah says. "This is going to be a long four weeks." Then she turns back around to where I am trying to disappear under the covers. "Are you okay?"

I shake my head, a few tears leaking out, and she scoots up next to me, throwing her arm over my shoulders. Bea sits down on the other side and then I am all wrapped up in my sisters, which I realize is one of my favorite places to be, even when my heart has fallen out of my body.

"Do you want to talk about it?" Hannah says.

I take a deep breath, trying to let it go. "Not right now. I kind of just want to enjoy the fact that you're here."

"Okay," she says, pulling the three of us even closer together, until I almost can't breathe.

"Ow!" Bea whines.

"Stop being a baby!" Hannah says, reaching across me to pinch Bea's leg.

I wiggle out from between the two of them. "We should go rescue Mom from her terrible cooking skills," I say, grabbing a sweatshirt off the floor. I wipe my face on the back of my hands and follow my sisters downstairs.

• • •

I SOMEHOW MANAGE TO MAKE IT THROUGH THE DAY WITHOUT being alone again. Which is good because I think if I was, something inside of me might give way and I'd just lie on the floor for days, refusing to talk to anyone.

El brings us on another Christmas adventure, to a craft sale at the Episcopal church, and we buy a bunch of hideous clothespin reindeer and angels made from cinnamon sticks, and then we go home and put them on the bookshelves and windowsills so the house feels a little less haunted.

We watch *Elf* and make cookies, and even though I'm heartbroken, I feel like this loose piece of me that has been rattling around for the past few months has finally started to settle.

At six o'clock Mom leaves us, wearing makeup and perfume and reminding Hannah that Bea and I are grounded and may not leave the premises under any conditions.

"I'm almost eighteen," I say, rolling my eyes. "I don't need a babysitter."

And Hannah says, "I charge twenty an hour, just so you know."

Then Bea says, "Don't forget to use a condom."

And Mom puts her hand over her eyes and says, "Oh my god, I need to get out of here."

The three of us sit on the couch, listening to Mom's car backing out of the driveway, and when the sound of her tires has faded Hannah turns to me and says, "Spill."

I knew this moment was coming and I'm prepared, having turned all of the delicate little details over and over in my mind until they don't feel quite so fragile anymore.

But right when I open my mouth to tell her, there's a knock on the front door, and when I look out the window, Jesse is standing there, the porch light shining down on his head like a halo. He's wearing his Carhartt hoodie jacket, and my sleeve of photos is peeking out of the pocket.

Hannah and Bea squeal, and I smooth my hair down, wishing I was wearing something cuter than sweatpants. But right then he looks over and sees me through the window. His eyes lock on mine and a smile slowly works its way across his face, leaving me a little bit breathless.

I step into the hall and pull open the front door, and the swoosh of cold air from outside makes me shiver.

"Hi," Jesse says.

"Hi," I say.

He steps inside and takes off his beanie, ruffling his hand over his hair. He looks nervous.

"Can we talk?" he asks.

I try to answer, but I feel like my jaw is glued shut. All I can do is swallow and nod.

Suddenly, another pair of headlights swoops over the wall.

"Fuck!" Bea yelps. "Mom." And she runs into the hallway.

Bea looks at Jesse and whispers, "Hide."

And I pull him by the hand, into the closet under the stairs.

I hear Mom burst into the kitchen. "I decided not to go," she says, and beside me, Jesse's whole body tenses.

"What?" Hannah asks, her voice a little shrill.

"Just kidding," Mom says, walking right past the closet as she heads for the stairs. "Forgot my wallet."

Relief comes in a rush, and right on its heels is the realization that I'm in a dark closet with Jesse Keller. It's pitch black and I can hear his breathing and feel the cold canvas of his jacket underneath my fingers. I want to pull him to me, to bury my face in his coat, to breathe and breathe and breathe him in. But I hold myself awkwardly apart. Because if I get any closer I know I won't survive him telling me it's over again.

And then, suddenly, he's leaning his forehead down onto mine.

"Marigold," he whispers.

I feel like I can't breathe.

Above us, Mom's feet clomp back down the stairs. "Okay, bye, girls! Love you!" she says.

And then the kitchen door shuts and she drives away. But Jesse and I don't move. We stay there for what feels like forever, awkwardly folded against each other.

"Should we just leave them in there?" Bea asks, right outside the door.

Her voice shocks us out of our stupor. Jesse pulls back as I open the door to where Hannah and Bea stand, about a foot away, watching us like creeps.

"Thanks," he says to Bea, who is grinning up at him, seconds away from saying something embarrassing.

"We're going upstairs for a minute," I say, pulling Jesse by his jacket.

Hannah crosses her arms, giving him a cold, hard, you-hurt-my-little-sister stare. "We'll be down here if you need us," she says.

• • •

JESSE AND I ARE STILL TWO CHARGED PARTICLES; THE TIME APART hasn't changed a thing. Squashed together in the closet, the air vibrated between us, but now, up in my room, we move in big, nervous circles.

I feel tender from last night, not sure what's coming next. I have to keep reminding myself of how much it hurt so I don't throw myself at him again.

Finally, Jesse stops pacing and sits down on the bed. He pulls the photographs out of his pocket.

"Did you really mean all of this?" he says.

"Yeah," I say, trying not to think about how many times I used the word *love*.

He pulls the photographs out of the sleeve, shuffling through them one at a time. "These are really good," he says. "Really, really good."

"Thanks," I say, my face warming.

I risk coming a little closer then, and Jesse reaches out and grabs my hand, pulling me all the way in. He's still wearing his jacket and his hair is sticking up on end and he smells like winter.

"I want to understand," he says, looking up at me.

"I want you to," I say, reaching out and touching one of his curls.

He lies back on the bed and looks up at the ceiling like he's watching the night sky.

"Start at the beginning."

So I do. I lie down next to him and I tell him everything. I tell him about forgetting my dad and fucking up with college and not being able to let go of Bennett. I tell him about how confused I've been, how lost, and he traces his fingers over the back of my wrist and makes me forget how scary this is.

When I'm done, when every secret is laid out between us, he turns his head to look at me.

"I think I'm in love with you," he says.

I'm stunned, watching his eyes open and close, his thick eyelashes sweeping down to his cheek.

"I think I'm in love with you too," I whisper.

"Don't lie to me again," he says, his face suddenly serious.

"I won't," I promise, reaching down and looping my pinkie through his.

And then he pulls me toward him, so our faces are just a breath apart. I can feel the zipper of his jacket, cold against my neck. He reaches out and traces his fingers over my cheekbones, my nose, the outline of my lips.

"Yep," he says, whispering it through the tiny sliver of air between us, "I love you."

I reach up to touch the scar under his eye. "I love you too," I say.

And then we are kissing and the only word I can think to describe it is *perfect*, the way his lips press against mine, soft at first, like I'm something precious, then faster and more frantic.

He keeps saying these little half phrases: *I need* and *I want* and *You are so—*

And I'm twisting my fingers in his hair, trying to pull him closer.

Then Hannah calls up the stairs. "Time to go!"

We break apart, breathless.

"Tomorrow," he says, pressing one last kiss to my lips before rising unsteadily from the bed.

"Tomorrow," I say, following behind him, all the way down to the front door.

• • •

WHEN MOM COMES HOME, WE ARE ASLEEP IN A HEAP ON THE COUCH. My head is on Hannah's stomach and Bea's feet are in my hair. I hear Mom set down her keys and pull off her boots and tiptoe into the living room, stopping in the doorway, trying to be quiet. I keep my eyes closed, but I can tell she's watching us. She comes closer, her feet almost silent on the rug, and then I feel her lean down to press a kiss to the top of my head. For one second, my face is in the curve of her neck, right under her throat, the place where her heartbeat surfaces. I blink my eyes open then, to the blur of her skin up close in the dark.

Epilogue

IT'S THE DAY AFTER NEW YEAR'S AND I'M IN THE DARK-room with Jesse. We've turned off the music so we can hear the heavy silence of the falling snow.

Today the darkroom feels serious. Today we're working.

There are a few fumbling kisses in between hanging up our prints and reloading the enlarger, but mostly we're in a steady rhythm: developer, stop bath, fixer, sustained quiet, predictable increments of time.

On the light table is a sheet of negatives, cliffs and ocean and slanted light, all of it in reverse. I choose one and slide it into the negative carrier, click it into the top of the enlarger. I'm impatient so I don't make a test strip; I guess at the time, shining the light on the paper for lucky number eleven seconds. And then I plunge the paper into the developer.

I lift the tray up and down at the corner, agitating the chemicals and making waves. I watch an image emerge: a blurry beach from above, covered in driftwood.

And my dad's not there.

He's not reading Shakespeare.

All I can see in the air is light and dust.

But somewhere in my mind I feel him start to emerge. I imagine what it would be like if he were. I can almost smell the Earl Grey tea, I can almost hear the turn of the pages.

Acknowledgments

Thank you:

First, to my family. Mom, for your relentless support of my every dream, no matter how weird or impossible. To my brother, Chris, for helping me build a strong foundation. To Phil: you have been cheering me on since the day we met and I feel like the luckiest person to be your daughter. And to my sisters, who were the inspiration for this book. Sarah, so much of my thinking about loss and memory is grounded in your art and the many meandering conversations we've had throughout the years. Ann, since we were small you've been my best friend and fiercest defender and I will look up to you until the end of time.

To my boys, Andrew and Angelo. You pick up the slack when I need it, you make me laugh, and you fill me up with love.

To the Lerner family book club for helping me remember where I come from. To my grandmothers: Grandma Jean for never giving up hope that I'd become a novelist and Grandma Mary for teaching me how to sparkle. To my uncle Jim for helping to keep Dad alive for me. And to my aunt Betsy, the real-life Aunt El: you are just as magical as I made you out to be.

To Nancy Portilla and all of the teachers at Sunshine, and everyone else who took care of my child during all of those hours I spent writing this book.

To my chosen family, Erin, Lee, Marisa, and Shelby: You help me remember who I wanted to be when I was young and wild. There are no greater friends in all the world than the four of you. To Hannah Barr DiChiara and KC Bull, thank you for helping me on the journey of motherhood and YA fiction. And to Amy Weber, Olivia Wiley, and Chelsey Norton: thank you for being there when I survived this story the first time.

To my many mentors, especially Mary Gordon, who was the first person to make me feel like I was really a writer. To Mary Firman, my high school English teacher who invited me out for tea. To Anna Richert, who reminded me that there is art everywhere, even in the day-to-day grind of teaching. To Moraima Machado and Elizabeth Coles, who taught me how to come back to myself, and to Becca Coleman for teaching me how to sit still.

To Sarah Simon, who has taught me so much about writing. And to my many other creative partners over the years, Sam Berman (who showed me the I love U-nicorns trick), Claire Plumb, Hannah Weiss, Lily Rachles, Jasmyn Wong, DB Leonard, and many, many others.

To my Small Works family, for your support and kindness. I could not have made it through the pandemic year without you.

To the readers who helped me shape this book, Amy Spalding and Kate Spencer: your guidance helped me make the story of Marigold come to life. To Dani Moran, thank you for all of your excellent feedback.

To my agents, Melanie Figueroa and Taylor Haggerty, and to the entire team at Root Literary: thank you for seeing me and believing in me and finding a way to get this book out into the world.

To my editor, Kelsey Murphy. You are a true artist! Your gentle prodding and steady guidance has made this book bloom into something that is so much better than I could have imagined.

To the Philomel team who has worked so hard to make this book come to light: Cheryl Eissing, Jill Santopolo, Ken Wright, Monique Sterling, Ellice Lee, Talia Benamy, and Liza Kaplan.

To Kristie Radwilowicz for the beautiful cover you created and to everyone at PYR: Theresa Evangelista, Deborah Kaplan, Christina Colangelo, Emily Romero, Kara Brammer, Shanta Newlin, Elyse Marshall, Lizzie Goodell, Felicity Vallence, Shannon Spann, James Akinaka, Alex Garber, Carmela Iaria, Trevor Ingerson, Summer Ogata, Rachel Wease, Felicia Frazier, Debra Polansky, Rachel Jacobs, Gerard Mancini, Elise Poston, Jayne Ziemba, Krista Ahlberg, Marinda Valenti, Sarah Mondello, Amanda Cranney, Pete Facente, Jocelyn Schmidt, Robyn Bender, and Jen Loja.

And finally, to my readers. I haven't met you yet, but I'm already in love. Thank you thank you thank you.

Turn the page for a sneak peek at Kate's next book,

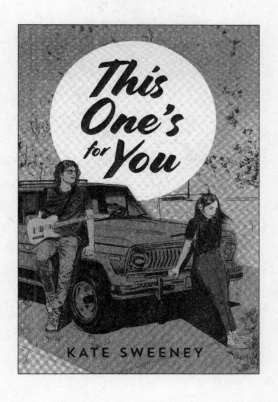

Coming Spring 2023

1
Caspian

SOME MORNINGS, WHEN I'M STILL DRIFTING back and forth between
asleep and awake, I think I can hear her voice. She's singing, or maybe
she's laughing, and it's the color of sunlight on the back of my eyelids.
Orange-gold. Glowing.

It's not her real voice. The human brain doesn't start making memories until the age of two, and she was gone long before that. She died
in a time when there was nothing but a half-made, invisible foundation, when my subconscious was still being shaped by experiences
that would never be remembered. She shaped me—in the impression
of her voice and her touch, and then her absence. But I'll never, ever
know her.

If I let them, things with Mom can become an obsession. I'm a
detective and she is the case that will make my career. I'm a scientist,
and she is the grand, elegant equation that will explain the universe.
But the rest of the time, she truly doesn't exist to me.

I run down the front steps and jump on my bicycle, the straps of my
helmet dangling down around my ears. My American History final is
in ten minutes; I just woke up and I haven't even brushed my teeth.

I begin pedaling furiously up the giant hill that leads away from the
cul-de-sac. June gloom is in full force, so I'm not sweating as hard as

I could be by the time I get to the top. Just enough that I feel a trickle at the edge of my forehead.

I fly through the burned-out strip that is downtown El Sobrante, dodging a man who is riding his horse down the street. I pass Santa Shoe Repair, Nerd Crossing, Mountain Mike's Pizza. I barrel into the school parking lot and lock up my bike next to a monstrous hydrangea bush, run down the hallway, and slide into my seat at 8:59 a.m.

Hannah looks over at me and says, "You look . . . interesting. Everything okay?"

She's perfectly neat as always, and there is something deeply calming about her thick golden ponytail, her crisp white T-shirt, the tiny silver H at her throat. I reach up and tug the end of her hair.

"I accidentally slept in."

She raises both hands. "Not my fault."

Then Mr. Henderson walks in, looking sad and rumpled, the human equivalent of a ketchup stain.

"Good morning, seniors! For most of you this will be the last test you ever take at De Anza High. Good luck."

He passes around the test books and pencils and then the next two hours are a fog of essay questions about the Civil War and the industrial revolution. I try, but by the end of it I'm basically propping my eyes open with sticks.

I hand in my test, brush my teeth in the bathroom, and then wait for Hannah and Jake out front. A pack of wild turkeys roams through the parking lot, shitting on cars. I sit on the gate of Hannah's dad's pickup truck, tucked between my bike and the surfboards, my hood cinched over my ears to muffle the chattering birds and the distant highway sounds.

And then we are driving along the Richmond Parkway, my hand on Hannah's knee, Jake whining about being crammed into the back seat of the extended cab. The fog is burning into a smoggy, hazy blue that can't decide if it's dirty or clean. A cormorant corkscrews into the water. Rust-colored fuel cylinders loom on the hillside, blending in to the orange rocks.

We cruise over the Richmond Bridge, past the San Quentin State Prison. Hannah is singing along loudly to the Killers, which she thinks is cool/retro but everyone knows is garbage music. Her voice is slightly off-key, but somehow it's charming.

Hannah is calmly, classically beautiful, with delicate features and soft, pale skin. We've been together since junior year but I liked her for a lot longer than that.

We're heading up to Bolinas, where Hannah and Jake will surf and I'll wait on the beach, and then we'll meet up with a bunch of other kids from school and drink warm beer around a fire under the moonlight to celebrate the great accomplishment of finishing high school.

My phone buzzes on the seat. It's Dad.

Congratulations dude.

Thanks. Going up to Bo for the night.
Probably gonna camp out. Good?

Yep. Just don't drink too much and DO
NOT DRIVE.

Got it.

We stop at the grocery store in town for lunch items: hard rolls, cheese and salami, salt-and-pepper chips. I get a Sprite and Hannah crinkles her nose at me, setting her kombucha on the counter.

"Don't do that," I say, reaching out a finger to push on the freckled end of her nose. "Or I'll make you drink it."

She makes a fake choking noise and watches as I take cash out of my wallet and set it down.

"You guys are disgusting," Jake says. He is clutching an armful of Hostess CupCakes against the front of his UC Santa Cruz sweatshirt. Jake is white, with pale, freckled skin and strawberry blond hair.

"Disgustingly great," Hannah says, lacing her fingers up with mine.

We walk down to the end of the road that leads to the beach. I carry Hannah's surfboard and she carries the food. We find a spot and spread out a big red-and-black quilt, our toes digging down into the dark brown sand that's always a little bit wet, even when the sun is out. We put sunscreen on our arms and ears and noses. It's too cool out to have much more skin exposed than that. Hannah and Jake head down to the water and I lie back and try to read a book about Sun Ra and the Arkestra, the sound of the waves and the soft but relentless breeze rushing in my ears.

I can't focus for long because of the fact of this day: the last day of high school.

I'm done.

I have a scholarship to Cal State East Bay, and my first semester starts in less than three months. Everything is starting. Everything is good. The future is waiting in a neatly wrapped and labeled package. But for some reason I can't really feel it. I never can.

I put down my book and watch Hannah and Jake bobbing up and down in the water like seals. Everything is backlit and the top halves of their bodies are two irregular black shapes, in steady motion on the dark sea.

Hannah is going to school in Ohio, and we are deep into negotiations about what that will mean for our relationship. At any given moment either of us can be found on either side of the argument. We're circling around something inevitable, but no one wants to be the first to let go.

The shadows get longer and longer until it's time to get out, get dry, head to Blake's cousin's house. By the time we park the pickup on the dirt road out front, kids from school have already started gathering.

The house is a California-interior-style wet dream, everything wabi sabi, weathered, reclaimed, decks and steps everywhere. Ceramic sculptures. Glass doors. Cool grass in the twilight, fruit trees sagging under the weight of ripening apricots and plums. It's the kind of house Dad builds for people who have a lot more money than we do.

"I'm hungry," Hannah whines from where she sits on a wraparound bench on the back deck. She's wrapped up in lavender fleece, white leggings, and Uggs, shivering with wet hair.

"I'm pretty sure Connor is bringing pizza," Jake says, adjusting his baseball cap.

"Yup," I say, "and here he is."

"Hey, bro!" Connor calls from across the yard. He ducks under the crooked branch of a live oak tree, balancing the pizza on one hand. There's lots of hugging and backslapping as we all greet each other. Something about it feels disingenuous, every single time.

More and more kids come, and I start to worry that this is more like a party than a hangout, but by that point the beer is surging through my veins and I feel *good*. Light. Free. This is the way I should feel on the last day of school.

Hannah is over talking to a group of her friends. After a day outdoors, she is this shade of golden pink that is completely enticing. I walk up behind her and wrap my arms around her waist, kissing her neck.

"Excuse me, ladies," I say, winking. "I need Hannah for a minute."

I pull her up the stairs into a bedroom that looks like a perfect replica of a fisherman's bunkhouse with old glass floats and porthole windows, and she pushes me down onto the bed and takes off my glasses and we tangle ourselves up in each other until we get right up to the edge of the line that we are both, for some reason, hesitant to cross. For a while, I lose myself until I'm completely gone, in a way that makes every voice, every thought, everything that isn't the soft blur of Hannah, recede.

Afterward, when we are strung out, breathless, lying limp on our backs, Hannah turns her head to me and says, "Today was the last day of high school, ever."

I nod, slow, rubbing a long strand of her silky hair between my fingers. "So weird."

Suddenly, her aquamarine eyes are overflowing with tears. "Everything is going to change, isn't it?"

The past half hour in this tiny room has sobered me up, made me thoughtful, and for a few long minutes her question swirls around my brain.

She leans over and kisses my shoulder.

"I'm really going to miss you."

"Yeah," I say. "I'm really going to miss you too."

But there's something empty about the words because I can't imagine what it would be like, really missing anyone.

Later, we are back downstairs. I'm loose in a good but dangerous way. Like everything might fall apart at any moment and I might not mind.

I'm sitting on a camping chair next to the fire when I see Sydney Greenfield drifting across the firelit lawn like a fairy. Her black hair is braided into a crown on the top of her head and she's wearing an old black T-shirt that's full of holes and a giant black old-man's cardigan sweater. She's holding hands with a guy I've never seen before. He's white, skinny, and scruffy, and looks like he doesn't belong at a high school party. He tugs her along, both of them looking cool and disinterested. A cigarette dangles between her fingers.

I first met Sydney when we were eight years old, after Dad and I moved from Oakland into the house next door to hers at the end of a dusty cul-de-sac. For years, I followed her everywhere. She introduced me to music and made me dye my hair black and dared me to do a hundred stupid and dangerous things.

But at some point Syd and I drifted apart. Sometimes it felt like she was still and I was moving, and sometimes it felt like I was still and she was moving. Now here we are, on opposite sides of a gigantic ocean. It's weird because for so long she was my twin, the other half of my brain. Sometimes I still wake up at night and expect to find the lump of warmth that is her body in my bed.

The older guy stops for a second to talk to a friend, and Syd stops too, turns her head, looks at me, stares. Her eyes are like exploding stars, the way they suck everything inward. For a second I feel this great missing, this frustrated longing. They pull me in, her eyes, like a swamp.

And then she looks away, turns back to the guy, moves along like a fish in a stream until she's out of sight.

2
Sydney

THIS PARTY IS STUPID. IT'S FULL of the worst kind of normal kids rem-
iniscing about high school. Everyone is singing along to bad music
and hugging each other, and all night Robbie's been looking at me in
this way where he's trying to tell me that he wants to have sex.

And me? I feel like I'm a human paper cut. There's a sting under
my skin that I can't get rid of today.

I look sideways at Robbie, his round blue eyes half hidden under
dark, shaggy hair. He's been drinking and smoking pot all afternoon
and he smells sad. He's talking to Rich about music in this way he has,
basically saying that anything he doesn't approve of is utter trash, and
I know he's just moments away from diverting off into a long diatribe
about Pantera.

"I'll be right back," I say, dropping his dead-fish hand.

"'K, babe," he says, kissing me on the forehead.

Suddenly, the earth tilts, just a little. That's how I know it's coming.
I turn away fast, making my way through the shadowy trees to the
back gate, wiping the sweat that's already beading along my upper lip.
When I'm out of the yard, in the utter, inky darkness of the street, I
sink down to the edge where the curb would be if there were curbs
here and let my head fall down between my knees.

My lungs begin to feel like they are full of water, so I concentrate on the feeling of the hard gravel on the backs of my thighs. Three in, six out. Four in, eight out. Six in, twelve out. I do the breathing exercises my therapist showed me in her moldy office. I take two puffs of my inhaler and try to tug the helium balloon of my brain back down to earth.

Then an idle part of me wonders if this isn't really a panic attack at all, if the tightness in my chest is actually killing me. Young people can have heart attacks, right? Every once in a while, it happens. I could die tonight, at this stupid party, on the side of the road in front of some rich hippie's house.

Once, when I was lucky-number-seven years old, I did almost die. At the beach, sucked out too far, my struggle for forward motion turned to a defeated up-and-down bobbing of my body in the ocean, and the waves washed mouthful after mouthful of salt water down my throat. I felt real terror and then an alluring calm right behind it. I knew that it would feel good to surrender. But then my dad yanked me out by the back of my bathing suit and I threw up all over the sand.

I wait for that calm feeling of near death now, but it doesn't come. I can't die tonight. I have to work at Amoeba tomorrow. I have a sound internship at the Fox that starts July 15th. I have a plan. So I draw circles in the dirt with a long stick until the blotches on the backs of my eyelids start to fade. I count and breathe, in and out, again and again.

When I can hear the night birds over the hum of the party, I know I'm going to be all right. I stand up on wobbly legs and start walking.

It's three long, dark blocks to the edge of the mesa, and I pass the time by humming the Roches and rhythmically crunching my feet in the gravel. I light a cigarette and inhale deeply. Something about smoking makes my aloneness feel somehow more alone. Better. Even though the first drag always makes me cough and wheeze.

I crush out the cigarette halfway through and slip the butt into my back pocket. I never, ever litter. Then I walk right up to the edge of the mesa, the edge of the earth, and look down at the calm, moonlit sea, far below in the bay. And I wonder how this perfect calm can be a part of something so turbulent as the ocean.

3
Sydney

WHEN WE WERE KIDS, CASS AND I used to take epic bike rides on the first day of summer. We would ride along the Richmond Bay Trail, chasing birds until our shoulders were burned to a crisp, or head out over rolling farmland to the orchard where we would ditch our bikes in the trees and sneak around the gate, filling up our backpacks with cherries. Once we took BART into the city and rode all the way out to Ocean Beach. I made us go swimming, even though it was cloudy and only sixty degrees outside. Cass insisted on keeping his wet underwear on when we got out, and his lips were blue the whole ride home. I remember feeling worried about him in this way that I was often worried about him, like I wanted to wrap him up in wool blankets but also yell at him for being such a scaredy-cat.

Today, on the first day of summer, I wake up at noon. I make myself a vegan scramble sandwich and eat it in the kitchen, waiting for my mom to come home from an overnight shift at the hospital. She left me a note that says, *We need to talk*, but I don't feel like talking today.

I sweep the kitchen, listening to a podcast about global atmospheric change and animal populations. The content is pretty much what you'd expect: a thousand elaborate explanations of the myriad of ways in which we are fucking everything up. Carbon dioxide, methane, ozone, chlorofluorocarbons, nitrous oxide. It's like a tragic Greek poem in which everyone is recklessly engineering a slow descent into their own death.

Twenty minutes pass. I wash my dishes and plunge deeper into the dark hole of global doom to distract myself from my own impending implosion. Two marine biologists are talking about dead zones in the ocean caused by changing respiration patterns and a lack of oxygen when I finally hear Mom's car in the driveway. I'm in such a panicked and hopeless mood that I slip out the sliding glass door and hide behind the house.

I stand there for a few minutes, plastered against the back wall, listening to my mother calling for me up the stairs. And then, for some reason, I find myself in the garage, quietly digging my rusty old bike out from a pile of discarded outdoor stuff. The tires are flat, but I figure out how to pump them up and then wipe off the ten million cobwebs clinging to the metal, whispering an apology to the spiders whose homes I've destroyed. My hand-me-down helmet is a revolting, sparkly teal color, but I dust that off too and buckle it under my chin. And then I wheel myself out onto the street, squinting at the rare June sunshine.

By the time I make it to the top of our hill, I'm panting and sweating like a middle-aged man, but then my legs remember the way and I cruise with no hands, all the way down to San Pablo Dam Road. It's the weirdest kind of beautiful here, all rust and garbage and overgrowth. Painted wooden signs, old cars, crumbling churches.

I don't know where I'm heading at first, just following an ancient feeling. I turn onto a side road and after a while the beauty becomes less complicated, more overt. The grass is drying out, so the rolling hills are golden against a deep blue sky. I can hear daytime crickets in the sound of the wind filtering past my ears and all kinds of birds chattering at one another. In the early spring these hills are covered with flowers, but they're mostly dead now.

When I've gone as far as I can pedal, I ditch my bike behind a knobby oak tree, walk halfway up a slope of grass, and flop onto my back in the sunshine. I've forgotten my sunscreen but I don't even care. I need the sun to bring me back to life. I'm a dead wildflower longing for a glass of water, and water is the light. I let it sink into all the tiny little holes in my skin, I let it burn my nose, I let it pull the sweat to the surface.

It's actually working, but then I imagine myself talking to my mother, listening to whatever it is I've done wrong this time. And the dead-zone feeling hits me again. Even out here in this field that is full of oxygen. Then, for some reason, I imagine Cass last night, looking right into my eyes.

For a second, just a second, I let myself miss him. I let myself miss his grass stains and the gap between his teeth, his quiet thoughtfulness and careful observation. No matter how much I hate him, today, in the presence of so much wildness, it feels like he should be here.

Do you feel it? he would say.

I feel it: the heaving of my lungs, the heat of my skin, the scratch of the grass, the thrum of the bugs around me. The vastness of the sky, the dryness of the dirt, the gentle undulation of the hills. I let my awareness stretch outwards into the earth, over the dirt and plants and insects, into the sky, into the first day of summer.